Canoodling Always & Forever

—— BOOK THREE ——
The Canoodling Series

Shawn M. Verdoni

© 2024 SHAWN M. VERDONI.

All rights reserved. No portion of this book may be reproduced, stored in a retrieval system, or transmitted in any form or by any means—electronic, mechanical, photocopy, recording, scanning, or other—except for brief quotations in critical reviews or articles, without the prior written permission of the publisher.

This is a work of fiction. Names, characters, businesses, places, events, and incidents are either the products of the author's imagination or used in a fictitious manner. Any resemblance to actual persons, living or dead, or actual events is purely coincidental.

ISBN: 978-1-957351-53-7
Library of Congress Control Number: 2024936463

Written by: Shawn M. Verdoni
Edited by: Marla McKenna
Cover Design: Michael Nicloy & Shawn M. Verdoni
Interior Layout: Giffin Mill

Published by Nico 11 Publishing & Design
Mukwonago, Wisconsin
Michael Nicloy, Publisher
www.nico11publishing.com
Quantity order requests may be made with the publisher: mike@nico11publishing.com or by phone: 217.779.9677

The Story
Words and Music by Brandi Marie Carlile, Phillip John Hanseroth and Timothy Jay Hanseroth
Copyright© 2007 UNIVERSAL MUSIC CORP. and SOUTHERN ORACLE MUSIC, LLC
All Rights for SOUTHERN ORACLE MUSIC, LLC Administered by UNIVERSAL MUSiC CORP. All Rights Reserved Used by Permission
Reprinted by Permission of Hal Leonard LLC

Printed in The United States of America

Dedication

To Rich
Always and Forever

Canoodling Always & Forever

PART ONE: DILLION

Chapter One

"I will always love you," she whispered gravely, her face taut and gray. Her voice still contained a hint of the sweetness he'd known for his whole life, yet each word was a struggle. "It's time, my love. I'm so sorry I have to leave you," she took a raspy breath before she could continue. "The children … "

The tears came freely now. He could no longer keep a strong face. It was too soon. She was too young. This wasn't supposed to be the end of their love story, the pages torn out as his soulmate, a young wife and mother, breathed her last in their bedroom while a hospice nurse lingered just outside in the hall. For the very last time, he lightly kissed the dry cracked lips of the first woman he ever loved.

He put his lips to her ears and whispered back, "I will always love you, Corinne. I won't let the children forget you. I promise." He felt her chest rise for the final time and heard the escape of the last breath from his childhood sweetheart. Dillion Clark closed the eyes of his wife of 10 years as he felt her soul leave her battered body to join the angels in heaven where she surely belonged. She had been his angel on Earth since childhood, but her battle with ovarian cancer for the last three had been brutal. He wouldn't have wished that curse on his worst enemy, yet, he had endured watching it eat away at the most beautiful soul he'd ever known, and it had almost killed him.

Dillion put his lips on her forehead and let them linger for a moment while he tried to get up the strength to leave her and get the hospice nurse to start the process of saying goodbye. Next, he laid his head on her chest, trying to find that heartbeat that kept him company every night for the past decade, but it no longer beat for him. The tears were coming in buckets now and he found it hard to breathe. When he finally could take a breath, he cried out in agony. It was the outcry of his broken heart.

The hospice nurse came rushing in along with his father. They both hugged him in place until the screaming stopped. The blood rushed in his ears, and he couldn't get a grip on what was going on around him. He felt like a wild animal trapped in a cage. His father's strong hands gripped his shoulders and brought Dillion's face to his chest. "I know, son. I know. I'm so sorry. So sorry. We're here for you. Let it all out."

The familiar smell of his dad's cologne and the feel of the traditional black cardigan sweater on his cheek were helping to bring Dillion back from his animalistic instinct to scream and run away, far away from this horrific feeling. When Dillion had finally cried and screamed the anguish out of his system, he took a cleansing breath and let go of his father. His rock. His anchor. His priest.

 "Son, I have to do what I promised Corinne I would." He peeled his son's hands from around his own torso and walked over to his daughter-in-law who had been a brave warrior in the face of imminent death and torturous agony. He put his hand on her heart and whispered, in the language of his God, the words that he believed would help this lamb reach her well-deserved final destination, heaven. "Rest in peace, my daughter. Amen."

Father Riley Clark made the sign of the cross over Corinne's chest and kissed her on her forehead before he allowed his own tears to release from his 50-something year-old eyes. He'd known this woman since her family had moved into the community years earlier. He had been a young Episcopal priest in his first church with a new family of his own. Those were the years that he had a spark in his blue eyes and not a single gray hair on his head or beard. His beautiful bride was a loving wife and a nurturing mother to their two boys. Dillion was in kindergarten when Corinne first showed her face at church, her corn-colored hair braided down her back and tied at the ends with bright yellow ribbons to match her dress. Move ahead several years, and Riley recalled how she looked like a fairy princess in her cotton candy pink prom dress studded with rhinestones and glitter. A smile came to his face, recalling Dillion looking very pale and nervous as he was getting a lecture from Corinne's father before they left for the dance. Speeding ahead a few more years and he stood in front of the young couple as they spoke their wedding vows.

Two years after that, Corinne placed his first grandchild into his arms and told him that they had named her Riley, after him. Riley looked down at Corinne's sunken face and pale gray skin, sighing as he remembered how, almost three years ago to the day, at the baptism of their third child, Corinne had said she didn't feel well and needed to lie down. A few days later, ovarian cancer was detected and their whole world turned upside down. It was very difficult to be a priest to a member of his congregation when his family was going through something this heart wrenching. How would he find the strength to lead his family out of this darkness and into the light when he couldn't see the light himself? How could he mentor his son in the ways of the church when he was struggling to find a way for this death to make sense?

Dillion looked out the window of their little ranch home as the autumn leaves fell from the tree outside of their, his, bedroom. Something was moving under the tree. It was a mature buck; six, maybe eight points. It had been lying under the tree for the past hour and now it was getting up and leaving as if it knew Corinne died. His beautiful Corinne was gone. Leaving him to raise their three children alone; Riley who was a precocious eight; Benji who had been the closest to Corinne was six; and the baby, Brianna, only three and didn't get the chance to really know her mother.

Dillion left the bedroom and looked for his own mother who was rocking the baby in her lap while the older two were snuggled on either side of their grandmother. When he entered the room, his mother stopped rocking and Riley and Benji looked up at his tear-stained face and knew their mother had died. In her bed. In their home. With her family around her. He didn't have to say a word.

What word could he have said anyway? None that would have made sense. None that would have brought her back.

Chapter Two

A few days later, dressed in his best black suit and tie, Dillion accepted the handshakes and hugs of a parade of parishioners who gave him their condolences and perhaps a casserole to help his family through this difficult time. He didn't remember the words. The faces were blurry. His children were all he could focus on. Helping Riley zip up her dress and Benji with his tie. Brushing Brianna's blonde curls into pigtails with ribbons that matched her black and red polka dot dress.

After the last guest left, he was grateful his parents and brother were still there to help him clean up and package all the leftovers and casseroles which would feed them for the foreseeable future. With them cleaning up the kitchen, Dillion started getting the kids ready for baths and bed. He peeled off his suit coat and dress shirt so that he was only in his white cotton undershirt. He looked at his face in the mirror. Thanks to his older brother, Roger, his dark brown hair had enough product in it that it still looked well-groomed. His eyes were much the worse for wear, though. Bags were hiding a good portion of the eyes that Corinne used to tell him reminded her of the bluest summer skies as seen from their favorite spot under the old oak tree by the stream.

Dillion assessed himself and realized that he still felt nothing. Empty inside. He looked again at his face in the mirror and wondered, would he ever feel emotion again? Would he be able to tell his children he loved them and actually feel it? Could he preach about God's love if he couldn't understand why God's love wasn't enough to keep his wife from the pain of cancer? From dying? He realized that tonight he wouldn't have those answers. Maybe the words would come, in time. Maybe they wouldn't. It was necessary for Dillion to focus on the things to manage right this minute. Baby steps. He needed to give his baby a bath and get her ready for bed. He needed to read with his older children and help them with their nightly prayers. They were real, and they needed him. That would have to be enough for now.

When it was time to put Benji to bed he saw his son standing at the window and looking up at the stars. Benji almost startled as if he didn't know his dad was in the room until Dillion touched his shoulders. "Hey, buddy. What'cha looking at?" Dillion asked.

"I was trying to find our star." Benji looked intently at the night sky until he pointed and said, "There it is! There's our star!" Dillion looked past his son's pointing finger and saw he was aiming in the direction of the North Star.

"That's the North Star, buddy."

"Dad, it's correct name is Polaris. But it's our star, too. I picked it for us."

"You mean you and me?"

"No! Me and Momma." Dillion's dead heart skipped a beat. It hurt.

"You and Mom?"

"Yeah. Before she died, she asked me to pick out a star so whenever I was missing her, I would look up at the sky and find it and know that she was looking at the same star from where she's at in heaven." Dillion got all choked up again and the tears that he thought he'd cried out came back. He ruffled the dark mass of hair on his son's head and kissed the top of it.

"Oh. I see. That's pretty great, Benji. But why did you pick that star? Why not another one?"

Benji seemed exasperated and turned around to look his dad in the eyes. "Because it's the brightest star in the Ursa Minor constellation." Dillion wasn't getting it. Benji sighed, rolled his eyes, and then put it in terms his dad could understand. "That's the star that led the wise men to Jesus."

"Okay," Dillion said, still a bit confused.

"Well, I figure if the star was bright enough to lead the wise men from different countries to Jesus, then it's probably bright enough for Momma to see in heaven." Dillion hugged his bright boy and kissed him on top of his head.

"You are a very smart little boy, Benjamin Clark. How did you get so smart?"

"From Momma, of course." Dillion pulled away and looked curiously at his son who may have had his hair color, but definitely had his mother's wise eyes. "She told me how she had to help you with your homework all the time otherwise you got bad grades."

Dillion chuckled as he remembered how he wanted to sneak kisses while Corinne would quiz him on his American history or algebra. "That is very true, son. Very true." He held Benji's hand while he walked him over to his bed.

Tucking Benji in under dinosaur sheets, Dillion couldn't help but ask, "Is there anything you got from me?"

Benji scrunched his nose while he thought hard about it and then Dillion knew when he got the answer he was looking for because the lines in his forehead relaxed. "I got your messy hair." Dillion laughed out loud at that revelation and then messed up his son's hair.

"That's true, son. Very true."

When all the children were tucked in, and all the clutter was cleaned and organized, Dillion walked back to his bedroom and stared at the bed he had shared with his wife for a decade. His mom had changed the sheets and had the comforter and pillows cleaned. But he still couldn't face sleeping in that bed alone. Not tonight. Not when he buried her just a few hours before. Not sure if he could ever sleep in it again.

Dillion went to the hall closet, pulled out a guest pillow and a thick throw before he walked over to the sofa, making his bed for the evening. He tried to close his eyes and get some sleep. He hadn't slept much at all this past week, a flurry of activity and grief, he knew he needed to sleep sometime so he could be there for his children. After tossing and turning a bit, he got up and felt the urge to walk outside and look up at the stars, beside a gnarly oak tree. He wondered. Would she be on the other side of the night sky looking for the North Star? Looking for her family? Well, he thought to himself, it couldn't hurt. So, he began …

"Corinne, I miss you so badly right now. I don't know how I'm going to be able to be the dad I need to be without you there beside me. Guiding me. You've been such a big part of my life. I don't know how to be me without you. I know you aren't in pain anymore, and I am so grateful for that. But this pain I feel is almost claustrophobic. It takes everything I have to breathe. Just breathe."

"I don't know what was said at your funeral. Everybody told me it was beautiful. I don't know what people were saying to me in the reception line. I just kept saying, 'thank you,' and nodded a lot. I know you would have handled it better."

"It should have been me. I know you don't think that, but it's true. You would've known how to handle all this and been the better parent to help our kids get through this. You wouldn't have hated God. You should have been a priest. You got me through school and helped me practice my homilies. They were always better after you gave me helpful hints like, where to pause and when to raise my voice and when to smile."

Dillion yawned, finally feeling the knot in his chest decompress a bit. He sensed sleep coming on and his eyelids heavy. "Thank you, Love, for listening to me." He gazed at the North Star and concluded his solitary conversation, "Maybe Benji is right. Maybe this star thing really works." He smiled as a tear escaped and ran down his cheek. "Thanks for listening to me. Would it be okay if I shared the star with you and Benji? It can be our little secret." A light breeze kissed his cheek as he felt his tear evaporate into a cool kiss.

He turned around and walked back into the house, feeling a little bit lighter, and snuggled into the throw blanket before he closed his eyes.

Chapter Three

The next week went by in a blur. Dillion's mom came to his house every morning to help him get the kids ready for school. He'd drive them the half mile up the road to the red brick school that housed all the grades from kindergarten to eighth grade. He followed the drop off order and kissed his older children goodbye, promising to be there at 3:30 p.m. to pick them up again. The principal offered the kids as much time off as they needed, but Dillion thought it would be better to immerse them into their regular routine right away. Then he drove over the railroad tracks and back toward his house to drop off Brianna at her preschool. The four hours he had alone, he used to compile the legal documents to change things like the mortgage, health insurance, car title, and so on, into his name. Because it was busy work, and it needed to be done sooner rather than later, it helped him pass the time.

When Brianna's preschool let out at noon, he'd take her home for a quick lunch and then set her down for a nap. He would use nap time to get things together for his deacon work and preparing dinner. His mom would have been happy to help, but he was afraid that if he relied on her too much, he wouldn't be able to stop.

After dinner and homework, they had family time before preparing for bed. It could be coloring, watching a movie on TV, or whatever the kids wanted to do. Bedtime was his favorite time. He started to get feeling back when his children would snuggle against him and listen to him read their favorite books until it was time for their nightly prayers.

When the kids were down for the night, Dillion would finish cleaning up and organize for the next day before looking at his empty bed and then shuffling to the couch. Every night, he tried to fall asleep on his own and then would get up, walk out the back door, lean on the door jam and look up at the sky to find Polaris and talk. Sometimes it was about the day's activities. Other times it was reminiscing. Still others it was how angry and hurt he was at Corinne for leaving him and at God for taking her away. Yet, regardless of the conversation, he found he could fall asleep after it was said. It may not have been a full eight hours, but he did sleep.

The weeks turned into more than a month and while he had some money available to him and his young family from Corinne's life insurance and memorial gifts, he needed to work as an Episcopal deacon to make ends meet. He still had his studies to become an Episcopal priest. And then the Christmas season was in full bloom. Dillion was overwhelmed with grief and everything that he was now responsible for, without Corinne's help.

Dillion didn't feel like he was managing his own life well. He didn't feel like celebrating anything, especially Christmas, but he knew he needed to do something. His mother was coming over less and less. At his request, not hers. But this day, while the kids were at their respective schools, he asked his mother to join him at the local diner for a coffee. Rose Clare was a loving mother, but also a strong woman. He knew that she would speak her mind if he asked her to, most of the time she spoke it anyway.

Today, he needed her advice. He was never good at the Christmas thing. That was Corinne's baby. She had this timeline and a plan for almost every day between Thanksgiving and New Year's Day. When the tree would go up, when the cookies were baked, when to shop for presents and when to wrap them. She was the one who stayed behind while he took the kids for their annual ride to see Christmas lights. When they came home, Corinne would fake being asleep on the couch while the first gifts of Christmas were laid under the tree—Santa came and went while she was sleeping—or so the children thought.

CANOODLING ALWAYS & FOREVER

Rose Clare came through the glass door with her tan wool coat covering her black pants and grey turtleneck sweater. Her sandy-brown hair was up in a clip—she hated taking the time to do her hair, but she hated having short hair even more. Rose Clare's chocolate brown eyes twinkled when she caught the eye of her youngest son. Dillion waved and stood up beside the red vinyl booth bench he'd been sitting on. When she got there, after several quick hellos to the locals, she gave him a bear hug and kissed the side of his neck. There was comfort in that. Comfort in something that continued to be the same, even after Corinne was gone. Not too many things that were familiar gave him comfort these days. They mostly made him sad.

"Hey Mom," he said as he kissed her cheek.

"Hey there, yourself." She sized him up, but chose not to say anything. However, he could tell she was not too pleased that his clothes were hanging off him a little too much. They were clean, but just a bit rumpled. His jeans were held together by an old, worn out brown belt that matched the worn out brown hiking boots he chose today because of the slushy snow on the ground. His tan V-neck sweater and button-down white shirt were simply hanging on his frame. However, he took the time to shave and put some gel in his hair so that the cowlicks could be tamed. He still wore his wedding ring. Hadn't had the strength to take it off just yet.

The owner/server, Melinda, came over to get his mom's order. Melinda had grown up in Big Rock, Illinois, not too far from the Clarks. She always kept her blonde hair long and in a braided ponytail. Melinda's family was working poor, and she went to work early as a busser/dishwasher at this little diner after her dad had hurt his back at the grain elevator. The family had needed to find other ways to bring money into the home so, at the age of 12, Melinda put on her best dress and rode her bike around town to look for a part-time job.

Jim, the owner of Babe's Diner, was a gruff man with a warm heart. He gave Melinda a job right away and let her do her homework at an empty booth when there weren't many customers. He was even known to quiz her on her math homework a few times.

After Jim died, he willed the diner to Melinda who had become his best server/host over the years. For a family who didn't have much, owning her own business meant a great deal to Melinda, and she made sure that every customer had an excellent experience at her diner.

"Hello Rose Clare, what can I get for you this morning? We've got a Denver omelet special today if you haven't had time to eat breakfast."

Rose Clare smiled at the young woman whom she'd known since she played Mary in the Christmas pageant. "Morning, Melinda. Thanks, but I think I'll just have a coffee." She looked over at the bakery counter and then added, "Are those sticky buns over there?"

Melinda smiled and in her gravelly voice responded, "They sure are. Made 'em myself this morning. Can I get you one to go with your coffee?"

Rose Clare was someone who never gave a handout, but she always tried to find ways to help people she cared about. Today looked a little slow in the diner, so she thought she could add a little more to her bill. "I've got a meeting later with the Christian Women's group at church, and I think I could get them to volunteer a bit more if I bribe them with your famous pecan sticky buns. Can I take a dozen to go?"

Melinda chuckled and then replied, "Of course. I'll make it a baker's dozen, so you get one to take home to Father Clark. I know those are his favorite."

"Perfect. Thanks, Melinda."

With the coffee poured and the bakery boxed, Rose Clare looked at her son and asked, "So, to what do I owe the pleasure of your company this morning?"

Dillion smiled, though she noticed the twinkle in his pale blue eyes still hadn't returned. But it had only been about a month and a half since Corinne died. She had to be patient. "Love you too, Mom. Can't I simply ask my beautiful mother out for a coffee for no other reason than to spend time with her?"

She chuckled and then stared him down. "You could. But you didn't. So, spill it. Do you need me to come back and help you with the morning routine again? Too much on your plate?"

Dillion took a sip of the hot, caffeinated liquid, shook his head, and then put down the cup before he began. "Thanks, Mom."

"For what? I haven't agreed to anything. Yet."

"For being brutally honest and straight forward. I appreciate you not pussy footing around me and the kids. It helps me feel a little closer to being normal."

"You're welcome. Now, I do have that Christian Women's group to get to in about an hour so let's get a move on. How can I help?"

He looked down into his coffee mug as if it was giving him the strength he needed to get this next part out. "It's Christmas, Mom. I don't know how to do it. Corinne loved this time of year and organized it all. To a 'T.' I would get my marching orders, show up when I was told, and then enjoy seeing the magic unfold the way she planned it."

Now he raised his head and looked into his mother's eyes. She could see he was pained. She hurt for him. She really did. Not that any parent plans on having a favorite child, but at this very moment in time, Dillion was her favorite. He needed her the most. She was a strict parent, the disciplinarian. However, her children knew she loved them, would fight for them, would do anything she could to help them. She may have an opinion or two, or more, about their choices; but she would always be there for her children and her grandchildren.

Rose Clare taught her boys to be independent. Roger, her oldest, took that to heart and moved away as soon as he graduated from high school. The big city called him, and he hadn't looked back since. She didn't mind Chicago, only in short visits.

She preferred small town life. Being a priest's wife, she had a great deal of responsibility and people looked up to her. She was strong enough to handle it most days. But there were two times in her life when she didn't think she'd have the strength to lift herself up, much less anyone else.

The second time was when her beloved Corinne died. She didn't have daughters of her own, but Corinne was truly a blessing from God. She was her daughter, if not by blood, by marriage. The first? When Corinne's parents died in that horrible car crash after a drunk driver swerved into their lane and hit them head on. She felt for that girl. It wasn't long after Corinne and Dillion married when the crash happened. Corinne was crushed. Cloaked in grief, Corinne reminded Rose Clare of the first time they met, when Corinne was a little girl in blonde braids and big brown eyes that were afraid of her new town, new school, and fitting in with the other kids. Rose Clare tried to be there for her, and she was, but it was Riley who found a way through that grief and got her past her pain. That was Riley's gift. He had a way with people to guide them toward the light. It was Riley who got her to move forward with her life and when Corinne laid that beautiful babe in his arms for the first time, it was Riley's name that was granted to their first grandchild. It was fitting, to be sure. It's just that sometimes, just sometimes, Rose Clare would like to be seen as the warm and loving one. She was. Honestly. But her logic and strong sense of self tended to bully the warm and affectionate part of her personality out of the way. Still, she felt her family knew she loved them and would do anything for them.

Looking into Dillion's eyes that morning, it was clear he would be asking for her help and she would agree to anything he asked of her. Perhaps his favor, once granted, would allow that spark in those lovely pale blue eyes again. "So, what is it you want from me, Dillion? To shop for you? Bake cookies? What?"

He sighed and then responded, "I was wondering. Hoping, really. If you would be willing to organize our Christmas for me? Plan it out so I know what to do and when. I'll do all the leg work. It's just, I am afraid I'll forget or miss something and that something would be *the one thing* that is most important to the kids. I don't want to fail them, Mom. I need your help. *Please.*"

His pleading brought a tear to her eye. Trying to hide it, she sniffled and faked a cough while bringing up the napkin to dry it off her cheek. "I can do that for you."

"Thanks, Mom. I really appreciate it." Dillion reached out over the table and placed his hands over his mother's. "One other thing…"

This time Rose Clare furrowed her brow and flashed him a questioning glance. "Oh?"

"Christmas Eve, how will Santa bring the first gifts of Christmas if I'm driving them to see the lights?"

"Well, Christmas Eve is a tight schedule for us, as you know. I've got to get the children organized for the pageant and your dad has the service, but we'll manage." She looked up at the ceiling to try to solve the problem. "Give me a little time to figure that piece of the puzzle out. In the meantime," She drank the last of her coffee, picked up the bakery box and scooted out of the booth before bending down to kiss his cheek. "I'll work on that organization chart and get back to you before the weekend with a plan. Okay?"

"Sounds great, Mom. I really appreciate this. I don't know what I'd do without you and Dad right now. You've been great."

Dillion drank the rest of his coffee and laid the dollar bills on the table. Melinda stopped by and scolded, "Hey there, Dillion. The coffee is on the house this morning. Your money's no good here." He looked up and saw the concern on her face. He wondered, for a moment, how different his life would be at this moment if he'd fallen in love with Melinda instead of Corinne. At least Melinda was here. She wasn't dead. He grinned a half-grin and gave her a hug.

"Thanks, Melinda. Next time, though, I'm paying."

"I'll charge you double." She chuckled at her own joke.

He chuckled with her. "Deal."

Dillion scooped up the bills from the table and opened his trifold leather wallet only to find another memory—their wedding photo staring at him. Two smiling faces with the world ahead of them. Another reminder that Corinne was gone, and he was still here.

Dillion put on his olive green jacket and gloves before he walked out onto the street. He had plenty of time before his baby girl, Brianna, would need to be picked up from preschool. A light snow was falling on this first day of December. The quiet town of Big Rock was all decked out already with Christmas garland and colored lights on each lamp post. When he got to the corner, he smiled as he grabbed one of the orange flags that pedestrians took to cross the road at streetlights. He half smiled as he remembered family walks downtown to grab an ice cream, go to the library, or just hang out and the two oldest fighting to be the one to get to hold the coveted flag. Corinne was the one who would break up the fights while he held on to Brianna. If Riley and Benji couldn't agree, then Brianna got to hold it both ways and they hated that even more than giving up their turn to hold the flag first. With that memory still in place, he walked across the street and investigated the shops on Main Street. In each window was the shadow of another memory, and another, and another. Every person he met on the street paused a bit, unsure how to approach him, or not at all.

Dillion was a small-town guy. He loved that Melinda knew how he took his coffee with cream and his mom took hers black. He appreciated walking into the barber shop, closing his eyes for several minutes while the owner gave him the same haircut he'd had since high school. It gave him comfort to get his oil changed, grab a carton of milk, or whatever else he needed in town, and he always ran into someone he knew. But not now. Memories of her. Corinne. Memories of them. Together. Memories of their family. Together. His heart ached. It was hard to breathe. Difficult to keep his head up. Almost impossible to get his spirits up. Everywhere he was, their memories were also there. He was beginning to loathe living in a small town. Big Rock was just too small these days.

Specifically taking the morning off from studying to prepare for his General Ordination Exam, which he would be taking right after the holidays, he thought he'd spend the morning with his mom, until it was time to meet Brianna. However, her leaving early forced him onto the streets of his childhood where he was left to wander the town's business district, all four blocks, and found that he was walking past the grocery store. Dillion headed inside as he thought it would be a good idea to pick up something easy he could make for dinner.

"Mornin' Dillion!" Bryson was at his post, bagging groceries for the customers. Taller than most, Bryson was expected to play basketball or volleyball in high school. An unfortunate swimming accident almost took his life, but instead, left him brain damaged. He enjoyed being around people and being productive. The job at the grocery store was great at offering him an opportunity to do both.

"Hey, there, Bryson. How are those Bears doing?" Dillion knew that Bryson was a huge Bears fan. Always wore a blue and orange jersey on game days.

"They won against the Seahawks on Sunday! But I don't know how they will do against the Vikings. I hate the Vikings."

"Not too many like the Vikings around these parts, that's for sure."

"Yeah. Say hi to Corinne for me, 'kay?" Dillion's heart did a flip flop before it was crushed. It wasn't Bryson's fault. The accident took away his short-term memory. He remembered things that happened before the accident really well. He didn't always remember recent events, like Corinne's death. He and his mom did stop by the church to give their condolences, but today, well he simply remembered that Dillion and Corinne were a couple.

Dillion couldn't get the words out, and it wouldn't matter much anyway. Bryson was likely to ask about Corinne the next time as well. Dillion couldn't be mad, but it hurt to be reminded of her, nonetheless. Instead, he just nodded and went back to the meat section to pick up a package of bacon, then to the produce bins for a few tomatoes and a head of lettuce. He knew they had bread and mayo at home already. BLT's. The dinner of champions, and widowed fathers.

Chapter Four

After the grocery store, Dillion decided to head home to drop off the foodstuffs and start bringing up the Christmas decorations that Corinne kept in the basement. Maybe the older kids could help get some of the outside things placed in the yard this weekend. Once he put the items in the fridge, Dillion walked down the wooden stairs to the basement and found the storage shelves packed with red and green lid bins holding all kinds of Christmas cheer they'd collected through the years.

When they first started out, Corinne's mom would put together gift packages for each of the holidays and include decorations for them along with some festive treats and hand towels. Then, when they bought their house, Corinne wanted to put her own decorative touch on things, so she watched for after-season sales and coupons so she could stock up on craft items to make her own decorations. He grinned as he found the simple manger he had built for her out of black walnut. He'd followed a pattern of one her father had made many years before. She had cried a river of joyful tears that Christmas Eve. They hadn't much money then, and yet he knew by her reaction his gift was priceless. The next year they went to a local craft fair and found a ceramic nativity scene an elderly woman had made to look like porcelain. Even the three wise men had their gifts to the Christ child painstakingly painted in gold. It always had a prominent place under their Christmas tree until Riley began crawling about, and they had to place it up high, so she couldn't get her chubby little hands on the figures and break them. With Brianna being three years old, it was still a safe bet to keep the scene on top of the bookshelf.

By the time he brought the last bin upstairs, he looked at the clock and realized it was time to get Brianna and bring her home for her afternoon nap. He got into the minivan and drove to the preschool. Since he had gotten home, the streets had become covered in a light blanket of snow. It looked like a scene from a Christmas movie. In previous years, it would have brought joy into his heart. This day, however, was just another reminder that he would be spending Christmas alone. Oh, Dillion knew he wouldn't be alone, really. His family, children and congregation would be there. But it wouldn't be the same. Christmas was Corinne, and Corinne was all about Christmas. He would try his best, but he already knew it wouldn't be good enough. He just hoped his mom would give him enough guidance that he could fake it through this holiday and hopefully, the kids wouldn't hold it against him in the future.

"Daddy!" He heard the familiar squeaky voice of his youngest angel.

"Hey there, Bri, what'cha got in your hands?" Today she wore her curly hair in a ponytail on top of her head. Little ringlets were cascading down around her beautifully rounded face. Chestnut brown eyes twinkled when they saw him. Today, Brianna was wearing a black turtleneck underneath a red and black plaid jumper and black leggings. She was his "girly girl." Brianna loved dresses, tea parties, wearing plastic crowns and pretend jewels and wobbling around in Corinne's high heels. Today, though, she was wearing little black shoes with a Velcro buckle, so she could put on her own shoes. Brianna didn't like being left behind, so she wanted shoes she could put on herself, even if she was a little too young to tie her own shoelaces.

Dillion looked at the construction paper tree that she was carrying around. "Look, Daddy! I made a Christmas tree!" She beamed with pride and wanted to show him all the hard work she had put into it before she even would set it down to put on her coat. "I colored the candy canes and ornaments all by myself!" Dillion smiled as she carefully pointed out every decoration that she colored and glued onto the tree. "Can we take it home and put it in a special place to show Riley and Benji?"

"You bet, Bri. You did a really great job on this. Let's get going home, and you and I can find a place together. Deal?"

"Deal!" She stuck out her hands to have him help her put on her pink, puffy winter jacket. Since they were just a few steps away from the car, he didn't force her to give up the tree to get on her mittens, but he did make sure she put on her pink crocheted headband to cover her ears. On the way to the minivan, she chattered away about all the exciting things they had done at school. She continued her stories as he buckled her into her car seat. Dillion smiled as he was thankful she seemed to get on with her life and not be stuck in grief as he seemed to be. He was grateful for her prattling as it drowned out all the reminders that Corinne wasn't there.

At home, she carefully put the tree on the kitchen table before she took off her coat and headband. Then, she ran back to it after she put her jacket on its hook and her headband away in a pocket. "Daddy?"

"Yes, Bri?"

"Where can we put it so that everyone can see it?"

"Hmm, what about on the refrigerator?" He started to clear a spot when Brianna replied with another question.

"Do you think Mommy can see it there? From where she is?" His heart broke into a million pieces. She may be moving on, but she didn't forget.

"I'm sure she can, Bri. Yes. Yes, Mommy can see it from there."

Brianna held up the Christmas tree with an artist's eye while Dillion shifted it around until she was satisfied it was in the right place. "Right there, Daddy. There." Dillion gathered a few spare refrigerator magnets to hold it into place and stepped back to assess its final placement with his daughter.

"I think it looks good, there, Bri. Real good."

"Daddy?"

"Yes, baby?"

"Will Mommy ever come back home?"

The lump in his throat made it difficult to swallow and choked him as he tried to answer her question. "No, baby. She's not coming back. She's in heaven, remember?"

"Uh huh. I 'member." She looked up at him with those doe eyes and continued, "It's just, I worked really hard on my tree, and I want her to see it." Her little pink lips started to tremble, and tears welled up in her eyes before they began to spill down her rosy cheeks.

Dillion was a mess. He didn't know what to do, so he simply reacted with instinct. When a baby cries, you pick it up and try to soothe it. So that's what he did. Reaching out, he picked up his baby girl and held her to his chest while he rubbed her back. "I believe, Bri," he finally choked out. "I believe that Mommy is looking down from heaven right now and is so pleased that you made her a Christmas tree to look at."

"Really, Daddy?" She hiccupped and looked up at his tear stained face.

"Really." He kissed her forehead and said, "Hey, I haven't had any lunch. Wanna join me in a peanut butter and jelly sandwich?"

"I like creamy peanut butter."

"I can make it with creamy."

"'Kay." He put her down. Brianna went over to the drawer and pulled out a butter knife, then over to the lazy Susan for the peanut butter, setting it on the table and next to the grape jelly Dillion put down a moment ago. Dillion spread the PB&J onto the two slices of bread before cutting it at a diagonal because that is how she liked her sandwich cut. When he finally sat down, he placed a glass of milk in front of each of them.

They ate in silence, but it was a comfortable silence. When the plate was clean and the milk drunk, Brianna slid off her chair and helped him place the dishes in the dishwasher. He waited for her to finish cleaning up before putting her to bed for her afternoon nap. As he stood over her bed, she looked at him, and he didn't want to leave her alone. He didn't want to be alone.

"Slide over, Bri, I could sure use a nap. Can I take one with you?" She grinned, slid over, and let him snuggle in next to her under the covers.

"I love you, Daddy," Brianna whispered before he heard the deep yawn and then her steady breathing started letting him know she was asleep already.

"I love you too, Bri," he whispered as he closed his eyes. Dillion thought he just needed a little cat nap; he had plenty of time to go and pick up the bigger kids at school.

RING! RING! RING! His phone was going off, and Dillion was a bit disoriented as he tried to figure out where he was in relationship to his phone. Brianna started to stir and stretched out her arms. "Is it time to get up, Daddy?"

He threw off the covers and ran to the kitchen where the ringing was getting louder. "I think so, baby. Make up your bed while I try to find my phone." Just as he got to it, the ringing stopped. "Shit," he said under his breath.

"Daddy, that's a bad word! You better say you're sorry and put money in the jar." Corinne had started the tradition as soon as he had gotten into the deacon program. She had thought it wouldn't be a good idea to preach the word of God to the people on Sundays but allow the words of the devil to come out of their mouths every other day of the week. When the jar was full, they would use it to plan a vacation or a long weekend. He reached into his pocket and pulled out a few quarters that were hanging out with some lint and threw them into the jar before he heard the "Ding!" of the notice that he had a voicemail.

After dialing his password, he heard the message, "Mr. Clark, your children, Riley and Benjamin, did not ride the school bus to school today so they did not get on the school bus to come home. They are waiting for you in the office to come and pick them up. Please call our main office line to confirm that you are on your way to get them. Thank you." Dillion dropped his head. It was only supposed to be a short nap, and now he was in trouble with school.

"Bri, we've got to get our coats back on. I'm late for picking up Riley and Benji. We've got to book it." She nodded and rubbed the sleep out of her eyes before she put on her shoes and jacket. He carried her to the car and buckled her in before he turned on the ignition and sped out of the driveway. A car was already on the road and honked at him because he pulled out right in front of it. "Shit! Sorry!"

"Daddy!"

"I know, I know, Bri. I know. Daddy's sorry. I just got to get to the school before they start charging me for after school care for your brother and sister. I'll put money in the jar when we get home. Promise." Looking in all the mirrors before going forward, he took a deep breath and realized that he needed to calm down or Corinne wouldn't be the only family member in heaven that day.

When he pulled up to the main entrance, the principal saw him and led Riley and Benji outside to the van. Dillion saw the angry face on Riley, and Benji just looked sad, like a lost puppy. At least they both had their hats and mittens on with their jackets zipped. The principal came to the van and opened the side door for the two kids to climb in. After he shut it, he walked around to the driver's side so Dillion rolled down the window for his lecture.

The principal was a bit older than Dillion and had kids of his own. Dillion remembered they were in high school. He was a decent guy, and the students respected him, but he was also a stickler for the rules. "Hello Mr. Clark."

"Hello Mr. Scott. I'm really sorry I'm late. I promise not to let that happen again. I just put Bri down for an afternoon nap, and I thought I'd close my eyes for a few minutes. Then the phone woke me up. I'm sorry."

Mr. Scott had a full beard and head of curly short hair that was graying at the temples. Once he would be full gray, he'd make a fantastic Santa Claus. But until then, he was the principal at Big Rock Elementary. "I understand, Mr. Clark. It's been about 10 years since Mrs. Scott died of breast cancer and that first year was brutal. Me and the kids got through alright, but not without a few bumps and bruises along the way." Dillion nodded; he had almost forgotten that had happened. A kindred spirit. Perhaps he'd get off with a warning this time.

"Listen, my kids don't need me much anymore. They all have their driver's licenses and carpool between home, school, sports, etc. How about you stop in the main office tomorrow morning when you drop off the kids and sign a permission slip that will allow me to take them home or to your parents, in the event you're running late. That way I don't have to charge you for after school care."

Dillion looked up at the man and saw the compassion in his eyes. He may be a stickler for the rules, but he also understood when someone needed a break. "Thanks, Mr. Scott. I really appreciate it. I promise I won't make this a habit."

"I know you won't. And Dillion?" Dillion's ears perked up when he heard his first name being called. "Listen, if you ever need someone to talk to. Just to listen to you. Someone who's been in your shoes, just call. I'd be happy to be there for you. It will suck for quite a while, but then one day, you'll be going around, working your busy schedule, and you'll realize you aren't faking it anymore."

Dillion looked up, and those compassionate dark brown eyes looked right back. This time with understanding. Mr. Scott put his hand on Dillion's forearm and squeezed a bit. Dillion nodded. "Thanks," he choked out before the principal stepped away to let Dillion roll up the window and pull out of the drive. He looked in the back of the van and saw Riley giving him the evil eye, and Benji just looked out the window and into space. His dark framed glasses slipped down his nose a bit before he pushed them back up, but he didn't move otherwise.

Chapter Five

After they got home, Riley helped Brianna get out of her seat. Then Brianna remembered her exciting news, "Riley! Benji! Come see my Christmas tree! Daddy helped me hang it on the fridge!" He was glad for the distraction. Hopefully the two oldest would give him a break today. Maybe he'd hold off telling them they had to put up Christmas decorations this weekend.

Once in the house, he noticed that Riley faked excitement for the tree while Benji just hung up his things and quietly set the table for dinner, his nightly chore. Dillion got out the fixings for the meal. "Riley, Benji, dinner should be ready in about 30 minutes, so you go ahead and start homework."

"I don't have any," Benji replied in a flat tone.

"Then why don't you read a book until dinner's ready?"

"I've read them all."

"Well, tomorrow's Saturday, we can go to the library in the morning and get you new ones. How about reading to Brianna? She loves it when you read to her."

Benji just looked up at his dad and then at Brianna. "'Kay. Hey Bri. Why don't you pick out a book for us to read before dinner?"

Brianna stopped chattering to Riley about her day and jumped at the chance to pick out her favorite book, *The Many Adventures of Winnie the Pooh* by A. A. Milne. They went to the sofa in the family room and Brianna snuggled into the side of Benji's olive green pullover fleece with her feet curled underneath her skirt.

Riley picked up her backpack and headed into her bedroom where she could start her homework at her desk. She wasn't sure if she wanted to say anything to her dad now, because she was still pretty mad about being forgotten. She had to color in all the Midwestern states with colored pencils, write in their capital cities, and name all the Great Lakes before her test next week.

Dillion went to work frying the bacon and placing the cooked slices between paper towels lining a plate. The toaster was working overtime, and he put out the mayo on the table with glasses of milk by each plate setting. He knew they should probably be getting fruit slices or vegetables as well, but the nap took away a great deal of his prep time. Instead, he laid out a bag of baked chips and found a forgotten box of chocolate chip cookies for dessert. "Dinner's ready! Wash up!"

Like little soldiers, they lined up in the bathroom to wash their hands. Brianna pushed a little wooden step stool up to the sink, so she could reach the handles and soap better. Almost in line, they sat down in their seats and folded their hands for prayers. Dillion began, "Let us pray. Dear Lord, thank you for the food on this table. The love we feel for each other, and the blessings of this day. Please, Lord, I ask for your forgiveness and for the forgiveness of my children for the mistakes I made today. Please know that I will try harder to be a better person tomorrow. Amen." In unison, the Clark children said, "Amen," before grabbing the food closest to load their plates.

"Riley, how was school today? What did you do?" Dillion inquired. Trying to lighten the mood.

"It was okay, I guess. Typical Friday stuff. In social studies we are learning about the Great Lakes and the midwestern states, so I have to work on my map for homework. Next week we have a test on their names and their capitals. Can you help me study this weekend?" He looked at her, and it seemed that her anger had dissipated. Her sandy blonde hair was a bit unkempt, but her lavender T-shirt and sweater were in perfect order. Riley liked things neat, clean, and organized. She was one of those weird kids who enjoyed washing dishes. She may not have her mother's knack for cooking—she burnt popcorn and toast more times than he could count, but she kept her closet and dresser neat as a pin.

"I'd be happy to help. As a matter of fact, I was going to ask you and Benji to do a favor for me this weekend." They both looked at him and stopped eating. "I found some of our Christmas decorations downstairs in the basement. This weekend's supposed to be mild. Thought you two could help with some of the outdoor decorations before it gets too cold." He thought they might get excited about it. In year's past, they'd practically crawl over each other for the chance to help put up decorations with Corinne.

Riley was the first to accept. Then Benji answered with a simple, "Sure."

"Benji, how was your day? What'd you do in school?"

Benji put down his sandwich and took a sip of milk before he answered. "I don't know. It was a normal day, I guess. We're learning fractions and decimals in math. That's kinda cool."

Dillion would take it. A few sentences and even a little casual conversation. "That's great, buddy! Since you're learning fractions, I think I'll have you help with measuring ingredients when we start making Christmas cookies." Benji nodded in a way that seemed to Dillion that he agreed with his new assignment.

"Listen, guys, I've got to be honest. I'm not sure how to have Christmas this year. I don't know if you want to keep it very small because we all miss your mom and Christmas was her thing or try to make it like she made it with her magical touch." He looked up from his plate and folded hands to see that his children were listening intently. He was talking to them at a mature level, and it seemed to be working. He went on. "Actually, I have another confession to make." They were engaged.

"I met Grandma for coffee today and asked for her help. I don't know the first thing about making Christmas happen. Your mom would tell me what to do, and I would do it. Grandma's going to help me stay on top of it. She's making a list."

They all shouted in unison, "And checking it twice!" Everyone laughed at their own joke. "That was good, really funny. Seriously, though, Grandma is writing down everything that needs to be done for Christmas and when. When I get it, we can go through it together and see what we want to keep this year and what we want to let go. I think it should be a family decision. Especially since it's just me, and I have studying and work to do. I know I'll need some help to make Christmas happen."

Benji spoke first, "I'd like to help make the cookies, Dad. I'm also pretty good at helping put the lights on the tree without getting them tangled."

"How about I get a piece of paper, and we can write down all the things we can help with and then when you get Grandma's list, we can compare and see what else is left? Maybe those are the things that we will have to let go this year?" Riley's logical mind was working it all out for the family, and Dillion smiled and sighed in relief. He didn't need to take this all on his own. He would have lots of help this year.

"What can I do?" Brianna looked very concerned and almost ready to cry.

"Well, Bri, you've already done something pretty darn special." Dillion pointed to her picture. "You made a beautiful Christmas tree decoration. You can help the rest of us with our Christmas projects and, if you have time, you can make more decorations." The trembling mouth turned into a wide grin. "Deal?"

"Deal!"

The rest of the night was spent listing all the things they thought they could do to help get through the holiday. When it was bedtime, Dillion started with Brianna first. After her prayers, she put her chubby arms around his neck and kissed his nose. "I know you made mistakes today, Daddy. But I still love you."

His heart grew a little bit at that moment. "Thanks, Bri. I really needed to hear that. Love you too." He kissed her back before he turned out the light and made his way to Benji's room.

Benji was looking out his window and staring up at the sky. "Did you find it?" Dillion asked as he came up behind his son.

"Yup. It's up there. To the left of the oak tree." Dillion followed his finger and found Polaris.

"It's pretty bright tonight."

"It's always bright, Dad. We talked about this, remember?" Dillion smiled. His six-year-old son was teaching him a lesson in astronomy. At some point, very soon in the future, he wasn't going to be able to help him with any of his homework. Benji was destined to be one of the great minds of his generation. Dillion just hoped he wouldn't screw him up too much to ruin any opportunity he'd have to reach his potential.

Next, Dillion made it to Riley's room where she was just finishing up her prayers and climbing into bed. "Dad ... "

"Yes, sweetie?"

"How old do I have to be to have a later bedtime then Benji and Brianna? I'm not tired, and it's a Friday night. Can't I stay up a little longer?" Dillion looked at her and kissed her forehead.

"I understand you're growing up, Riley. I do. But right now, I need you all to keep some things the same for a little bit. Until I get used to this single parent thing. Until I get better at it." He could see he was losing her. She was looking frustrated. "How about when you have your next birthday, when you turn nine, we try and see how it works for you to stay up 30 minutes longer?" Riley gave him a nod and a small grin. She was willing to compromise. Who knows how long that willingness will last? One? Maybe two more years? He kissed her forehead and turned off the light when he left her room.

Oh God, he thought to himself. In four years, he'd be raising a teenager all by himself. "Shit." He said aloud, reached into his pocket and pulled out a dollar bill to put into the jar.

Chapter Six

Saturday morning came with the sun shining through sheers in the family room and the sound of a key turning in the back door to the kitchen. Dillion jumped up and saw that at least he had the sense to change into his pajama pants and a T-shirt before he fell asleep on the couch again last night. Rose Clare pushed open the door and stomped the snow off her boots as she came inside the house. "Take this off my hands, will you Dillion?" She handed him a large, slender box. "Be careful with it, it's an antique!"

Reaching to take the box, his bare foot stepped into some of the snow puddled around her feet. "Wow! That's cold!" he screeched.

"That's why you should always wear slippers." She shook off her coat before hanging it on one of the empty hooks near the children's winter things. Next, she reached into her large bag and pulled out a pair of slippers to put on her own feet before venturing further into the house. "See? Now I have warm AND dry feet."

"Not too many people keep a pair of slippers in their purse, Mom. I didn't think I'd have snow inside my house this time of the morning. What time is it, anyway?"

"Well, I've got a busy day today, so you were my first stop. It's 7:30 in the morning. I have my first meeting at eight, so I wanted to get your Christmas chore chart here before I ran out of time." Rose Clare's nose was sniffing for something, but Dillion was still a little groggy to figure out what it might be. "Too early for coffee, I guess?"

"Um, sorry? You woke me up, Mom. I didn't have time to make it."

"Dillion, coffee machines now have timers on them. You can set it up the night before and then when you wake up, the coffee is already brewing. It's a nice way to wake up—to smell the coffee."

"No, Mom. I didn't know that. Sorry. I can make you some now." He started over to the coffee machine and was about to put the box down on the kitchen table.

"No time for that now, Dillion. As I said, I've got to run. Open the box."

A little discombobulated, Dillion did as he was told and opened the box to find an antique wooden advent calendar inside. It was made to look like an old-fashioned chalet—almost like a gingerbread house. It had 25 mini doors with brass knobs to pull them open.

"Now, today is the second of December, so open doors one and two to see what's inside." Rose Clare spoke with a bit of a teacher's authority, but also with a bit of excitement. Dillion carefully pulled on the first two knobs and found that they weren't doors, but drawers. In each tiny wooden drawer was a small, folded piece of paper. "Open them, Dillion, and read."

He stared at his mother in amazement. He wasn't sure he was following her just yet but began reading the first note. "Put up the Christmas stockings." Then he read the second, "Buy Christmas cards." Dillion looked at his mother as he was attempting a coherent thought.

"I wrote down a chore for each day of the month, and put them into their own drawer. So, the advent calendar is your chore list, and it's a timeline!" She looked from the little wooden house to her son who was perplexed. "Look, Dillion, I didn't want to overwhelm you, so I just took the bare necessities and wrote down one thing to do for Christmas for each day. I figured with everything else you've got on your plate, one extra thing wouldn't be too difficult to manage."

He put the papers down on the kitchen table, next to the calendar and hugged his mother, very hard. "Thank you, Mom. This is great. So great!" He kissed her on the cheek and hugged her again. Rose Clare didn't fluster much, but Dillion's excessive gratitude was getting her there.

"I'm glad you like it. It was my mother's, and I thought it was also a great decoration; one less thing to have on your list. She walked a little further into the room and gave the house a once over, staring at the couch that looked recently slept on. "Still sleeping on the couch?" It wasn't much of a question; it was more of an observation. A concerned observation.

"Yeah. Each night I say prayers and good night with the kids and head into the bedroom. I go through all the motions like I will sleep in the bed, but once I get there and turn down the sheets, I just can't go there."

She nodded and looked into his eyes. "Are you sleeping at all?"

"Better than before. Not all through the night, if I'm honest. But longer blocks of time than before."

She nodded and patted his cheeks before she heard her youngest grandchild yell, "Grandma!" Rose Clare bent down and accepted the running hug that Brianna offered.

"Hello, my angel. How'd you sleep?" Before Brianna could answer, Benji and Riley opened their doors and came over to get their hugs. Brianna, releasing her grandma, saw the advent calendar on the kitchen table and pointed to it.

"What's this, Grandma?" That got everyone's attention, so the whole family gathered round the table.

"This was my mother's when she was a child. It's called an advent calendar, and it's to help your father keep track of all the Christmas chores he needs to do before Christmas Day."

Riley spoke up then, "We're going to help Daddy, too, Grandma! Last night we sat around the table and wrote down a list of all the things we can help Daddy do for Christmas this year." Rose Clare looked into the eyes of her oldest granddaughter and saw Corinne's eyes. Right now, Riley's eyes held a maturity that only those children who've experienced loss or trauma have. Rose Clare's heart broke a little bit, recognizing that Riley was preparing to be the lady of the house to help keep the family moving forward. So young. Too young.

"That's wonderful, Riley. You all will be a great help to your father. I'm very proud of you." She drew them in for a group hug and kissed the top of their tousled heads. "Oops! Look at the time!" She saw the digital clock on the microwave when she opened her eyes again. I'd better be on my way. The Optimist Club will not stay optimistic very long if I don't get there on time to make the coffee and get the pastries laid out. Sugar and caffeine keep them thinking positive!"

Dillion laughed at that and kissed his mother on her cheek. "Thanks, again, Mom. See you at church tomorrow."

After she changed out her slippers into her boots, Rose Clare waved behind her and yelled back, "Someone better get out here and shovel! We're supposed to get more snow tonight!"

Dillion showed his curious kids the drawers and the little pieces of paper already opened. They were fascinated, and a decision was made to review their list against the chores nestled in the advent calendar to make sure they didn't miss anything. They agreed that Brianna would open the drawers every morning and the bigger kids would take turns reading the chore.

After a breakfast of cereal, the children had a new-found excitement about the day and chores, so they spent little time in their PJ's and instead got ready and into their snow gear to put up the wreaths over the lamps on the house while Dillion snowplowed the driveway and shoveled a path to the front door. After it was all shoveled, they piled into the minivan for a trip to the library for some new books and Christmas movies.

December was moving along as the advent calendar and Dillion's study schedule kept them all on track. While they didn't always eat meals with fruit and vegetables, they did eat three meals a day. Sometimes he made them breakfast for dinner because they loved it, and it was easy to do. The calendar kept them focused and working as a team. He had to admit, it wasn't the perfect Christmas, but it was an okay Christmas. He still made mistakes, forgot that shortening isn't the same as butter, shorted out the tree lights, forgot to pick up the kids one or two more times—boy did he appreciate Mr. Scott's foresight at making him sign that permission slip—but the kids forgave him each time. They just looked at the chores in the advent calendar and moved on.

Christmas Eve, he cheated and brought home a roasted chicken from the grocery store and made mashed potatoes from a box. He knew they would be treated to a real meal on Christmas Day at his parents' house, so taking a few shortcuts wasn't terrible. After the prayer, the kids didn't seem to be put off, but instead prattled on about what Christmas movie they were going to see and which cookies they should put out for Santa to eat when they went out to see the Christmas lights.

Dillion's heart stopped. He had forgotten to confirm with his mom that she was coming over. Just then, there was a knock and his parents were at the door taking off their coats. "Merry Christmas! Did we miss dinner?" Grandpa asked.

In unison, the Clark children screamed, "Grandma! Grandpa!" And ran over to gather their kisses and hugs.

"I think we have some leftovers. Are you hungry? We can wait for you to eat before we go to see the Christmas lights," Dillion said with a bit of trepidation. He wasn't sure how they could carry this off.

This time his mother spoke, "Oh, we are a little hungry. We had the pageant practice today and prepping the church for tomorrow's mass. Didn't have time to cook anything. Do you mind if we stay and eat?"

Brianna voiced her concern, "But then we'll miss the Christmas lights!" Dillion recognized his opening and responded.

"How about this? Why don't we let Grandma and Grandpa sit down and eat in peace and quiet for a bit while we go and see the lights? Then when we get home, we can all watch a movie together before your bedtime?"

"And open presents!" Brianna seemed to think this was a good compromise and ran to get her candy cane off the tree before she put on her winter things.

"Sounds perfect. I could use a little quiet time. I've had that choir singing in my ears all day and I've started to get a headache." Grandpa answered. "Grandma and I can get the cookies out while you're on your ride. Okay?"

It was Brianna who spoke for the group again. "Thanks, Grandpa! See you soon!"

Dillion mouthed "I owe you!" to his parents who just grinned and waved.

The older kids helped Brianna buckle into her seat and unwrap her candy cane. Dillion found some Christmas music on the radio and started to drive along their street. Every house that had lights on, they slowed down to get a good look. Dillion used the rearview mirror to observe the wonder on the faces of his children. He gazed out the driver's window to see one of the homes had a blow-up snow globe and candy cane lit driveway. A smile grew on his face. Then one of the kids said, "Look over here! They got music going with the lights, Daddy!" So, he turned to look over to the passenger side; his smile faded. He saw a shadowy figure in the seat. Bouncy blonde curls underneath a white knitted cap. Wearing her favorite white ski jacket with the brown and white fur on the hood. She used to pretend she was a ski bunny in that jacket. Wearing heavy winter boots on her feet because she complained that her toes were always cold. His eyes misted over, and he stopped breathing for a moment. She was here, with them. The vision of his late wife opening her mouth to sing the Christmas carol that was blaring from the house across the street. He wanted to reach out and touch her but was afraid the apparition would disappear, and he'd be without her once again.

"Okay, Daddy. We're ready to see the next house. Let's go!" Brianna said. He blinked, looked at his daughter, and realized she didn't see her mom sitting right there, in the front seat. He looked at Benji and Riley to see if they recognized her. They were just as oblivious. He was afraid to look back at the passenger seat because he already knew. She was gone. The little light of Christmas that was in his heart a moment ago, left him feeling empty and hollow. And alone.

Chapter Seven

"Daddy! Let's go!" Brianna commanded.

Her voice shook him out of his momentary despair. "Sorry, angel. Here we go." He realized he needed to focus on the road and fake it tonight. Quite possibly tomorrow as well. The vision had just been so real. He had hoped, for an instant; his heart had been ready to live a little again. Then it wasn't. He was back in a world where he was, and she wasn't. It hurt. It hurt like hell.

After a few more roads and Christmas carols, they pulled into the driveway and unloaded. When the back door opened, and the gaggle of Clark children ran through the door, Grandma and Grandpa Clark gave their best performance as sleepy bystanders. Dillion looked one more time at the passenger seat and carefully reached out to touch the soft, cold fabric to see if the apparition had left an imprint to prove Corinne had been there moments ago. There was nothing. Dillion allowed a single tear to run down his cheek and said a silent prayer.

Dear Lord. I don't know why you needed her by your side so soon. I'm trying to understand. To live again. To be the father our children need. But this burden you gave me. It's too hard to bear. I am angry with you for taking the love of my life, the mother of my children, away from us when we had so much more to do as a couple. As a family. I know you sacrificed your only son for us, and I suppose I now understand a little bit what that grief was like. I am struggling as a man, as a father, and as a man of faith, right now. Please give me a sign. Please show me the way through this quagmire. I'm lost. So lost. Please help me be what they need. Amen.

Dillion left the van and took a deep breath of the brisk, cold air outside before getting his game face on for the evening's festivities. When he came through the door, he shook his head as he saw the disheveled bundle of jackets, boots, mittens, and hats on the floor. Presents trumped order. Brianna met him at the doorway to the kitchen. "Daddy! Daddy! Santa came! Santa came!" Her chubby little hand reached out to him and held on tightly to drag him through the clutter and into the festivities in the family room.

An organized home earlier in the day, now was a higgledy-piggledy mess. Partially eaten cookies, sparkling with brilliant crystals of colored sugar, lay near glasses of half-drunk milk, cocoa, and mulled wine. Millions of crumpled pieces of colorful printed paper scattered around the tree. The children were still in awe of all the gifts they uncovered, jumping from one toy to the next. Dillion sat back and tried to take it all in. Benji was looking at his telescope, reading the directions to get it set up just right. Riley was thrilled with the newest book in the series she was reading, and Brianna was busy playing tea party with Grandpa on her new tea table and chair set.

Grandma rose from her place and walked out of the room, only to come back with a shopping bag and a solemn face. She cleared her throat to get everyone's attention. The children knew that sound as did the men in her life. When she wanted your attention, you'd better give it. "This seems about the best time to do this. Before your Momma went to heaven, she asked me to do her one last favor." Rose Clare's voice caught, and her eyes misted, but she had made a promise, and she would keep it. "You all know how very important Christmas was to your mom, and she didn't want to leave you without giving you all presents. I'll start with the youngest. Bri, baby, come sit down by Grandma a moment, please."

Brianna put down her pink teacup, scooted from her chair, and walked over to her grandma and sat down by her on the couch. "Here, baby, here's your present from your momma. Open it up, and I'll read the note that goes with it." Brianna pulled the white glittering tissue paper out of the red bag with a gold star emblazoned on the front, put her chubby little hand into it and pulled out a bronze plastic manger scene.

Rose Clare began to read, "My littlest angel. My gift to you is my very favorite Christmas ornament. My mommy's family didn't have much money, so she would only get one gift for Christmas. One year, she was given this miniature plastic manger that she fell in love with and filled her with joy and light when she put it on her tree. When I was around your age, she gave it to me and I've put it on every Christmas tree ever since. My wish for you, my darling Brianna, is to always have the spirit of wonder and joy of Christmas in your heart." Brianna took the ornament, cleared a path to the tree, scooted around until she could see the perfect spot to place her treasure, and then stepped back to see the lights shine through the little plastic ornament.

Rose Clare reached back into the bag and pulled out a tiny velvet box before continuing to read, "Speaking of heart, I am gifting you the very first Christmas present your daddy gave me, a gold heart necklace. When you wear it, I hope you know that I am living on in your heart. Love You Always, Momma." Dillion's eyes filled with tears when his mom handed off the box to him. His fingers trembled as he opened the tiny treasure chest and saw the sweetheart necklace he bought for Corrine. Closing his eyes, he took a deep breath as tears rolled down his cheeks. Brianna left the Christmas tree to stand in front of Dillion so he could clasp the dainty gold heart around her neck. Once done, Dillion enveloped Bri in a great big bear hug.

Benji knew it was his turn, so he sat next to his grandmother intently. "My bright baby boy. I promised you a star up in the heavens to look at and know that I would be looking down on that same star to watch over you. My Christmas present to you, Benji, is just that. I named a star for us, 'Clark's Star' and now you have the certificate to prove it. You've been the bright spot in my darkest days, Benji. My wish for you is to continuously find the wonder in the world, to be curious about how it works, and to reach for the stars. I will be watching over you. Love You Always, Momma." Benji held onto the certificate and read it silently to himself. He pulled it to his heart, laid his head on his grandmother's breast to let his tears fall. Rose Clare almost lost it then but kissed the top of his head before she went on.

"Okay, Benji, it's time to let Riley come get her present. Riley, dear, come sit by Grandma." Riley did as she was told. She was given a small white box. Dillion's heart skipped a beat. There was only one thing that it could be, and he hadn't seen it since the day she died. "My big girl. You will certainly have the world at your feet. You are smart and always planning, carefully strategizing, and organizing your world. I know you will be the best at whatever you decide to do. But I want you to always remember the importance and power of love in your life. It will lead you to greater fulfillment than anything you can achieve on your own. To always remember the power of love and to keep it in your heart, I give you my most treasured possession, my engagement ring." Riley opened the box and lying inside was a solitary diamond pendant set in a 14-carat gold on a gold necklace chain. She reached out to Dillion who gathered the strength to move over to his eldest daughter and hold the diamond in his hand that he had presented to Corinne on another memorable Christmas Eve years before. He opened the clasp and locked it around his precious Riley's neck before kissing her cheek.

Dillion thought he couldn't take any more. He wanted to run away and crawl into a cave and just cry until he passed out. This was more than he could bear. "Dillion, honey, it's your turn." Rose Clare looked at her son and he could see the anguish in her eyes. He moved next to his mother and braced for the last gift from his wife. "I don't know what's in it, but she wrote you this letter. It's okay if you want to read this on your own, son. We understand."

With shaking hands, he opened the envelope and smelled the wafting scent of her favorite perfume coming from the pages of her lofty, lyrical writing.

My Love,

I've thought the hardest about what would be my final Christmas gift to you. Today I realized I don't have days left, but hours. I asked God to help me, and I've finally figured it out. My gift to you has two parts. First, is my wish that you know how thankful I am for the life I was given. Oh, I know you feel like it was gone too soon. We didn't have much time together. But, in all honesty, I've had a full life and you've been there every step of the way. Every memory I have, that I am taking with me, has you in it. My first day at church, at school, when I learned to ride a bike, my first kiss, the eighth-grade dance, homecoming, prom, graduation, our engagement, wedding, the death of my parents, the birth of our children. You were there. Through it all. I am so honored that you chose me as your wife, and I'm so very blessed to have lived a full life with you by my side. Always.

The second part is my blessing. My second wish for you is to find love again. Go on living. Find the joy and the wonder of the world once again. God gave you a gift. I've seen you inspire groups of people with your words. With your actions. I know you will need time to grieve. To heal. But I want you to promise me that you won't get stuck there. You need to move forward. You need to help our children grow to their potential and find love for themselves. You need to inspire others with your words and actions as their priest. Don't let my death and your grief define you. Let our love lift you up and move you forward. Find your faith again. Find love again. Love You Always, Corinne

The sobbing began and couldn't be contained. He wailed out like a wild, caged animal. He ran from the room and out the door and shouted up to the heavens until he landed on his knees and put his head into his hands to let the grief out. He didn't know how much time had passed, but his whole family came to be kneeling around him and holding him in the warmth and security of their love. He hated God at that moment. He hated Corinne, too. But then he felt the strength and warmth of the love that was showering over him from the family that was there to hold him and help him up. To move him forward.

Chapter Eight

Since Christmas Eve, Dillion's life had moved past him in a flurry. Between deacon work, studying, and his family responsibilities, he barely had time to rest. They celebrated when he passed his exams by going to the diner and Melinda gave him a slice of bumbleberry pie on the house. It was the month of April, and his brother, Roger, was in town as well. After dinner, when the children were put to bed, Roger asked his parents to stay with the kids while "the boys" went into town for a celebratory drink.

Patty's Pub on Main was your typical Irish bar. Dark wood elements, Irish beer on tap, soccer playing on the TVs, and a small stage for live music on Saturday evenings. Roger bought two beers which were poured to perfection. He raised his glass and encouraged Dillion to join him. "To my baby brother. Who'll be the finest priest this side of Chicago!" They clinked their glasses and took a long drink before setting them down on the bar.

"Wow. It's been a while since I've been in a bar. Since I've had a beer," Dillion said.

"No shit?" Roger questioned in surprise.

"No shit," Dillion confirmed.

"Hey, I thought men of the cloth couldn't swear. Giving up already, Father?"

Dillion laughed, pulled a dollar out of his pocket, and laid it on the dark oak slab that held their glasses. "Well, it isn't recommended. However, once you do, you pay the fine, and you gain forgiveness." Roger looked quizzically at his brother. "Okay, every time I swear,

I have to put a dollar in the swearing jar and when it gets full, then we take the money and do something fun as a family."

Roger laughed. "That sounds like something Corinne would have made up to keep you on track to sainthood."

Dillion laughed with him. "She did." Then the laughing stopped, and he took another long drink and stared at the bar that held the eyes of many men before him trying to drink away their memories.

Roger noticed the pregnant pause and decided it was time to broach the subject. "It's been about five months now. How are you doing?"

"Honestly? Or would you like the version that makes you feel better about asking?" Dillion questioned coarsely.

"Hell, bro, you know I don't deal in hometown mumbo-jumbo. I live in Chicago. I live by cut-throat honesty every day. Give it to me." Roger's dark hair and dark eyes matched his all black attire. It also matched his personality.

Dillion felt he could share it with his brother because he was an outsider. He gave it to him, honestly. "The truth is … I hate it here. I feel like I am dying a little bit every day. Oh, I go through the motions and make sure the kids are doing alright, but I am suffocating." He looked up from his drink to gauge the reaction from his brother. When he realized he was in a judgment-free zone, he continued.

"I see her everywhere, Roger. Even here. When we turned 21, we came here to pay for our first legal drink." He looked over his shoulder and nodded to the booth in the corner. "Corinne ordered a glass of wine, and I had a beer with dinner." Dillion looked at his brother square in the eyes and continued. "I see her every damn day in every corner of this place. How can I get over the grief, move on, if the memory of her is everywhere I go every day?"

Roger nodded in understanding. "And when I do have a momentary lapse of a memory? I have someone who sees me on the street and makes a comment that they think will make me feel better. It doesn't. It just reminds me again." Dillion looked at his brother and put his hand on his shoulder and asked, "How the hell can I get on with my life when she's everywhere I go?" Absent-mindedly, he put his hand in his pocket and removed another dollar bill.

This time, Roger put his hand on his brother's shoulder and looked into his eyes. "You can't. You've got to get out of here. The sooner the better in my opinion. I'll help you."

Dillion turned back to his drink and took a slow pull this time. "It'll kill Mom and Dad, you know. They fully expect me to be an ordained priest, and then he can retire and the vestry will vote me in to take over. What about the kids? Haven't they been through enough? Take them away from the only place they've ever known? Their friends? Grandparents?"

Though Roger hadn't been at Christmas Eve, he was there for Christmas Day and had read Corinne's letter, so he used it to get his point across. "Dillion, if you don't, you'll be breaking your promise to Corinne."

"What?" Dillion asked, shocked.

"Her Christmas wish for you was to live your life. Live up to your potential. Find love again." Dillion looked confused, so Roger continued. "In order to do that, you must move on. Move out. You'll just die a lonely old man. You won't inspire anyone."

Dillion looked up at the mirror behind the bar and into his own face. He saw that he was still pale and had sunken eyes. He kind of liked the scruffy beard and mustache he'd kept since the start of winter, but it looked a bit disheveled like he was riding the boundary between a trendy outdoorsman and a vagrant. "I know. I know." He looked deeper into his own eyes and then shifted his gaze back to his brother. "Actually, I've known for a while. I guess I just needed you to come home to get me to admit it to myself."

"Look, I tell you what. As your big brother and as I didn't get you a gift, I will start looking for a place for you. I'll help you sell your home and help you buy a new one." Roger saw that Dillion was looking a little like a deer in headlights now. "Don't worry. You can tell me what you are looking for and we won't have a time limit on this. But I do think that if we can find you a church that needs a priest in a community that you feel is safe and good place to raise your kids, hopefully before school starts, it'll be a good thing. It's time to move forward, Bro. Time to live again." Roger held up his glass for one last toast. Dillion's glass met his and then they both downed the last drops of their brew before leaving the bartender a $3.00 tip (the swearing fee) and headed for home.

Chapter Nine

The June sky was bright blue with glorious cumulus clouds slowly meandering above them. The moving truck was packed with the last bits of their life in Big Rock, and the Clark kids were all buckled into their seats. Riley and Rose Clare had just kissed and hugged their grandbabies and were about to say goodbye to their son when he spoke. "Look, Mom and Dad. You've been great. Really great. I couldn't be doing this if I didn't feel strong enough, and you've helped me get to this point."

"I know," Riley put his hands on his son's shoulders and looked deeply into his eyes. "It's just that its six hours away. Couldn't you find your new life a little closer?"

"Actually, it's more like five, five and a half hours away, Dad. Roger found us a great house in Minocqua, not too far away from the church, which is in Woodruff. The congregation is small but vibrant. The kids will be able to fish, swim, learn to snowmobile, and all kinds of great outdoorsy things. It'll be a great place for you to visit." He looked at his mother who was trying her best not to cry. "There's an afterschool program at the church. The ladies there have already met the kids, and they will be well taken care of, Mom. I promise."

Rose Clare nodded as she couldn't get the words out without crying, and she didn't want to make her son feel any worse than he already did about leaving. However, her logical, practical mind was already rationalizing this moment. He was leaving so he could live. He needed a fresh start. This was the part of parenting that all parents strive for; letting go. Unfortunately, it was also the hardest thing to do. It hurt. It hurt like hell. She reached out to give a hug and a kiss to her son and said, "You call us when you get there so we know you got there safely. Don't hesitate to call on us if you need help. We'll be there."

Dillion hugged his mother, his rock, and kissed her cheek. "Thanks, Mom. I will. I promise." He left her arms and took the hand of the man who had been his role model and teacher for the past 30 years.

"I know this isn't what you wanted, Dad, but I hope you'll respect my decision and support me."

Riley pulled his son into his arms and hugged him fiercely. "This may not be my plan for you, but it's God's plan. He has more insight as to what's right for you than I have. Godspeed, Son." He released his son, his protégé, and watched Dillion get into the minivan and pull away from his childhood home and toward his new life. "Godspeed," he repeated as he waved to the van in the distance.

PART TWO: AURELIE

Chapter Ten

Aurelie looked around her best friend's bedroom at all the commotion and wondered, *How did we get here?* Scenes of playing Barbies on the floor, tea parties for their stuffed animals, spontaneous dance parties and sleepovers flashed through her mind like the shuffling of a deck of cards. Priceless memories of a childhood well-lived and loved. Their final sleepover as single women was last night. Today, her best friend of more than a decade was getting married.

After putting the finishing touches of make-up on Cat's face, Aurelie nestled little sprigs of mistletoe blossoms into the waterfall flow of auburn curls that came down to rest on Cat's left shoulder. Cat's mom surely knew how to get her daughter's unruly curls to stay put when warranted. Aurelie put the last mistletoe blossom in Cat's hair and took a step back. "There. What do you think, Mrs. C.?"

Claire Carneri looked up and down and all around with an eagle's eye. "Well, well. I think you did a fine job, Aurelie. A fine job." Tears glistened in the corner of her eyes and her voice caught a bit. "You made my baby into a beautiful bride. She's picture perfect. Catrina, honey, turn around and take a look at the back with this hand mirror to see if you like it."

When Catrina, "Cat", Carneri turned around, Aurelie saw the overall glow on the porcelain skin of her best friend since childhood. Where did the time go? She found herself reminiscing about how they met when Cat was getting bullied at school and Aurelie was struggling with her learning disability, so they found a champion in each other. "Aurelie? Hey, Aur! Hello?" Aurelie shook her head and put her attention back where it belonged. On the blushing bride.

"Sorry. Lost my focus for a moment, but I'm back. Don't start looking for another maid of honor just yet. What's up?"

"I just wanted to say what an amazing job you did on my hair and make-up. I've never seen myself as a glamorous person, but, wow, I look and feel like one of those top models on TV."

Aurelie smiled. "Sweetie, I've always known you were a hot momma. You just didn't believe me."

Cat put her two hands over her rounded belly. "Isn't that the truth. I'm hot and I'm going to be a mom in a few months. Holy shit! When did all of this get so real?"

Claire saw that the two friends were going to have a moment, so she found a way to excuse herself. "I'm going to check downstairs to see if anyone needs me."

Cat stood up and let her white, fluffy robe billow around her belly before she took the few steps over to her mother. "Thanks, Mom. Can you come back up here in a few minutes to help Aurelie get my dress and shoes on?"

Claire smiled, put her hand on Cat's face and nodded. "Whatever you need me to do today, baby. This is your day." Then she looked over at her daughter's best friend and saw the second daughter she never had but always wanted. "Aurelie, you are a vision. Truly. You both should be on the cover of a magazine. There's a guy out there for you, too. I feel it in my bones."

Aurelie smiled and said, "Thanks Mrs. C. but in my 30 years, I haven't found a single guy that is as great as Mr. C." All three women laughed. Claire told the story of their first meeting more than 30 years ago when Anthony asked her to dance and when they touched, she knew, just knew, that he would be the man she was going to marry. However, what she didn't know was that Anthony was stubborn and old fashioned. He certainly didn't realize he had fallen in love with a very strong willed, independent woman. Needless to say, their personalities kept their family life interesting.

"Seriously, Mrs. C., you look amazing in that dress. You make Mr. C. take you on a date to a fancy restaurant and maybe stay overnight in a swanky hotel so you can wear that dress again." Claire blushed a little and smiled as she smoothed the chiffon overlay skirt on her burgundy, tea length, satin dress. The three quarter length sleeves were chiffon with a scalloped edge and gilded in dark bead work that looked like falling snowflakes. The satin bodice incorporated beadwork following the overlap from the right ridge of the V-neckline to the natural waist where a large, beaded snowflake pulled both sides together as it lay on top of the slightly gathered chiffon before it fell as a curtain swag falls over its windowpane.

"Thank you, Aurelie. I think I'll keep you around a little bit longer. Maybe you can kick Anthony into shape now that Cat's off to Montana again." She left the two girls and Aurelie's heart sank a little. In a few hours she would be celebrating the marriage of her best, and probably only true friend, and then wave her off into the night toward her new life in Bozeman, Montana where she was now an instructor in the equine science department of a university.

Aurelie turned around to see what Claire saw in her to call her a vision. She was wearing silver strappy high heels that wrapped around her ankles in a crisscross pattern. At mid-calf, the vintage forest green velvet pencil skirt ended and followed her slight form up to snuggle her rounded hips where it gathered on her right hip before riding up her fitted waist to cross over her breasts in a femme fatale V and then fanned into small cap sleeves that settled off her shoulders. She was impressed that her B-cup breasts were pressed together enough to show a bit of cleavage—it would have been the waste of this incredible dress without some. Her usually bronzed skin was pale by comparison to her summer tan but was a fierce complement to the deep, warm green that hugged her every line and curve. She was blessed with a long neck that held up her heart shaped head. Her lips were luscious in a shade of dusky red lipstick to match the deep jade liquid eye liner outlining her almond-shaped emerald eyes reminiscent of a cat's eyes. Aurelie's jet-black short hair was coiffed in the roaring twenties style deep waves of a flapper and adorned by a side headpiece of crystal and silver snowflakes.

Cat stood behind Aurelie and rested her chin on Aurelie's bare shoulder. "You're breathtaking, Aur. If I wasn't getting married today, I would take you out on the town and show you a good time."

"Thanks, but you are. To a pretty great guy. Oh yeah, and you're preggers. That might put a damper on things." They both laughed.

"I can't believe it, Aur. It feels like we were just having a sleepover in this room and talking about boys and zits and dancing around until all hours of the night hopped up on chocolate and soda. "

"I know. That's what I keep thinking about. You caught me before when I was daydreaming about our first day together."

"You were so bold, and I almost peed my pants when you asked me to be your friend. I've never known anyone like you, Aur. You are one of a kind."

"Back at you, sister." Cat reached around and hugged her friend tight around the waist then looked down.

"Damn! Look at your boobs! They look great in your dress!"

"I know, right? They are actually showing off a bit." They both laughed and heard the familiar footsteps of Claire coming to help get Cat's wedding dress on.

"Alright, we have a tight schedule, Cat, do you need a potty break before we get you into your dress? I don't think we can figure out how to get all three of us in that bathroom without someone standing in the bathtub." Cat moved away from the mirror and down the hall for a quick stop.

"Are you doing okay, Mrs. C.?" Aurelie noticed she had started to pick up around the room and tidy up the place. Claire would always do that when she was upset or nervous.

"I'm just fussing. It's been a whirlwind, you know. Oh, don't get me wrong, Damon is a wonderful man and I know he loves my baby girl, but it came so fast. I'm just trying to catch my breath."

Cat came in, shed the robe, and stood in the middle of the room so that her assistants had plenty of space to work around her to help get the white satin, A-lined wedding dress on her body without making any wrinkles. Cat aided by shimmying her shoulders to get the gathered, overlapping bodice over her very rounded breasts so the cap sleeves could rest below her shoulders.

Once she was situated in the gown, Aurelie stepped back and exclaimed, "Damn, woman! Your boobs are taking on a life of their own up there! I don't think there's room to fit any more of them in that dress."

Cat shuffled to the long mirror and viewed herself from all angles. "Wow. Just wow. Who is that staring back at me? She looks amazing!" On either side of her, Cat's mom and best friend snuggled into the frame of the mirror to see all three women at the same time. It was one of those moments that stop time and breath to take a mental snapshot and save it for later.

Cat began to sniffle when Aurelie pulled back and turned her around and said, "Hey there, no crying before the wedding! I worked hard to make you look this good!"

Cat chuckled. "Okay, okay. It's just seeing all three of us so grown-up and serious and then these crazy hormones, I can't help it!"

"Well, I can help with that," Claire said. "Just remember that you could be marrying Jason Potter instead of Damon. You know, the kid in preschool who is now changing my oil at the garage in town? He was at his cutest when he was that age."

Both Cat and Aurelie did a full body shake as if they were covered in creepy crawly critters. "Ooh! That'll do it. He lost his hair on top and grew it long in the back to try to compensate." Cat recalled.

"Yeah, and he smells like cigarette smoke and oil all the time. Not a great combination."

"Hey Claire! It's almost time. Can I get up there and get my daughter?" Anthony Carneri yelled up the stairs.

Claire did a once over, smoothing a few of the edges of the satin skirt. "Aurelie, why don't you help me downstairs with the flowers, so Anthony can have a moment or two with Cat. He'll need it. I better make sure there's some Kleenex around here for him, just in case." Anthony was a stoic Italian man. He loved to work with his hands, especially carpentry. However, when it came to his only daughter, he became a protective marshmallow. He had been tough on Damon in the beginning, but during their break-up, Cat found out she was pregnant with his twins and at the same time, she was interviewing for her dream job in Montana. Anthony knew that Damon and Cat loved each other and that his daughter was just as stubborn as he, himself, could be, so he intervened. He showed up at Damon's house with a beer and a plan to make her see that she still loved him and that they belonged together because the babies needed to feel both their parents' love and support. Damon did go to Montana and brought Cat back home with the news of a job confirmation, an engagement, and a home they found just outside of Bozeman. Only Claire knew that, after the celebrations, her husband cried himself to sleep that night. Now, she could sense that he would do the same tonight.

Aurelie followed Claire down the stairs and into the chaos that was festering on the main floor. The cacophony of people's voices, musical instruments being tuned and a dog or two barking from all the excitement helped to drown out the sadness that wanted to mature in the crevices of her mind. She really was happy for Cat and Damon. Honestly. But she was sad, too. She couldn't quite put her finger on it. It was like graduation day, when there's all this pomp and circumstance and then the great big relief from school stress flows into a celebratory mood that concludes as everyone leaves the party, in complete terror for the unknown. Aurelie stopped and smiled for the selfies with Cat's family. She found the flowers and pinned boutonnieres on the men and handed out the wrist corsages to the ladies. She found her own spray and held on to Cat's as well when she heard Claire announcing that everyone should take their places.

A waft of cold air came into the kitchen as people shuffled out onto the large deck covered in white icicle lights and evergreen boughs. The judge was already in place under the cover of the attached gazebo as the violins began to play. She could see the photographer's lights go off as Ryan, Cat's younger brother, escorted Claire to her seat. She smiled at Damon who looked like he was about to faint, clad in his formal kilt attire—red and green plaid, perfect for a winter wedding. Then she heard the footsteps of the father of the bride and the bride herself, coming down the steps.

"Hold still, Cat, while I fix your train." Aurelie went to work making sure that the satin gown flowed behind her friend and then handed Cat the bouquet of cedar boughs, mistletoe, and white roses. When she stood back to see father and daughter in their formal stance, tears formed in the corners of her eyes. "You two look picture perfect." Anthony breathed deep and looked like he was holding back a few tears as well. Cat smiled and mouthed the words, "Thank you," before the processional began. Aurelie had to take her place to walk down the aisle with a smile plastered on her face while her heart was breaking.

The nice thing about being a performer is that Aurelie knew how to fake smile, laugh, and look happy while she was aching inside. She couldn't hear the words that the judge said or the vows that were spoken. She recognized the cue that was hers to begin singing. She felt as if her spirit was in limbo and that she was overlooking the scene from the crystal-clear night sky. At one point during the ceremony, she looked up at the stars and caught sight of Polaris, the northern star, and wondered, was there a man out there who would love her as much as Damon loved Cat? Who would support her passions? Who would be the doting husband and father hers had always been?

Aurelie wasn't very religious, but she had been raised Catholic growing up. Still, she thought it couldn't hurt on this magical night where dreams were coming true for her best friend, if she made a tiny wish—or prayer—for her own future happiness.

The rest of the evening went by like a blustery March day in Wisconsin. Whirlwinds of people eating, talking, laughing, and taking photos. She tried to be present in mind and body, but her mind wasn't having it. She hoped that the photos wouldn't show the truth. She prayed that she put on enough of a front that everyone in the room, especially Cat, would see how much fun she was having instead of the pit of sadness that was ever-growing inside her heart.

When the last dish was put away, and the last guest left, Aurelie hugged the new Dr. and Mrs. MacGregor and wished them a happy and fun-filled honeymoon. She held onto Cat a bit longer than she intended to; a single tear escaped the stronghold she had kept it under all evening. And its gentle glide from her eyelashes made its way to the place where the two best friends' cheeks met. "I love you, Aurelie. Thank you for everything. I miss you already," said the new Mrs. MacGregor.

Aurelie's breath caught, and she hugged a bit harder. "I love you, Cat. Promise me that you won't forget about me."

As she began to cry in earnest, she felt Cat pull away and whisper in her ear, "I promise." Through blurry eyes, Aurelie watched as her best and only true friend walked out to the truck that would take her away from this childhood place and bring her to her new adult home 21 hours away. Away from Aurelie. And tears ran down her face. This time taking her flawless make-up with it while they landed in damp drops on the crushed velvet bodice of her dress.

Chapter Eleven

Weeks passed. Sunrise, get up to teach. Sunset, hang out with the band or in one of the bars in the Greater Milwaukee area. Before Aurelie knew it, the wedding was several months in the rearview mirror. But today, the sun was making its appearance through a window that Aurelie didn't recognize. She heard a strange "whirr" sound coming from somewhere. She squinted and tried to lift her head up, but it was like an ice pick had been slammed into her forehead. Even after putting a pillow over her head, the "whirr" wasn't going away. And the pillow. It didn't smell like hers. It smelled of cheap aftershave and that made her stomach churn.

How much did she have to drink last night? Whose bed was she lying in? What time was it? What was that awful whirring sound she kept hearing? "Hey there, glad you're up. Can you make us some breakfast while I take a quick shower? There are eggs in the fridge and bread on the counter. Coffee's already brewed. Thanks."

Shit. Not only didn't she recognize the bed, but she also didn't recognize the voice. And now that voice was expecting her to make breakfast. Shouldn't it be the other way around? Wasn't she the guest? Aurelie slowly put the pillow down and began peeling one eyelid open and then the other in an attempt to reduce the risk of sensory overstimulation. When both eyes were open and in focus, she looked around the room and realized that she was definitely in a guy's bedroom but didn't recognize which guy.

Now she sat up and noticed that she wasn't wearing anything, but looking down, all The Hot Rockin' Horns performance wear was on the floor. She reached down to grab the basic black kami, threw it on with her denim jacket over it. Then she slid on the black, shiny hot pants and slipped into the patent leather wedges. Her purse was over on a chair a few steps away from the bed. She quietly opened it up and found her keys, wallet, and phone. Didn't look like anything was missing.

Aurelie stood up and saw herself in the reflection of the window that held the sunlight. She looked like a drug addict. Pasty skin. Hair that stuck up on end on one side and pasted to the side of her head on the other. Large dark rims of last night's eye make-up highlighted the blood shot red around her usually sparkling emerald eyes. She heard the water turning on and realized this was her opportunity to get out of a bad situation before it got worse.

Walking out of the loft apartment onto the street, she realized she was in Walker's Point just south of Milwaukee's downtown, a neighborhood known for its vibrant night scene. Luckily, she found her car with a few hits of the alarm button on her fob. It wasn't too far away so she could get away quickly. The crisp spring air woke up her foggy brain a little bit more than it had been in the loft, so she felt certain she could drive home without concern. When she sat in the driver's seat, she started to shake. She knew that she was in a bad place in her life and now she felt she had hit rock bottom. She had slept with someone she just met a few hours ago and didn't know their name. How did she get here? Before she contemplated her life's choices, she recognized the importance of getting back to her own place and taking care of herself.

In the 40 minutes it took to get into the driveway of her comfortable upper flat in the Village of Mukwonago, Aurelie kept her mind and her feelings on autopilot. The minute she pulled into the driveway of the little bungalow where Cat used to live and which was now her home, she broke down and cried. Sobbed, really. Recognizing that she wasn't enjoying her carefree lifestyle any longer. It wasn't fun anymore. It was scary. When she could pull herself together, she got out of the car and wrestled with her purse for her second floor apartment keys. Before she could find them, Mrs. Romansky, her landlord who lived downstairs, had the backdoor open for her.

"Thanks, Mrs. Romansky. I'm sorry if I woke you. I was just trying to find my keys," Aurelie said sheepishly.

"Aurelie, I wasn't asleep; it's one o'clock in the afternoon. I was going to start cleaning out the flower beds since it's supposed to be a nice day today." The elderly woman loved her small plot of land and grew the most amazing flowers in every nook and cranny she had. She was a retired widow, whose son and family lived in the Greater Milwaukee area while her sister and brother-in-law lived next door. She felt safe in her little house, but just to be sure, she only rented the upstairs apartment to women who she knew or who were recommended to her. Oh, she was a stern woman and didn't mince words in her Polish accent when she had something to say, but she also cared very much for her tenants. She would make homemade cookies and offer them on days when rent was due. If money was tight, she'd have the tenant do chores around the house like painting or helping with the yard work to reduce the rent owed. Often, Mrs. Romansky would have a soft touch, but today, it would be tough love.

"Aurelie Beres, I want you to go upstairs and take a hot shower. As hot as you can stand. Then get dressed in clean clothes and meet me down here for a late lunch at 1:30 sharp. No excuses."

Aurelie knew she was being scolded. Even at 30 years of age, she felt sometimes like a small child. "Yes, Ma'am," she squeaked out. Dragging herself up the stairs, Aurelie used her key to get herself into the cozy kitchen area and made a beeline to the bathroom to run the water for a quick bath. Knowing there would be no excuse good enough if she were a second late, Aurelie quickly shed her clothes and stepped into the extra-large clawfoot tub and used the shower head extension to wet down every inch of her body before she lathered it up and scrubbed it all down. When she stepped out, she found her toothbrush and went to town brushing all the scum and who-knows-what else from her teeth and her tongue. She found a simple gray sweater and pulled it over her still damp short black hair. Finding a pair of black yoga pants, she slipped those on and found a pair of ballet slippers to put on her feet. Her cell phone read 1:25 p.m. Just enough time to get down stairs and face the music.

Before she could knock, Mrs. Romansky opened the door and nodded for Aurelie to sit down. An array of simple food was placed in front of Aurelie. Apple slices with chunks of cheddar cheese were on a plate with a small cup of chicken noodle soup steaming and a crusty roll with a pat of butter were placed in front of her. A glass of ice water was set nearby. "Eat. Drink. You need it."

"I don't feel … " Aurelie started to complain before she was interrupted.

"Eat. Drink. While I talk." This time, it wasn't a request, it was a direct order. Though Mrs. Romansky was smaller in stature, she had a commanding presence. Today her silver curls surrounded her lightly weathered face. Her yellow collared sweatshirt had a graphic print of a bird house and some cardinals on it. Her olive-green polyester pants and crocs polished off the ensemble and showed Aurelie that after this meeting, her landlord was ready to get to work cleaning out her gardens.

Aurelie reached for the spoon and took a sip of the hot steaming goodness that could only be from Mrs. Romansky's secret soup recipe. It had cured a great number of Cat's colds while she was a renter here. It couldn't hurt to try it and see if it could make Aurelie's head stop pounding and her stomach stop rolling. "You will start respecting yourself, your apartment, and your car. Today you stop treating it all like trash."

With the spoon just an inch away from her mouth, Aurelie sensed that she was expected to accept the unconditional terms of living here.

"I'm not a prude, Aurelie Beres, I was a young woman of the sixties. My peers and I worked very hard for gender equality—I went to many rallies in my day and burned my bras a time or two. I chose who I slept with and who went home with me. But I always respected myself. They respected my choices. You need to clean up, shape up, or you will *not* live under my roof any longer. Understand?"

"Yes, Ma'am," she almost whispered. Though her elder wasn't yelling or screaming, her tone sent shivers down Aurelie's spine. This was it. There were no more second chances. "I'm sorry that I've disappointed you and disrespected your home. I'm sorry." Aurelie hung her head and put the soup spoon down.

"What's wrong, Aurelie? What's happened to the happy, life-loving young woman I used to know?" After asking the question, the liver-spotted hands of a concerned friend reached out and covered Aurelie's thin olive-skinned hands and gave them a light squeeze.

Tears began to flow again, and Aurelie found it hard to breathe, much less talk. But she knew that an answer was expected. "I just feel so alone. Sad. Confused." Another squeeze and a nod from the woman whose eyes turned from sternness to compassion. "When I saw Cat in her wedding dress and during the whole affair, I realized that her life moved on while mine is at a standstill. She has Damon now, to be her best friend in all things. She has a job that she loves and is about to be a mother. She's living a grown-up life. The kind she always talked about when we were kids." Aurelie looked through the lenses of her watery eyes and saw, possibly, that Mrs. Romansky's eyes were a little misty as well. "I still don't know what I want to be when I grow up. But I feel like I don't want to be a child anymore either. She's the person who helped me focus. Now I have nobody."

Mrs. Romansky added a light rubbing of her slightly gnarled fingers over Aurelie's. "I understand." She released her hands and sat back in her chair. "You need a dog."

Aurelie was shocked. Not sure what she heard. "Excuse me?" Now she sat back in her chair, in confusion.

"Since Catrina left, she took Mia with her. Two women living alone need protection. You need a project. A protector. A best friend. A dog." She nodded her head in confirmation of her decision.

"Why would I want a dog? I have to teach during the day and on the weekends, I perform and sing. I don't have time for a dog. Plus, I don't think I'd like to pick up after a dog all the time."

"Yes. A dog. A dog will teach you to take care of your things, or it will destroy them. A dog will give you unconditional love and attention; you can tell it all your secrets. A dog will force you to respect yourself otherwise it will not respect you. I will be happy to help take care of the dog when you are at work or performing. The rest of the time, you will be responsible for it."

Aurelie looked up at the ceiling trying to see if she could get a handle on taking on a new responsibility. "I suppose a small dog, like a Shih tzu or Pomeranian would be okay."

"No. We need a big dog. It could scare away potential troublemakers. Small dogs go on furniture. Big dogs can be taught to stay off my furniture."

"Okay … I guess I could start looking for a bigger dog … "

"No. First, you clean your apartment. Next you clean your car. Make room for a dog in your apartment, car, and your life. Then, you can get a dog."

"Alright. I suppose that makes sense." However, Mrs. Romansky was seeing that she may have made a tactical error, not putting a timeline on getting Aurelie's life together.

"Good. You have one week to get your life together. Another week to get the dog. It is settled. Go on now. Eat. Drink. Feel better."

Aurelie smirked a little and started to nibble on a piece of cheese and then took a bite of the apple. She didn't know how the older woman did it, but somehow, she gave Aurelie something to look forward to. A small purpose.

After eating, Aurelie put the dishes into the sink and gave the petite dynamo a hug. "Thank you for not giving up on me."

"No worries, Aurelie. I have faith in you. You will find your purpose. You will find your life. Have faith in yourself."

Chapter Twelve

Over the next two weeks, Aurelie acquired a fresh energy about herself. Her students noticed it. Her bandmates did too. Even when she talked to her mother on the phone and invited her parents over for dinner, they were inquisitive about the change.

Dr. and Mrs. Beres were as punctual as they were a gorgeous couple, arriving in their sleek, black luxury car with brown leather seats. Dr. Antoine Beres wore tan chinos and leather loafers with a pale blue golf shirt, complementing his slight athletic build as well as his salt and pepper hair. Aurelie's mother, Beatrice, or Bea, as she preferred to be called, had Aurelie's model thin build with stunning jade green eyes and jet-black hair set into a short bob, no hair dared to be out of place on Bea's head. She simply wouldn't allow it. While Dr. Beres made his name in the world of oncology as a globally known clinical researcher and surgical oncologist, his wife was well-known for being a brilliant partner, raising their children to be respected professionals.

Aurelie remembered one time when her father's boss disrespected her mom. Even though his hands are the tools of his trade, he made a fist and hit the bastard right across the face—may have broken his nose but certainly gave him a black eye and something to think about for a while. Bea was furious that Antoine hurt his hand and may have lost his job. That is, until she heard the whole story and realized that he esteemed her enough to make sure that everyone knew she was the reason for his success. Bea cried happy tears and they never spoke of that incident again. Bea never questioned how her husband felt about her after that. She knew her purpose. She knew she was valued. She knew she was loved.

"Bon jour, Mama! Bon jour, Papa!" Aurelie greeted her parents in their native French-Canadian tongue and kissed them both on their cheeks. "Come on in! I'm making crepes for dinner. Everything is almost ready. Can I pour you a glass of wine?"

They looked at each other and then observed the quaint upstairs apartment. The sunlight was starting to fade looking out of the double hung windowpanes in the kitchen. There were fresh daffodils on the tiny round table that had a bright yellow tablecloth draped over it. She led them into the dining room where a lovely simple table setting was already laid out. Candles were lit, and a bowl of pink tulips were in the center.

"Your place looks lovely tonight, Mon Cheri. Why the fuss?" her mother asked. Tonight, Bea was wearing a very flattering black and beige cashmere sweater set with black skinny jeans and ballet slippers.

"Oh, yeah. Well. That's sort of why I invited you two over tonight. I have the salad ready to go on the table and some French bread I picked up at the farmer's market. Will you help me bring them out? Dad, can you pour the wine? I've got it sitting out by the sink." They both nodded, looked at each other and followed their orders.

The baby spinach salads were dotted with fresh strawberries and drizzled with a poppy seed dressing. The French bread was sliced and placed in a breadbasket next to a small crystal dish holding the butter. Dr. Beres poured the chilled white wine, smiling that it was a French chardonnay he'd seen on sale at the grocery store earlier in the week.

They sat down and enjoyed a bit of catch-up because it had been a while since they'd last shared a meal—just the three of them. Bea prattled on about the other Beres adult children and shared updates on the grandchildren. Dr. Beres talked about his latest published paper and then dove into a difficult case that he was helping manage remotely in northern Wisconsin. After the salads were eaten and the fresh bread was nibbled, Aurelie excused herself and put a pan of crepes stuffed with asparagus, sliced almonds, and melted Swiss cheese into the vintage white enamel oven in the kitchen.

When Aurelie came back, she smoothed her sweater and sat down. "I guess you guys are trying to figure out why I invited you over here for dinner." She saw the curious stares and raised eyebrows and decided it was time to continue. "Well, I had a serious coming to Jesus meeting a few weeks ago, and I'm making some changes."

"What are you talking about? Are you okay?" Bea's concerned tone was on the verge of being anxious.

"Thanks, Mom. I'm feeling better now. It's just after Cat's wedding, I hit a rough patch. A really rough patch." She gazed up and saw that they were both genuinely concerned now. "I didn't like myself and wasn't taking care of me, or my things. I was making poor choices."

This time it was Dr. Beres who spoke up. "What choices, Aurelie? Were you taking drugs? Are you pregnant? I noticed you haven't touched your wine. You've been drinking water." Leave it to her dad to get straight to the medical concerns.

"No. Dad. I promise. No drugs. You never have to worry about that with me. You've taught me well in that area. I was drinking way too much. Staying up until all hours. Sleeping all through the weekend. I'm not pregnant, either." She saw the question in his steel gray eyes. "I took a home pregnancy test after the last time, with the last—very last unnamed guy I slept with. I'm not pregnant." She heard the notable sighs coming from both. Still, they were concerned.

"I've been depressed since Cat left. You know how hard it is for me to make real friends. Not the superficial ones that will go out to the bars with you and hang out. Someone that always has your back, and you can talk to at any time. I was lost and wasn't taking care of anything, including me. Mrs. Romansky saw it and put the kibosh on it. She set me straight. Basically, I got the 'clean up or clear out' message from her." They now looked like they wanted to have a word or two with her landlady. Nobody speaks to their baby girl like that without recourse. "I deserved it. I needed it. And it ended with homemade snickerdoodle cookies," she said with a slight smile.

"And now?" her mother inquired.

"Well, that was two weeks ago and now, I've cleaned up my act. I've deep cleaned and organized my apartment. I even put my clothes away after I wash them now. I also cook meals on a regular basis at home. I've started to save that money for a new car. I cleaned that out too. I've had that car since college and it's not going to last too much longer. I figure, if I can get it into one of those 'push, pull, drag' sales where the minimum trade in is $5,000, and I save another $5,000, I could get close to a brand-new-to-me car."

"I'm glad that you've taken the initiative to move forward and clean up. Why are you telling us now? Why didn't you ask for our help before?" Bea asked.

"I didn't ask for help from anybody, Mom. Mrs. Romansky gave me an ultimatum and a few homemade cookies to start me on my new path." Aurelie reached out and held her parents' hands and continued. "I'm going to stop dating for a while. A long while, while I get my life together."

"That sounds like a wise decision. What about your jobs? Are you keeping them both? Singing in the band will put you in front of a lot of triggers," her father noted.

I know, Dad. I've been thinking a lot about that too. I really love singing with my band. On the whole, they're a great group of guys. Most of them are married or in long-term relationships. I've set up a band meeting, and we're going to talk about our schedule. If they want to continue to perform year-round, I am going to see if they can pick up another singer during the school year and then I can pick up the gigs in the summer. That way I can focus on teaching during the school year and not get distracted by the band stuff. I can still work at Kohl's during summer break and gig on the weekends."

Aurelie looked back and forth between her parents and recognized that they seemed to be onboard. Now it was time to hit them with the other news. "Um, I have something else I want to tell you." Now they looked nervously at each other and back again at their daughter. "I'm getting a dog."

"A dog?" Her mother was very concerned and surprised. "You've just started taking care of yourself. Only a couple of weeks, right? How are you going to take care of a dog? What's Mrs. Romansky going to say?"

"Look, I know. It's a bit of a shock, right? But it was her idea. I guess she really liked having Mia around and now she feels that we could use the deterrent, and I could use the project. She says I need to learn how to take care of a dog before I can learn how to take care of a relationship. Long-term commitment and all."

"Mon Cheri, I love you. I love your free spirit and your excitement when you start something new. But you get bored quickly and then it gets put aside. You can't do that with a dog. They love you unconditionally and need you to be there for them for their food, water, going to the bathroom, exercise." Bea was showing her hand. She was nervous. She was losing her cool.

"Momma, I know, I know how I have been in my past. But after I thought about it, she's right. I was the youngest and most difficult in the family. I never quite fit in, and I didn't need to take care of anything or anyone because my brother and sisters were all so responsible, everyone just took care of me. Then I had Cat to take care of me at school and until recently, while I was learning how to be an adult. I never had to take care of myself because there was always someone else there to take care of me. I could be reckless, spontaneous, carefree, because I always had someone there to be the adult. Until now."

"Aurelie, I agree with your mother. A dog is a big commitment. There's no going back. They live for many years, and you'll have to make sure that they are always taken care of. Why not start smaller? Like with a fish or a cat maybe?"

"Dad, I've put a lot of thought into this, and I know that Mrs. Romansky doesn't want any animal that will go on her furniture. Cats are out. I can do this. I know I can. I promise. I just wanted to tell you both before I brought one home."

"You've decided then," Dr. Beres commented.

"Yes," Aurelie confirmed.

"Then, we will support your decision. It will still be your responsibility, but occasionally, if you need help, you can call on us," Bea offered. "By the way, you've done wonders with this apartment. Antoine, doesn't it remind you of our first apartment when we were newlyweds?" she reminisced.

"Yes, Aurelie, the place looks wonderful. It suits you." He stood up, walked a few steps over to kiss his daughter on the top of her head. Then he smiled at his wife and confirmed, "Bea, I do remember pouring a glass of wine in that tiny apartment and then sitting on our porch, overlooking the city, and talking about our future."

Dr. Beres looked his daughter's face and smiled as he continued. "Aurelie, you've always been the brightest spot in our family. I know that you will find your own way in your own time to the life you deserve. I predict that the next young man who comes into your life will see you, what you've become, and won't want you for just one night, but for a thousand and one nights. Just you wait and see." He kissed her head again.

Just then, the stove timer beeped and Aurelie got up to get the pan of crepes from the oven. The night ended with crepes stuffed with sliced strawberries and whipped cream. She and her mother washed the dishes while her father put them away. Such a simple gesture, but it meant the world to Aurelie. It was the first Friday night in a long time that she stayed home. And she enjoyed it.

Chapter Thirteen

The next day was another bright, sunny spring day. Aurelie noticed the crocus buds pushing their way into the world and smiled. Mrs. Romansky would be pleased. With her keys in her hand, she jumped into her car and checked the times for the open adoption event and the address of the all-dog rescue, Hoover's Hause. Before she put the key into the ignition of her tan sedan, she checked one more time for the adoption paperwork, a dog leash, and her wallet. Good to go!

Aurelie was belting out Lita Ford's "Kiss Me Deadly" which was playing on a Chicago rock radio station. Sometimes on clear days, her crappy car radio could catch the tunes playing on radio stations well outside of the Greater Milwaukee area. *This is going to be a great day*, she thought to herself.

After a brief drive to the dog rescue, she found a spot in the parking lot which was already filling up fast. Bringing her bag, she walked out into the sunshine in her navy-blue tennis shoes, matching yoga pants, and an oversized navy and white sweatshirt. In the sunshine, she squinted until she found her black sunglasses to ease the glare. Taking in the site, she noticed the cluster of cages and heard the sharp barks of excitement from dogs who were hopeful they would find their new homes by the end of the day. In the center of a patch of grass, was a baby gate play yard filled with loveable bundles of fluff, puppies! Oh, she knew that a puppy would steal her heart, but she had promised Mrs. Romansky a large dog. That meant she needed to steer clear of that place and focus on the larger cages nearest the building.

Aurelie had never adopted a dog before, and she was a bit overwhelmed. A volunteer came over to give her some helpful hints. "Each dog has their photo and some basic information printed on a sheet attached to their cage. Pay attention to any notes about their behavior with kids, other dogs, and how active they are so you have the right fit for your homelife. Other than that, when you find one you'd like to meet, ask a volunteer to help you, and over there on the grass you can take your time to get to know one other. If it's a match, bring the paperwork and the dog with you to that table, and we'll start the adoption process. If it's not a match, no problem, just find another volunteer to help you return the dog to their cage. Any questions?" Aurelie shook her head. It was a bunch of information but it all seemed simple enough, so she started her journey in the aisle between the cages.

Something about this place had her feeling a bit sad and excited at the same time. Sad that some of these dogs wouldn't find a home today, yet happy that many would. Hopefully, she'd find a good fit for her and her apartment. Casually, she stopped at a cage to read a sheet and look down at the dog inside to see if anything triggered a reaction. She meandered a bit further, watching other people and how they interacted with their dogs, taking it all in. Then she felt something. Like a stare. She looked around and saw a very large dog looking right at her.

Aurelie walked closer and noticed that the dog was sitting and was nearly looking at her eye-to-eye, with its head cocked. She saw it had the most beautiful blue eye—as if the Caribbean Sea kissed it as a pup and gifted it with the color of a slow-moving wave on a white sandy beach. The other was a warm, cinnamon brown. Then the animal cocked its head in the opposite direction, and she followed it. Looking more carefully, she noticed that its body was a myriad of black spots—but not perfectly round spots, almost like they were splattered onto a white canvas. Its nose was black which was a nice contrast to the large pink tongue that was panting. The artist in her craved the nuances of the misshapen black swatches; they fascinated her. The two different colored eyes seemed to be looking into her soul. But it was the ears that sold her. One was sticking straight up as if it was picking up even the slighted breath sound as she exhaled. The other? Well, that one was plain ol' droopy, as if it was lollygagging around. In Aurelie's eyes, this dog seemed perfectly imperfect.

"Hello, I'm Aurelie. What's your name, buddy?" She looked for the sheet attached to the cage and began reading.

Name: Mumford

Breed: Great Dane

Age: 1 year

Personality: Happy-go-lucky. Gets along great with kids, people, and other dogs. Needs daily activity. A little nervous of loud noises. Would benefit from obedience training.

"Well, I plan on taking obedience classes anyway." She took a step or two backwards to get a better look. "Mrs. Romansky did say she wanted a big dog to scare away any troublemakers. I don't think they get any bigger than you, hey, Mumford?" She noticed that while the head was still cocked, the tail was wagging back and forth. "Okay, let's give this a go." Aurelie turned around and flagged down a volunteer who put Mumford on a leash and led him to a quiet patch of grass on the far corner of the parking lot.

"Just take your time to get to know each other. I've walked Mumford a few times since he got here, and he's really a gentle giant. He's got a lot of love to give. Because he's so big, you'd be wise to always have him on a leash outside. He doesn't realize how strong he can be, either. A leash will help you keep control."

"Thank you." Then Aurelie realized there was something she wanted to ask. "Um, can you tell me why he's at the rescue?"

"Of course, I was here when the family that owned him surrendered him. They didn't realize how much work it is to own a dog. Especially a Great Dane. They felt terrible, but they'd bitten off more than they could chew." The middle-aged woman scratched his neck, and he leaned into it a bit showing how much he was enjoying the attention. "Mumford is a great dog. If you think he's a good fit,

I'd recommend signing up for training right away. Get you both on the right path."

"Oh, I planned on it. I've been around dogs most of my life. My best friend and her family always owned dogs. I've helped dog sit many times, but I never owned one before. I'm at a time in my life now that I realize I'm ready to own one."

"As I said, Mumford will be a great addition to the right home. Enjoy your time together and let me know if you want me to help you get him back into the cage or start the adoption."

"Thanks. I'll look for you when I'm ready." Mumford was standing now, and the top of his head reached Aurelie's shoulder. He walked very nicely on the leash next to her, like he had some training. Next, she held out her hand to let his wet nose take a sniff or two, so he could start getting to know her. When his tail wagged, she took the next step and began to pet his neck. She couldn't tell how much time had passed, but she had walked him in a small pattern around the parking lot to see how he reacted to people, kids, other dogs, and cars. He seemed to be on his best behavior. She tried some simple commands, like "sit," "paw," and "down," which were all happily completed by her companion. For good measure, Aurelie did look around again to see if she had any other reactions to any of the other dogs. She didn't. Mumford was the one.

"Well, there, Mumford, how would you like to come home with me today?" She felt a sloppy kiss hit her on the cheek, and she couldn't help but giggle and then scratch him behind the ears. She found his happy spot because one of his back legs started to thump. "Such a good dog. I don't know why anyone would give you up. I know I won't give up on you. I promise."

A few more minutes later, she was in line with her paperwork and payment to make it official. When she received his medical records and a receipt, she was whisked off to a wall that had a backdrop over it and asked to smile. "Say 'cheese' Mumford! It's our first family photo!" His one ear perked up and his tongue came out as if he were trying to smile as commanded.

Aurelie walked out to her car and realized that the only way she'd get him home was if he sat in the front seat, pushed all the way back and with the window open. Maybe she hadn't thought this through enough …

At the End of Leash pet store, she found out that there were no indoor dog crates large enough to fit a full-grown Great Dane. They recommended using a small room and a mattress because their largest dog bed couldn't come close to being long enough for Mumford to lay down on. Then it was time to get his food and food dishes. While the clerk led Aurelie around and placed things in her cart, Mumford was a gentleman. He was happy, and he was on his best behavior. When they got to the toy aisle, Aurelie asked him if he had a preference. The clerk recommended an indestructible chew toy that she could put treats or peanut butter in to keep Mumford busy. But Aurelie also wanted Mumford to pick out something as well. She remembered Cat's dog, Mia, always had her favorite toys through the years. She wanted Mumford to have the same opportunity. He sniffed around and then he seemed to be nosing a green and orange dinosaur with a squeaker in the middle. Aurelie put it in the basket, and they headed for the checkout.

She was lucky enough that everything fit in the trunk, because with Mumford in the front seat, there wasn't any room in the back. With the window rolled down, Mumford was almost giddy as the wind whipped through his ears and made his jowls and tongue flap in the breeze. Aurelie laughed and kicked up the heat a little bit. It was time to go home and get settled.

When she arrived in the driveway, Mrs. Romansky had her straw gardening hat on and was working diligently on her tulip beds in the back. Aurelie scratched Mumford on his neck and said, "Welcome home, Mumford. It's time to meet our landlord, Mrs. Romansky. You should be on your best behavior. You want to keep on her good side." The large head tucked inside and cocked again as if he was trying to understand what she was saying. Aurelie got out of the car and walked around the side to open the door for Mumford. Mrs. Romansky heard the commotion, turned around and was staring into the bluest eye she'd ever seen before feeling hot breathing on her neck.

"What in heaven's name is this?" She questioned.

"Mrs. Romansky meet Mumford. He's my new dog! Our guard dog!" Aurelie said proudly.

"Oh, my Lord, Aurelie! I told you to get a dog. A large dog. Not a *giant* dog! He barely fits in your car! Will he fit in your apartment?" Just then Mumford looked at the shocked woman and gave her a very big, wet, kiss on her cheek. "Ugh!" Mrs. Romansky took her gardening glove off and tried to use it to dry off the dog slime left behind.

"See, Mumford likes you! He walks really well on a leash, and I signed up for dog training classes before I left the rescue. Honestly, Mrs. Romansky. I think he'll be great. The volunteers said he is a good dog; gets along with kids and other dogs. I don't think anyone will think of playing a prank or causing you any trouble with him around. The volunteer helping me called him a gentle giant."

At this, Mumford pushed his nose onto Mrs. Romansky's ungloved hand in an attempt to get her to scratch him. She got the hint, and he closed his eyes, stretched his neck, and his back leg pounded like Thumper in *Bambi*. This made the older woman soften a bit and sigh. "I guess since I told you to get a big dog, it's kind of my fault. He seems like a good boy. And you've signed up for training classes. I guess he can stay." The large head shifted again, and a smile crossed his face as if he could understand what the woman was saying, he finally had a home.

"Thank you. You won't be bothered. I promise. I will work really hard with him, and you'll see that this is a good thing for all of us." Aurelie hugged her landlord and Mumford, not wanting to be left out, stood up and licked them both.

Aurelie walked Mumford across the street to the park to get him used to his new potty stop and he seemed to understand what was expected of him. Next, she walked him upstairs, while still on a leash and let him sniff all the rooms before she went back downstairs to grab the rest of his things. She set up a water and food station in the kitchen and realized that an old milk crate would do just fine to store his toys, tucked away in a corner of the spare bedroom. The problem now was what to do about a bed. All the dog beds at the store were too small and the floor of the spare bedroom was linoleum. Not very comfortable. For now, she found an old fleece throw to lay down on the floor. Aurelie went downstairs one more time to grab the food and make sure she had everything else out of the car. She definitely needed a new car—one in which his extra-large body would fit inside.

She hadn't been told if he'd eaten yet, so Aurelie read the back panel of the dog food bag to gauge how much food he should eat. Shit. Food was measured by the weight of the dog. She looked at him and cocked her head. He looked at her and cocked his. "I don't own a scale, bud. Never needed to weigh myself. I guess I'll just take a guess and then on Monday, when I set up your first vet appointment, we can weigh you there." Feeling proud of solving that problem, she went over to the dog food bag, picked up a plastic measuring cup and scooped out a cup or two and let it drop into the silver dish. At the sound of food, Mumford galloped over and was ready to start eating when Aurelie took his leash and made him halt.

"We're going to work on your manners, Mumford. First lesson is that you will sit and wait until you get permission to eat." He looked quizzically at her and gave a deep whine. "Mumford, sit." He cocked his head, and his floppy ear danced a bit, but then he seemed to understand the command and sat; right on Aurelie's foot. "Ouch! Okay, okay! You can eat. Damn that hurt!" As she was rubbing her foot, Mumford put his head down and started chomping away, almost gulping down the food. When feeling came back to her semi-injured foot, she put some water in the second dish. Before she knew it, the food was gone, and he was looking for more or for water. She brought his muzzle to the water dish, which he sniffed, but seemed to discard. He was on the lookout for something, but that water dish wasn't it.

"What do you want, boy? Didn't you see the water right there? There's nothing wrong with it." Aurelie attempted to bring him to the water again, but this time he definitely resisted and went about the kitchen and then the rest of the apartment searching for something that she couldn't figure out. Finally, he walked into the bathroom tucked under the side dormer of the second story and barked once at the faucet in the large clawfoot tub. The sound he made took Aurelie by surprise. It wasn't just a bark. It was a baritone "YAWP!" To get her attention.

"What are you barking at? It's a tub. A bathtub. It isn't a water bowl, silly." She tried to drag him out and back to the kitchen, but he wouldn't budge. Instead, he stuck his head into the tub and started to lick at the faucet. "Fine. I guess this one time," She turned on the water for a light dribble to come out of the silver spicket and the determined Dane began lapping at the dripping water until he had his fill. Then he backed up and was on the lookout for something else. She followed him as he was sniffing the floors in the dining room, front room, her room and then finally into the spare room where the milk carton was tucked into a corner. The large black nose sniffed the carton, and his mouth tenderly surrounded the green and orange dinosaur. Fluffing up the throw and circling a few moments, he found his preferred resting place with his toy in his mouth, sighed and laid his head on his front paws before he closed his eyes.

Aurelie sighed too. "It's been a big day for you already. I guess it's a good time for a nap. Sweet dreams big man. She bent down and kissed him on the top of his head, to which he sighed again and snuggled with his stuffy. Even though it was barely lunch time, Aurelie was feeling a bit tired herself. Lots of excitement. She went back to the kitchen to get his paperwork organized. When the apartment was back in order and she'd feasted on a half a ham and Swiss sandwich, she decided to practice some of the songs she would be singing the next weekend for a local wedding.

Wanting to keep things quiet, she plugged in her headphones into the keyboard so as not to be too noisy for the downstairs. When she started singing "Perfect" by Ed Sheeran, she thought she heard a bit of a commotion coming from the bedroom. She kept hearing a howl and it was getting louder. Every time she started singing, Mumford started howling. "Quiet, Mumford! You'll get us in trouble! I have to practice!" Attempting it again, Mumford wailed his baritone howl as if he was singing along in tune. At the end of the song, Mumford came out, with the dinosaur in his mouth, wagging his tail, and sat by the keyboard. With a stern look and voice, Aurelie scolded, "Mumford, you are a bad dog! You can't keep howling every time I practice! And I have to practice! I'm a band teacher. I sing in a band. Music is my life. It's what's going to pay for your food, your toys, and this apartment. If you don't quiet down, we may lose this place for good, and I don't know where else I can go that is this nice for this price. Buddy, you've got to work with me on this. I'll give in to the tub faucet if you give in to the music. Deal?" She scratched behind his ears, and he laid his head on her lap to enjoy the attention.

As quickly as the morning turned into afternoon, a line of clouds moved in and Aurelie's phone alerted her to a severe thunderstorm brewing. She got up and kissed the big head of her new fur baby, who seemed a bit perturbed that his pillow had been eliminated. "Sorry, boy, but that storm looks like it's going to be nasty, and it's moving quickly. I have to shut all the windows before the rain gets in. Mumford's head cocked again as if he knew she was talking to him but couldn't quite figure it out. Then she found the leash and hooked it to his collar. "Better be safe than sorry. Come on with me, Mumford, you're going to try to go potty before it gets bad out there. Oh, and drop your stuffy. It stays inside." He seemed to understand that command and dropped his dinosaur down next to the keyboard before he followed her through the kitchen and outside. Looking both ways, and practicing his sit before they crossed the street, Aurelie focused on keeping him at her side and using the commands she remembered Cat used with Mia. Simple action words. Consistent actions and reactions. Always be in control of the dog when outside. She gave him a bit of a lead when they got to the park and the raindrops began to fall in very heavy plops, painting the sidewalk when they hit. Mumford seemed to understand his purpose and did what was asked of him. He shook his head once or twice when the drops fell on his head, but he kept his composure and looked to his new master for direction. "Good dog, Mumford. Let's get back inside where it's dry."

She jogged the short way back to the flat and noticed that Mrs. Romansky's TV was on the news, and the windows were shut. She double checked her own car windows just in case. After jogging up the stairs two by two to keep up with Mumford's gait, she sat down on a kitchen chair to catch her breath. CRACK!! BOOM!! The first of the thunder bellowed from the sky. The giant dog jumped and let out a squeaky "YIPE!" and tried to hide under the table, still on the leash. "It's okay, Mumford. It's just silly ol' thunder. It can't hurt you. You're too big to be so scared." Aurelie reached around his neck and gave him a hug and felt his damp fur. "You're wet. I bet you'll feel better once I dry you off a bit." She unleashed him, draped it back in its spot on the pantry wall, and went to the bathroom to search for a towel large enough to dry him. Just then another loud rumble and a crack let go overhead. "ROWR!" This time the giant dog was not going to quiet down. He was genuinely concerned and didn't intend to stop calling out while the storm was going on.

Once she found a towel large enough, she double-timed it back into the kitchen where the commotion was occurring. "Mumford! Bad dog! Quiet! You'll get us in trouble! It's just a little thunder, boy, it can't hurt you." She put the towel on his back just as another loud crack and lightning bolt lit up the sky. "ROWRRR! ROWRR!" Aurelie went from anger to being concerned.

"Stop it!" She finished drying his back and paws before another round of thunder and lightning shook up the sky. "ROWRRRR!" Which was beginning to sound like a howl. Moving the towel up to his head, she thought of possibly stuffing the towel in his mouth to quiet him down but realized it was not a good idea. However, something interesting happened when the next thunder boom cracked. This time, Aurelie had the towel around his head to dry it off and when the sound shook her apartment the only sound heard was that of the thunder. "Hmm," a thought began taking form. Her towel was too wet to continue to use. It was spring, so winter scarves were put away for the season. She started looking for other options. Mumford followed her, and she noticed his hind legs were shaking. He was physically upset, and he already figured out she was his only option to get some relief, if only she could figure something out.

First, she tried towels, but they were either too small or too big and kept falling off. Then she went to her bedroom and tried a couple of old T-shirts. The howling continued as the piles of discarded fabrics lay higgledy-piggledy around the house. She tried ankle socks and slipper socks. Stuffing cotton balls in his ears that he just shook out. "Damn it, Mumford. I'm trying here! Work with me. Help me figure this out before Mrs. Romansky has both our hides!" At her wit's end, she opened her top drawer containing a myriad of bras: lace ones, push-ups, sports bras, etc. "Okay, okay, something that has some padding has to work. Got to work. Come on, push-up bra, don't fail me now!" She picked one that had black lace and little red hearts embroidered on it and tied it around his head so that each padded cup was covering an ear. Making sure it was snug, she gave a little tug and then cringed when the next set of boomers went off … and … nothing. She looked at him, straight in the eye, "Don't screw with me, Mumford. This better work." Though he was still shaking and panting heavily, the next time the sky lit up like the Fourth of July and the rumble shook the room, he stayed quiet. Just staring into her eyes looking scared.

"Good boy, Mumford," she said as she kissed his black wet nose. "Good boy. I think we get to stay after all." She hugged him and heard a "hrmmph" in return. She also heard footsteps up the back stairs and a knock at the door. "Be on your best behavior, Mumford. I think it's judge and jury time."

"Come in, Mrs. Romansky." She heard the door squeak open and the first few footsteps before she saw the woman. It was clear that the landlord had an agenda but as soon as the older woman looked around the trail of miscellaneous materials meandering from the kitchen to the bathroom and into the bedroom, her face turned from anger to curiosity.

"What is going on here, Aurelie? What is all this racket and this mess? I thought we talked about this?" She inquired as if she were judge and jury at the Spanish Inquisition.

"I know, Mrs. Romansky, I'm sorry. Really sorry. It's just that," as she was prepared to respond to the list of questions, the storm brewed up another thunderclap and she cringed afraid that her make-shift earmuffs were going to malfunction. Instead, Mumford almost skipped over to where she was standing and rubbed up against her leg, still visibly shaken, but quiet.

This time, the cocked head was Mrs. Romansky's. She stared at the gentle giant, with his misshapen spots, and his different colored eyes wide in fear and the contrast of his white fur to the black lace push-up bra tied snuggly under his chin. It was clear her brain just was not comprehending what she was seeing. "What is he wearing on his head? Is that a bra, Aurelie?"

Hanging her head, feeling exhausted, defeated, and downright frustrated, Aurelie responded. "Yes, yes, it is. It's just that, well, Mumford seems to be afraid of loud noises, like thunder and music. Once I figured out that covering his ears stops the howling, I've been trying to find something that would stay on his head and muffle the sound, so he won't bark."

The silver-haired woman looked around and then started to follow the trail to its end, the top drawer of Aurelie's dresser. Then looked back at the odd couple waiting for her deliberation. "I see." She walked over some of the strewn clothes and came face-to-face with her ashen face tenant. Mrs. Romansky sized-up the disheveled apartment. Her nervous tenant's oversized companion who could gaze directly into her own eyes. What she saw when she held his gaze was that the giant dog was clearly tender-hearted. Mrs. Romansky could feel his concern washing over him. It was obvious Mumford really wanted to find his forever home here, with this young, broken woman. As lean, dark, and strong as Aurelie was, her goliath companion was hulking, pale, and fragile. They needed each other to make each other better than when they were apart. Putting her gnarled, liver-spotted hands gently on his neck, Mrs. Romansky gazed into Mumford's eyes and saw that he really wanted to stay, he did want to be good. He was just trying to find his way.

"Well, it seems you've found a short-term solution to this long-term challenge. However, he cannot walk out of this apartment with a black lace bra on his head every time it rains. We've got to do better."

"You mean he can stay?" Aurelie's heart was in her throat and hadn't realized how close to crying she truly was until her voice caught at the end and tears began to form in the corners of her eyes.

"Yes, Aurelie, he can stay." Mumford seemed to understand that and reached out with his massive pink tongue to give Mrs. Romansky a kiss. "Augh!" She shrieked and then used the sleeve on her pink and tan cardigan to dry off her cheek. "You start working on getting your home back in order, I think I might have something that could work."

Aurelie was so relieved that she reached out and hugged the sweet, older woman who gave her another chance at improving her life. After Mrs. Romansky left the apartment, the rain came down harder, but the thunder and lightning seemed to have moved farther east. Focusing on her chore, she could no longer stand still to give comfort to her companion. Mumford seemed to understand and he must pull his weight in this relationship as well. He had to find a way to self-soothe. Sniffing around the piles, he found what he was looking for, his stuffed orange and green dinosaur. Putting it gently in his mouth, he looked around for a safe place to curl up, out of the way. There was a strewn afghan that had seen better days. He used his front paws to manipulate the blanket until he was satisfied, circled a moment or two, and then curled up in the center with his favorite toy tucked into the crux of his front leg and resting his cheek on it.

After all that extra work was done, Aurelie looked at Mumford sleeping soundly and thought that he had the right idea. She gathered another afghan around herself and lay on her couch until she heard the familiar knock on the door.

"Come on in, Mrs. Romansky." She called out to the kitchen. After a brief stretch and a loud yawn from the form on the floor, the door opened and in waltzed a very smug looking woman with something green and crocheted in her hands.

"I've been working on this for my grandson who is wild about dinosaurs. I found this crochet pattern and wanted to try it out for him. However, I think we have an emergency on our hands. Since he doesn't know what I'm making, I figure he can wait a bit longer. If this works, that is."

"What is it?"

Mrs. Romansky held it out to show the shape of her creation. "It's a dinosaur snood!" She spoke proudly.

This time, Aurelie cocked her head to try to take in this olive and sage green full head cover. "What's a snood? Who's that for?"

"This is a snood. A dinosaur snood." I see that Mumford already has a thing for dinosaurs and he needs something that will stay on his head without falling off if he shakes his head or whatever. They're made to cover ears to keep them warm and dry. I figure we can give it a go to see if he'll let you put it on, keep it on, and the big test is when you play your music if he'll howl. Willing to give it a try?"

Aurelie shrugged her shoulders and reached over to untie her make-shift sound barrier from Mumford's sensitive ears. "What'd 'ya say, buddy? Are you ready to give this a chance?" He willingly let her take off the bra and shook his head a moment. Next, Aurelie took the snood from its creator and let Mumford sniff it a moment. She spoke calming words while she shimmied it over his nose, face, and then into its final resting place; taking special care to get the three olive green horns to stand at attention. Carefully Aurelie pulled away and looked at him for any insight as to what he was thinking or might do next. When it was clear Mumford was letting it stay on his head, she stood back, and both women looked critically at the placement of the snood and how it covered his ears.

"I think it's time to test it, Aurelie. Why don't you turn on your keyboard and start playing something to see what kind of reaction he has to the music?" Aurelie gave a big sigh, nodded her head, and walked over to her silent black keyboard and sat down to play. This time she chose, "Ain't Too Proud To Beg," by the Temptations, feeling it was appropriate for the time. At first, she had the volume turned down low and sang softer than usual. Mumford heard something, sat up and looked at her, but didn't make a sound. "Good, good dog." Mrs. Romansky reached down to pet him on his shoulder. "Turn up the volume a bit more, Aurelie, let's see how well this works." Bringing up the volume to normal levels and singing in her normal capacity, Aurelie noticed that Mumford stood and was panting, but did not make a peep. He did move to sit near Mrs. Romansky, and she pet him to let him know everything was okay.

With the song demonstration done, Aurelie audibly said, "Phew!" and shut down her instrument. "Well, I'll be damned. Mrs. Romansky, you saved us. Thank you so much. Honestly, I think it would have broken my heart to give him back. I can tell how much he wants to stay."

"No worries, Aurelie. I was the one to tell you to get a large dog. I just didn't think you'd take it so literally." Mrs. Romansky chuckled at her own joke. "Seriously, though, I know you are trying very hard, and I do want you to succeed. Only you and I will know that he is a scaredy cat. The rest of the neighbors and any troublemakers will fear him." As an afterthought she asked a final question, "You are going to take him to training classes, aren't you?"

"Absolutely! I've already found a place, and we start next week."

"Good. With his size, I can only imagine how easy it would be to lose control of him."

"I know, but I promise, I'll work really hard with him. I can tell he wants this to work out as much as I do. We won't disappoint you, Mrs. Romansky. Thank you for giving us a chance." With that, Aurelie walked the few steps toward her landlord and gave her a big hug. Mumford recognized the signs of affection and wanted in, so he stood up, and licked them both on their cheeks to seal the deal.

Chapter Fourteen

In the next few weeks, spring had sprung from a lengthy rainy season. The dinosaur snood was getting a good workout; anytime Aurelie left the house without Mumford, the snood went on just to be on the safe side. The weekly obedience training classes were going well. A few missteps here and there, but overall, the instructor was pleased with their progress and Aurelie made sure they did their homework for a few minutes every evening after school. She even worked with Mrs. Romansky so that when the landlord was dog sitting, she was using the same commands, and Mumford would get used to the structure.

On Easter Sunday, Aurelie was invited to her parents' home for a family dinner, and they extended the invitation to Mumford as well. Aurelie was a bit nervous. He had been great with Mrs. Romansky and at class with the other dogs and people, but around all the chaos of her nieces and nephews and her siblings? Well, that could rattle even the most obedient of dogs. Still, sooner or later he'd be introduced to the cacophony that was her family.

Being the youngest of four, she felt the least successful of her siblings. The oldest, Felix, became a family medicine doctor in Sussex, and had two boys, Oscar and Arthur, who loved running around trying to get their girl cousins to eat worms and other creepy crawling things. His wife, Audrey, was happy leaving her stressful financial manager position to be a stay-at-home mom while their boys were growing up.

Next was Zoe, a very successful computer programmer in Verona. She enjoyed her rural upbringing but preferred to live in one of the new high tech/modern luxury condos being built in Madison to cater to the techie millennials flooding the city. She and her husband, Jack, met on the sprawling intergalactic campus where they worked. They had just recently come back from a trip to Chile with their three-year-old daughter, Chrissy, and Zoe had just found out she was pregnant again.

Sophia was the closest in age to Aurelie, but the most different. Sophia was obsessed with being on time and cleanliness. Straight A's all the way through dental school, Sophia loved her little sister, but she constantly reminded Aurelie of her missteps and the house rules. Sophia married a man she had met in dental school, Davis, and they built a successful family dentistry practice in Waukesha. Their two daughters, Megan and Olivia, were always perfectly coiffed with head bands, bows, and braids; but when they were in close proximity to their boy cousins, all prim and proper was thrown to the wayside. More mess = more fun.

It was a bright spring day and the lawn had shifted from looking like prickly winter wheat to a lush verdant meadow. Purple and yellow crocus were scattered around the yard along with blue wood violets, and the budding tulips and daffodils that made up the borders around the Dutch colonial log home. Nestled into the Kettle Moraine Forest, the Beres home was built on five acres of hardwoods and included two ponds; one welcoming visitors to the front covered porch and the other in the back of the property where all the Beres children learned to swim, fish, and row a boat. The covered front porch always had rocking chairs in the summer and offered a great place to sit on one of the handcrafted log benches to put on ice skates or snowshoes in the winter.

Once inside, the warm earth tones of the pine logs and stone fireplace always made Aurelie relax. The open concept downstairs had a lovely flow into the modern kitchen with all charcoal gray granite countertops and cherry cabinetry. The kitchen led to the dining room that was like a peninsula surrounded on all three sides by windows. The formal table was encircled with cherry high-backed chairs with woodland tapestry cushions that matched the drapes. The windows peered out onto the side yard with lovely views of the mini-forest and a myriad of birds enjoying an ever-abundant supply of high-quality seed and suet regardless of the season.

The great room was Aurelie's favorite; all the overstuffed leather furniture with soft, fluffy throws available for an afternoon snuggle or nap in front of the fireplace. Double patio doors opened onto a screened porch that housed whitewashed wicker furniture in the summer for those hot, humid nights when the bugs were biting unwilling victims on the lawn. Yes, the porch was a safe haven and also a place to still enjoy the sounds and sights of summer days and nights like when the cicadas were calling, or the stars were sparkling and you just needed to be a part of it.

The master bedroom had a view of the front pond and the flowering crab tree that was her mother's favorite. Upstairs belonged to the Beres children and grandchildren. The girls were offered one bedroom and the boys the other. But most family sleepovers ended up with everyone congregating in the loft area, in their sleeping bags. Even though Dr. Beres certainly made enough to own a home where everyone could have their own rooms and bathrooms, Bea was very strict and refused to raise privileged children. School and chores were priorities. Manners were a must. Rent was to be paid by any Beres child who didn't adhere to the rules.

Aurelie recalled paying rent for an unmade bed or poor grades. She was a shy child because she lacked confidence and an understanding of why she struggled in school. Still, she knew she was loved. Aurelie thanked God the day that her parents told her that she wasn't less smart, she had a learning disability, which was why school was so hard for her. So, they helped her learn a new way of reading and studying. Her mom decreed a new rule for Aurelie; make a new friend, lose a chore. The day she met Cat was the best day of her life. She'd found confidence enough to go up to her and shake her hand while telling Cat they would be best friends. Cat helped her with her studies, and with Aurelie's newfound confidence (and reduced chore list), Aurelie helped Cat meet new people—especially boys.

Easter was always a great holiday for the Beres family. Bea would make the traditional French-Canadian Easter dinner of mustard-crusted lamb, maple baked beans, potatoes niçoise, and for dessert she'd switch it between apple tarts and an Easter basket cake. Her father loved hiding the Easter eggs all over the yard. He'd create a treasure map, of sorts, to make sure that all the eggs would be found—too many of the early years found rotten eggs or lost plastic eggs with money or melted candy months later stuck in the branches of a bush or buried among the ground cover.

Aurelie arrived a bit early, just to give Mumford an opportunity to get the lay of the land before the chaos started. Besides, she wanted to thank her parents and let them meet Mumford while he was still relatively calm and obedient. To be safe, she brought the snood and his favorite dinosaur toy, just in case. When she pulled into the driveway, Mumford's head was still hanging out the window with his mouth wide open and his pink tongue flopping out the side, the sign of a very happy dog. Dr. and Mrs. Beres opened the front door and walked onto the meandering stone path to greet them. Aurelie could tell that they were a bit surprised at the size of their furry guest.

Aurelie stepped out with tan canvas flats on her feet and khaki capris belted with a navy and white tan striped boat neck cotton shirt. "Hi guys! Can you believe we're the first ones here? Let me get Mumford out of the car so you can meet him. He really loves car rides." She walked to the passenger door and hooked the bright blue leash onto his collar. Carefully leading him out of the sedan, she motioned for him to sit next to her in the heel position. "Mumford, this is my mom and dad. Mom, Dad, hold out your hands like this," she demonstrated how to lay their palms flat and upright, "so he can smell you first to get to know you." They did as they were directed, and Mumford sniffed carefully. Before long, his tail began wagging, making a loud thumping noise on the driveway.

"Oh my, I didn't realize how large he really is," Bea commented. She was wearing a pale pink sweater set with sage green capris and tan sandals. She giggled a bit when Mumford licked her palm. "It tickles."

Dr. Beres smiled and scratched him under his ear to which Mumford's back leg began moving like a jackhammer—louder and faster than his tail had done just a few minutes before. "How does he fit in that car of yours? He can't be comfortable."

"Dad, I'm working on it. I've got a budget, and I'm looking at my options. However, it may take a bit longer than I originally planned because to get the headroom he needs, I have to look at SUV's or trucks, which are a bit more expensive than I had calculated. No worries, I'll figure it out. Once he's fully trained, I can use that money to save toward the new vehicle too."

Once the introductions were done, the three of them took a walk around the property and let Mumford sniff and mark his territory to his heart's content. He was curious about the ponds, but not curious enough to go swimming in them. He got excited every time he saw a new stick to play with and was happy when Dr. Beres found an old tennis ball in the garage to throw and play catch.

Just as Aurelie was feeling more confident about Mumford being at her parents', the rest of the Beres pack came in carloads. She heard the shrieking of the nieces and the "YES!" screams of the nephews. Aurelie jogged over to where Mumford was nosing around in a pile of leaves looking for the slobbery ball, so she could get the leash back on his collar and to be near him when the rest of the introductions began. While he seemed a bit nervous with Zoe's daughter, the youngest of the cousins, he seemed thrilled that the Davies girls and the Beres boys thought he was the best thing since ice cream. And Aunt Aurelie was the bestest aunt in all the world because she got them a giant to play with.

"Looks like you got this, Aur. Go ahead and hang out with the kids while we get dinner ready with Mom," Sophia called out. "Girls? You behave for your aunt or no dessert for you. Got it?" Two little dark haired ponytails wagged up and down, but their faces were focused on their new furry friend.

It was decided that the first game they played would be hide and seek. They would hide first and let Mumford find them and then they reversed. Though Aurelie never let Mumford get farther away then she could reach for him, her confidence was getting stronger as she saw how much he loved playing with the children and how much they adored playing with him. When dinner was called, she found a nearby tree to tie an outdoor lead to and brought out a bucket of water and his dinosaur. After a good long drink, Mumford yawned, carefully put his dinosaur in his mouth and circled until he found the perfect spot to lay down and nap.

Aurelie felt relaxed now and was enjoying the old family stories of Easters gone by and hearing about the vacation of a lifetime to Chile, the news of the pregnancy, the boys and their pee wee soccer team, and the girls' dance classes. Looking up at her parents, from time to time, she saw the satisfaction on their faces. Not all Easters were peaches and cream. Many had hurt feelings, pulled pigtails, a few had food fights. But today? Today seemed as close to perfect as one could get.

After the main course, the tradition was that everyone would help Mom clean up the dishes, and Dad would enlist Felix's help in hiding the Easter eggs. Mumford's straight ear cocked up and his bright blue eye opened to see what was happening. Keeping his toy close, he slowly moved his head and cocked it once or twice trying to understand what was going on.

The Easter egg treasure hunt was ready. The children were outfitted with their baskets and eager to be given the "OK" to scour the property for the coveted colored cache. "Can Mumford help us, Aunty Aur? Please?" Arthur begged. She nodded and walked over to the newly minted Easter egg treasure hunter and leashed him for his first big break. In the beginning, he had no clue what he was doing, but after a few successes, he was on a quest. His nosed pressed to the ground and tail wagging high in the air, he made a little pounce when he found one. The children were shrieking in joy and in surprise when a cold, wet nose or large pink tongue connected with their cheek.

At one point, Aurelie was struggling to control Mumford as he insisted on switching directions and going toward the pond. She was getting angry and mumbling to herself that she should have brought the training collar for better control. That is, until she looked over to the pond and saw Chrissy toddling toward the water's edge. Aurelie let go of the lead so she could run over, but the dog's extended gallops and gate eclipsed her own and beat Aurelie to the water. At first, she was very afraid that Mumford wouldn't know his strength and knock over the child, but then she saw something that had her in awe. Mumford put himself between the water's edge and the toddling girl. Every time he blocked her, she'd turn around and try a different tack. He turned swiftly and blocked her again, his head down and low "woofs" were heard. Not in a scary tone, but more of a fatherly one. No matter what, he was not going to let that little girl anywhere near the water. "Chrissy! Chrissy honey! Get away from that water, baby!" Jack ran over and swept his little girl into his arms. By this time, Aurelie was no longer in shock and walked over to her fur baby and gave him a huge hug and kiss.

"Good dog, Mumford! Good boy! I'm so proud of you!" she looked right into his eyes to make sure he knew she was singing his praises.

When she raised her head, Aurelie noticed Chrissy and her dad were right next to her. "It's your turn, Chrissy. You need to thank Mumford for taking good care of you." The little girl knew she was in trouble and had that hiccup, crying about to start. Some families wouldn't require their children to be accountable, but Bea Beres made sure that her grandbabies knew she loved them more than anything in the world AND that they knew their manners and acknowledged when they did something wrong.

Still being held around the waist of her pink polka dotted Easter dress, little Chrissy reached out with her pudgy arms and reached Mumford's jowls. "Tank you, Mumfurd," and she kissed him on his wet nose. He returned the favor with a big sloppy kiss.

The rest of the Easter celebration was much less eventful and because it was a Sunday, the clan packed up early so the working parents could get ready for the week. Being the first one there meant that Aurelie had to wait until the other cars left before she could exit the driveway. Mumford's first family affair was a success. The big boy had a full day, and he was visibly tired. When she opened the door, he couldn't wait to jump into his seat and lay his head out the window waiting for the wind to lull him to sleep on the ride home.

Once she hugged her mom goodbye, she reached out to her dad, and he turned her around to walk her to her side of the sedan.

"Aurelie, you are the most stubborn of all our children. You fought me to pay your own way through school and refused my offers to help with rent, or any number of things parents help their young adult children with as they get established in the world. This time, I will not take 'no' for an answer."

Furrowing her brow, she inquired, "What're you talking about, Dad?"

"I am going to help you buy a new vehicle so that our hero over there," pointing to the snoring dog hanging out of the window, "has a comfortable place to sit when he's driving with you." He gave her a stare down.

"Dad, I've got this. You know how I feel. You and Mom paid for private tutors and all kinds of tests for me when you found out I was dyslexic. You don't need to take care of me anymore. "

"This is what I'm talking about."

"What?"

"Your stubbornness is getting in the way of what's best for you."

"Isn't it what you and Mom always taught us? Be independent? Don't expect us to give you everything? You need to earn it? I've been working hard lately to turn over a new leaf. Taking care of myself, my apartment, my dog, my future. Aren't I doing a good job?"

He hugged her hard and kissed the top of her short black hair. "I am most proud of you. You've overcome many more difficult obstacles than your brother and sisters could ever have imagined. And you've never let me help you out. So, this is what's going to happen now. I have a patient who owns several dealerships, and he always told me to call on him if I need a new car. I'm going to call him first thing tomorrow and set up a time next week to see him, trade in your car, plus the funds you've already saved, and I'll pitch in the rest. You need a safe car. One that handles in the snow. One that fits your dog. Period."

She looked into his eyes and realized that she didn't have the stamina to fight him on this. He was right. Mumford deserved something more comfortable for him. She needed a safer car. She nodded and received another kiss on top of her head and a hug from her biggest fan. "You know, Aur, I wasn't keen on this dog business. But something tells me that it was serendipity between the two of you. You both have impressed me."

This time when she looked into her father's eyes, they were no longer stern. They were warm and loving and, if she looked hard enough, maybe a tear or two forming? What? The famous Dr. Beres was a softy? She stood on her tip toes and kissed the tip of his nose. "I love you, Dad. Thank you."

Chapter Fifteen

It was decided that they would head to the dealership in Mukwonago after obedience training on Wednesday night. It was the most practical since Mumford was usually so exhausted after having to think hard for a long period of time that he liked to take a nap. Dr. Beres met Aurelie at the apartment and they drove the sedan to the dealership. After a few test drives and a lengthy negotiation, Aurelie signed away her tan car that had gotten her through college and her 20s and signed on the dotted line for an almost new AWD, 4-door SUV. It was practical from the standpoint that both the second and third row seats folded flat, so Mumford could lay down comfortably in the vehicle. It came with a tan leather interior which would wipe up easily and not collect dog hair. Plus, it would look classic with the Cajun red exterior, and it had a sunroof. She may have needed a family car for her extra-large dog, but it was nice to be able to jazz it up a bit with a spiffy paint job and classic leather seats. She had to admit, she was giddy with excitement—never owning anything this new before. It was slick, and she couldn't wait to see how much Mumford would enjoy having the roof open and being able to lay down during a drive. Life was looking up.

Usually, she'd stop over at Cat's house to show her best friend the newest "thing" in her life. She'd been laying low since the wedding to let the newlyweds get used to their new life and home. But Aurelie needed to share. So, when she got home, she woke Mumford up from his nap, took him to the park for a quick bathroom break and then showed him their new SUV. His tail wagging, he sniffed every inch of the outside and when she opened the trunk, he took a moment before he hopped in and lay down. Mrs. Romansky came outside to see all the hubbub and agreed to take a photo so Aurelie could send Cat the photo of her new man and car.

Aurelie hopped in and took Mumford for a quick ride around town to get him used to the new vehicle. He was so happy. Aurelie opened the sunroof, and he stretched his long-spotted neck to sniff the fresh air that was coming from above. At stop signs and lights, people just stared and a few snapped photos. Aurelie felt like they were the cool kids. "Mumford, I think we need to get matching sunglasses. We'll be the rock stars of Mukwonago!" He seemed to know what she was saying and barked in agreement.

Back home, Aurelie carefully put her new SUV into the garage for the night. She knew it was time to get ready for the next day and get to bed, but she was still jazzed. After making her lunch, setting out her clothes and checking on her class schedule for tomorrow, she took a quick bath, and no sooner had she made it out of the tub than her phone rang.

"Hello?"

"Aur?"

"Cat! Is that you?"

"It sure is, all 200 pounds of me."

"Well, you are growing two babies in that belly of yours. Give yourself a break. How's married life? How's the job? Montana?"

"Hold on! Hold on! Let me catch my breath a moment. Oh, and at any time, I may need to hang up to go pee. I pee a lot these days. Don't be offended."

"I promise. I won't."

"Okay, married life is great for me. I don't know about Damon, though. I'm a bitch and when I'm not complaining, or yelling, I cry. I'm hungry, tired, and need help getting dressed. I'm surprised Damon hasn't left me yet. He just keeps checking on me and dodging bullets when I go off the deep end. He's really been patient and talked me into acupuncture to help with some of the discomfort. I think he also talked to my acupuncturist about finding other points to make me less of a bitch. My work at the university is so great. I love being with the horses, and they seem to have a sense of being careful around me. I've only got two weeks until the last class, and then we can pack up and drive back home to have the babies. How about you? I saw that photo of you with that hot red SUV. Whose car is that? Was there a giant dog driving it?"

Aurelie snickered. She so missed these rambling conversations. She missed talking to her best friend face-to-face. Still, this was better than nothing. "Well, if you must know, they are both mine. The dog is a Great Dane, and his name is Mumford. He is a wonderful dog but has this minor defect,"

"Defect?"

"Yeah, he's afraid of loud noises and doesn't like music. Or, maybe he likes music so much that he feels he needs to sing to it."

"Oh no!" Aurelie heard the laughing on the other end. "So, what do you do?"

"He wears a dinosaur snood so he doesn't get scared and he stops singing."

"What the hell is a snood?"

"Hold on a sec, I'll show you," Aurelie put down the phone and called for Mumford to sit in front of her while she put on his dinosaur snood. Then she sent a photo to Cat.

"Holy shit! That's hilarious!! Oh God, now I gotta go pee again. Damn. I'll video chat you when I'm done. That's fantastic!"

Aurelie chuckled and then kissed Mumford before she removed the snood and gave him his toy dinosaur which he gently accepted before following her to the couch where he laid his head on her lap and gave her sad eyes. "No, you aren't allowed on the furniture. We've talked about that." When her phone vibrated, she switched to video mode and saw the rounded, flushed face of her friend and almost cried. God, how she missed Cat. How she wished they were in the same room, so she could feel the babies moving and touch her hand when telling an important part of the story, seeing her eyes sparkle while she laughed.

"Sorry about that. I warned you. The slightest giggle sets me on the run to the toilet. I've started wearing pads in my gigantic underpants just to stop having to change underwear all the time."

"I don't want to think about that! What does Damon think about your gigantic underpants? Has it tempered the love slave?"

"Don't start with me, Aurelie. You've always had a lot more sex than I ever had. Just when I finally get to enjoy the lusty benefits of marriage, my body starts doing things that I can't control. The second trimester was fabulous. My hormones were raging all the time, he was happier than a stallion on a stud farm! But now? Now if he looks at me funny, I may bite his head off or just start crying about how big and fat and ugly I am. How I can't fit into any of that sexy lingerie I bought before we got married and now, I have to wear granny panties with pads!"

Aurelie howled in laughter and that set Mumford off to join her. "Hush, Mumford! Quiet boy!"

"I want to see him without that dinosaur hat on. Get him on the screen!"

Aurelie motioned for Mumford to sit his hind legs on the seat cushion next to her. Even seated, he seemed to be at eye level with Aurelie. She turned the screen sideways, so Cat could get the whole view. "Oh, Aurelie, he's so beautiful! Look at those piercing blue eyes, I mean one blue eye and one … brown? I love the way one ear is straight up and the other is floppy. And those spots! Ooh, I just want to give him a great big hug and kiss!"

Aurelie was pleased to get such a rave review from her best friend. It meant the world to her. "Thanks, he kind of picked me, actually."

"And Mrs. Romansky didn't have a cow? How'd you get her okay?"

"That's the funny part. Or, not so funny," Aurelie cleared her throat and told her torrid tale which ended with how she landed her sweet ride.

"Wow. I'm sorry. I didn't know. Wow." With her voice cracking and tears starting to build in the corner of her hazel eyes, Cat realized just what her friend had sacrificed to let her go to live her new life.

"I'm so sorry I wasn't there for you, Aur. Really sorry." And the tears came in earnest now.

Aurelie held up as long as she could, but seeing Cat lose it, she couldn't stop herself and began to cry as well. "I've missed you *so* much, Cat. I was so lost without you. I was in a self-destruction mode and didn't know how to get out. Mrs. Romansky gave me one of her tough love speeches and helped me get back on track. It was her idea to get a dog. A large dog to scare away the bad guys."

Cat was speechless, but the tears were rolling down her face which made Aurelie cry harder. "Dammit, Cat. Now I have to get some tissue for this leaky faucet you started." She got up and walked to the bedroom for a box and then when she returned, Mumford was laying on his back, spread eagled on the couch. "Mumford! What the hell?" She wanted to discipline him but instead started to laugh hysterically.

"What? What's going on over there? Show me!" Cat was itching to find out what had her best friend in a fit of hilarity.

"Fine. But don't say I didn't warn you. It's definitely not PG." Aurelie slowly turned the phone so that it now faced the very relaxed Dane as he stretched his entire length over the couch that wasn't to be touched by furry friends.

"Oh No! It's ... It's ... puppy porn!" Laughter rolled out of Cat which made Aurelie only laugh harder. "Shit! I got to pee again! I can't take much more of this, Aur. I gotta go. I'll see you in a few weeks." and then the phone went dead. The laughter died with the phone. Aurelie had a moment of a familiar connection back, and now it was lost. An emptiness rolled over her. She sighed as she fought back tears of sadness. Was it possible to feel heartbreak for a friend who wasn't lost to you, just far away?

Mumford was on the verge of snoring, and she didn't have the energy or the heart to move him. Instead, she walked over to her bathroom and drew herself a hot bath. Nothing destressed her better than soaking in a tub with water as hot as she could stand and bubbles almost kissing her nose. She stripped and placed her dirty clothes in the hamper and pulled out a rose colored short-sleeved T-shirt pajama top and matching rose-colored poppy printed pajama pants that she lay on top of the toilet seat before she submerged into her luscious lavender scented bubble bath. Closing her eyes, she tried to release the stress of school, excitement of buying a new car and seeing her best friend again, and the loss she felt when they hung up. It was this feeling that, for several months, sent her to find love in all the wrong places and to make poor choices. She was talking to herself, sending out positive messages about all the good things that happened that day when she heard the clicking of toenails on the linoleum and felt the cold wet nose and breath of her fur baby on her cheek. "Thanks, baby. I'll be okay. I'm just a little sad right now." He seemed to understand a little and gave her a big sloppy kiss before he lay down on the plush bathroom rug next to the clawfoot tub. "My protector. So, are you going to take care of me just like I take care of you?" He lifted his head, cocked it so that the one ear stood straight at attention on an angle and the other flopped. Her aching heart felt a little less empty now; and that was a good thing.

Chapter Sixteen

On May 19, Aurelie received the text message for which she'd been waiting for the past few days. The twins had arrived! She didn't delay a moment after school except for a quick call to Mrs. Romansky to ask if she would be able to dog sit Mumford. Aurelie practically ran to the SUV in her oversized white tunic with musical notes printed in a topsy-turvy pattern, black leggings, and black ballet flats. It was a good thing she planned ahead and kept the baby presents in the car for the past week.

Standing in the doorframe of the birthing suite at the hospital, Aurelie was in awe. She was in view of the creation of a family. Just a few days ago, she'd been welcoming her friend back home and enjoying a lengthy gab session. Now? Now, she was overlooking a scene from a movie. The proud husband was beaming at his wife while holding an hours-old red-haired pixie while the new mom was holding its twin. Life was moving on whether she was ready for it or not. If she wanted to still have Cat in her life, she needed to accept that there was no longer the unlimited time and affection her friend had been able to provide her in the past, but rather what Cat could still offer her now as she moved into the world of motherhood. May 19, and this scene, would be embedded in Aurelie's memory as a day when their friendship changed once again. Would it be for the worst? Better? Honestly, she had no clue what the birth of these two ginger-haired angels would mean to the longevity of their relationship. But, if she was honest with herself, she could see that those two pink faces had already changed Cat's aura. She looked complete. No matter where their relationship would go in the future, one thing was crystal clear in that moment; Catrina MacGregor was meant to be a mom.

Aurelie stepped into the room with a smile and a yellow and green polka dot gift bag. "Happy Birthday, Munchkins! Auntie Aur is ready to spoil you rotten!" She placed the bag on the windowsill and then reached over to kiss Cat on her flushed cheek. "How are you doing, Cat? They treating you well here?"

"I'm so glad to see you, Aur, I can't believe they're finally here! Do you want to hold one?" Cat asked as she gently lifted a tiny bundle wrapped in a pale pink striped blanket and matching cap. Aurelie's eyes went wide. She didn't expect to be handed a baby so soon after they'd been born. Figured that the rest of the family needed to have their baby fixes before she'd get a chance. Still, she put down her purse and accepted the precious baby in her arms and began rocking the groggy babe back to sleep.

"Wow, Cat. Just … wow."

"I know, right? I can't believe it either."

"Two of these guys came out of you? Aren't you in pain down there?"

"Well, I tried to deliver them vaginally, but it wasn't working, so they did an emergency C-section and got them out that way."

"Ouch!"

"I'm feeling a bit sore, but they have some great drugs."

"I guess no bikini this summer."

Damon chimed in. "My wife has a smokin' hot body—bikini or no bikini." He bent over and carefully kissed Cat on her pale pink lips.

"So, who's been by to see the babies?"

"Our parents, of course, Ryan is stopping by after work, and Damon's brothers and sisters are mostly planning to see us after we get out of the hospital."

"What about Pete and Angie?"

Damon responded, "Tonight. Angie got her mom to babysit Rosie, and once Pete's done at the equine hospital, they are stopping by." Aurelie saw a look pass between the two new parents and knew something was up.

Cat resituated herself and looked at her friend. "Aur, we'd like to ask you something. Something important."

Aurelie looked at both of them, a little nervous but more curious than anything. "Okay … "

Cat continued, "Well, you have been such a huge part of my life and a big reason why Damon and I are together. There aren't words enough to thank you for all you've done for me and how much you mean to me." The words were starting to get stuck in Cat's throat.

Damon saw an opportunity to jump in, "To us. What you mean to us, Aur. I know this move to Montana has been very difficult, and we haven't been as good at connecting with you since the move and everything, but you still mean the world to Cat and to me."

Aurelie's heart was racing. She was confused, but felt it was a good confusion. Cat got her voice back and said, "I'm so sorry, Aur, that I haven't been there for you these past few months. Real sorry. But I love you like a sister, and I want to show you how much you mean to me, Damon, and now to Grace and Gordon. Aurelie Beres, would you do us the honor of being Grace and Gordon's godmother?"

Her heart stopped. She paused rocking Grace and looked wide-eyed between Cat and Damon who were waiting for an answer. When Grace started to squirm and whine, it helped Aurelie get back to reality and give the answer that they were waiting for. "Yes! Oh my God! I'm finally someone's godmother!" She kissed Grace on her forehead and left a little red lipstick behind. Then she carefully walked over to Damon to kiss baby Gordon on his forehead and left a matching print.

"I almost forgot. You've got to open your presents!" Damon took the cue and handed Gordon over to Cat and then picked up the bag.

"Do you want Cat to open them, or can I?"

"I don't care Damon. Just open the damn presents!" She was so excited that the language just jumped out.

He reached in and tackled some of the tissue paper before he found what he was looking for, a black onesie with white writing on it,

"LEGEN-

Wait for it … "

Then he found the second one,

"Wait for it …

-DARY!"

Cat started to laugh, but it hurt too much and tried to calm down. "That's awesome, Aur! You found onsies for our favorite late night binge show 'How I Met Your Mother.' Classic!"

Aurelie was pleased with the response and even started to laugh, herself, which led to Grace crying and then Gordon followed. Damon jumped into play and put down the gifts to check on Grace's and then Gordon's diapers. "Diapers are good. Looking at the time, I wonder if they're hungry, babe?" Cat nodded and Aurelie took that as a cue to skedaddle.

She carefully handed the pink bundle back to Cat and kissed Cat's forehead, making sure to leave a mark. "There, you match your kids!"

Damon looked miffed. "What about me?" She smiled and lightly tugged on his bright red beard to make him bend down to her level. She still had to stand on her tip toes, but she managed to get a matching pair of red lips on his forehead as well.

"There, now the whole family matches. Better?" Then she had an idea. Encouraging Damon to sit by Cat and the babies on the bed, she reached into her purse for her cell phone and grabbed a few photos. "Perfect. Best family photo ever!" She turned the screen around to show the new parents. They started to laugh, but that made the babies start crying again and Cat's incision to feel sore as well.

Aurelie waved goodbye, smiled, and walked out of the room feeling a little lighter than when she had arrived a few moments earlier. She wouldn't be forgotten. She had just received the biggest honor of her life—being named the godmother to her best friend's twins. She was as close to being part of their family as she could get. Things were going to be okay.

Chapter Seventeen

On a bright sunny day about a month later, it became legit. Within the Holy Hill Basilica, Aurelie Beres was officially made the godmother to Grace and Gordon MacGregor.

The rest of the summer was glorious. Aurelie was invited to spend time with the MacGregor clan in their summer home on the family horse farm in Erin, Wisconsin. She was even invited to join them up north for the Fourth of July when they planned on showing off the babies to Ruth Luther, the woman who lived on the pristine 250 acres of woods around Loon Lake and had been like family to Cat since she was a child. It was important to Cat to introduce her own babies to the woman who, along with her late husband, Marshall, had made such a huge impact on Cat's life. Aurelie wanted to go, but she promised her bandmates that she would play with them for the Fourth of July at Summerfest. She couldn't beat the free admission, parking, and fireworks.

When August came around, Aurelie's heart began to sink. They went to the Wisconsin State Fair as they tried to do every year. It was Cat's favorite festival. But once the fair ended, Cat and her family had to drive back to Montana, so she could be ready for the students arriving for the fall semester. After several moments of tearful hugs and goodbye kisses, Aurelie found herself waving to the family that had taken her heart with them as they left for their trek out west. She'd brought Mumford with her as he loved coming out to the farm and running free with Mia around the fences that held the horses. He was so gentle around the babies, even if they tried to pull at his ears or when they cried. Aurelie was always ready with the dinosaur snood when that happened. Aurelie knew she needed Mumford to comfort her on the ride home and for however long it took for her to get over this heartbreak. He seemed to understand and pushed his body so that it was touching her side and so she could pet him with one hand while waving goodbye with the other.

Fall swept in a blustery fashion and Aurelie wanted to be excited about seeing her students again, but that empty feeling came back. She stayed focused and kept her routine rocking. It wasn't depression. It wasn't loneliness, per se, but she just didn't feel like herself. Mumford kept a close eye on her and was a wonderful distraction. His goofy personality and keen sense of her need for his affection and comfort helped her get through this tough spot a great deal better than when she had become depressed and had embarked upon her self-destructive behavior after the wedding. He was a great listener and secret keeper. Patiently listening to all her rambling with his head on her lap.

The months rolled on and between the frenetic business of teaching, being caregiver to a furry giant, and her own music, Aurelie somehow managed. She knew winter break for Cat was right after the first week in December. Aurelie's heart soared again at the thought of seeing her friend and those chunky babies with those curly auburn locks growing in. Ooh, she just wanted to pinch their thighs and hear them giggle in person while she gave them raspberries on their bellies.

While many Christian families keep an advent calendar to count down to Christmas, Aurelie spent her time counting the days until Cat's visits home. While the visit was brief, it gave Aurelie the positive energy fix she needed to get through the winter doldrums.

Aurelie really wasn't living her best life, but she was leading a clean life. Spring sprung in Mukwonago with the early blooms of purple and yellow crocus buds popping up through the thin skin of late winter/early spring. Easter at her parents' home marked the one year anniversary of Mumford being introduced to the Beres family. *Last year,* Antoine thought to himself, *Aurelie was apprehensive bringing her new self and her new companion into the family.* This year, however, he noticed Aurelie was behaving differently. Alouf?

Sad? Unconnected? After the Beres grandchildren, and their Great Dane nanny found all the Easter eggs around the Beres family yard, Antoine thought it was time to broach the subject.

"Mon Cheri,"

"Oui, Papa?"

"Are you happy?"

She looked at him quizzically. "Yes. I think I am. Why?"

He stared into her usually bright, sparkling emerald green eyes and saw they lay flat. The spark was missing. "You seem to be sad today. In fact, you seem sad most of the time when I see you."

Aurelie sighed. It was true. She felt melancholy most often. He reached around her blue and purple floral dress and gave her a hug. "Have you started dating again?"

"I've tried it a few times, but nothing special. In fact, a lot of those dating sites? Well, let's just say that I don't think I need to see a dick pic again any time soon."

At first he choked a bit. But then he chuckled. "You never worry about having a filter, do you?"

"Dad, you're a doctor. It's not like you haven't seen them before. Why should I shy away from telling you? You asked me, didn't you? You want me to lie?"

This time he kissed the top of her head. "No. I don't want you to change, Mon Cheri. I was just surprised is all. Listen, I've just finalized a speaking engagement after you're done with school. It's part of a cancer survivor workshop and I've been asked to be the keynote speaker. Would you like to come with me? We can drive together and make it kind of like a daddy-daughter weekend. What do you think?"

Aurelie gazed out onto the vast green lawn and saw Mumford playing hide and seek with the Beres boys trying to find their girl cousins and smiled. There were times when she had a moment of being content, like this afternoon. However, they were few and far between lately. Perhaps she needed to shake it up a bit. A weekend away from home may be the thing. "Sounds like a plan, Dad. I'll see if Mrs. Romansky can watch Mumford for me or maybe Mom would be willing?" He nodded.

That night, after preparing for the next day of school, Aurelie kissed and hugged Mumford good night, made sure he had his stuffed dinosaur and went to bed with a smile on her face. Something that had been missing for a long time.

PART THREE: UP NORTH

Chapter Eighteen

Dillion hadn't slept well, too nervous about today's activity—the cancer survivor workshop, an event that he was coordinating for the church. The good news? Because it was also *June Bloom Arts and Crafts Festival* weekend in Minocqua, there were a ton of people coming into town and his parish community had done a bang-up job of asking for sponsorships and registering guests. It wouldn't be a huge fundraiser for the church, but it was going to be a significant friend-raiser. Lots of new people would be learning about his church and their community outreach, and some might be interested in stopping in at one of their services or other community events soon. The bad news? Dillion was an idea man. He didn't have a clue what he had gotten himself into. It was taking an army to organize the conference. It was divine intervention that had helped him gather an unstoppable event committee whose chair was a force with which to be reckoned.

The sponsorship from the local hospital and the keynote speaker, Dr. Antoine Beres, were the two primary reasons that the local media showed interest in promoting the event. Dillion was grateful that his committee chair had negotiated the fundraising team from the hospital to help with organizing and promoting it as well. Even better was that she knew the general manager of a local hotel was a cancer survivor, so he was more than willing to offer the conference venue for free, only charging for food and beverages. If his calculations were correct, after they paid for the speaker fee and the food service, they'd have about $2,000 to give back to the community as part of their annual community grants program. Not too shabby.

Speaking of shabby, he noticed he looked a bit ragged after the sleepless night. Bags under his eyes and the scruffy beard that seemed to sprout overnight. Sighing and running his fingers through his hair, Dillion lumbered from his bedroom to his bathroom for a hot shower. The cold camel-colored tiles were a shock to his system, and he scrambled to stand on the chocolate shag bathroom rug. He loved this bathroom, the combination of the warm knotted pine accents, classic pewter drawer pulls, and the craft paper-colored walls. It was a contemporary twist to an updated, traditional north woods ranch home. Getting the hot water started first, he then reached for his electric shaver and worked at getting what looked like a three-day growth beard down to a day's worth. When steam began to rise from the tub faucet, he shed his cotton boxers and T-shirt to step into what felt like heaven at that precise moment.

Most mornings one of the three kids would be banging on the door to complain about one of their siblings. However, in a moment of brilliance, he had invited his parents up north for the weekend and splurged for a room at the hotel, so they could help him with the kids while he was working his magic at the cancer conference. The children would love the water park and think it was a special treat to have a sleepover with grandma and grandpa in a hotel. It didn't hurt that the general manager also offered significant discounts for people attending the cancer survivor event.

After a relaxing shower, Dillion dressed in his parish's sapphire-blue polo shirt and khaki pants with a brown leather belt and matching shoes. The last touch was a bit of spray gel worked into his short, dark golden-brown hair; lifting his bangs so they stood up. The matching belt and shoes as well as the haircut/style were gifts from his older brother, Roger, who kidnapped him for a weekend get-away to his condo in downtown Chicago. Roger felt that his baby brother needed to look more like a millennial than a widower priest if he wanted to start dating again. The whole dating thing had been disastrous thus far. After Dillion made a phone call to Roger saying that staying celibate was a better choice than the dating scene in Minocqua, Roger took it upon himself to work with Dillion and gift him with a high-end haircut and a few accessories to dress up his wardrobe. Dillion had to admit, once he got the hang of using the spray gel, it was a relief to get rid of his traditional black comb. The shoes? Well, he didn't want to think about the price tag, but he had to admit, they were the most comfortable shoes he owned.

Looking at the time, he moved along to the kitchen, where his coffee was already brewed and sitting on top of the black granite countertop. There'd be a continental breakfast in the conference center, so he just poured his go-go juice into a travel mug before walking out to the minivan. Backing out of the driveway, Dillion took a quick glance at the home they'd occupied for the past year. A modest butter-cream ranch with an overhang above the front door, a wooden stoop, and windows accented by forest green shutters adorned with evergreen tree cut-outs. No flowers, no landscaping, but plenty of trees and a nature path that the previous owners carved out of the forest which he and the kids enjoyed taking hikes on regularly, especially when it was blackberry and blueberry season. Nothing beat the taste of freshly picked berries on top of vanilla ice cream on a warm summer's night. Yum!

Taking the backroads into town, he was able to avoid any early morning anglers driving to the big lake for a day of fishing. This time of year, dawn was great for musky and bass fishing. How'd he know? His parishioners of course! In his youth, his dad was busy teaching him about the word of God, so basic boy skills of fishing, camping, and fixing cars were not the life skills Dillion had acquired. However, as a beloved young priest to a very engaged congregation, he had access to the best mechanics, fisherman, and contractors in the north woods.

Dillion arrived just after 7 a.m. at the hotel and parked near the log overhang welcoming guests with its rustic charm. Inside the two-story lobby, he scanned the room to find someone who could let the general manager know he had arrived, to receive an update on what was completed last night and what needed to be done in the next 30 minutes before guests began to arrive. He scanned the immense room with a splattering of seating areas encouraging small groups to sit in their buttery soft leather overstuffed furniture, to the view of the floor-to-ceiling river rock fireplace adorned with an antler chandelier hanging in front of it. The hunter green walls complemented the golden glow of the exposed beams and other wooden features throughout the space. When his eyes encountered a silver-haired man in a vest and open collared white shirt, he smiled. Even at 7 a.m., Mr. Marcus Stephan was always dressed for success.

"Good morning, Father Clark! It's going to be another beautiful day today. A great day for a conference." Mr. Stephan held out his hand and shook Dillion's vigorously. Dillion began to think that perhaps the hotel's coffee had something to do with the energy Mr. Stephan had in his handshake.

"Morning, Mr. Stephan. I can't thank you and your staff enough for helping us host this cancer event."

"Please, father, call me Marcus. And as for your thanks, no thanks are necessary. I am very grateful that I can stand with you today, cancer-free. It's my way of giving something back to the community that helped me when I was battling this terrible disease. Come with me, and let's do a walk through to make sure everything is ready for you and your committee."

Dillion followed the dapper gentleman into the main concourse to the conference center. Long banquet tables were already set up with white linens, and clear round glass vases were filled with vibrant zinnias and tied with teal ribbons, in memory of his late wife, Corinne, and her battle with ovarian cancer. He got a little choked up thinking about her but was able to continue to move forward and focus on what Marcus was sharing with him.

"So, we'll have the oatmeal and fresh fruit stations here, healthy bakery over there. Coffee, tea, and water will be closest to the doors as they will be constantly refreshed throughout the day. Over by the windows and across from the doors to the conference center is the reception desk. We've arranged for a garbage can nearby for the nametag stickers."

Dillion nodded and looked at the posted agenda to make sure there were no errors:

    8 a.m. - Registration and Continental Breakfast

8:30 a.m. - Welcome
8:40 a.m. - Keynote Speaker, Dr. Antoine Beres
9:30 a.m. - Breakout Sessions
10:30 a.m. - Morning Break
10:45 a.m. - Breakout Sessions
11:45 a.m. - Lunch Break
1:00 p.m. - Cancer Center Speaker
1:45 p.m. - Afternoon Break
2:00 p.m. - Patient Panel
3:00 p.m. - Closing remarks, Adjourn

"Everything is right on time, Father. Just welcomed Dr. Beres and walked him to the podium to meet with the AV person." Dillion breathed a sigh of relief at the assurance he received from the event chair. He turned around and smiled when he looked down and into the steel blue eyes of his right hand person and all around community advocate, Mrs. Johanna Bradley. He put his hands on her shoulders as she was almost a foot shorter than he was. Wearing her signature short, curly auburn hair with whispers of silver gray on the sides and accenting her face with an all silver curl in the center of her bangs, Johanna was the standard that all the lake ladies aspired to be. No hair was ever out of place and her light bronze skin tone was accented with a few light lines around her smiling eyes—recognition of her 70ish years but not too many or too deep—as if any new wrinkle knew it was not welcome, but those that were there showed that Johanna accepted her age. However, she was keen to keep her aging to a minimum by accenting her features with impeccable taste and wisdom. Her pale pink lips never saw a Botox needle but, as with her skin and hair, were always treated to the best hair and skin care that the Northwoods had to offer. She was dressed in a chartreuse collared cotton shirt with three quarter length sleeves, a teal camisole underneath, a wide leather belt, teal capris, and tan sandals to show off her recently pedicured pale pink toenails. She reached up with a name tag to offer to Dillion.

"Father Dillion Clark," Dillion read out loud.

"Is there something wrong, Father Clark?" Johanna inquired.

"Actually, you've done a great job here. Everything looks perfect. I'm wondering, though, if we can just lose the 'father' part of my name today? I want our guests to see me as one of them." He looked down and saw the quizzical look in her eyes, as if the wheels in her mind were going 20 million miles an hour trying to see if she should put her energy into making him keep the name tag as is, or if she had the energy and resources to fix this problem with less than an hour before guests would be arriving. Dillion realized he needed to help her understand why this change was so important to him.

"What I'm trying to say, Johanna, is that if the word 'father' is on my name tag, people will have a preconceived notion that as a man of God, I've got this cancer-thing under control and I'm better at it than they are. Instead, if they only see my name, then they may perceive that I'm just trying to do the best I can. A widower. Learning how to date again, being a single parent, and just trying to keep my sanity. Does that make any sense to you?"

Johanna's eyes softened as her head tilted to the side and her hands came together to rip up the small paper in her hands. "Of course, Dillion, it makes perfect sense. I see what you're saying, and I can make a new name tag in a jiffy. Why don't you go and introduce yourself to Dr. Beres and make sure he doesn't have any problems with his AV?" Dillion smiled, hugged her, and whispered *thank you*, before he began to walk into the main ballroom.

When he entered the large room, he found Dr. Beres exactly where Johanna had said. Johanna had mentioned a second person, and there was one sitting next to him behind a computer whom, Dillion assumed, was the AV person. When Dillion reached them, he extended his arm for a handshake, "Dr. Beres, I'm Dillion Clark. I am honored to have you be our guest speaker today. Thank you for taking time out of your busy schedule to come up to the Northwoods this weekend and share your expertise with the guests."

Dr. Beres turned around, accepted Dillion's hand, and smiled. This morning he was wearing a light blue short-sleeved oxford, khaki's, camel-colored leather belt and matching boat shoes.

"Dillion, I am happy to be here and am looking forward to sharing what I know with you and your guests."

Dillion looked over to the person sitting behind the laptop and asked, "Is the AV specialist getting your presentation up and running, okay? Do you need anything?" The crop of jet black curls turned. Dillion's breath left his lungs and his heart skipped a beat as the person stood up. Dillion realized he was looking into the most intense emerald-colored eyes he'd ever seen in his life.

"Actually, this is my youngest daughter, Aurelie. I hope you don't mind, but I invited her to join me this weekend. It has been quite some time since we had any time alone together, and I thought a road trip to Minocqua for the weekend might be a nice father-daughter getaway."

Before he found the ability to speak again, this vision before him spoke and reached out her hand to shake his. "Hello Dillion, it's nice to meet you." When their hands touched, it was like an electric shock ran through his fingers, up his arm, and started his heart once again. When he peeled his gaze from her eyes, his brain was sending him signals at a rapid pace to gather as much data as it possibly could. Her heart-shaped face and bronzed skin held her perfectly symmetrical bright green eyes framed by long, luscious black lashes. Her cheeks seemed to have an added blush since they started touching, but as he was still collecting data, his sense of sight continued moving down to her full lips outlined in fire engine red lipstick. Her long neck made him want to bend down and nuzzle it where it met with her collar bone. She was wearing a black and white checkered form-fitted top with thin straps and a sweetheart neckline with just a hint of a ruffle that matched the ruffle on the bottom hem which skirted the top of a pair of black skinny capris. The capri's formed around her lean, long legs (which he was shocked to have a brief vision of wrapped around his waist). His data collection ended in a pair of black open-toed canvas wedges highlighting her lipstick-matching red toenails.

Dillion's sense of smell went into overdrive as he breathed in an arousing spice scent which made his earlier vision re-appear within a backdrop of a yurt filled with oriental rugs and plush, brightly colored pillows. Trying to regain focus, Dillion's sense of sound went to work at recording her voice for perpetuity—that soft, sultry, sound suggestive of single malt whiskey.

The sense of time frozen was broken the moment Johanna touched his shoulder and interrupted the introduction to hand him his new name tag. "Excuse me, Dillion, but I thought you'd like to know that your family just arrived, and they are at the check-in table."

Dillion's ability to speak returned with Johanna's light touch. "Thank, um, thank you, Johanna. Dr. Beres, Aurelie, won't you please excuse me?" He broke the handshake to pivot and walk towards his family. However, he paused halfway across the room to look over his shoulder, making sure she was still there. That she was real.

When he got to the registration table, Dillion saw his parents and his three children helping each other with their name tags, animated. Even though he felt a little guilty about pushing his kids out the door last night, he realized that they needed that time away from him as well. Except, Benji. Benji looked to be on the fringe. He was going through the motions. It seemed to Dillion that he wasn't as excited as his sisters were. Maybe it was a boy thing. But then again, he feared, maybe it wasn't. "Hey, who opened a barrel of monkeys and brought them here?"

"Daddy!" A chorus of high pitched voices was heard throughout the hall and then three pairs of arms opened and three pairs of feet could be heard pounding down the carpet toward their dad. Dillion spread out his arms in response, bent down with a great big smile as the first one hit his body followed quickly by the other two. He showered them with kisses before he stood up.

"Did you all behave for Grandma and Grandpa?"

"Oh yes, Daddy! And guess what? Daddy guess what??" His youngest, Brianna, was about ready to burst. "We got to go to a waterpark and know what? Grandma and Grandpa said that five years old was old enough to go down the big slides!"

"By yourself?"

He could see that the perfectly coiffed pigtails were shaking back and forth. "Oh no, Daddy. Grandma said I had to go with Benji or Riley. But I still got to go!" He noticed that her baby pudge was starting to go away, and she seemed a little taller in her pink denim skort with a pink and white flower-patterned T-shirt.

"Wow, that's big news, Bri. That's a big girl thing to do. Was it fun? Were you scared?"

"It was so much fun that I forgot I was scared."

Then he looked at his oldest. "How about you, Riley? Did you have fun at the waterpark?"

Riley's face lit up, but she had a bit more control than her youngest sibling. "Oh yes, Daddy. Grandma and Grandpa said we could stay at the waterpark until it closed! We went down the slides, did the lazy river, and floated in the tubes in the giant wave pool. So much fun!" He smiled, and really tried to pay attention to what his 10-year-old was saying, but he couldn't help noticing how much she was starting to look and act like Corinne at that age. She wanted to grow her hair longer this year and started asking to have him part it on the side with a crown braid. Looked like she got his mom to do the braid this morning. She was wearing a jean skirt with a ruffle on the bottom hem and a teal striped T-shirt.

"How about you, Benji? Did you have a good time at the waterpark?" The dark shaggy hair of his middle child shook "yes" as his pointer finger pushed up the black-rimmed glasses. He, too, was wearing a striped T-shirt, but in his favorite color, green. His tan cargo shorts were barely staying on his lean waist; Dillion wondered if Benji hadn't been eating enough again. Dillion ruffled his hair and stood up. Noticing the line of people waiting to check in; he ushered his family to the side and pointed to the food stations. The children didn't need to be shown twice, so they practically skipped over to where the plates were stacked. Dillion's mother saw the potential of disaster and followed right behind.

"Don't worry yourself, son. Your children were perfect angels." Senior Riley's eyes wrinkled a tad in the corners as he chuckled.

"Well, almost perfect."

Dillion pulled in his father for a quick handshake hug. "Thanks, Dad. I couldn't imagine trying to rally the troops and get here on time. Get yourself some breakfast." The elder Father Clark patted the younger's shoulder and went to help his wife with all the breakfast wishes and dishes. Dillion paused for a moment to take in the sight with his parents in their element, he knew it broke their hearts that he had moved their grandchildren farther away, but at times like this, he felt that the quality of the time they got together would make up for the quantity they lost. Then something, actually a someone, took his focus off his parents. That long-legged beauty was in line right behind Benji, and it looked like she was talking to him and helping him reach a muffin at the bakery table. Hmm, curious that a stranger was willing to help Benji and he was accepting the stranger's help.

Dillion turned his attention to welcoming the guests and showing them to the breakfast buffet. This was a good task for him because he could get in front of a ton of people this morning and have a few touch points that may be able to get a few more community members to visit the church or volunteer at the thrift store. When the line started to die down, he took a few moments to grab another cup of coffee, some fruit, and a muffin or two, and went into the ballroom to look for the reserved table where Johanna was sitting with the Bereses. A seat was open right next to Johanna and as luck would have it, on his other side, Aurelie. His nerves started up again as he got closer to her, and his coffee spilled a little on the white tablecloth as he was attempting to carefully put it down. "Oh here, let me help you," that warm, husky voice said to him and as she brought up her napkin to soak up some of the coffee spill, their arms brushed against each other, and he shivered.

"Thank you. Normally, I'm not this clumsy. I guess I'm a little nervous about getting up in front of such a large group and talking." Dillion was afraid to tell her that she was the real reason he was so nervous. At this time, he wished that Roger was here and could feed him suave one-liners that would get her to smile again.

"Hey, I totally get it. Even though I've been teaching for years, that first day of school with all those new kids, I still get butterflies in my stomach." And there was that amazing smile again. How was he supposed to concentrate?

"So, you're a teacher, then?"

"Yeah. I teach high school band. What do you do, Dillion?" Just then, Johanna tapped him on the shoulder and motioned that it was time to welcome everyone and to introduce Dr. Beres as the keynote speaker.

"Excuse me, I have to get this party started." *Get this party started? What kind of a line was that???* He wanted to walk out the door, instead he put on a dopey smile and walked up to the podium. *Get a grip, Clark! Breathe. Remember why everyone's here. Remember why you're here.* Dillion said to himself as he reached the podium. *Wait a minute, did I hear her giggle? Stop it! I need to concentrate.* Dillion said a silent prayer asking for strength and courage to lead this crowd and for a successful day. Then he remembered why he was here, and he began.

"Two years ago, I held my beautiful young wife in my arms as I kissed her goodbye for the last time." The audience was silent. All eyes were on him. All he had to do was what he had practiced all week. Share what was in his heart. Dillion continued. "We grew up in the same small town. Went to school together. Played together. She was my first kiss. My first dance. My first love. With her, my world made sense. She was smart, funny, and had a competitive streak. When I asked her to be my wife, I was scared, but knew that she'd say yes. I didn't think I could love her more, and then she gave birth to three amazing babies, Riley, Benji, and Brianna. My heart was bursting with joy. We had plans. So many plans." Here he paused for impact but also so that he could gather the strength he needed to get through this next part.

"Then she got sick. Really sick. Shortly after Brianna was born. The doctor took us into his office and said those words that changed our lives forever, 'You've got cancer.'" He felt his throat grow tight, and his eyes began to fill. He let them. He knew that part of the healing was grieving. Letting it flow, Dillion cleared his throat.

"Corinne Clark died two years ago in the house we bought to raise our family. In the town where we grew up. Through her illness and after her passing, the town and my family took great care of me and my kids. There were months, days, hours, and minutes when I didn't think I could hold on anymore. I wished the darkness would envelope me. Then someone would break through that murkiness and reach me and give me a little of their strength to hold on for a bit longer." Dillion paused again and looked around the room. He heard the sniffles, saw the napkins raised to wipe the tears he knew were flowing. He caught a glimpse of Aurelie wiping away a tear and his heart leapt. Then he searched the audience for his family and saw his littlest in the arms of her grandmother while Benji had his head down and Riley was resting her head on her grandpa's shoulder.

"Two years ago, I needed to decide either to stop living and let my grief take over or to push on and be the dad my children needed me to be." He looked right at his children and the tears rolled down his face. "I knew that no matter how hard it was on me to lose my wife, it was worse for our children to lose their mother. I made a vow that day, that moment. I vowed that I would go on and do my best to give them the love and the life they deserved." Now he looked out over the audience to capture their gaze.

"I failed more times than I succeeded. Being in our hometown, everyone was there to help us. To help me. I really wished I could have stayed there. In that house. With our family, friends, and neighbors supporting us. But I couldn't. Everywhere I went, I saw Corinne. It was our first Christmas without her, and we were doing a great job of creating new memories and mixing them with some of those time-honored family traditions we wanted to hold on to. Coming back from a trip to see Christmas lights, I swear I heard her laughing. I smelled her scent; she smelled of vanilla. I saw her in the seat next to me." Another pause. More tears. "I knew then, in order for me to heal, to move forward, to move on, I needed to leave our town and find a new place to raise our children—to build a new life and home." Dillion sighed and looked at his parents.

"Besides saying goodbye to Corinne that last time, telling my parents that we were leaving home, was the second most difficult thing I've ever had to do in my life.

"Minocqua has been a good place to raise our children. And the people here have been so welcoming and supportive. I've realized that leaving our home didn't stop me from grieving, in fact, I've found that I'm not the only one who's lost a spouse to cancer in this community. Unfortunately, I've learned that Minocqua has many families impacted by cancer, and we are all just trying to make it through, day by day. Hopefully having more successful days than not.

"About a year ago, I had the great opportunity to hear Dr. Antoine Beres speak at a conference. I was so impressed by his knowledge of cancer research and how down-to-earth he is. He truly cares about his patients and about those of us who are affected by cancer. I started to mull around an idea. What if the people touched by cancer in Minocqua could get the same inspiration from Dr. Beres that I had? What if I could give back to them a little of the support and encouragement they've given to me and my family this past year?"

Dillion looked at Johanna and smiled. "So, I shared my idea with Mrs. Minocqua over here," pointing to Johanna and inviting her to stand up. "Johanna Bradley, a woman who never shies away from a challenge and is always looking for an opportunity to make a positive difference in our community. She took the reins and turned my vision into a reality. Please join me in thanking Johanna and her committee for putting this great event together." Dillion started clapping and the whole room joined in.

"And now, it is my great honor to introduce our keynote speaker, Dr. Antoine Beres. Dr. Beres ..." Dillion waited until Dr. Beres joined him behind the podium to shake his hand and then walk back to his seat.

When he was settled, and the lights dimmed for the PowerPoint presentation, he felt a hand on his forearm and a warm whisper in his ear, "Thank you for sharing your story, Dillion," Aurelie squeezed his forearm for impact. "You had nothing to worry about.

You are an amazing speaker. You had us all crying. Hell, I'm still crying!" She squeezed it again for emphasis and held it there just long enough so that he found the courage to put his hand on top of hers and whisper into her ear, "Thank you."

The rest of the event became a blur. Dillion was shaking hands in the lobby when he caught a glimpse of something. He ended the last handshake and turned to focus on the scene that captured his attention. Benji was at a baby grand piano with Aurelie sitting by his side. It looked like she was talking to him and helping him move his fingers over the keys. As he walked a bit closer, he focused on Benji. It seemed like he was opening up a bit to her. He wasn't just going through the motions. Benji was looking at Aurelie's fingers on the keys, and then he would copy her. He watched her face as she spoke to him. Then he would look back down at the keys and play them again. Was it possible? What if this stranger was able to get through to Benji? Just as he was asking these questions, internally, he felt a presence at his side and then heard the French accent and knew Dr. Beres had joined him in watching the scene unfolding at the piano.

"Amazing, isn't she?" All Dillion could do was nod in agreement. "It's hard for me to believe that Aurelie ever had a severe learning disability and begged me to let her quit school because it was too hard and she was being teased." That confession broke his trance and he turned to look at the older Beres as he was reminiscing.

"What?" Was all Dillion could say.

"Aurelie. Isn't she amazing?"

"Amazing ..." Dillion confirmed.

Dr. Beres smiled, looked down at the smitten priest and patted him on his shoulder. He knew when he had lost the attention of someone to which he was talking. He also knew that Aurelie was a supernatural force, like a magnet, people would gravitate to her. He had a thought and, while he wasn't often a spontaneous man, he felt compelled to give this younger man a little push. "You know, Aurelie's band is playing tonight at the *June Bloom Arts and Crafts Festival*. You should come out and celebrate your accomplishment.

After all of this work, you deserve to grab a beer and relax. Let me buy you one as a thank you. What do you say?"

Dillion was trying to get his bearings, Benji is interacting with Aurelie, she's in a band, and Dr. Beres is inviting him for a beer. "Um, that sounds great. Let me just check in with my parents to make sure they are okay with having the kids alone one more night."

Of course his parents would jump at the chance to spoil his kids a little longer. Sure, he should go over his sermon one last time before church tomorrow, but he felt this energy that he hadn't experienced in a long time. Dillion felt compelled to go to the festival. He wanted to see more of Aurelie, and he was very curious about what kind of band she was in. He walked over to Benji and Aurelie at the piano and heard her in almost a whisper of a voice, talking to him, encouraging him. She was also touching him, lightly. Sometimes moving his fingers to the right keys, a squeeze on his shoulder, or a nudge as if they shared a secret. When Dillion got closer, he interjected, "Hey bud, what're you up to?"

Benji, still looking at his hands on the keys, responded, "I'm learning to play the piano."

"Impressive. Did you thank Ms. Beres for teaching you?"

Aurelie didn't look up, she was present. For Benji. "No thanks needed, Benji. I am happy to see that you are enjoying it." Dillion was taking in the moment as well. He was impressed that she wanted to spend time with Benji and liked it. How many dates had he been on where the woman didn't want to even hear about his kids? Yet, here was someone who he wasn't even dating but was interested in Benji, and Benji was responding to her. Dillion checked into his own thoughts and feelings, and he realized what it was. It was a possibility.

"Benji, thank Ms. Beres. It's time to go back to the hotel room with Grandma and Grandpa."

The shaggy-haired boy lifted his head up and looked into Aurelie's eyes and said, "Thanks."

Aurelie nudged him one more time and replied, "Thank you, Benji. I didn't know anyone today, and I was nervous. You helped me today. Like a friend. And since we're friends, you can call me Aurelie."

Benji looked up at her and then to his dad as if asking for permission. Dillion's heart skipped a beat. A friend. Since moving here, had Benji even mentioned any friends? Did he have any? What else had he missed about Benji's acclimation to his new home? Dillion nodded and forced a grin.

"Thanks, Aurelie."

"You are welcome, Benji. Thanks for being my first friend in Minocqua." She gave him a light hug and Dillion noticed that his son allowed her to do so. Afterwards, he got up from the piano bench and ran across the lobby to where his siblings and grandparents were waiting for him.

"Whoa." Dillion exclaimed.

"Whoa what?" Aurelie questioned.

"Oh, sorry. It's just that Benji has been struggling since we got here. I've been worried about him but haven't found a way for him to tell me what's wrong. This morning, I saw him and it looked like he had lost weight. And then, here you are, just meeting him and yet you are reaching him. He's responding to you. He's playing music. How'd you do that?"

Aurelie got up from the piano bench and stood within hugging distance of Dillion. He felt the air between them sizzle. It was as if he had just drunk a triple espresso. "I used to be just like him. I get him. I had no friends at school, my brother and sisters were all older than me and so much smarter. I just needed one person to connect to. One thing I could be good at, better than my siblings. Something to help me work through my feelings. For me, that was music. Benji can feel the music. It speaks to him."

Dillion was now flooded with emotions. How was it that a perfect stranger could reach his child? Could understand what was troubling Benji? And he, Benji's father, had completely missed it?

Aurelie furrowed her brow, reached out for his arm and squeezed it. Where she touched him, he felt the heat. "Hey, don't beat yourself up about this, Dillion. My dad's a doctor and my mom is brilliant, but they couldn't help me. It wasn't until I met my best friend, Cat, and found music that I began to feel better about myself and do better in school. After what I heard you say today, I'd say that you are doing the best you can with what you were given. I don't know if I could come back from a loss like that. I've never had anyone in my family die."

"Honestly, I didn't know if I could go on. But I had the kids. Most days, they were the only reason I got up in the morning."

She nodded and looked up at him, cocking her head. "You are very brave, Dillion. You are doing a great job." She squeezed his arm again and said, "I'm really glad that you got up this morning." Then she smiled and her eyes sparkled.

"Me too."

"I have to get going to get ready for tonight. My band's playing at the festival. Did you want to stop by and check us out? My dad will be there, and it might be nice for him to have someone he knows to hang out with."

Dillion smiled and his heart soared. "Yeah, your dad told me about it. Said he'd buy me a beer to celebrate a successful event. What's the name of the band?"

"The Hot Rockin' Horns."

"The kids are with my parents for the night, so I can stop by for a bit, but I've got to get up early tomorrow morning."

"Oh, I understand." She dropped her hand, and he felt the cold space where her hand used to be. "It's just, I was kinda hoping that you might hang around until after the set and maybe grab a bite to eat?"

He felt the possibility bloom into a promise at that moment. He gathered his courage and responded, "Yeah, I think I can do that. I can make strong coffee tomorrow morning to get me through work." She smiled and that spark showed up in her emerald eyes again.

"Great. I'll see you later then. It'll be nice to have more than one friend here."

Chapter Nineteen

Aurelie jumped into the shower after a final check-in with her band to make sure they were all in sync for tonight's set. Instead of visualizing singing the songs, which was part of her pre-performance ritual, Aurelie was playing back her interactions with the dreamy, young widower. How excited he was to see his kids, how he moved her to tears during his speech, how vulnerable he was after seeing his son playing the piano. She lathered herself in her signature spice scented body wash and began to feel lingering stirrings that hadn't been felt in months. How difficult would it be to keep her promise not to sleep with someone she just met? But Dillion didn't feel like a one-night stand. She didn't quite have the word or words to describe how she felt about him. But her body seemed to know what to do whenever she was near him. It compelled her to touch him. Sit closer to him. Flirt with him.

After wrapping herself in a towel, she reached for her hair gel and blow dryer with diffuser to scrunch her hair into a spikey, coiffed style that was perfect for playing the part of the singing siren. As she was drying herself off with the towel, her imagination ran wild again as she fantasized Dillion holding the towel and wiping her down as his eyes seared into hers. The heat she was daydreaming about made her shiver. *Enough.* She told herself. She had to get ready and play her part. Sipping on hot water, lemon, and honey, she laid out her leopard print "cat suit" leotard and over-the-knee black boots.

But something felt different tonight. Instead of getting ready to play for a large audience, Aurelie kept thinking about how this hair style, those boots, or that crimson lipstick would appeal to a single audience member, Dillion. If she were honest, she was more anxious about tonight than she had been about a gig in a long while. By the time she got the knock on her door from her bandmates, Aurelie was working herself into a tizzy. *Snap out of it.* She told herself in the mirror. She looked at herself from all sides and futzed with her hair one last time before she grabbed her things to go out the door and into the night. She felt the energy shift and though she wasn't much of a churchgoer, she did a quick prayer that she wouldn't be too distracted, and they would kill it tonight.

The crowd was spilling out of the tent when the band got there. Aurelie felt a bit less confident than usual and silently wished that Cat was there to help her focus. She shook her body loose and waited for the MC to introduce the band before she jumped onto the stage. Closing her eyes, Aurelie listened for her cue and when it came, all her muscles kicked in. She practically ran onto the stage and began belting, "I Love Rock N' Roll" as if she were Joan Jett and her band was the Blackhearts. The audience responded ecstatically. The grass space in front of the stage filled with impromptu couples and groups who felt the spirit compel them to dance. Aurelie sang with a fervor that she hadn't felt in a long time. When the song was done, she opened her eyes and saw her dad and Dillion hanging out on one of the picnic benches. Both were clapping and smiling at her. It gave her the confidence she was missing earlier.

The Hot Rockin' Horns were on fire during their first set and Aurelie set the tone. It was as if Janis Joplin, Pat Benatar, and Nancy Wilson had infused her soul with their spirits and had given her their voices to sing at levels Aurelie only hoped to achieve. It was a transcendent experience. Quite a few times she looked in Dillion's direction to see his reaction and what she received in return fueled her passionate vocals.

At the break, Aurelie worked herself through the crowd toward the two men she was hoping she had impressed. "Hey," she said, almost breathless, "how are you enjoying the show?"

Her father, smiling with pride, was the first to answer, "Mon Cheri, you sound better than ever tonight. Congratulations!" With that, Dr. Beres put his hands on her shoulders and kissed her on both cheeks. While Aurelie was pleased that she had impressed her father, she was more interested to hear how Dillion felt about the set and her performance.

"Thanks, Dad. I appreciate that, really. It means a lot." Then, she turned to look into those steel blue eyes to catch a glimpse into his mind. "So, Dillion," stopping to take a drink from her bottled water, "What do you think?" Adding a bit of coyness, "Do you like what you see? Hear?" She forgot they were standing with her father until she saw the shock register on Dillion's face.

"Uh, excuse me?" Dillion asked.

"Oh, sorry. I mean, how do you like the band? Are you enjoying the music?"

"Oh yeah. You sound amazing! You're so talented. Thanks for inviting me to listen to your band tonight." Aurelie was trying to focus on what Dillion was saying, but she couldn't stop taking in his physique and his energy. Now that he wasn't in conference mode, she noticed he was more relaxed. She wanted to hang out with him longer, but she felt a tap on her shoulder and knew it was time to start the second half of the show.

"Thanks, Dillion. I'm really glad to hear it. Listen, I gotta get going for the next set. I can't wait to grab a bite to eat afterwards. I'm always starving after a show."

Dillion realized Aurelie was confirming their late night date, or not a date, or whatever, and was waiting for him to confirm. "Yes, I do want to meet up with you after the show. With me having to go in to work early tomorrow, I thought we could eat someplace close. Within walking distance from here." His eyes focused on her high heel boots and flushed. "Umm, will you be able to walk into downtown in those?"

She smiled, enjoying the fact that she made him nervous. Good. He deserved a little of his own medicine. He may not know it, but she had been battling butterflies in her stomach and was quite frustrated at how much energy she was using up thinking about whether he'd like her in this outfit, what he thought of her singing, how close he would get to her when they went out to eat, and how he would feel naked against her. "Great, listen I gotta go. Stick around the tent after the show. I'll look for you."

The second set confirmed that they were most definitely red-hot tonight, fitting with their band name. They played some big band standards, a few Chicago hits, and her favorite Santana songs before they culminated into Journey's "Lovin' Touchin' Squeezin". The crowd surged toward the stage and begged for an encore. After a quick water break, she whispered the next song title to her bandmates. She gave a cat-like grin scanning the crowd, looking for her target. When she caught his eyes, she winked, did a little hip roll and swaggered so that her backside was showing her tight ass swaying side-to-side. Aurelie was in her estrogen element when she lowered her vocal register so that each note of Billy Idol's "Hot Summer Night" almost sounded like a growl. She was turning herself on and was hoping she was doing the same to a certain person in the audience. At the end, during the band's bow to the crowd, Aurelie looked up to see her dad clapping and cheering loudly and her intended target with his eyes as wide open as his mouth. Success.

After Aurelie shook several hands and acknowledged many congratulations, Dillion made it up to the front of the line. Still looking like a wide-eyed child on Christmas morning, he got up the courage to speak. "Wow. That was great. Your band was great. You were great. Wow." Aurelie tried hard not to laugh, but a giggle snuck out anyhow.

"Thanks, Dillion. It felt 'great.'" He looked down at his feet now and she felt his shame. *Shit.* "I'm sorry. That was mean. But honestly, it did feel great. Really great."

He lifted a corner of his mouth into a side smile. His excitement, squelched. *Shit. Shit.* "Listen, I'm going to quick change and will be back in five to grab that bite to eat you promised me. After that show, I am famished!" Dillion nodded and put his hands in his pockets. God, she just wanted to run her fingers through his hair and tousle it. And more. *Geez, get a grip, Beres. You can't jump him with your dad right here. Breathe.*

Aurelie got a bear hug from her dad as he whispered his words of encouragement in his native French. It felt more special because he spoke in a language only she could understand. He had a knack for making each child feel as if they were his favorite. She knew he would never admit it, but she felt like his favorite in this moment and forever.

By the time Aurelie appeared in a cut-off grey sweatshirt, black yoga pants, and black sandals the crowd had dispersed enough so she could zero in on Dillion. "So, where are you taking me?" she asked.

"Well, it's late, but I think this place is still open. If not, there's a hot dog stand not too far from here."

"Lead the way." When she got close enough, Dillion put his hand on the small of her back to guide her in the direction of the main drag, Oneida Street, in downtown Minocqua. They didn't have that long of a walk before reaching an old European-style front entrance and a wooden statue of a man wearing lederhosen. Dark-stained wood and murals of the German countryside adorned the restaurant. A teenaged boy with floppy hair welcomed them to Otto's Beer and Brat Garden. Aurelie was fascinated by the framed tapestries, beer steins, and other German memorabilia that greeted them as they wove deeper into the restaurant. Then it was her turn to have her eyes and mouth wide open. With their next few steps, they seemed to leave the traditional indoor restaurant and walked into a magical place of trees draped in twinkle lights to match the star-filled sky above. Heavy wooden booths were available under the tutor-style awnings and black wicker seats with square tables were scattered in the beer garden space. After spending most of the evening with crowds of people under a tent, this was like walking into a secret garden. Aurelie was impressed. The young host chose a table in the center of the beer garden, which suited Aurelie well. She had the opportunity to look up into the starry night and enjoy the evening breeze to cool her heated skin.

"So, what do you think? Is this okay?" Dillion asked a bit nervously.

"This? This place is amazing, Dillion. I had no idea it was here. It's like a magic trick, you know? So cool. You really know how to impress a girl on a first date." She chuckled at her own joke while looking down at the menu. Not hearing a response, she gazed up over the laminated list of German foods and saw the shock on his face.

"You think this is a date?" he asked.

"Isn't it?"

Dillion paused. Gulped down some ice water and looked at her. "I've been on so many bad first dates that I guess I didn't recognize it as a date." He looked down at his menu for a moment, and then looked over it. "This is way better."

Aurelie laughed. A good, hearty laugh. It felt nice to be on a date with someone who didn't have expectations. She began to relax. "I agree." Looking down at her menu, she asked him a suitable question for a first date. "So, what's good here?"

Aurelie noticed that Dillion seemed to relax a little. "Well, since we are in a Wisconsin beer garden, I'd recommend Otto's famous bratwurst or spatenbrat which is a brat soaked in beer."

"Mmm. I haven't had a brat in a while. That spatenbrat sounds perfect. I'll give it a shot."

A young woman with a ponytail stopped by their table and took their order. A few moments later, she delivered frosted mugs of craft beer to the couple. Aurelie had a good, long drink and then sighed. "Man. That sure does hit the spot. Now I am really looking forward to that brat." It was nice to see his smile. It was the kind of smile that made it all the way up to his eyes. Eyes that seemed to have an extra sparkle tonight.

"So, tell me a little bit about yourself, Aurelie. Since this is a first date and all."

She straightened up a bit and took on a serious look. Clearing her throat, Aurelie replied, "Like what? What do you want to know?"

"Where do you live?" Dillion asked.

"I live in Mukwonago. Pretty much have lived there all my life. I even work there. Man, I can't imagine the guts it took for you to pick up your whole family and move away from everything you've known. You are very brave, Dillion. I don't know if I could do that." Just then the teenage server came over with plates of steaming brats and German potato salad. Aurelie didn't care how it looked, she just took a huge bite of her spatenbrat and let the juice run down her chin while she enjoyed the experience. "Oh. My. God. This is fantastic!"

Dillion smiled and grabbed his napkin to dab the drippings off her chin before they fell onto her sweatshirt. "Glad you like it. Here, let me get this for you," Aurelie's breath caught as he got close to her mouth.

"Thanks," she almost whispered.

"Sorry, I guess spending most of my meals with kids, I just automatically kick into dad-mode when I see something that needs to be cleaned up. Maybe that's why my dates go so poorly."

This time, Aurelie gave a full laugh. "Well, if we're keeping score, I'd say that drooling on a first date gets a demerit." After a bite of German potato salad, Aurelie asked the next question. "Besides running special events and being a motivational speaker, what else do you do for a living?"

Dillion dipped his head and looked like a child who got caught with their hand in the cookie jar. "And now comes the reason why I rarely go on second dates."

"Oh no. Don't tell me. You're a cat burglar. Wait, a male stripper…"

"Worse."

"Worse than a male stripper? Geez, now you've piqued my interest. What do you do?"

After a heavy sigh, Dillion answered her, "I'm a priest."

Aurelie's cat eyes went wide, and she sat back in her seat. "No shit?"

"No shit."

"Huh. I didn't know that priests could date. I guess it's been a while since I've been to church."

"I'm an Episcopal priest, not a Catholic priest. We can get married and have a family. But it does tend to turn women off. Come to think of it, I haven't been on a third date before."

"Well, Dillion, I can honestly say that you stumped me on that one. I had no clue. Oh wait, you did tell me that you couldn't stay out late because you work tomorrow morning. Color me stupid."

"You're not stupid. I wasn't forthcoming with the information. The truth is, I enjoyed spending the day not being seen as Father Clark. I even had my name tag for the cancer event changed so it said 'Dillion'. I just wanted to be a normal guy for a day. But I'm not. Not really. Sorry to be such a downer. I guess a next date is out of the question, no matter how good the brat is."

Aurelie peered into Dillion's eyes. Past the silver flecks that dotted the steel blue color that got her attention in the first place. His honest admission gave her pause. She felt as if she was getting a glimpse inside his soul. He was honest and authentic on their first date. Could she see a second date in their future? Living four to five hours apart? A widower with three kids and an Episcopal priest? When would they have the time to date? How much baggage would they both be bringing to the table? Yet, if she were honest with herself, she felt a pull towards this mess of a man. As much as a second or third date didn't make sense, wasn't practical, she couldn't deny that she wanted to see where this went.

"Don't sell yourself short, Dillion. I may have been on more second and third dates than you have, but they've never been worth my time. You and I have had more truth in this first date than I've had in any of my 'relationships,' if that is what you could call them." She paused to take a drink and to let what she said sink in. Would she have the guts to be as honest with him as he was being with her? Would their first date also be their last? "I guess it's time to find out if I'm second date material. Hit me with another question." This time, she was the one who looked sheepish waiting for him to react to her authentic self.

"Hmm, so why do you think you may not be second date material?" He was looking deeply into her eyes and Aurelie couldn't tell if he was indeed interested in her answer as a man or as a priest.

"Well, I've only dated guys who were fun, spontaneous. Anytime things looked like they would get too serious, I usually jumped ship. I liked feeling free and enjoyed the nonchalant nature of the 'relationships.'"

"Are you interested in having a real relationship? Or are you still looking for fun and spontaneous flings?"

Aurelie smirked and pushed her plate away before she looked up at him again. "It's not what you think it is."

"Okay, then tell me. What is holding you back from having a real relationship?"

This time she looked deep into those cool pools of water, breathed deeply, and began to let herself open up to him.

"It's because I know what a perfect relationship looks like. Feels like. My parents. You've met my dad." Dillion nodded but waited for her to continue. "Well, my dad is one side of a perfect match. My mom is the absolute partner for him. Don't get me wrong, they have their fair share of disagreements. But no matter how many awards he gets, or papers published, he always asks for her opinion and her approval. I envy the way he looks at her when she's unaware of him. And she always knew she was his equal while she kept the house running, and all of us kids knew who the real boss was." Aurelie chuckled as she reminisced about a childhood memory that she wasn't ready to divulge just yet. She looked deeper into those eyes and saw an opening that she hadn't seen before. She was willing to risk it. "I want what they have. I don't want to settle for anything less. I want a man to look at me the way my dad looks at my mom. And I want him to see me as his equal partner in all things."

"That makes some sense, but I still don't understand why you choose to date men who sound like they are the opposite of your dad? Guys who will never live up to that standard." Dillion inched forward on the table as if to reach deeper into her head. To get to the root of her past actions.

"Thanks for pulling out the hard questions already on the first date. Isn't this third date stuff, Dillion?" She tried to make light of the situation and possibly deflect the difficult question.

"Sorry, I don't mean to pry. It's just, just," He paused, looked up at the star-filled sky as if looking for inspiration for his next word. "What I'm trying to say, very poorly, is I see an incredibly talented, charismatic, caring, and beautiful woman in front of me. And what I don't understand is why she would date men who were so far beneath her? Not her equal, if her dream is to have what her parents have?"

Aurelie pushed her hand through her hair as she looked up to the stars. Taking a deep breath, she responded, "It's because I'm not perfect and I'm terrified of finding the right partner and screwing it up. As a kid, I was always the outcast of the family. The ugly duckling. My brother and sisters were all high achievers, and I could never be as good at anything that mattered to my mom and dad. However, I was exceptionally good at being silly, late, and getting into trouble."

"But your dad doesn't treat you like that now. He seems very proud of you. He told me you have a learning disability, and you overcame that through music. Couldn't all the things you just described be attributed to the fact that you had a learning disability that wasn't diagnosed right away?"

"You're right. But I also had an incredibly smart best friend who helped me figure out how to get through school and I helped her find her silly side." Aurelie's smile came back, but with a sense of melancholy.

"Hmm, why am I sensing you are getting sad? See, I told you I'm not really good at this first date thing. Instead of feeling happy about being together, I'm making you sad."

Aurelie reached out to hold his hands and she felt that spark again. "No, no. Not you. Not you at all. It's just that my best friend, Cat, was always a constant in my life. I could come to her day or night with a problem, and she was there for me. And vice versa. But she met this great guy and they moved away to Montana after getting married. And I crashed. Crashed hard. I knew I was grieving losing her, but I couldn't stop spiraling out of control. I was in self-destruction mode; I was partying all night long after gigs and going home with all the wrong sorts of men. Then one morning I woke up in a bed and an apartment that I didn't recognize with a voice I didn't know asking me to make breakfast while he showered. I felt so dirty. Disgusting. I grabbed my clothes from the night before and sprinted out of there." Aurelie felt Dillion squeeze her hands encouraging her to go on.

"Well, my landlady gave me a thorough talking to and used tough love to get me out of that spiral and onto a new path which included a new guy in my life." Dillion released her hands and shifted his eyebrows. Was it jealousy? She reached into her oversized bag and pulled out her cellphone to show him what she meant. "Here he is, Mumford."

Dillion held the phone and cocked his head. "He's a dog. A giant dog!"

Aurelie took the phone back. "Yep, Mrs. Romansky told me to shape up and be responsible for something other than myself. She encouraged me to get a dog and I came back with a Great Dane." Aurelie noticed he looked a little frightened, so she expanded. "Yeah, I didn't expect to get such a big dog, but there was just something about him. He just kept following me with his goofy face and I loved that he has one ear that stands straight up and the other is so floppy. He's so imperfect that he's perfect for me." Dillion nodded like he understood where she was going with her line of explanation.

"He loves kids. He gets so excited to see my little nieces and nephews and he acts as their nanny, keeping them from getting into too much trouble. He's so sweet."

"Mumford, is it?" Aurelie nodded. "Mumford sounds like the perfect dog for you." Now she laughed heartily.

"You'd think so, but there is one problem."

"What's that?"

"He's afraid of loud noises and music."

Dillion's eyes went wide, and his mouth shaped into a quirky smile. "What? He's afraid of music? And you're a musician and a music teacher? Isn't that a problem?"

"It was in the beginning. But we've figured it out. When it is going to storm or I'm going to be practicing, I put his dinosaur snood on him and he's good as gold."

"What is a snood?" Dillion asked quizzically.

"It's easier to show you." She scrolled in her phone again to show him a photo of the gigantic dog wearing a green close-fitting hood with dinosaur scales running down the center back of the hood.

"Wow."

"See why I thought you might not want a second date with me?" Aurelie asked, half sassy and half serious. "I have a lot of baggage and a dog the size of a small horse who needs to wear a snood to keep from freaking out at loud noises and music."

Dillion paused, then he realized the time when the server came to take away their dirty dishes and give them the check. He took a card out of his wallet and said, "This one's on me. I'm old-fashioned in that I never let a lady pay for the first date."

"Thank you." Then Aurelie got up the courage to ask, "So, Dillion, do you see a second date in our future?"

She caught him looking at his phone and thought that perhaps she could just chalk this one up to her best first date in a long time, perhaps ever, and leave it at that. Too complicated.

"What? Oh, sorry, I just saw the time, and I have to be getting you back to your hotel and me to bed."

"No worries. I guess it would be too complicated for us. But this was a great first date. Honestly. Thanks for dinner, Dillion. I haven't had someone to talk to about things that matter to me in a very long time. It was refreshing."

He got up and helped her get out of her chair, put his hand on her lower back, as if they were comfortable with each other. He paid the bill, left a tip, and guided her onto the deserted main street before he turned her to him. "I really enjoyed our first date, Aurelie, and I agree. It was definitely the best one I've been on lately. At the risk of tempting fate, I'd like to see if we could go out on a second date if that's okay with you?"

Standing so close to him, with his hands holding onto her arms, she had to tip her head up to see into his eyes. "Yes, Dillion, it's okay with me."

He smiled and squeezed her arms before he pulled her into a hug. A warm and soothing, if also a bit sexually arousing hug. "Would it be okay to walk you back to the hotel since my car is in the parking lot?"

"I would love it. Thanks for offering." Dillion released the hug and Aurelie grabbed his hand as they strolled the deserted street while enjoying the quiet.

When they arrived at his minivan, Aurelie turned to face him and reached out to put her palms onto his chest. She could feel his heartbeat quickening and it stirred all kinds of feelings in her. Aurelie got up the courage to move her hands so that they clasped behind his neck, and she moved forward to give him a goodbye kiss. When her lips touched his, her mind went numb. She intended it to be a quick little peck that spiraled quickly into a heated entanglement. His full lips opened slightly, and she moved to fit closer to his body and deepen the kiss. Feeling his warmth and hardness against her, she boldly opened her mouth to lightly taste his lips with her pink, little tongue. In response, Dillion opened his mouth and invited her into it to tangle with his tongue as if they were learning about each other through this most passionate, mind-numbing kiss.

Aurelie's arms brought his hard body as close as possible to hers. She could feel his heat permeating through their clothes. As their temperatures rose, something else was also. She wasn't thinking anymore, she was just reacting in that freeing-space of being present in the moment when she felt his hands move from the small of her back down to her ass and begin to massage it in a way that had her head spinning. Aurelie, forgetting that they were in a public space, wanted to take these feelings and these actions to the next step, when she heard an audible groan from her partner and felt a strong push away from her.

"Wha, What's wrong? Don't you like kissing me?" Her eyes trying to focus after being in a heated frenzy.

"I like kissing you very much, Aurelie. Too much, actually," Dillion responded looking down at a full-on bulge in his pants. At first, Aurelie was confused, but after following his gaze, it dawned on her, and she started to giggle.

"Sorry. I didn't mean to laugh. It looks…" What was she trying to say? What should she say so that she could empathize without patronizing? Without losing a second date? "It looks kinda painful," she said while taking a step back.

Dillion shifted and leaned his arm up against the van door and pushed his fingers through his hair in a fit of exasperation. "Yeah, it's a little uncomfortable, and embarrassing. I'm feeling like a 13-year-old who can't control his bodily functions."

Aurelie's fit of giggles dissipated. She took it all in. Reached out to touch his arm and give it a light squeeze. "Dillion, that kiss had more excitement and passion in it than any sex I've ever had." He looked down at her quizzically, and then with a smirk of pride.

"Really?" His voice almost went up an octave, which only made him sound like a teenager.

"Really. And, if I am honest, and this might be a sin to think it or even say it, but I can't imagine how mind-blowing sex would be with you. If any man could break my chastity promise, it's you Dillion." She had no idea how he would react, thinking that a priest would likely just get into the van and hit the gas and never look back. She was the devil. A temptress. But God, did she feel heavenly right now. That feeling intensified when he pulled her in for a deep, long-lasting kiss that took her breath away. She had no concept of space or time, just how their bodies and mouths felt as if they were the last two pieces of a 10,000-piece jigsaw puzzle snapped into place completing the picture. This time, she was the one who slowed the kiss to a halt and stepped out of their entanglement.

"Holy shit, Dillion." She paused to catch her breath, then looked up at him. "What does this mean?"

He tipped her chin, stared deep into her emerald eyes, and replied in a husky whisper, "It means we are definitely having a second date." With that, Dillion dipped his head and barely touched his full lips to hers before leaving her breathless for a second time.

Chapter Twenty

Dillion, for the second time this weekend, woke up to the sound of his alarm, the only sound in his home. Earlier in the week, he was looking forward to peace and quiet. However, now he was missing not having kids climbing all over him, begging him to get up and get breakfast started. He wondered if he could turn this into a meditative, peaceful moment, knowing that in a few hours he would be the responsible parent once again. His own parents would have to leave right after church due to the long drive back to Illinois. But then something else came into his semi-dream/semi-awake state. It was a snippet of memories from the previous day.

Sifting through them in the rolodex of his mind, the first truly clear picture was of a pair of striking emerald-green eyes. Next was the electric shock when she first touched his arm. A smirk found itself on his face as he remembered how her cat-like leotard hugged every single, subtle curve. The smile grew as he recollected the growl in her voice when she belted out rock anthems. Then the scene shifted to their conversations in the beer garden where it lingered while he felt a little more deeply before his dream-state landed on the hot and heavy make-out session in the hotel parking lot. Groaning, he felt his physical need growing inside of him as well as on the outside. As if by muscle memory, his hand moved to cover his hardness and began to slowly stroke it as he continued to re-envision their passionate kissing.

BUZZ! BUZZ! BUZZ! The snooze on his phone alarm went off and severed his connection to his lust-filled dream. His hand found a different purpose and Dillion felt a bit despondent. He was exhausted from the late night before. He hadn't wanted the night to end, and he didn't feel like being a priest in this moment. He wanted to feel like a man. A man who would wake up next to a woman on a lazy, Sunday morning and make slow, adoring love to her. Just as he was beginning to feel sorry for himself, he remembered that the woman who was lingering in his dreams was the same woman he wanted to wake up next to on a Sunday morning. And that woman would be in his church in just a few hours.

Dillion shot up and threw off the covers. Renewed with an energy that was lacking before, he practically ran to the shower, making it a bit cooler than usual, and quickly went through his normal Sunday routine. Thinking to himself that the sooner he got to church, the sooner he could see her again. The exotic woman with the equally exotic name, Aurelie.

Though he spent a little more time making sure his hair and his shaven face were worthy of a second meeting, and hopefully a second date confirmation, he hastily went through the rest of the tasks needed for a workday. When everything at home was done, he practically ran to the minivan and had to remind himself that most of the roads in town had a 25 MPH speed limit.

The choir director met him at the door and looked a little quizzically at his priest. "Father, you're here a bit early, aren't you? The choir hasn't even started practicing yet."

"Oh, I just thought I'd get here early in case Dr. Beres had any questions about the service and such."

The director nodded and walked into the church hall, toward the classroom where his choir would soon join him. Dillion walked in the opposite direction, on the way to his office, where his green vestments were hung and ready for him to put on over his black dress pants, shirt, and white collar. Once he walked into his office, the dark-stained wood and rich leather furnishings helped bring his focus back to the job that was in front of him. His calling. Dillion methodically got dressed in his officiant vestments while silently going over the structure of the service and his sermon. When he felt fully prepared, he left his office and shifted perspective to being the leader of his congregation.

This sun-filled morning had his parishioners lingering outside to chit chat about the event the day before and all other smalltown happenings. Though most of his parishioners were seniors, during the summer months several young families would gather and share communion as they vacationed up north. He was fully engaged in conversation with one such family when his own arrived and he heard the shrill sounds of "Daddy!" coming from the parking lot. Dillion excused himself and bent down to welcome his own family to celebrate with him. No matter how old he got, he knew that he would never grow tired of this scene. In fact, he knew emphatically that he would miss this terribly when his children would choose not to welcome him this way anymore, when they grew up. But that day was not today. He would relish the moment when everything clicked and there were no trials or tribulations he had to maneuver between his children. He hugged them hard and welcomed the feeling of just being present with them. And it was good.

"Dr. Beres, Aurelie, so good to see you both this morning," Dillion heard the elder Riley say. It shook him and he released his offspring to stand and welcome the Bereses to his church.

Outstretching his hand, Dillion shared his father's sentiment from a moment earlier. Except that he paused, ever so slightly, when he took Aurelie's hand in his to meet those exceptionally striking eyes that had a bit of a twinkle in them this morning. It could be the sun playing tricks on him, but then he looked down at her pale pink lips and saw the smirk of someone who was sharing his secret.

"Father Clark," Aurelie responded. He hoped he hadn't audibly gulped, but he did take a moment to view her outfit which was the perfect blend of feminine and a little bit fun. She was wearing a rose floral swing dress with white pumps, matching purse, and sunglasses that she held in her opposite hand. *Heaven help me.* Dillion thought to himself. His mother helped break the uncomfortable pause by gathering the children and taking them to their pew. As if on cue, Johanna showed up to walk the Bereses to their reserved seats inside the church.

All through the service, Dillion worked harder than normal at looking and sounding like a spiritual leader. But inside, he felt like a hormonal teenage boy. While everyone else was praying out of *The Book of Common Prayer*, he was praying silently that he wouldn't have a hard-on in church and thanked God for his loose-fitting vestments to hide anything that might be happening beneath them. He was both embarrassed and working harder than he ever imagined, looking like the perfect example of an Episcopal priest. He was most grateful for any of the moments when he was not the focus of the service. He so appreciated that today's sermon was shorter so that he only had to introduce Dr. Beres, who had prepared something similar to yesterday's presentation, but added to it with the benefits of spirituality to one's cancer journey.

When the church service was complete, Dillion breathed a sigh of relief and practically ran back to his office to release his green frock and was back in his short-sleeved black shirt, collar, and pants. As close to looking like a man as he could while he networked during what his kids lovingly called the *donuts for Jesus* coffee hour. He was a bit nervous about having to pick between sitting with his family and the Bereses but was lucky enough to find that they were all sitting together. Benji was thoroughly engaged in conversation with Aurelie as his dad and Dr. Beres were discussing something somewhat intense. Rose Clare had her eagle-eyes on Brianna making sure she didn't make too much of a mess or fall off her chair. And his Riley sat like a cherub, carefully nibbling on her pastry and sipping milk out of a paper cup. For a brief moment, Dillion let the thought enter his mind. A thought he never would have imagined being there in the first place. It was as if divine intervention whispered it into his ear for only him to hear: "My family."

Brianna looked up and saw him with his coffee and Kringle and gave him the direction he needed to get out of his zone. "Sit by me, Daddy! I saved you a seat." He smiled, nodded and out of the corner of his eye, saw that Aurelie was watching him.

"Thanks, Bri, it is so crowded in here today, I didn't know if I had to sit cross-legged on the floor by myself." That's when his favorite laugh in the whole world broke free. It was as if a chorus of cherubs were rolling around and giggling.

"Oh, Daddy. You're so silly! You can't sit on the floor. You're in your work clothes!" This time he was the one who laughed. After putting down his pastries and coffee, he kissed the top of her head.

"You're right, Bri. What would I do without you?"

"Don't worry, Daddy. I'll always be here to help you. I promise."

A warm feeling began to grow from his heart and quickly reached his eyes, that began to mist a bit. "Thank you, Bri."

"You're welcome, Daddy." And as if the conversation never happened, Brianna focused on eating the rest of her donut and drinking her milk.

As the coffee klatch began to die down, Dillion's parents congratulated him on a successful event and sermon, kissed each grandchild, said goodbye to their guests and left to begin their journey back home. He heard a rustle and felt someone tapping on his back. When he turned around it was his little boy who looked like he had something important to say.

"What is it, Benji?"

"Dad, can I show Aurelie where they keep the piano? She offered to teach me a few things before she leaves to go home. Can I, Dad? Please?" He looked at his son and furrowed his brow, feeling a bit jealous of this young boy with the messy crop of dark hair and black rimmed glasses. Then he looked up at the most beautiful woman he had ever seen and realized that she was just as eager to be with his son as he was to be with her. Maybe he had misunderstood the gestures from the night before. Perhaps he'd been alone a little too long. She was incredibly gorgeous this morning, reminding him of a 1950's model, definitely out of his league.

"Sure, as long as you understand that when Aurelie says it's time to go, it's time to go."

"Yes, sir. Thanks!" Benji practically skipped over to Aurelie, took her hand and guided her down the hallway. Dillion felt the pangs of disappointment. He hoped she would spend every last moment with him. Oh well. It felt good to be a man enjoying the company of a beautiful woman for even the little bit he had with her. Perhaps he should start thinking about dating again. Seriously.

"Looks like your son is a bit taken with my daughter, eh?" Dr. Beres chuckled at his own joke.

"Yes. It sure does, doesn't it?" Realizing he sounded like a lovesick teenager, he tried to recover. "I should have told him to get permission from her dad to date his daughter."

The dashing doctor made a jovial laugh and lightly slapped Dillion on his shoulder. "Touché, Father Clark. touché."

"Please, call me Dillion. We've worked hard on planning these last two days and we also shared a beer or two. I think we've spent enough time together that you can certainly call me Dillion."

The good doctor's wide smile turned into a grin while he looked Dillion squarely in the eyes. "Fair enough, Dillion. And you should start calling me Antoine." He paused and saw that Dillion agreed to do so with a nod before he completed his train of thought. "Especially since you plan on dating my daughter." Antoine looked stoically into Dillion's eyes and saw a gobsmacked younger man. Trying very hard not to laugh out loud again, he paused for the second time to see how the young priest would respond.

Dillion's heart raced and he could feel beads of perspiration gathering on his forehead. *How much does he know? What did Aurelie tell him about last night?*

"Easy Dillion. Didn't mean to spook you. It's just the two of you make it very obvious you're interested in one another." Still enjoying having the upper hand, he continued, "Aren't you going to ask me?"

At first, Dillion was dumbfounded and then he realized just what the doctor was asking for, the same show of respect that Dillion teased about his son just a few moments ago. "Of course. Forgive me, Antoine." Looking at him straight in the eye and with conviction he said, "Antoine, I enjoyed spending time with your daughter this weekend and I'd like to spend more time with her. I would like to know if I have your permission to formally date your daughter?"

This time, it was Antoine who was taking a pause. It was as if he didn't expect Dillion to go through with it. "Of course you have my permission, Dillion. But you know you don't need it. Aurelie is a grown woman with her own mind."

"Very, very true. And thanks for your blessing. At first it felt like we were joking around, but when I started to ask for it, I felt differently. Like it was important. I don't know if that makes any sense."

Antoine grinned and nodded. "I do understand, Dillion. You see, Aurelie has never brought a date home. She's never been with a man long enough for us to get to know any of the men she's dated. But I can see the way she looks at you. Behaves around you, that this is different. Don't take this the wrong way, what I am going to say next. I realize it is too soon to assume but, Dillion, you should know, she's never been in love before."

"She did say something like that last night. I didn't know if she was kidding or not, but she seemed serious about it."

Antoine looked down the hall where his daughter was doing what she loved, getting a student excited about music, and then said something that took Dillion by surprise. "I know that a parent shouldn't have favorites, but Aurelie has always had a special place in my heart. She's had to struggle harder than her siblings for everything she has. But the one thing that has evaded her all this time is falling in love with someone. If I'm honest, it is the one thing I am most fearful of for her. She's strong on the outside and fiercely loyal to her family and friends. But when she falls in love, I believe she will fall hard and fast, without thinking about any consequences. And if/when she has her heart broken, I honestly am worried that it may be the one time she isn't resilient enough to come back from it whole."

Dillion was a bit stupefied by Antoine's confession. But he could understand. He knew that kind of heartbreak. His parents hadn't thought he'd make it out of his grief alive. He hadn't thought so either. "If there is something that I can totally empathize with is living with a broken heart. I didn't know if I'd make it. But between God, my parents, and my kids, I found a way to make it past that first year without Corinne. But here I am, two years later, and I am asking to date your daughter. And if I'm honest, I will tell you that your daughter brings an energy with her that makes me feel more alive than I ever thought I would feel again. I guess that's why asking for your blessing had so much weight behind it. Because it feels like she could be important to me and to my kids, especially Benji."

Antoine turned to look at Dillion, grabbed his hand and shook it hard, as if to make a pact. "You're right, Dillion. She does have a unique light to her and for a moment I forgot your background. I have a feeling this 'dating' thing may be just what you both need." With that, the distinguished doctor looked at his watch and recognition hit that it was time for them to leave up north and get back to their reality. "Sorry, Dillion, but I have to interrupt the lesson. I promised my wife that we'd be home for dinner tonight."

"No worries. But is there enough time for me to officially ask Aurelie out on a second date?"

The smile came back in Antoine's eyes, "Of course." With that, Antoine walked down the hallway to his daughter, as Dillion turned around to see that Riley was helping Brianna with a coloring project back at their table.

Benji came out first, "Dad! I promised Aurelie that I would practice every day. Can I come to your work and practice, Dad? Can I?" Dillion was happy to see his son's flat emotions had been left behind and excitement had taken over.

"I think we can ask the choir director if it's okay with him. As long as it doesn't interfere with his practicing and your chores, young man."

"Thanks, Dad!" Benji turned around and grabbed Aurelie's hand to pull her closer. "Aurelie, Dad says it's okay!" Then he paused and Dillion could see the wheels turning in Benji's overactive brain. "Wait a second, how will you see how I'm doing with my practicing?"

Aurelie bent down, tussled Benji's mop of hair and looked him straight in the eye, "Well, that's something that your dad and I have to discuss right now. Do you mind giving us a moment or two?"

"Dad, can I go find the choir director and ask him if I can use his piano?"

"Sure can, buddy. Then check on your sisters. Riley may need a break from Bri while I finish up here." Benji let go of Aurelie's hand

and practically ran down the hallway to find the director. After watching to make sure that Benji didn't take out a wall or elderly parishioner, Dillion turned his focus on the glamorous woman in front of him. "So…"

She smiled at him and replied, "So," with a rather coy tone to her voice.

"So, while you were with Benji, I asked your dad for permission to date you." It sounded better in his head. As a matter of fact, he thought she would be impressed by the idea. Instead, it looked like she was getting upset. *Oh, no. I screwed it up already! I'm so bad at this dating stuff. God, help me.*

"Did I hear you right? You asked my *dad* for permission to date me?"

"Umm, it sounded like a good idea at the time. Do I need to apologize because I screwed up already?"

Aurelie cocked her head and looked deeply into his eyes as she contemplated her next move. "I'm not sure. I guess I need to understand the 'why' behind what you did before I decide if I'm mad or not."

"At first, we were joking around. We both saw how enamored Benji is with you so we joked that he should have asked your dad's permission to date you and then it turned to me asking for his permission. It started as teasing, but when I decided to ask, it felt important. Serious." He saw Aurelie's head cock in the opposite direction and her normally wide eyes were squinting. Dillion felt he needed to explain himself a bit more. "Look, Aurelie, I get that we just met a day ago. But I felt more alive in these past 24 hours than I have in the past two years. I don't want that to end. I see how you are with my kids, but especially Benji. I have to be extra careful bringing women home and into their lives because they've already lost their mom and I don't want to bring someone home with me who I don't feel could stay. So, yes, I did ask your dad's permission, not because I see you as a woman who needs a man to look after her. But because I see you as someone who has the strong possibility to be in my life and my kids' lives for a long time."

He wasn't sure, but he thought he saw the start of a tear growing in the corner of her eye. "You're lucky, Dillion, very lucky. I am wearing very pointy shoes and I could have kicked you hard in the shin for that. But what you said. How you said it. I can tell you meant it. It means a lot to me that you shared your rationale with me." She looked up at the space where they were having this conversation and she paused and whispered. "Instead of wanting to kick you, I feel compelled to kiss you. I think that the kind of kissing I want to do may be sacrilegious to do in a church, so, instead, I will grant you a stay and allow you to ask me out on a proper date."

Dillion didn't realize he had been holding his breath this whole time but recognized that he made an audible sigh as soon as Aurelie stopped talking. "Great. Aurelie, would you be willing to come back to Minocqua next weekend? I could take you to one of my favorite restaurants for a fish fry on Friday night. I can get a sitter. If that goes well, Saturday I'll have to spend time with the kids, and I am hopeful that you'd be okay with a family-friendly date? I can check to see if my sitter can also watch the kids on Saturday night. You should know, though I have to work on Sunday. It's Pentecost."

"The weekend sounds great, but what am I going to do with Mumford? I can't leave him two weekends in a row. I'm not sure if any hotel would take him." She looked concerned.

Dillion grabbed both of her hands in his and said, "Look, since I am asking you on a date weekend, how about you let me see if I can figure out the details. I've got 'people.'"

"Fair enough. I'll look forward to hearing from you." Aurelie squeezed his hands and turned to leave, but then turned back to him. "Just so you know, Dillion, you've made a significant impression on me, also. It feels different for me, too. Important. It'll be interesting to see where this all leads." She let go of his hands and walked away through the heavy red doors and into the glaring sunlight.

Chapter Twenty-One

After finishing his priestly duties, Dillion asked his family what they'd like to do for the rest of the day. He thought it might be a good idea to butter them up with things they wanted to do before hitting them with the information that they were spending all next weekend with Aurelie. They decided that they wanted to spend the day at the beach. Back at home, Dillion packed a picnic dinner of salami and provolone sandwiches, apples, chips, and some snickerdoodle cookies in a picnic basket. Also, he packed a small cooler of bottled water and juice boxes. The kids put together the beach bag of toys, towels, and blankets. They loaded up the minivan and headed into downtown Minocqua to enjoy the day. However, he completely forgot how crazy busy downtown was because of the festival and summer vacationers. Looking at a car full of sad faces, he remembered an open-ended invitation from one of his long-time parishioners, a widow, Ruth Luther, who lived alone in the middle of the Northwoods and had her own small lake. Her number was already in his phone. "Sorry to bother you, Ruth, but would you like company this afternoon?" After hearing "yes," he turned the car around to head toward the opposite end of town to travel the back roads to Ruth's place.

Driving down the pine and white birch-lined sandy road, Dillion felt that he was being transported to a simpler time. When there were no cell phones, when the day began at sun-up and ended when the stars came out to illuminate the path home. Once the trees cleared, he saw the covered porch that fronted the cottage and a woman in a straw gardening hat watering red and white begonias spilling over cedar window boxes. When he pulled into the makeshift sand driveway, the gardener turned, put down her red watering can and waved to the car's inhabitants.

"Father Clark, kids, welcome to Loon Lake!" The kids filed out of the car, a little shell shocked at the vastness of the property and the view of this private lake.

"Please, Ruth, call me Dillion. Thanks again for letting us stop by at such short notice."

"Don't think anything of it. I'm just glad to have some company and the lake will be happy that someone will enjoy playing in her."

"Your lake is a girl?" Brianna asked as she approached Ruth.

"Sort of. She was made by mother nature, and she gives life to the plants and animals that live around her and in her. So, Brianna, I think of Loon Lake as a woman." That seemed to satisfy the youngest Clark. "Now, I understand that you are going to the beach today, so there are a few things you need to know. First, the path to the beach is right behind the house and next to the outhouse. Second, when you're done using the outhouse, cover the toilet paper with the Saltine tin so the squirrels don't steal it for their nests. Third, there is only one main rule at Loon Lake."

Riley, the oldest and keen to know all the rules, inquired, "What is it?"

As seriously as she could muster, Ruth said, "Kids rule!"

A huge cheer came from the Clark siblings, and each took turns grabbing the items that they needed to take to the beach. "And when you're done swimming, come up here and your payment for swimming in my lake is to have dinner with me. If your dad can run the grill, I thought we could have bergies, potato salad that I made fresh this afternoon, and mock apple pie for dessert."

"Oh, Ruth, you don't have to go to all that trouble, I made sandwiches and have snickerdoodle cookies from the store."

"Nonsense. I have more food than I can possibly eat. Besides, I'll enjoy the company. Now go introduce yourself to the lake and enjoy the afternoon. I may join you after all my gardening chores."

Dillion led his brood into the woods and noticed how the path meandered, especially as they ascended where he could look down the steep cliff to the rocky shoreline. As they wound downward, the craggy shoreline gave way to fallen trees, long grasses and then the path opened up to a secret sandy beach with a few pocket chairs, a plastic lounge chair and a very large silver mailbox filled with a variety of lake-friendly castile soaps and sunscreen bottles.

The Clark family dropped all their wares and got to the business at hand of having a family fun day-at-the-beach. Dillion made sure he spent quality time with each child separately, whether it was making sandcastles with Bri, or having a game of catch with Benji, or a swimming contest with Riley to the raft and back. But he thought it was the most fun and relaxing as the kids decided to bury him, which is exactly what they were doing when Ruth came down to visit with them. "Well, it looks like you all are following my rule to a 'T.'"

Dillion took that moment to pretend he was a superhero breaking free from some villain's torturous device. "AAGH!" Everyone roared with laughter as he exaggerated breaking free.

He took a dive into the crystal-clear water to rinse off all the sand that crept into crevices he didn't even know he had. Then he told the kids to make sandcastles for Ruth to judge for the best in show. Their competitive sibling rivalry took over and each focused on building the best one.

"Thanks for this, Ruth. It looks like they are really enjoying this."

"And you? Are you enjoying being here also?"

"Of course. Why do you ask?"

"Well, you are so very serious most of the time. You're a great priest, but I get the feeling that you find it difficult to take a break and just enjoy life."

"So true. So true, Ruth. You're good. Very good. Maybe you should become a priest?"

"No thanks. I've raised my family and now I am just enjoying doing what I want to do, when I want to do it. But I do miss having people around all the time. I guess that's why I do so much volunteering and join so many clubs. What do you do for fun, Dillion?"

"Honestly, I haven't had much time to have fun, but I am working on that now."

"Well, that's good to hear. As someone who knows what it is like to have lost a spouse, it is very important that keeping busy isn't all that you do. You need to find ways to have fun as well."

Dillion realized that Ruth's lesson was also an opening for him to enlist her experience in helping him find help for next weekend. "I am hoping to remedy that next weekend, but having a young family makes dating a bit complex. And to add to that, the woman I want to date lives five hours away and has a dog, a Great Dane. I've invited Aurelie Beres, Dr. Beres' daughter, to come up again next weekend, but I need to find her a place to stay that will allow dogs. Big dogs. I also need to find a babysitter that could watch the kids for two nights in a row."

"Oh Dillion, I think that's wonderful! I've met Aurelie a few times in the past. Her best friend, Cat, is like family to me. I also got to talk to her a few times yesterday and she seems to have grown into a lovely woman. I'd be happy to help. Marshall and I always had dogs before he got sick. Maybe not as big as a Great Dane, but as long as it is friendly, I'd be happy to help. I have a smaller cabin on the other side of the house. She could stay there. It is a bit rustic, but as long as she is willing to forgo some modern-day amenities, she's welcome to use it. I also adore your kids. I can definitely help babysit."

Dillion got up out of the pocket chair he was sitting in and hugged her. "Thank you so much, Ruth! I can't wait to let her know. I so owe you for this."

"You owe me nothing, unless it's a complete disaster."

After a great day at the beach and a barbeque, Dillion hugged Ruth goodbye and left while the loons were calling on the glass-like lake. His kids were practically passed out on the way home and were more than glad to crawl into bed after quick showers. Bri didn't even ask for a story; she was already snoring as her head hit the pillow.

Dillion knew the first thing he wanted to do was to call Aurelie to give her the good news and to hear her voice. "Hello?"

"Hey, are you still on the road? It sounds like you're far away."

"Oh no, I'm outside taking Mumford for a walk. Miss me already?"

Smiling to himself he replied, "Yes. It's nice hearing your voice, but I also called because I have some good news."

"I like hearing your voice, too. What's the good news?"

"I've secured you a place to stay that takes dogs and the owner is willing to babysit."

"Holy shit! You work fast, Dillion. That's amazing!"

"Yeah, after we get off the phone, I'll text you the address and directions. It's on Loon Lake. She's one of my parishioners, and she says she knows you already. Her name is Ruth Luther."

"Auntie Ruth? Are you kidding me? Cat took me up there once or twice when we were kids. I think I saw her at Cat's wedding two years ago. Didn't I also talk to her at your event?"

"She said you two talked. She has a small cabin on the lake that is a bit 'rustic' but is all to yourself and it comes with complementary dog and babysitting."

"I can't wait to see you again, Dillion. I'm really looking forward to it. But I've got to go because Mumford is taking me for a walk now and I've got to get him under control. I'll let you know when we're leaving Mukwonago."

"No worries. Good luck with your walk and I am excited for next weekend, too!"

After hanging up, Dillion lay down on the couch looking up at the ceiling. He had all these crazy feelings but didn't know how to sort them out. He wanted someone to talk to. Someone that might help him understand what he was feeling.

"Hello?"

"Hey Rog, did I catch you at a bad time or can you talk?"

"I guess I can make time for you, little bro. Is it about Mom and Dad? Did they drive you crazy this weekend?"

"Nope. It went really well, actually. I had the kids stay with them at the hotel all weekend, so I didn't have any issues. It's something else. A woman."

"A woman, huh? Tell me more."

Dillion gave a Cliff's Notes version of how he met Aurelie and ended with their upcoming date. "Whoa. This sounds serious. Is it?"

"I don't know. I think so. I guess. Hell, I don't know. That's why I'm calling you, Roger. I feel like a horny 13-year-old when I'm around her. And yet I asked her dad for permission to date her. I arranged for her to spend an entire weekend up here so I can see her again."

"Hmm. Let's go back to you feeling like a horny 13-year-old. What do you mean?"

"Shit, Roger, this is so embarrassing. I keep having hard-ons around her and I woke up on Sunday morning touching myself. It's not normal, is it?"

Dillion could hear the roar of laughter on the other end of the phone and felt his ears burning and flushed cheeks. "Shut up. Just shut up. I'm going to hang up."

"Okay, okay. Sorry. Don't hang up. It's just I can't get this image of you in your priestly clothes walking around in church with a hard-on. It's funny. Damn funny. Did anyone see it?"

"No. Thank God for vestments. They cover everything from the neck down. But I'm pretty sure she felt it while we were kissing goodbye on Saturday night."

"This is great. So great. You've made my night, bro."

"I'm hanging up now."

"No! I'm sorry. You called me for advice, and instead I am teasing the shit out of you. My bad. Okay. The first thing is that you are now officially out of your grieving period. Congratulations!

You are ready to move on with your life, not just going through the motions."

"If I'm having these," Dillion paused to think of something that was more refined than *boner*, or *hard-on* to stop his brother from laughing, "reactions to Aurelie," he prided himself for his inner Thesaurus, "does that mean that I am cheating on Corinne? That I stopped loving her?"

"Seriously, Dillion, it doesn't mean that at all. All it means is that your physical body is not dead. It is done grieving. It wants to get back to living. Yes, you loved Corinne, and you will continue to love her. But you were only kids when you met. As long as she was alive, you never even saw another girl or woman in that way. But now she is gone and Aurelie is here. You are definitely physically attracted to her, and it sounds like she's into you as well. I think you should see where this goes. You deserve it, bro. You've been through hell and back. You deserve to enjoy life again."

Dillion paused as he took in what Roger was saying. But there was still something that he had to ask, without getting laughed at. "Thanks, Rog. But, and don't laugh, since I absolutely can't talk to Dad about this stuff, I need your help. I'm 32 years old and I can't control my body around her. I'm a priest. I can't walk around with my dick as hard as a steel rod all the time. How can I make this go away? It's too soon to have sex. Besides, she told me she's on a self-proclaimed sex hiatus because she was choosing all the wrong guys before. What can I do?"

"You're right. You can't go around with your dick pointing at anything with breasts. So, here's my suggestion. It worked for me in high school, and I bet it could work for you. Okay, here it is. As you get ready for your date, make sure you shower and while you do …I can't believe I'm giving this advice to a priest."

"What? Just say it. I'm almost willing to try anything at this point."

"Okay, okay. While you're in the shower, jack-off. Release the sexual pressure. The closer to the date you can do it, the better the chances that you won't embarrass yourself because your dick raised its ugly head."

"You can't be serious!"

"Do you have any better ideas? You called me for help, remember? If you want something else, then call Dad. Maybe there's a prayer or something that can help you."

"God no! I can't talk to Dad about this. I didn't think I could be more embarrassed, and you've proved me wrong."

"Listen, the date isn't until Friday night, right?"

"Right,"

"Okay then. You've got until Friday night to find an alternative. If you don't, then you can use this proven technique. It worked for me on countless occasions. It'll work for you unless it's a mortal sin for a priest to masturbate."

"I don't really think they go over this in theology class. I'm sorry, I shouldn't be so judgmental. You're right, I did ask you for advice. I will think about it. If I can't find an alternative, I'll give it a shot," at that point, he could hear Roger roaring in laughter on the other end. "Shut up, dickhead."

"Sorry. It was too funny not to laugh at that, bro. I've gotta go. I have a showing early tomorrow morning before the client goes to work. Let me know how it goes. I can't wait to hear about next weekend!"

Chapter Twenty-Two

The rest of the week felt like it was going in slow motion. Every time he looked at the clock, it seemed like it hadn't even moved. He made a checklist to keep on top of everything he needed to do for the Pentecost service, the date weekend, and his homelife. The closer it got to Friday, the more checks were on the list, but instead of feeling accomplished, he was becoming more nervous.

When he got the text that Aurelie and Mumford were on the road and should be there around 3:00 pm, Dillion was both excited and anxious. He didn't remember ever feeling this way with Corinne. Corinne was comfortable, like lemonade. Aurelie was like dropping a roll of Mentos into a two liter of Coke and watching it explode. In the past, he would have likely run away from anyone who made him feel like that. Instead, he was running toward it.

Checking to make sure that his children were all ready to go, he let them watch a kids' movie while he went into the bathroom to get ready. The one thing he did not check off his list was an alternative method to relax the sexual tension. So, he turned on the fan and the shower. Shook his head, dropped his drawers and got under the hot water spraying all over his body. He began by remembering what she wore the first time he saw her and how she looked in that summer floral dress. He enjoyed reminiscing but neither were doing the trick. Then his mind went to how she looked in her skintight cat suit. How she strutted around the stage like she was on a catwalk. Then the scene changed to the two of them kissing by his van. But this time, instead of her in an oversized sweatshirt and leggings, she was still wearing the catsuit and instead of standing by his minivan, they were standing in front of a king-sized bed with satin sheets. He imagined how it would feel to run his hands down her back and land on her buttocks, massaging that tight ass while pressing her closer to his hardness.

His hand found what it was searching for and went to work. As his fantasy climaxed to her lying naked under him on their bed, pulling him closer, he felt the release he'd been working for and let the water wash everything away. Helping him feel renewed and relaxed.

Dillion spent extra time in front of the mirror to make sure his hair and his shave guaranteed he'd be putting his best face forward. For tonight, he kept it business casual, a black short sleeved collared shirt, tan khakis, and brown boat shoes. When he went into the family room, he saw all three kids engrossed in *Moana*. "Alright, everyone, it's time to go to Mrs. Luther's home now. Remember what we discussed about behaving with her. And we are all going to meet Aurelie's dog, Mumford. I know he's big, but as long as you treat him with respect, everything should be just fine." He hoped and prayed.

They drove the backroads until they got to Loon Lake. The kids were just as excited to see Aurelie out on the porch with Ruth as was Dillion. Then he saw something lying down and covering almost the entire length of the porch. It looked like a spotted calf. Then when they pulled into the grassy parking area by the flower garden, its ears perked up, and a loud cry came out of its mouth as it got up and tried to crawl into Aurelie's lap. "It's not a dog, it's a baby cow, Daddy!" Riley said with a hint of horror in her tone.

"I thought so, too, Riley, but I don't think Aurelie would be able to raise a cow in her apartment. Let's all remember our manners. I'm sure everything will be just fine." Brianna went to hold his hand and Riley took the other. Benji looked frightened at first, but then was more curious than scared.

"Welcome back to Loon Lake!" Ruth said as she got up to assure the children. Dillion couldn't get his eyes off the giant dog attempting to sit on Aurelie's lap. "Thank you so much for this, Ruth. The kids are excited to be back here again so soon. They packed their pjs, and they know they can't go swimming tonight. So, they should stay away from the lake."

"No worries. We will have plenty to do. I thought they could help me make up a batch of hummingbird nectar and watch them come and eat from the porch feeders, then we could make homemade bubbles because I've just learned that Mumford loves to catch them. And after dinner we can watch a movie or catch lightning bugs or both." The girls lit up with excitement over all the fun things they could do, but Benji seemed drawn to the giant dog.

"Hi Benji. This is Mumford. Would you like to meet him?" Aurelie said as she was trying to get the giant dog to stay off her. Benji nodded. "Okay, stand right here." She pointed to a spot in front of them without crowding the dog. "Now, put out your hand slowly with the palm side up. Good. That's perfect. Now let him sniff you. Mumford, here's my new friend, Benji. He wants to meet you. It's okay."

The big, scared dog looked at his owner with trepidation. She encouraged him one more time, and he groaned a bit before he reluctantly sniffed the extended hand. Then he licked it. "Good, Mumford. Very good. I think he'll let you pet him now, Benji. Just let me get him off my lap first. Your car scared him, and I forgot to put on his snood."

"What's a snood?" Benji asked.

"Oh, Mumford is afraid of loud noises so it's kinda like a hat that protects his ears by hugging his head. Like a helmet." After the explanation, Aurelie maneuvered the mountain of a dog so that she could get up off the patio couch and position Mumford closer to Benji so he could get petted. Benji slowly reached out and Mumford's head bent down so the boy could pet the top of his head. Mumford started to move closer so that Benji could get to his ears, then scratch him under the chin and finally ended in a hug where Mumford laid his head on top of Benji's tousled hair. The introductions continued until the entire Clark family had been introduced.

When Aurelie felt comfortable leaving the dog with his adoring new friends, she went inside to bring out the dinosaur snood to put on Mumford. "This is for insurance, Ruth, I don't want any loud noise to scare him and you not being able to calm him down."

The littlest Clark chimed in to say, "It's okay, Mumford. We won't let anything scare you tonight. We'll protect you." With that, Mumford licked the top of her head.

Dillion was so taken in by this scene that he almost forgot why they were there in the first place. Then he saw Aurelie stand in front of him and smile. "I think they will be alright now. I think it's okay to go." Then she grabbed his hand and his focus shifted so quickly that he thought he might have whiplash.

"Oh. Right. Dinner." Then he looked down at her and just spent a moment taking her all in. She was wearing a white short-sleeved sweater with turquoise top underneath and white capris with white sandals. He smiled when he saw that she had her toes painted a pale pink, to match her heart-shaped lips. "Hey, you look great tonight. Really great."

"Finally. Thank you, Dillion. I was afraid I came all this way and all you could do was pay attention to my dog."

"I wouldn't dream of spending our precious time together only to play with your dog. Mumford and I will have plenty of time to get to know each other tomorrow. Let me get your door."

"Now you're talking." She smiled as they both thanked Ruth and Dillion hugged his kids. When they drove out of the driveway, Aurelie closed her eyes for a moment, sighed and put her hand on his leg. "Dillion, I can't tell you how much I've been looking forward to this weekend."

"Really?" Feeling his confidence rise a little. Luckily nothing else was rising at the moment.

"Really." She looked him up and down and continued, "You look very handsome, Dillion. I was nervous about what to wear. Nothing too dressy but I didn't want to show up in a concert T-shirt and ripped jeans, either.

"You look perfect to me, Aurelie. Definitely worth the wait." Dillion drove into Lake Tomahawk and parked behind the soft serve stand in the public parking lot. He took her hand and walked with her across the street and into the Shamrock, a local bar and grill that, in his opinion, had the best fish fry in the Northwoods. They arrived before the rush, so they luckily got a seat in the back dining room with a window looking out onto the snowshoe baseball diamond.

He ordered a Spotted Cow on tap, and she ordered a brandy old fashioned. Aurelie looked out the window and asked, "Why is the baseball diamond covered in sawdust?"

"That's because it's our snowshoe baseball diamond."

"Huh, Cat told me about that, but I don't remember ever going to a game before."

"Well, next time you come up, you'll have to arrange it so that you can stay through Monday night's game. The kids just love coming here. And since it's free, unless you want a piece of pie, it's great on this single dad's pocketbook."

Aurelie looked at him and smiled. "I'd like that a lot, Dillion."

"Already? But we just started our second date. You haven't made it through the whole weekend yet. Isn't it a bit risky?"

She leaned across the table and grabbed his hands to hold them in hers. "I like my odds." Their drinks were brought to the table, and they easily went to task talking about their past week's trials, tribulations and how nervous and excited they both were about this weekend, except for Dillion keeping one very embarrassing conversation to himself.

When the fish fry came, Aurelie dug in and moaned in gastro-pleasure. "You were right, Dillion, this is a really great fish fry. See? Second date isn't too bad."

During dinner, they took turns talking about their childhoods and favorite things. The conversation went so smoothly and quickly that Dillion was surprised when the check came. As they were walking out of the bar, Dillion asked, "So you get to choose what we do next. I've got a pontoon boat lined up for us to take a ride around the lake, or we could walk to get ice cream for dessert."

"I think we should go on the pontoon first. I'm pretty full right now." Dillion walked her back to the minivan and drove the short way to the public boat launch on Lake Nokomis. Another parishioner was there with his pontoon boat for the second half of their date. Dillion listened to the directions, and they waved to its owner as they motored out of the bay and onto the lake. He was a little disappointed that the captain's seat was a single and the next closest seat was on the other side of the boat. But then Aurelie walked over to him, moved one of his arms from the steering wheel and sat down on his lap.

"This is better." She snuggled in and made sure that he could both steer the boat and see where they were going. Dillion leisurely drove the boat around the shoreline until they reached the sandbar. He motioned to Aurelie to throw in the anchor, and he turned the boat off. They both flipped off their shoes and he rolled up his pants to take her onto the sandbar.

Dillion stood back in awe to watch Aurelie's uninhibited reaction to the cool waters and sand sluice over the tops of her feet. It was as if she had a calypso melody playing in her head as her feet and hips swayed while her arms stretched overhead. He cocked his head and grinned. If he was honest, he was a bit jealous of her unrestrained abandon. He leaned against the boat and continued to enjoy the silent dance recital that was unfolding in front of him. In a moment, when the sky was gloaming behind her, she opened her eyes and outstretched her arms to invite him to join her.

Shaking his head and looking down in an "awe shucks" response, he slowly walked over to her and said, "Don't laugh, I'm not much of a dancer. Especially when I can't hear the music."

"I promise not to laugh, and I think I can help with your music issue. I know a few things about that."

Dillion chuckled and replied, "I bet you do." Taking his hands out of his pockets, he reached out to touch the fingertips of the water nymph beckoning him forward. When they touched, even though at this point he half expected the electric shock, it still surprised him. As he reached her, she placed his hands on her hips and shifted hers up to his neck, pulling him in closer. He could smell the spicy fragrance that he knew was her signature scent, reminding him of a Bengal tigress in the jungle.

He must have been trying too hard with his movements when he heard her say, "Just close your eyes. Feel your way to the rhythm." When she finished, he could feel the vibrations on the nape of his neck where her lips finished with the "mmm" sound at the end of the word. Dillion visibly shook and felt a little unbalanced until he closed his eyes and focused on what she began humming and then started to sing Ed Sheeran's, "Shape of You," with her lips brushing against his neck and ear. It was both erotic and tender. Having her in his arms, moving in unison to the music in her head seemed to be the most natural thing in the world. He forgot that he'd been nervous about anyone seeing him dancing in the middle of the lake. Though the motions were subtle, there was a sexiness to their subtly. He moved his hands down to her buttocks pulling her tighter against him. He heard her voice catch suddenly and felt a little bolder, knowing how he got to her. Shifting his head, he slowly bent it down, lightly brushing his lips on top of her curls, moving down to her forehead, the bridge of her nose, and finally landing on those full, heart-shaped lips, where they stayed for what felt like an eternity.

Aurelie seemed to be entranced into stillness. He shifted his focus from her lips to her chin and then to her jaw line, lining light kisses down her long, almost regal neck until he reached its nape and nipped at it until he heard a soft "mmm" and then "oh my," from her. It was exhilarating to know that a woman of her experience and caliber, found herself so affected by him. He felt her shiver, in a good way, and he couldn't help but grin like a Cheshire cat. How was it that she could make him feel like Casanova when he was with her, when he was just the opposite?

When she pulled away, Dillion thought that maybe he went too far, but instead, Aurelie unlocked her arms around his neck and shifted to have her hands pull his face down toward hers, while she expertly maneuvered her mouth so that he could feel the wantonness of her movements. She began nipping at his lower lip while using her tongue in an expert manner to encourage him to open his mouth and join her in an intimate kissing dance that knew nothing of time, or place, just existence. Dillion felt the burdens of his life peel away as their kiss deepened. At present, he was no longer a widow, a single parent, a priest. He was a man who was tumbling into a love abyss. It was liberating, exhilarating, and erotic. If he took a moment to understand it, he would have been amazed at how this woman, in such a brief amount of time, was turning his life upside down, inside out, as if she was taking him to a multiverse where various versions of himself were possible. He didn't know how long they stood like this, with their hands roaming their intertwined bodies while their mouths were doing the same.

Aurelie paused and took a deep breath, laying her forehead onto his chest. "Oh boy, you are definitely a troublemaker, Dillion."

He was trying to get reality back into focus and comprehend what she was saying. "What? Why am I a troublemaker? Am I doing something wrong?"

"No, not even close. That's the problem."

"I– I don't understand."

"It's because whenever I touch you, kiss you, I just end up wanting to rip off your clothes and have wild monkey sex with you. Is that a sin? Am I going to hell?"

Still trying to understand what she was saying. *Wait a second, she wants to have sex with me? She thinks of having "wild monkey sex" with me??* Instead of responding to her questions seriously, Dillion began to laugh. Partly because of the "wild monkey sex" statement and partly because he was taken aback by someone as sultry and experienced as Aurelie confessing that he, Dillion Clark, made her want to give up her chastity pledge. While he was contemplative in his own little world, he missed the fact that she had pulled away and was beginning to sound miffed. "Hey, that's not very nice. Laughing at me."

"Oh God, no, Aurelie. I'm sorry, so sorry." He reached out for her hands and then took one of his to lift up her face so he could look into those liquid pools of emeralds while he said what must be said. "It's just that I've never felt like a guy who would have a woman say they wanted to have 'wild monkey sex' with me. My brother, Roger, yes. But me? Not even in my craziest dreams. Hell, I don't even have a clue what wild monkey sex would even look like." He gazed deeper to see if there was an indication as to what she was thinking. Did he screw up his opportunity to be happy with this woman? Then he saw it, there was something in her eyes that let him know that she was still willing to listen. "I'm sorry, Aurelie. It's just that I had a 'guy moment', a prideful moment and laughed because I couldn't believe that a woman as worldly and sexy as you would even notice me, much less be willing to have sex with me."

"Hmm. I guess you're kinda off the hook then." He hugged her and enjoyed another moment of feeling how perfectly her slight body fit into his. Then she pulled away once again and asked, "But I have to know, can you have sex without marriage? With someone of a different faith?"

"Well, I was going to tell you that I am so thankful that you've somehow managed to have me leave my roles and responsibilities back home and that I could just be a man tonight. But now you're putting me back into priest mode."

She took her pale pink fingernails and lightly scratched them down his chest with one eyebrow lifted, "I think I can fix that," Then she reached up and began kissing him with more fervor than before, making his toes curl in the sand. He wished he could blink and have their clothes vanish into thin air and a bed appear, but he, instead, found himself letting instincts take over and let the canoodling commence. Aurelie bit his bottom lip a little harder this time before asking, "What about now?"

Trying to gather the semblance of a coherent thought he commented, "What's a priest?" At that moment, he heard her go into a full belly-laugh and he joined in the jovial moment. His joke lightened the mood and Aurelie took that instant to break into a classic Dusty Springfield song, "Son of a Preacher Man," as they danced freely on the sandbar while the sun's golden rays frolicked with the water striders on the ripples of the shallow waters of Lake Nokomis.

When the gilded orb touched the edges of the pristine lake, Dillion led Aurelie back to the pontoon boat where she comfortably cozied into his lap as he drove them back to the public landing. While they waited for the boat's owner, Aurelie asked her questions again waiting for Dillion's response. "Well, I personally, have only had sex with Corinne and we did wait until we were married. But it's not a requirement. The way I teach it to my young parishioners is that sex without love is a sin, but when sex is the physical manifestation of love it is not a sin. Does that make sense?"

Aurelie searched Dillion's eyes and patted his chest, "Yes. Yes, that makes perfect sense, Dillion. Thank you. It's beautiful, actually." Just then, they could hear the gravel being stirred up by truck tires and saw headlights coming through the trees. Dillion thanked the boat's owner and gave over the keys before leading Aurelie back into the minivan.

"What would you like to do now?" He was hoping this wasn't the end of the date but understood if it was. It was a long drive to get up here and she was likely very tired.

"Can we go for that ice cream now?" She smiled as he squeezed her hand before he moved the minivan onto the gravel drive toward the main road into town.

Once there, he delighted in Aurelie's fascination with the combination of antiques, homemade jams and jellies, soda shoppe tables and chairs throughout the ice cream store. She ordered a double scoop of devil's food in a waffle cone, and he had his usual butter pecan in a dish. They talked easily about everyday life and what they might do for the rest of the weekend. Dillion appreciated how easy it was to talk with and just be with this woman who rocked his world. It was during this little moment when he knew he loved this woman. Not the same kind of childhood love he had with Corinne at the start of their courtship, but a more mature love. One that knows of pain, heartache, and that fairytales aren't real. But a love which knows with equal conviction of itself as a partnership to get through the chaos of life and recognizes the fragile, fleeting moments that make life worth living. Where love is a choice.

When the last of the ice cream was licked and the proprietor began her closing procedures, Dillion led Aurelie off the rustic porch to meander back to the minivan. He wondered if he would be brave enough to share his feelings with her so soon, or chicken out. Instead, he enjoyed the simple melody Aurelie was humming while petting his hand as it sat on the consul between the bucket seats. He wished he had the foresight to have a vehicle with a bench seat so that she could snuggle up to him while he drove her home. Oh well, minivans did have a huge advantage over cars in that all the back seats could fold down … To switch gears so she wouldn't know what was forming in his mind and elsewhere, he turned on the radio to hear the melodic musings of Chris Stapleton singing, "Tennessee Whiskey," which seemed the perfect song to end a perfect date.

When he turned onto the sandy lane that would take them back to the reality of three squirrely children and one skittish giant dog, he told himself he was slowing down to avoid the potholes, but Aurelie confirmed what they were both thinking, "Hmm, I wish this date didn't have to end. It was an amazing second date, Dillion. Thank you," squeezing his hand for emphasis.

When they pulled into the grassy spot in front of the flower garden, they could see one lone light on in the back bedroom. He looked at the digital readout on the dash and saw that it was after ten. His kids would be out cold and a real challenge to get back into their own beds. Though he had a quick moment of remorse, he realized that he would do it all again to have this time alone with the most amazing woman he'd ever met.

When they got out of the car, they saw the screen door open and a petite woman in a hand knitted throw over her shoulders walk onto the patio with a flashlight. "How did it go, Ruth? Do I have to knock any skulls together tomorrow?" Dillion asked.

"Oh, we all had a blast. No worries, Dillion. Mumford kept them entertained and he was a trooper. Benji read him some of the plant and bird books I have around, while Bri invited him to be the guest of honor at her tea party. Riley and I played cards and then after catching some lightening bugs, it was lights out. They are all snoring all over the family room.

"Thanks a bunch, Ruth, really. I better start getting them up and into the minivan."

"Dillion, they are out cold. Why don't you take the flashlight and walk Aurelie to the small cabin and then sleepover in the spare bedroom?" You can always get back home after breakfast tomorrow to wash up.

"Are you sure? I don't want to impose,"

"Stop it, Dillion. I'd let you know if you were imposing. It's just with the kids all grown and out of the house with their own busy lives, it was really nice to have a little bit of chaos back into this ol' house."

He looked at Aurelie who was beaming at the anticipation of a few more moments with him alone. He moved in to hug Ruth while Aurelie carefully opened the door to gather the biggest baby of them all, Mumford, and bring him to the small cabin with her.

On the short walk through the woods to the cabin, Dillion was feeling so much unbridled energy. He held Aurelie's free hand while keeping the flashlight on the rutted sandy road ahead. When they arrived at the quaint cottage, he went inside first to light the propane lanterns in the kitchen and gathering space.

In the distance, he heard, "Good boy, Mumford. It's time for bed big guy." Then the clippety-clop of large-patted feet and sandals on the weathered wooden porch before the creaking of the ancient screen door. Aurelie led Mumford into the small bedroom closest to the door as he hopped onto the top of the queen-sized mattress, and sprawled out as if he were a starfish before his snoring began. Dillion chuckled as Aurelie shut the pine doors to the bedroom and looked at him.

"He's not subtle, that's for sure. Sorry about the snoring. It looks like your kids tired him out."

"No, not at all. Glad they all got along. Maybe we can sleep in tomorrow morning, past 6:30 would be a miracle." With that he saw her smile and then move over to the opposite side of the bedroom door, past a hand-chiseled mantle and brick fireplace.

"Would you like to stay for a nightcap before you go back?"

"Yes," *What the hell,* Dillion thought. *In for a penny, in for a pound.* She brought out a bottle of whiskey and two glasses. Splashed a dram into each glass and handed him one while holding hers up for a toast.

"To the best second date ever." They clinked their glasses before taking a long drink. He could tell she was considering something to say so he didn't want to do anything to screw it up. Instead, she moved over to the small dining table where her phone lay and found an oldies streaming station playing "Unchained Melody" by the Righteous Brothers. Aurelie put down her glass and motioned for Dillion to give her his. Then she gestured for him to join her in a slow dance as the duo sang heartfelt lyrics about finding love at long last, with similarities to the ebb and flow of rivers and seas. It felt like a shock to his system how the lyrics were giving words to his own heart song for this woman he'd only known for a fraction of time in his 32 years. Just as he was about to speak of his heart, she stopped moving to and fro, set a soft, lingering kiss on his yearning lips and said, "I'm falling madly, deeply, in love with you, Dillion Clark."

Dillion couldn't believe what he heard at first, but then his heart jumped, and he knew what he had to do. "I love you, Aurelie Beres, and I can't wait to make love to you as my wife." With that, he lowered his head and showered her with thousands of feather-soft kisses on her face and hands, ending in a deep, soul-binding kiss full on her luscious mouth.

Chapter Twenty-Three

Aurelie was in that delicious place where dreams and real-life commingle. She was wearing a white satin, full-length gown and Dillion was in a smart black tux and they were dancing in one of those 1940s musicals with a big band behind them and palm fronds were lightly blowing in the ocean breeze. Dillion was cupping her face, bringing his mouth to hers. Aurelie was practically shivering in anticipation. When his lips were just barely above hers, she opened her mouth to a deluge from a surprise tropical storm.

"Ugh! Damn it, Mumford! I was having a great dream, you big lug. Get off me!" Aurelie pushed her unexpected bed partner off of her, after he woke her with a great big slobbery kiss.

"Mmrgh." The Great Dane managed to get out before being pushed off the bed.

"Alright, alright. You gotta go potty? You hungry? Both?" Mumford unceremoniously tumbled off the queen-sized bed and padded onto the hardwood floors toward the door to the cabin. Aurelie slipped on her flip flops and shuffled her rumpled self to the pine door. "You're lucky I love you. Here you go, stay by the cabin, Mumford. I'm not traipsing all over the woods in my jammies to bring you back." She looked out the small glass window in the door to see sunlight streaming through the pine needles of the tree nearest the wooden deck. "Sit. Stay. Let me get these doors open before you break them down to go to the bathroom." Aurelie heard an audible sigh as she stepped out onto the deck to hold the whitewashed screen door open for him. "Okay, Mumford. Go potty."

"Woof!" and then the giant dog, with his ears flapping in the breeze galloped off the deck and onto the grass, sniffing for the best tree to meet his urgent needs. Aurelie watched him for a few moments and when it looked like he'd found a squirrel or some other woodland creature to run after, Aurelie walked down the ramp and passed her vehicle to keep an eye on him. As she came around the corner, she could see what caught her bed partner's attention: three young kids and their very handsome dad. Forgetting that she was still in her cotton pj shorts and white tank top, she waved at the group and began to smile as she remembered how Dillion and she had ended the night with long, lingering kisses that made her toes curl and were the inspiration for her dreams. Just thinking about it gave her such a shiver that she tried to cover it up in a stretching yawn that had her tank top lift so Dillion and his kids could see her flat, bronze abs. With the remnants of her dream still fresh in her mind and her dream man now directly in front of her, she could feel the rest of her body waking up in anticipation of his touch. What she didn't realize, but he did, was that her perky breasts and her now hardened nipples were showing through her top. Not until Dillion did a fake cough and then dramatically crossed his arms over his chest did she realize her faux pas.

"Morning, I hope we didn't wake you." Dillion said with that luscious mouth of his, but looking at his eyes, she could see they were clouded with lust, darting back and forth between looking at her breasts and looking her in the eye.

"Morning. No. No, you didn't. Mumford woke me so he could go to the bathroom. Thanks for bringing him back so he can have his breakfast." The spotted Dane was acting like a little pup with his new-found friends until he heard "breakfast," which is when his focus shifted to sit in front of the screen door until he was given permission to eat his five cups of kibble.

After clearing his throat, Dillion responded, "Umm, we just came over to see if you wanted to have breakfast with us at Ruth's? She's cooking up something called eggy bake and should be ready in the next 20 minutes or so."

"Thanks. That sounds perfect. It'll give me time to get dressed since it looks like I'm the only one still in my pj's."

"Can we take Mumford back with us, Aurelie?" Bri asked as he finished the last of his meal.

"I don't see why not. Thanks, Bri. I appreciate it." Aurelie made Mumford sit as she had her mom moment with him to make sure he understood how he was to behave. It was like looking at the four musketeers as they romped and skipped down the tree-lined road toward the main house.

After a brief look down the path, Dillion pulled Aurelie up the ramp with him to the deck and captured her wrists over her head to give her a kiss that nearly destroyed the chastity promise right then and there. While his mouth ravished hers, he took one of his hands off her wrists, slid it down to the closest tight nub of a nipple, and began to run it between his finger and thumb. He took a brief reprieve from savaging her mouth in the most spine-tingling way. "Damn it, Aurelie, I planned on keeping myself under control today, but then seeing your nipples through your shirt and watching it ride up, I just couldn't wait. I had to have a taste of you. To feel you. I'm so sorry. I hope I didn't scare you." While still breathing heavily, Dillion let go of her wrists, pressed his forehead to hers and seemed to use every ounce of self-control to put a little distance between them.

Aurelie felt a bit blindsided if she was honest. First, she saw the family man with his kids coming up the drive, then it was the sensual man who gave her the feeling that he would starve if he couldn't taste her right at that moment, and now it seemed that the puritan man was talking to her. She felt as if she had whiplash. Add to all that she had a gazillion sensory nerves going off from her wrists down into her core telling her to wrap her legs around him and invite him into her sacred space.

She could tell he was waiting for her response, but her mind felt like it was muddled, trying to grasp all the emotions and sensory feelings that were messaging her brain like a firestorm. *Dammit.* She told herself. Just react. Release. Aurelie used her eyes to let him know just what she thought of his apology. Brought her hands to his hips, squeezed his ass, and pressed him to her while she tipped-toed to grab his lower lip into her mouth and suck it in. Those sultry movements had an intense effect on Dillion, rising in response to the sexual fission she was creating. Aurelie enjoyed leading him on this erogenous journey with her. Tugging, touching, grinding, canoodling. It was more exhilarating than her morning coffee had ever been.

"Ouch!" She heard him say under his breath as he pulled away and shifted his jean shorts. He put his forehead on hers as she placed the palms of her hands upon his chest, which was heaving with his heavy breathing. "How do you do this to me, Aurelie? I can control myself around every other human being in this world, but when it comes to you, I become this teenage boy who can't control his sexual impulses."

She laughed. "I'm sorry, I didn't mean to laugh. It's just that I was thinking the same thing. How is it that I am having sexual fantasies about a guy who's a dad AND a priest?"

This time, he laughed, and shifted himself one more time. "I guess I shouldn't wear jean shorts around you. I need a little more … flexibility." Aurelie roared at this revelation, which was dually funny and complimentary. "Why don't you go get dressed and I'll wait for you out here. Try to calm things down to a low simmer."

"Okay," she agreed. As she turned to go inside the cabin, Aurelie swore she heard him reciting The Lord's Prayer under his breath, which gave her another reason to smile.

She decided to put on her lime green and black halter bikini top and matching boy short bottoms and a black romper cover-up. After a quick pick up of the bedroom and brush of her teeth and hair, she was ready to go. Beach towel in one hand, Aurelie grabbed Dillion's hand in the other, it felt comfortable. Right. As if they'd been holding hands for years instead of days.

As Aurelie was reveling in the quiet comfort of this moment, it compelled Dillion to confide in her. "I gotta tell you, Aurelie, before last weekend, my life was going along at a snail's pace, and it made sense. Well, as much sense as it could for a widower with a young family, that is."

"But since that moment I met you, time seems to be going so quickly when we are together. And I have an energy that I never knew before. I feel things with such intensity now. I've never had this sensation with anyone." He stopped walking, turned toward her, and lifted her chin so that all she could do was look into those liquid pools of blue light as he said again, "Anyone," to emphasize his point.

Aurelie felt compelled to reach out and touch his stubbled cheek before she responded, "I get it, Dillion. It's the same with me. You're the man I never knew I always wanted." Again, on her tiptoes, Aurelie lightly kissed him on his full lips before continuing on their leisurely walk down the rustic lane.

After a lively breakfast that was filled with multiple voices all communicating together like a madrigal, they all helped with clean up duty. It was decided while Aurelie would take the paddle board out to do yoga, Mumford would help the Clarks dig up worms under patches of decomposing leaves on the trail through the forest to the swimming beach.

After that fateful morning when Aurelie had decided to turn her life around, she had reconnected with herself through yoga. When she was in high school and college, she used it to center herself to help with her concentration on schoolwork. This morning she felt the need to use it to help ground herself in the present and calm down the feelings and voices that were vying for her innermost attention. She needed to be still. Focus on balance. As she went through the poses she remembered, down dog, chair, crescent lunge, warrior, thread the needle, and full wheel, she could feel herself decompress. The nerves that were in a hyper flux state earlier, were now at peace and she found she was breathing deeper. When she finished her set, she happened to look up to see Dillion captivated by her while the kids and Mumford were focused on digging in the dirt.

By the time Aurelie paddled to the swimming beach, the Clarks and Mumford met her with their plastic margarine container filled with squirmy, juicy earthworms, a treat for any fish in Loon Lake.

Riley, wearing a simple yellow racerback swimsuit and her hair plaited down her back was the first to say something, "What were you doing out there?"

"I was doing yoga."

"What's that?" she inquired.

"Well, it is a form of exercise that helps with balance, focuses your mind, and stretches muscles."

Bri, in her pink and white polka dot swimsuit joined in the inquiry. "Aren't you afraid of falling in the water? Drowning?"

"It was scary in the beginning, but then after a while it just came naturally. You know, like riding a bike. It can be frightening at first and you fall a few times, but once you get the hang of it, you don't forget."

But it was Benji that wanted to get into the crux of it. "But why do it?"

"Well, for me, it helps remind me to be present, to be calm. To breathe. Not to become overwhelmed." Aurelie could tell he wanted to ask more questions, but now that they had a second grown-up, they wanted to go swimming and Mumford found himself completely fascinated with a pair of frogs that were keeping him busy between fallen logs on either side of the beach.

They spent the rest of the morning with mini swimming lessons, playing wiffle ball and building sandcastles. When the sun was directly above them, they packed up their swim gear and made the short trek through the woods back to the main house for salami and cheese sandwiches and ice-cold glasses of lemonade.

After lunch, Dillion wanted to tweak his Sunday sermon a bit, Riley wanted to lay in the hammock and read one of the Nancy Drew mystery books that she found stacked in the back bedroom. Bri wanted to have a tea party again with Mumford who was happy to play this game again as he tried to eat the pretend petit fours and cookies. Aurelie offered to take Benji fishing in one of the old row boats beached by the small cabin. Though she had enjoyed spending time with all of Dillion's children, Aurelie felt a special connection, an understanding of Benji's being.

With the fishing gear and Benji settled in the aluminum boat, Aurelie pushed off and let it glide onto the open water. She sat back, grabbing weathered wooden oars and began a stroking rhythm that moved them in the direction of the old beaver lodge. She saw some fallen trees on the shoreline which looked like they might make a nice fish bed. She was enjoying the quiet except for the splish splash of the oars entering and exiting the water. Benji and Aurelie had picked out two old baseball caps from the hat hooks out in the entry way of the main cabin, Benji was situating his brim to keep the sun's glare off of his glasses.

"Aurelie?"

"Hmm?"

"Why did you decide you needed yoga when you were in school?"

"Well, I didn't have a lot of friends growing up. I had one best friend, Cat, who's still my best friend today, but beyond that, I struggled. You already know that I wasn't that great in school either because of my dyslexia; I worried a lot. So, when I discovered music and yoga, I found two coping strategies that helped me focus on being present, release all that bad energy and I realized I really enjoyed it. Why do you ask? Do you want me to teach you yoga, too?"

Her young companion shrugged his shoulders and looked out to the shoreline. "I dunno."

Not wanting to probe, Aurelie just let the natural silence take over. When they got to the cove, she asked, "Now, do you know how to put a worm on your hook?"

"Not really. Dad tried, but he's not good at fishing. And I don't really have any friends to teach me," Benji replied shrugging again and pushing his glasses up.

"Well, I happen to be an expert fisherwoman, so you'll be taught by a pro." She caught a glimpse of a smile. "Now open the worm container, careful not to spill them. Take one, like this and if it is too long, rip it in half then thread it on the hook like this," and she showed him how to hook the worm in a looping motion.

"Why do you use worms?"

"Well, fish like to eat them."

"Why do I need to loop the worm onto the hook?"

"Because it is less likely to be eaten off the hook before the hook even gets into the fish's mouth."

Benji continued his rapid-fire questions on fishing, baiting the hook, and fishing spots. Aurelie was thinking she should have done more yoga or packed a cooler of ice-cold beer to bear the brunt of Benji's continual questions. But after a while, he seemed to be ready to get on with the actual fishing part of their time together.

The young boy, concentrating with the utmost precision, began hooking the worm as Aurelie showed him. Her teacher's intuition kicked into full gear as she could see signs of frustration and anger starting to form. She kept her breathing and her voice slow and controlled while she talked him down from a potential blow-up and toward success.

"Good. That looks good, Benji. Now, watch me cast. Then you can follow on the other side of the boat, so our lines don't cross." Aurelie spoke in the same, teacher-like manner she used in school and broke down the casting into small steps that Benji could follow. She could see the intensity of his focus while the young boy attempted to mimic her motions of a few moments before. When he got his line in the water and the red and white bobber was visibly floating on the ripples, Aurelie reached out to pat his shoulder in silent congratulations for a cast that met with her approval.

"Now what?" he inquired.

"Now we just wait."

"How long?"

"I don't know. As long as it takes." Benji seemed a bit bothered by her answer, but Aurelie could sense that she was teaching him something more than how to fish. She was giving him a lesson in self-control, and the power of peaceful silence.

After what seemed like an eternity to the young boy, he felt a tug and his bobber went under the water. "I got something! What do I do?" Aurelie looked over and saw the panic and excitement in her new fishing partner. She lay down her pole and moved to be closer to him to help reel in his first fish. It was a little sunfish, too small to keep, but big enough to entice a smile on Benji's face. Aurelie grabbed her cell phone out of its waterproof pouch and snapped a photo before she released it back into the lake.

With one successful cast under his belt, Benji baited his hook and cast his line with a little more confidence and a little less anxiety than he had at first. He seemed to be at peace with the silent focus that fishing offered to him. Aurelie, who could be a bit of a chatterbox at times, saw this opportunity to really bond with Benji by just being with him.

She was about to let him know that they should think about getting back when Benji spoke up. "Aurelie?"

"Hmm?"

"Do you believe in God?"

"I do."

After a pregnant pause, Benji asked, "Do you believe in heaven?"

"Yes." She could tell Benji was fishing for something else. Something to feed his soul.

"Do you think my mom is in heaven?"

"Well, Benji, I didn't know your mom, but after everything your dad has told me about her, I believe she is." She felt it was time to take a bit of a risk. Just like in fishing, she gave this lifeline a bit of a tug to see if she had hooked him. "Do you?"

"Yes," pause. "No." Another pause. "I don't know."

"Can you try to explain what you are thinking?"

"Well, Grandpa and Dad have always taught us about God, heaven, hell, and that good people go to heaven and bad people go to hell. So, I guess that means that Mom would go to heaven after she died. Right?"

"Right. But?"

"But we can't see heaven or hell. How can I believe in something I can't see? It's like Santa Claus."

"Excuse me? I'm not sure I am following you."

Benji sighed, put down his rod, and pushed up his glasses. "Well, I don't believe Santa Claus exists because I've never seen him or his workshop. But besides that, I don't believe because of all the economic constraints impacting his business model. What about labor costs? Overhead for the utilities? How much does it cost to maintain reindeer and the sleigh? Toy production? I just don't see any income streams to be able to cover these expenses. You know?"

Aurelie realized that she hadn't blinked or breathed since Benji began his tirade over the ineffectiveness of Santa's business plan.

"You make a very good point, Benji. I can see why you don't believe in Santa anymore. You make a solid argument. But what does this mean to you about God, heaven, and your mom?"

She could see the brilliant boy begin to quiver and shrink in stature as he started to talk about his mother's existence in the spiritual sense.

"Well, Grandpa and Dad are telling me to believe in something that I cannot see, quantify, test. The scientific theory just doesn't work to prove their hypothesis."

"True, but?"

As his voice began to crack and his eyes began to glisten with the collection of tears he said, "But I don't want to believe in or live in a world where my mom doesn't exist."

Aurelie got all choked up and tears began to run down her cheeks. She could tell this poor child was broken from the inside out. He doesn't feel he has anyone he can trust to talk to about the excruciating pain he has bottled up inside of him. She just wanted to reach out and hold him. Let him cry on her shoulders forever. She said a silent prayer to help her craft a response that would bring this child comfort and not push him further inside of himself.

"Well, you are right about Santa Claus. He doesn't exist in the scientific, economic sense, Benji. But I believe he does live in the spiritual sense. When adults talk about Santa, the spirit of Santa begins to live in them, and they want to do good things to make other people happy." She paused to see how he was reacting to this message. When she felt Benji was willing to accept her answer, she moved forward with the more complex answer to his very important question.

"Through music I learned that vibrations create energy, and that energy is generated through the frequency of these vibrations. This energy can either reinforce negative feelings or positive feelings for people who play and listen to music. I choose to believe that the creation of positive energy and vibrations exist beyond what I can see and feel. I have faith that a higher being, God, has created them to teach us the power of positive thought. And, since you believe in scientific theory, here's my take on how scientific theory can prove there is a heaven. Energy always exists. It just takes different forms. So, I have faith that good people, like your mom, is made up of positive energy. When their physical form has died, then the positive energy is added to a place we cannot see but exists beyond our world, and that place is heaven. Does that make sense?"

He looked up at her as the tears began to fall down his face and a small smile began to grow. "Yes. It does. It really does, Aurelie. Thank you!" He dropped his rod and shifted to be able to reach around her and hugged her with a force that felt as if he were releasing all of the pain, grief, anger, and sadness that a young boy could possibly hold inside his body. He cried like there was no end. He shook and hiccupped as Aurelie held him with everything she had. Rocked him and hummed a simple tune into his ears to help calm him down, one that her own mother had used on Aurelie from time to time, "Hmm, mmmm. Hmm, mmmm. Hmm, mmmm, hmm, hmm, mmmm."

When Benji finally was calm enough to dry his eyes, slow down his hiccups, and break the embrace, Aurelie looked at him and kissed each tear-stained cheek. "My mom always kissed my cheeks after one of my crying jags and told me that she loved me and that her kisses have special healing powers. I can't prove that scientifically, but it did make me feel better."

Benji gave a side grin and replied, "Thank you, Aurelie. I do feel better. Can we go back now? I think I'm done fishing today."

"Sure thing." They carefully put all the fishing gear away and Aurelie began the journey back to the small cabin's beach. The only sound they heard was the soft splashing of the oars piercing the water and that was all they needed to hear.

After a dinner of grilled fish and tater tots, Aurelie and the Clarks loaded up the minivan to go into town to watch a lumberjack show on the shores of Lake Minocqua. Aurelie felt at home with this young, broken, family and comfortable enough to lace her arm through Dillion's as they walked back to his minivan. "Daddy, we were very good today. Can we get an ice cream, please?" Brianna batted her long baby eye lashes and pouted her lips in a way that made Aurelie feel like she had to stifle a giggle.

"Well, I guess so. But we have to ask Aurelie if she wants any ice cream. She might be too tired and want to go to back to the cabin." He winked at her, and she elbowed him.

"I was hoping for s'mores by a bonfire, but I guess I could go for some ice cream instead."

The older kids started to bounce around and there was a mutiny against the youngest Clark. "S'mores! S'mores!" Bri gave in as they piled into the minivan to go back to Loon Lake.

As they rolled in, Mumford was heard barking in his loud voice as Ruth opened the screen door. "Ruth, is it okay if we build a bonfire down by the lake? Aurelie promised the kids s'mores." Dillion asked.

"That sounds fun. Can I join you? I think I can rustle up some s'more fixins. Aurelie, what do you want me to do with Mumford?"

"I'll take him with me to the small cabin to get my guitar. What's a bonfire without a sing-along?" She heard a resounding "YEAH!" from the Clark kids and took her leave of the clan to grab her contribution for the family fun-time.

Dillion built a wonderful pyre that created shadowed reflections off the liquid glass lake in the background. Ruth helped the children gather their s'more ingredients while Dillion checked the marshmallows for the right amount of toasting and Aurelie strummed camp songs for all to take part and enjoy. Aurelie took stock in the experience and how she was feeling. While it was a menagerie of marshmallow madness, she felt wonderful. Complete. Happy. And yes, she felt love.

When the sugar rush had died, Dillion and Ruth ushered Brianna, Benji and Riley back to the main house to get ready for bed. Aurelie strummed some instrumental music that was beginning to craft itself into a song that was complemented by Mumford's snoring. Dillion walked off the porch and towards her with a different look on his face than before. It drew her in. It was deeply intense. Not in a sexual, lustful, way. More like a life-changing way.

Standing over her, Dillion offered her his hand to bring her up to stand next to him. He placed his hands on either side of her face and drew her to him for a long, deep embrace before he released her. "Today was magic. You have a special quality, Aurelie, that has touched me and my kids to our core. I can't remember the last time they were so happy. I was this happy. I don't know if I'm going to scare you, but you are healing us with your presence. Aurelie Beres, I am utterly, inevitably in love with you." Before she could answer, he reached out to her again and intensified his kiss as if he were trying to seal her soul with his.

After pulling away for a second time, Aurelie searched his eyes, his face, took a deep breath and confirmed, "Dillion Clark, I have never offered these words to anyone other than my family. But I want you to know that I am whole-heartedly in love with you." This time, she offered him the lightest, sweetest kiss to seal her promise of the ever-elusive emotion, love.

They held each other and adoringly showed each other the depths of their feelings through tender touches, amorous kisses, and the calm connection of two people who have found their purpose in one another.

Chapter Twenty-Four

Sunday morning, Aurelie woke to her phone's alarm. She had to pack and get ready for church. Even though she wasn't a regular church goer, she wanted to spend as much time as possible with Dillion before she had to drive the four to five hours back to Mukwonago. She wanted to enjoy his presence before leaving. Long-distance sucked.

After taking care of doggie duties, she dressed in a floral maxi skirt and a matching pale lavender sleeveless top with a casual knot at the waist. She packed up the SUV and put Mumford's dino snood on him before kissing him on his cold, wet nose to leave him cradling his dino-buddy on his fleece blanket in the little wooden cabin.

She drove to the fieldstone church, near Carrot Lake, where the love of her life was going to preach the word of God to his flock. She shook her head and made a mental note to call Cat as soon as she got on the road for her long trek home.

She was quickly surrounded by the children when she walked through the red doors.

"Aurelie, come sit by me!" Riley asked.

"Aurelie, can you stay after church to teach me more piano?" Benji begged.

"Aurelie, where's Mumford?" Brianna inquired.

She smiled and gave each one a hug and a kiss on the top of their heads. Before she saw him, she felt him. The energy, the vibration in the room was at a higher frequency and she knew. Just knew he was there. When she looked up, she saw his blue eyes brighten and a generous smile grow on his face. Wait, did she see dimples? She was a sucker for dimples.

"Hey," she managed to squeak out as he reached for her hands.

"Hey," he replied. Such a small word. A word that was a copy-cat of what she had just said to him. Yet there was so much emotion behind that one-syllable word, it took her a moment to realize she wasn't breathing. "I hope you don't mind, but the kids asked if you could sit with them in the front row. It's okay if you're too uncomfortable being front and center. I can tell them no."

"No, no, it's okay. I like spending time with them. Maybe they will teach me a thing or two while I'm up there."

"Do you have to leave right away, or can we talk about getting together next weekend?"

"I can make a little time for Benji to hear him play piano, teach him something new and I will definitely make time to set something up for next weekend." He squeezed her hands and then left to begin greeting parishioners before leading the church in Eucharist.

Aurelie agreed to sit between Riley and Brianna and promised to tutor Benji after church. Riley was so helpful in keeping Aurelie apprised of when to sit, stand, and where the prayers were in the *Book of Common Prayer* and when to go to Eucharist. After service, the kids almost dragged her to the gathering space for *donuts for Jesus*. Then Benji took her to the choir's practice room for his piano lesson. After the short lesson, she saw that it was after one o'clock. Aurelie explained to Benji she needed to go back to the cabin for Mumford and get on the road to beat the traffic going home. Then she felt it. Him. It was his warm presence that she sensed entering the room that got her to end the lesson.

"Benji, can you let Aurelie and I have a couple minutes alone to talk about next weekend?"

"Sure, Dad. Thanks, Aurelie. I promise to practice every day this week."

"I know you will, Benji. Good work today."

He reached in for a big hug and said under his breath, "Thank you. Thanks for everything." She could feel the emotions rise in her throat as she hugged him back.

"Thank you, Benji. See you later."

He almost ran past his dad who was now dressed in his black priest casuals. Aurelie stood up, took Dillion's hand as he led her out to the quaint flower garden, near the parking lot. "I really, really, loved spending time with you this weekend, Aurelie."

"Same here."

"I asked the bishop for a weekend off for Fourth of July. Would you like to spend the holiday up here? I can check with Ruth again for help."

"Actually, I was hoping you and the kids might come my way this time. My parents throw a big Fourth of July BBQ at their house every year. The place will be crawling with kids, and I want my family to meet you."

"I'd like to meet your family, but where would we stay?"

"I've already started texting with my parents. They have room upstairs for adults sleeping over and plenty of tents for the kids to have a camp-out in the back yard. I think I can even finagle a date night for you and me to have some alone time."

"I think the kids will get a kick out of it, and I'll sleep anywhere if I can get to spend more time with you." Dillion drew her into a hug. "I can't believe I'm saying this, but I am missing you already."

She hugged him back, "I know. I am dreading letting you go."

He pulled back, tilted her chin and said, "I love you, Aurelie Beres," and gave her the most tender goodbye kiss she had ever received.

"I love you too, Dillion. I miss you already." She kissed him lightly on his full lips before she turned to walk back to her SUV so he wouldn't see the tears already forming in the corners of her eyes.

After picking up Mumford, she drove in silence until she hit Hwy 51, a straight shot for several hours. She used her Bluetooth to dial Cat who was glad for the distraction and tired of wrangling her twins to go down for a nap. "Damon! Aur's on the phone. Can you PLEASE take the kids for their naps?"

Aurelie smiled and was grateful to hear her best friend was losing her shit a little as she was practically perfect in every way. "Okay, I'm all yours. Spill."

"Nice to hear your voice, too, Cat. How are you doing?"

"Screw you, Aur! I know you don't know this, but having twins means I have very little time to be an adult and to have adult conversations. I think I am beginning to have a crush on one of the Wiggles."

"What's a Wiggle?"

"Don't ask. Give me the juicy details on the sexy priest you're seeing."

"Oh, I've missed you, Cat! Mumford just doesn't get into these conversations like you do."

"Yeah, yeah. Get to the good stuff before I have mom duties again."

"Well, he told me he loves me."

"Holy shit! What did you do?"

"I told him I love him."

"Oh God! Oh God! You told him you love him? You've never told any guy that before. How did it feel? How do you feel? When do you see him again?"

"Hold on, Cat. I'm driving here. I have to pay some attention to the road. What question do you want me to answer first?"

"Just spill. Wait, I'm getting a glass of wine and some chocolate. This sounds like it's going to be juicy."

Aurelie kept some of her time with Dillion private but did share enough that Cat was living vicariously through her best friend. "Wow. I'm getting all hot and bothered right now. If I wasn't on the phone with you, I might be ripping Damon's clothes off. Hey, that's not a bad idea. I just may do that after this phone call. I wonder where we have the liquid Tylenol for the little monsters to take before their naps?"

"Catrina Carneri MacGregor. Do not drug your kids so you can have sex with your husband. That's terrible."

"Don't knock it until you try it, sweetheart."

Aurelie laughed out loud and woke up Mumford who looked a bit annoyed at the disruption.

"So, it sounds pretty serious, Aur. How serious is it? Enough to take off your chastity belt? Wait, can he have sex before marriage? With a woman who isn't an Episcopalian?"

"Umm, you ask a lot of questions. Let me see if I can remember them. It is very serious on my end. It's like I can feel the energy shift when he's near me. I get all tingly and the hair on my arms stand at attention. And other places. Private places take notice too. I am finding it arousing and sexually frustrating at the same time. It's like high school all over again, except he is an amazing kisser, and I don't have to worry about his braces cutting up my lips."

Aurelie could hear Cat laughing on the other side. "That brings back some embarrassing memories. Let's get back to the good stuff. So, he's an amazing kisser, huh? Anything else he's good at? Are you still a self-proclaimed virgin?"

"You don't quit, do you? Not getting enough at home?"

"Well, if sitting on top of the washer during the spin cycle counts, then yes. I am getting some, at least once a week."

"Get out! You two were like rabbits. What happened?"

"Aren't you hearing me? TWINS! They have an innate sense of when we are starting to get it on, and then they knock on the door, 'Mommy, I gotta go potty!' 'Daddy, why are you on top of Mommy?' And when we do get time, it seems like all we want to do is go to sleep."

"Ugh. You are not helping me here. I've fallen for a guy who has three kids and is a priest. It sounds like I will never have a sex life again."

"Well, let's get back to the good stuff. So, besides getting you all hot and bothered, how serious are the two of you?"

"Serious enough that I've invited him and the kids to my parents' place for the Fourth of July weekend."

"Damn, woman! It's 'go big or go home' with you, isn't it? Do you have a ring picked out already? Where's the honeymoon? How do your parents feel about all of this?"

"Well, my dad has already met him, remember? He knew Dillion first. Dad was the one who introduced us. And Mom? Well, I think she peed her pants in excitement when I asked if they could come for the weekend. I think she may even offer Dillion a dowry just to get me married off. The last of her children, you know?"

Aurelie thought she heard a snort on the other end. "You are terrible, Aur. Just awful. Your mom has always wanted you to find someone to love and to love you as much as she and your dad love each other. A dowry. Get real."

"You're right. But I certainly didn't have to twist any arms or plead my case to get permission for Dillion and his kids to stay over for the weekend. They were both thrilled that I asked. Hey, that reminds me. When are you and Damon coming home for your summer vacation?"

"We're looking at the first two weeks in August so we can take the twins to the state fair with my family and stay at Damon's house on the family farm."

"Do you think you could find a couple of dates that might work for you and me to have a girls' day and then maybe have a double date so you guys can meet Dillion?"

"Absolutely. You can't get too serious with him without your best friend's approval. You should know that. I got yours early in our relationship."

"True, but we were both living in the same town back then. It was a little easier to plan to get together."

Aurelie heard a deep sigh on the other end. She knew she hit a nerve. "I know, Aur, I miss you too. I love our life out here in Montana, but I do wish I had my best friend just down the road."

"I'm sorry, I didn't mean to punch you in the gut when you weren't looking. But I do miss you. A lot. It's hard going through all of these new emotions without you. I think I can hold off a little bit longer, Kitty-Cat, before I walk down the aisle and become barefoot and pregnant."

Aurelie's attempt at lightening the mood did help, a little, but the sadness was still lingering. "No worries, Aur, I know you weren't trying to hurt my feelings. But I do get it that our relationship and you, specifically, sacrificed a lot for me to take my dream job in Montana. I wish there was something just as good in Wisconsin, but there wasn't. Isn't. I hope that someday you'll forgive me for hurting you so bad when I left."

Tears began to well up in Aurelie's eyes and her breath caught. She remembered that deep dark place she went to when Cat left to begin her new life 21 hours away from her. But Aurelie was not going to let that darkness define her. "I know it was the right decision for you. Even though it hurt like hell to go through. I realize now that I needed you to leave so that I could grow up and find my purpose. I don't know all the answers to that yet, but I do know that I'm in a better place and I found a better man than I've ever had before. I forgave you long ago, Cat. I promise. Don't beat yourself up about leaving me. Honestly, I'm doing much better."

"Okay."

"Okay. Now, I've got another three and a half hours to go, so let's talk about what we can plan for our girls night and double date!"

Chapter Twenty-Five

"Okay, we're almost there. Remember the rules about how we act at Dr. and Mrs. Beres' house this weekend?" Dillion asked, nervously.

"Yes, Daddy," Almost in unison, the Clark kids replied in the most lethargic way possible. Though they had taken potty stops and played at a wayside park for an hour, they were at the end of their patience and so was their father. Except that he had his nerves to give him a little more edge.

The GPS announced they had arrived just as Dillion saw the mailbox and a line of red, white, and blue pinwheels between mini flags lining the gravel road that led to the paved driveway. He saw a temporary parking lot situated on the grass and pulled the minivan into place. He could hear a cacophony of kids and one large dog playing in the yard. He closed his eyes, kept both hands on the steering wheel, and breathed deeply. This weekend was a big deal. Even though he'd already met Aurelie's dad, this was the first time he would be meeting the entire Beres' family, and if he didn't lose his nerve, he would also be having a very important conversation with Aurelie's dad before the weekend was over.

"Dad. Dad! Did you hear me?" He recognized the very matronly tone in which Riley was speaking. It didn't matter if he was ready, he had to get out of the minivan and start meeting the family. Aurelie's very accomplished, very wealthy family.

"Yes, Riley, I heard you. You all can get out of the car and don't forget to grab your things out of the back." It was going to be a hot one today, as his shirt was already sticking to his back, and he had to shake his legs out to loosen the wedgie that formed in his butt crack since the last potty stop. Benji had already opened the back hatch and Riley was helping Brianna gather her things when they all heard a familiar voice.

"Hey! You found it! Welcome to the Beres Backyard BBQ weekend, Clark family!" Aurelie welcomed her guests with her arms wide open and all three Clark kids dropped what they were carrying and ran in for a group hug. Not wanting to miss out, Mumford galloped down the driveway with his ears, jowls, and tongue flopping in his self-made breeze. When he reached Aurelie and the children, he greeted them all with big, sloppy kisses. Seeing an opportunity for his own welcome with Aurelie, Dillion stepped forward, grabbed her loose arm, and pulled her into him for a kiss and a hug. "Mmm. I've missed this," Aurelie whispered in Dillion's ear.

"I've been daydreaming about this moment for the entire trip. It was the only thing keeping me sane," Dillion whispered back before he kissed her on the nape of her neck, which caused her to let out a sultry sigh that made him wish he could drag her into the woods for a more intimate welcome. But there was the sound of footsteps coming down the driveway, so Dillion thought it best that he pulled away and be on his best behavior, just as he expected from his children.

"Dad, you remember Dillion and his family?" Antoine was dashing in his dark sunglasses, blue Hawaiian shirt, and jean shorts.

"Of course! Dillion, I'm so glad you were able to get the time off to join us. I think the Fourth of July is bigger in our family than Christmas. We can be a bit overwhelming at times, but it's all in good fun."

A more sophisticated version of Aurelie reached out her delicate hand. "Dillion, I can't tell you how excited we all are to have you here." Wearing bright red Bermuda shorts with a red and white striped boat neck shirt, Bea Beres bent down so that she could be eye-to-eye with Bri and her siblings. "Hello, I'm Bea, you must be Brianna." Bri shook her head, not knowing what the protocol was to greet Aurelie's mom. "You must be Benji. So nice to meet you. Aurelie tells us that you're learning to play the piano. Is that right?"

Benji didn't look at her, but he nodded and added, "Yes. I've been practicing every day in the choir room at church when Daddy is working."

"Well, Benji, I don't know if Aurelie told you, but we have a piano in the house. You are welcome to use it to practice this weekend. Okay?"

Now, Benji looked up and Dillion noticed he had a bit of a spark in his eyes that he didn't before. "Thank you!"

Standing almost upright, Bea introduced herself to Riley. "Riley, I hope you and your family make yourselves at home during your stay. We have lots of kids here to play with, toys, games, books, and if your dad says you can, we have a pond for swimming and fishing for you to enjoy."

Dr. Beres reached into the minivan, "Here, let's take some of these things for you and show you where you'll be sleeping. We've set up a tent for your family, Dillion, and you have a space up in the loft area with the adult children."

With everyone pitching in, Dillion was able to get everything out of the minivan in one swoop. He couldn't help but watch Aurelie from behind and be grateful that a woman that had such an amazing heart-shaped ass and long tan legs was with him. She was wearing the shit out of her ripped denim shorts and red sleeveless crop top that showed off her toned, bronze torso. *Keep cool, Clark. Making out in her parents' home will NOT go over at all.*

"Okay, Clark kids, follow me to the Beres campgrounds. We've got a tent all set up for you. When you've got your stuff put away, we can introduce you to the rest of the kids," Dr. Beres directed.

Dillion followed Aurelie and Mumford to the log cabin home and up the stairs to the loft. "Here's where all the Beres adult children get to stay. There's an air mattress that has your name on it." Aurelie pointed out. Dillion unrolled his sleeping bag and put his pillow on top before he dropped his duffle bag on the side.

"Where do you sleep?"

"Right over there, next to Mumford's bed." At the mention of his name, Mumford stepped over to his comforter bed, gently put his dinosaur in his mouth, circled a few times before laying down. Aurelie pointed out the air mattress directly across from Dillion's. "My parents are a little bit old fashioned. Notice how the couples get queen sized mattresses so they can share, and you and I get the twins opposite of one another." Dillion snickered a little before pulling her into a long, lingering kiss.

"Well, I think you should figure out a few places where we can enjoy some privacy."

"Mmm. I definitely can find the time and the place if you promise to kiss me like that again." She draped her arms around his neck, pulled him in so that he could feel the heat of her body through their clothes. This time, he added a bit more heat and she let him take the lead, relishing the steamy moment they created in her parents' home. It was intoxicating because he knew that he was the first man Aurelie had brought home, and she was on the verge of making out with Dillion in her parents' house. It gave him that *naughty* feeling he seemed to crave around her. But it also felt a bit different. If he had to name it, this new feeling, it was spicy risqué.

Dillion pulled away when his stomach growled, and he heard his children downstairs with Aurelie's parents. "Are you hungry? We've got some sandwich fixings in the kitchen. Help yourself. Dinner will be ready around 6 p.m.," Bea offered the Clark kids. The mention of food had his stomach growl a second time and it must have called all the kids on the compound because by the time he got downstairs, he was in line with seven of them. Then the rest of the Beres family came in behind him. It was a cacophony of conversations all happening at the same time until Aurelie whistled to get everyone's attention. "Since everyone is here, I'd like to introduce you to Dillion Clark and his kids, Riley, Benji, and Brianna. This is my sister, Zoe, her husband, Jack, and their daughters, Chrissy and the baby, Lily. This here is my brother, Felix, and his wife, Audrey, and their two boys, Oscar and Arthur." The adults shook hands and the kids waved before they perused the plethora of picnic foods on the granite counter tops.

Aurelie scanned the room, "Wait, where's Sofia and her family?"

"Oh, they will be here a little bit later. She said she wasn't feeling well this morning," Bea replied, with a twinkle in her eyes.

"Seriously, Mom, you've got that look in your eyes. What's up? Do you know something?"

"I can't say for sure. But I have an inkling."

"Mom, you've got that grandma look in your eyes again. Jeez." Dillion noticed the gaze between the two women and figured it was best to stay silent.

"Aurelie, you know we Beres women are quick to get pregnant and not feeling well in the morning, well, that's a telltale sign if I've ever heard one."

"But Mom, they already have Megan and Olivia and their dentistry practice. I think they have enough on their plate already."

"Maybe. But you know, Mon Cheri, these things aren't always planned."

"We'll see."

Dillion thought it best to focus on getting his kids their plates and finding a place outside for them to eat. He saw Dr. Beres signaling them to follow him onto the patio and sit by him on a picnic bench. Dillion eye-balled the space to make sure he left enough for Aurelie to sit next to him.

"So, Riley, how's your summer so far?" Antoine asked.

"It's okay, I guess. Dad works a lot, so we go to Bible school during the week and then sometimes we get to stay over at Mrs. Luther's house when Dad has a date. She's got her own beach, and we get to have bonfires and s'mores!"

Dillion choked on a slice of watermelon at Riley's answer, just as Aurelie snuggled next to him on the bench. "What did I miss?"

"Well, young Riley just informed me that they get to have bonfires and s'mores when Dillion goes out on dates." Dillion stopped breathing entirely and thought he could feel his heart skip a beat as well. When he looked over at Dr. Beres, he could see that dapper, classic man, that world renowned cancer doctor was working hard not to laugh at his own joke. *Touché.* Dillion thought to himself.

"Huh," Aurelie replied and then began to bite into her turkey sandwich, unfazed.

"So Benji, I hear you are enjoying the piano. Do you see yourself as a musician when you grow up?"

"No."

"Really? Why not?"

"I want to find the cure for cancer." Dillion's heart stopped, and he could feel tears forming. He no longer felt hungry. He felt empty. Just then, Aurelie put her hand on his and squeezed.

"I see. Well, it is a noble mission, Benji, and I should know. I've spent my whole career trying to find the cure for cancer as well. Maybe later, if you're interested, I can take you to my office where I have a few books you might be interested in reading."

Benji pushed his glasses up to the bridge of his nose and a sparkle came into his eyes. "Really?"

"Yes, really. As long as you promise to be careful with them. And, of course, you can ask me questions about what I do to fight cancer. Would you like that?"

Benji became animated, more than Dillion had seen in a long time. Beyond his excitement when he learned his music lesson piece both forwards and backwards. He looked between Dr. Beres and Dillion trying to figure out if he could really spend the entire holiday reading books.

"Dad, can I?" Dillion thought carefully on his answer. On the one hand he wanted to encourage his children to be what they were meant to be. Do what interests them. On the other hand, the Beres family had not only opened their home, but had a ton of activities planned and kids to play with outside. He really wanted Benji to work on making new friends. Learn how to play with others. Especially these kids, since he hoped that he could put into play something that he'd been mulling over almost since the day he met Aurelie.

"If Dr. Beres says you can, I don't see why not. But ... " He saw Benji begin to lose his animation and close off his body like he was waiting for a punch. "But we are also here to have fun. Play games. Get to know Aurelie's family. So, how about after you eat, let Dr. Beres show you where the books are that you can read. Then come outside and play for a while and then you can read a little bit before dinner. Okay?"

"Okay," Benji responded a little less depressed but not as animated as before.

"Well, Benji, I think you'll enjoy a game we Bereses invented when we were kids. Get ready to get messy and wet when you come back outside. We're going to play sprinkler kickball!" Aurelie described.

"What's that?" Brianna asked.

"Well, you can wear your clothes or change into your swimsuits because it is an actual game of kickball, but we turn on the sprinklers, so we get wet and muddy. Afterwards, we swim to get all the mud off," Aurelie replied.

While the Clark kids were trying to figure out if they were excited or scared, the Beres cousins were screaming "YES! Let's play!" after overhearing Aurelie's promise of one of their favorite games. All the parents were helping their kids clean up their lunch messes so they could go get on their swimsuits.

Dillion helped his girls get their swimsuits on and then he found an empty room to change into his blue swim trunks. He didn't know what they were in for but was hoping that it would tire his kids out so they'd go to bed early and he might get some alone time with Aurelie.

The game had already begun. It was boys against the girls, with Aurelie's mom as the designated pitcher for both sides. He noticed that the adults tried to control their kicks so that the kids on the other team wouldn't have to run into the bushes and trees marking the borders. When the littlest kids were up to the plate, everyone over acted to make them feel that they were helping win the game.

After the first inning, Dillion saw that Dr. Beres and Benji had on their swim trunks and were coming to join the game. He prayed that Benji wouldn't have one of his outbursts, that he would just have fun like everyone else. But now it was Dillion's turn to be up to the plate. The sprinkler hit Dillion's face just as he was set to kick the ball. He heard his team screaming for him to run to first base, but he was having trouble seeing it, until he was able to focus on the first baseman's red, white, and blue bikini top and boy shorts. He homed in on the stars that made up the top and tackled her to the ground as she caught the ball. "Safe!" He heard Bea yell.

"If I didn't know better, Father Clark, I would think you purposely tackled me to get a quick feel." Aurelie accused.

"If your family wasn't here and I wasn't trying to make a good impression, I'd say you were correct." He made her laugh, and she kissed his nose as he was trying to get his footing on the incredibly slippery ground.

The game went on until the boys won 10-9. He looked around for his kids and found that they had at least one cousin that they were hanging out with and laughing as they gathered over at the swimming pond. The small pond was barely big enough for everyone to get into, but it was the perfect depth for the youngest children to wade at the water's edge. Benji found him and asked if he could go see the books now. Dillion nodded yes and reminded Benji to dry off before going into the house. He looked for his girls and found that they were playing with the girl cousins and Aurelie on the other side of the pond. He smiled and felt a warmth spread in his chest. Though he wasn't sure when he would talk with Antoine, seeing how well Aurelie bonded with his girls and Benji, he knew he had to talk to him this weekend.

Aurelie was right about the BBQ. It was delicious. Though it was traditional fare, brats and hamburgers, potato salad, baked beans, etc., they just tasted better tonight. He couldn't tell if it was how the meal was prepared or if it was because Aurelie sat with him and his family. It didn't really matter, in the scheme of things. He appreciated the feeling that he wasn't going through the motions today. He was enjoying himself. He was having fun and so were his kids. Dillion thought that it may be possible for them to stop "surviving" and appreciate life again. Not the same as with Corinne, of course, it would be different. But a good different. Perhaps, instead of only surviving, they would become resilient.

After dinner, the dads took the young ones to the fishing pond to keep them occupied until it got dark enough for the fireworks. Dillion looked around for Antoine and Benji. He realized they must be back in the office. Jack offered to watch over Riley and Brianna while Dillion went to check on Benji. When he got inside, he heard the Beres women singing, and harmonizing, while cleaning up from dinner. Before he even got to the office, he heard Benji asking Antoine a barrage of questions and Dr. Beres calmly answering them with the patience of a saint. Dillion's shadow came through the doorway before he did, so they weren't surprised to see their visitor. "Okay, buddy, I think you've taken enough of Dr. Beres' time talking shop tonight. It's his holiday, too. Say 'thank you' and put the book in a safe place before you join the others at the fishing pond."

"Are you going with me, Dad? To the pond, I mean?"

"Actually, I have something I need to talk to Dr. Beres' about first. Jack said he'd help you out if you need it."

Benji nodded. Clutching the hardcovered book to his chest, he turned to Antoine and said, "Thanks, Dr. Beres. I promise to take really good care of your book."

"I trust you, Benji. You're a very smart and curious young man. I think you will be a fine oncologist one day." Benji gave a cock-eyed smile and walked out.

"I hope he wasn't too much trouble, Dr. Beres."

"Dillion, I thought I told you to call me Antoine? We've known each other long enough. And talking with Benji is a real treat. He has a gift, you know. He just soaks in everything that interests him. Almost like a human computer. He is far more advanced than I was at his age. It's going to be fascinating seeing what he will become when he gets older."

"I'm appreciative of the time you are taking with him. He's a great kid, but since Corinne died, he's been a bit of a challenge for me to figure out. She had a special touch to help him calm down when he would have one of his outbursts. She always knew how to manage his needs. I know I haven't been as successful, but it seems that he and Aurelie have a bond and that she gets him. It's a real comfort for me to know that he has someone who he trusts to help him when I fail."

"Don't think of yourself that way, Dillion. Having a kid with special needs is a challenge for any parent. All our older children were easy to parent. They behaved similarly to Bea and me. We understood them and parenting them wasn't perfect, but we found our rhythm and it worked. Then we were surprised with Aurelie and from the beginning, she had her own set of challenges for us. I can't tell you how many times I felt that I was failing her as her father. But then her friend, Cat, came into her life and she somehow helped us find our way to Aurelie. And now, look at her. She is a successful teacher and is the lead singer in a popular band. How she trained that giant of a dog, I'll never know. But he loves her and would do anything for her. She's the favorite aunt. As I told you before, Aurelie holds a special place in my heart."

Dillion felt that this was the chance. The break he'd been looking for. He took a deep breath and began. "She has a special place in my heart as well, Antoine. That's why I wanted to have a moment to talk to you. About her. About us."

Antoine motioned for Dillion to take a seat on one of the leather chairs in his office while he sat precariously on the corner of his oak desk. "I see. Go on."

"Well, I know we've only known each other a short time, but in that time, I found that I can't stop thinking about her. How she is with my children. How she makes me feel alive again. I thought that would never happen. She taught me that I could love again. A deep and powerful love. One that I don't want to lose, I want to have for as long as she'll have me. Antoine, I am asking for your blessing of my marriage proposal to your daughter. I want to marry Aurelie."

Antoine breathed deeply and ran his fingers through his salt and pepper hair before he answered. "I can't say that I'm surprised that you asked, Dillion, but I am surprised at how quickly you did. Why the rush?"

Dillion could feel the blood flush that was rising from his chest to the top of his ears. He practiced the first part, but now he'd speak with raw emotion. "Because I know what it's like to have your life planned out, how to follow 'the rules' for a good life. A spiritual life. And then the woman you thought would be with you for the rest of your life dies early. Too early. I know what it's like to be so broken that the only way you have the strength to get up in the morning is to care for those three precious children who didn't ask to be born. Didn't deserve to have their mother die so soon. Don't deserve to have a father who has been living a half-life, a broken life. They deserve to have light, love, and happiness again. Aurelie is healing me. Healing us.

"I love your daughter, Antoine. I no longer believe in waiting the proper amount of time before getting married. I don't want to waste a minute of time before making Aurelie my wife and a part of this family. The amount of time we have on earth isn't guaranteed, even if you follow all the rules. I don't want to make the same mistake I did with Corinne. I want to love Aurelie and have her be in my life as soon and as long as possible."

"Well, Dillion, I know that cancer can devastate a family. I've seen it too many times when loved ones may not come back from that kind of loss. I am pleased to hear that Aurelie is making a difference in your life and in the lives of your children. I can honestly say that I see you are also making a positive change in hers as well," Dillion's tension released a little as he relished in the fact that Antoine seemed to be giving his blessing, but not quite stating it directly.

"Thank you, Antoine."

"Just a second. Even though I am encouraged by Aurelie's transformation and that of you and your family, I am concerned about how quickly you want to move forward with this relationship. I've been with Bea for the majority of my life. She keeps me grounded and is my soulmate. Having said all of that, I know how challenging marriage is. It takes a lifetime to get it right. We took our time to get married. To make sure that we knew how to work together to solve the problems that would come our way. My concern is that by only knowing each other a few weeks, you haven't experienced what it will be like to problem solve as a couple. You'll have to figure things out after you've already made a legal and spiritual commitment to one another and to your children. I would hate it if at some future point in your relationship you two decide to dissolve the marriage. But I'd dread it even more because of what it would do to your children to lose not one, but two mothers during their lifetime."

"I don't ask for your blessing, lightly, Antoine. I know what I am asking is a huge risk for all of us. But I feel as if we have a second chance at being happy. Being whole. Your daughter has given me hope for a future full of love and joy. Hope for a life well spent.

"If you believe I am to choose between being patient or being spontaneous, I disagree. I believe the choice is between love and fear. And I choose love."

Antoine's head nodded as he slowly rose from the desk and invited Dillion to stand with him. He put one hand on Dillion's shoulder and the other shook his hand as he gave his answer. "Well then, Dillion, if it is love you choose, with all of its inherent risk and reward, then I will give you my blessing." Dillion accepted Antoine's hand and shook it confidently. When he thought that the conversation had concluded, he turned to leave, but was surprised to hear Antoine ask him to stay a bit longer.

"Dillion, did you ever hear the story about how I decided to become an oncologist?"

"No, sir, I haven't."

"When I was a young man, not much older than Benji, my favorite grandmother was diagnosed with cancer. In those days, there wasn't much to be done to save lives, and the treatments could be as painful or more so than the cancer itself. On her deathbed, she asked me to take her engagement ring and wedding band. She hoped I would give it to my future bride. However, Bea's family also had an engagement ring and wedding band that was inherited, and part of the promise I made to Bea's dad when I asked for his blessing was to agree to use their family's inherited rings for Bea. So, I guess what I am asking is if you'd be willing to accept my grandmother's rings for your proposal to Aurelie?"

Dillion looked in awe of the art deco designed rings glittering with diamonds and emeralds. He didn't see it as Aurelie's style, but he valued the family connection. Antoine must have figured out what the pause meant and continued, "Oh, and if you choose to accept the rings, you are welcome to redesign them, so they are more to Aurelie's taste."

"Thank you, Antoine. This is a huge honor, and I humbly accept them. If she agrees to be my wife, I promise I will choose love every single day of our lives together."

This time, Antoine became overwhelmed with emotion and hugged Dillion. "I pray that you do, Dillion. Good luck."

After hiding the ring box in his suitcase, he went outside to help his kids get ready for the main event, fireworks. Bri had some snarls that needed tending to, but Benji and Riley seemed to have everything managed.

There were blankets and chairs strewn over the lawn. Bea was handing out sparklers to the grandkids while the parents watched over them. Aurelie snuggled next to Dillion on a plaid blanket, licking a bomb pop. Dillion looked for his children once more before he focused on the beautiful woman sitting next to him. "Where's Mumford?" he asked.

"Oh, I have him lying on his bed with his dinosaur stuffed animal and his snood on."

"But won't he freak out if he's all alone in the house when the fireworks go off?"

"Already thought of that. He's had a small dose of anti-anxiety medicine I hid in a spoonful of peanut butter. He should be out cold and snoring." Aurelie replied as she quickly licked a stream of red liquid that was running onto her fingers. Dillion watched in utter amazement as she then sucked the tip of the popsicle into her mouth and continued the sucking motion as she pushed it deeper into her mouth and pulled it out again to lick the sides. He could feel his primal urges being activated by what her mouth was doing to the phallic symbol she was manipulating with her tongue. He realized that it just wasn't his mind that was engaged in her actions, his other head had its interest peaked as well.

"Oh no!" he quickly shifted and with inhuman strength, he reached to his side and picked her up to move her in front of him.

"Dillion! What are you doing? Put me down!"

"Stop squirming, you're making it worse. Just, please, sit still in front of me. Very, very still for a moment."

"What? Why? I don't appreciate …" and then he could sense she understood the gravity of the situation. "Oh. OH. Okay." But she was still for only a moment before the giggling started. Her whole body was shaking as she tried to stifle her laughter.

"It's not funny, Aurelie. I'm humiliated. Stop laughing."

"I'm. Trying." Then she giggle-snorted which got them both to laugh. The problem for Dillion was not over, it just took a different direction. Every time she giggled, her whole body jiggled up and down. Up and down.

Asking her to stop and be still wasn't working. He had to try a different tactic. He tilted his head downward and found the nape of her neck which he snuggled and then moved into setting light kisses on her bare skin. Her giggling stopped and he noticed she bent her head farther away, so he had more access to her pleasure center. "Mmm. That feels amazing," Aurelie responded in her husky voice.

He moved his mouth upwards toward her earlobe, while leisurely licking her highly sensitive skin. Once he got to his intended target, he sucked in her lobe in such a way that she hitched her breathing. "Oh my God!"

"Shhh, it's dark, but you still have to be quiet so that no one knows what we're doing here." Dillion was very pleased with her reaction, and he almost forgot why he began his sexually charged tease in the first place. "Just stay still a little bit longer, and I'll move to the other side. Promise?"

"Mmm. I promise not to move a muscle if you can continue doing this." Dillion couldn't help but smile to himself before he brought his teeth down onto her already stimulated skin and began to take tiny bites from her earlobe down to her shoulder. Then he switched tactics going back to the light kisses and gliding his tongue until he reached the other shoulder before he stopped.

"Keep going. Why'd you stop?"

"Because your popsicle is melting all over you and your clothes."

"Screw that. Don't stop." She threw the half-melted popsicle into the grass before leaning into Dillion for the second half of his incredibly intoxicating make-out session with her neck. This time, he blew on any new area that was still wet from his kisses. He felt cocky because of her reactions to his touch.

By the time he was ready to tease the other earlobe, he could hear his kids coming closer and looking for him. Dillion gave Aurelie a quick tug on her earlobe and whispered, "until next time," before pulling away. Just in time as Riley found them first.

"They're over here!" and plopped down by his side. "Why are you all way back here? Won't it be hard to see the fireworks from here, Aurelie?" Benji and Brianna followed suit as the girls found a spot on either side of Dillion and Benji scooted into the space in front of Aurelie.

"This is the perfect spot, Riley. I've been all over this yard and I am positive that we've staked out the best spot to see them. See? My dad is coming back from the farm field where they get set off, so you just look over that tree line and you've got the perfect view."

Dillion's lust-o-meter was about ready to overheat. But instead of focusing on what was not going to happen tonight, he settled into what he realized was the best part of his day. Every person that he loved more than life itself, was sitting next to him, leaning into him and Aurelie as if they were already a family. It would have fit the perfect romantic storyline if he could take her to a secluded space, underneath the fireworks, and proposed at that moment, but that was a little too cheesy even for him. This moment, this memory, was just as it should be.

Chapter Twenty-Six

The next morning, Dillion woke up to the sounds of sizzling breakfast meats and the chatter of children. It wasn't terrible sleeping on an air mattress with strangers around him, but it wasn't a sound sleep either. Mumford's snoring woke him up several times during the night. Dillion knew he was going to need a strong coffee, maybe two before he'd have the energy to make it through the day's planned activities.

Downstairs, he saw a few young stragglers, but mostly, tired adults sitting around the kitchen and great room trying to wake up. "You know I love Mumford, Aur, but can't you do anything about his snoring?" Zoe said.

"Look, if I didn't drug him, he would have been so scared he probably would have ruined everything. I think a little snoring is a small price to pay to get a chance to enjoy the fireworks."

"Well, I'm going into town to get some more worms for fishing and a set of ear plugs. I gotta get some sleep," Jack said. Pretty soon the entire table had their hands raised so that Jack could get them earplugs as well.

Bea asked, "Dillion, have you ever been to Mukwonago before?"

"Nope. Didn't even know it was a thing until I met your husband."

"You should have Aurelie show you and your family around. Aur, I think the electric railroad is running today. Maybe you could take them to the farmers market to pick up a few pies for tonight's dessert and hop on the train for a trip to East Troy and to that old fashioned ice cream shop?"

"Not a bad idea, Mom. Thanks. Do you all wanna go?" She looked around to see that Riley and Bri were playing Barbie's in the corner of the great room with Megan and Olivia. Benji had his nose buried in one of the medical books from Dr. Beres' library with Mumford's oversized head lying in his lap. The girls seemed intrigued, but Dillion and Aurelie noticed that Benji would take a little more effort to get him to want to leave his book. "Hey, Benji, they also have this really cool bookstore on the square in East Troy. It almost looks like it came out of a Harry Potter book." Dillion saw Benji break away from his reading and felt relief that it wouldn't come to a parent-child struggle.

"That sounds great, Aur. Thanks for the idea, Bea. Kids, put away those things and help Mrs. Beres clean up the breakfast dishes." The Clark clan did as they were told, and everyone hopped into Aurelie's full-sized SUV for their day of adventure. Dillion took in all the country sights from the varieties of greenery that make up the Kettle Moraine Forest. Clusters of cows and horses dotted the landscape in vast pastures. Red barns with multi-colored quilt patches painted on the sides and the soft rolling hills that gave the moraine its name.

When they got into the village, Aurelie pulled into a fenced-in park that sat kiddy-corner from the local grocery store. They got out near the playground and encouraged the kids to enjoy themselves. "This is a nice sized park," Dillion commented.

"Yeah, it is pretty busy during the year with activities. We have a summer flea market, a Father's Day parade and carnival, a Halloween event, and a bunch more stuff."

They took turns giving the kids underdogs on the swings and walked around the park while Aurelie pointed out the road to the high school where she taught band. Then they hopped back into the SUV to park it in the middle of the village. She pointed out the library, the "haunted" restaurant, and a quaint nostalgic candy shop, E and S Sweets.

"Dad, can we go to the candy shop? Please?" Brianna squealed.

"Sure, I wonder if they have some of the candy I used to get as a kid?"

Aurelie led them onto the covered porch and into the whitewashed cottage home that was turned into a boutique candy shop. Dillion looked around and smiled as he picked up shredded bubble gum and candy cigarettes. "These were essentials when we played baseball in the neighborhood." Aurelie smiled and then headed to the top shelf to pick up a bag of salty, sweet kettle corn.

"No summer vacation is complete without kettle corn," Aurelie declared.

"Can we pick out something, Dad?" Dillion knew that it would be impossible to leave the store without buying something. Even though he promised them ice cream later.

"I tell you what, you can pick out one thing for yourself and have Aurelie help you pick out candy for each of her nieces and nephews, too." Dillion was enjoying this day. Just watching Aurelie interact with his children and learning more about where she came from. It just solidified his commitment to proposing to her before the end of the summer. After they left E and S Sweets, they found a hot dog stand and Aurelie treated everyone to lunch. They sat at a nearby a picnic table under a shade tree and watched the whole village go past them in cars, on motorcycles, with boats, on bicycles, or walking their dogs.

"Come on, I want to take you to one more place before we hop on the train," Aurelie said as they cleaned up their lunch mess. The group turned off of Main Street and onto a residential side street that led to Phantom Glen Park. Aurelie guided them onto a fishing platform off the shores of Phantom Lake.

"So, the restaurant isn't the only place that's haunted in Mukwonago. This here is Phantom Lake. It's named after an old Native American legend stating that two neighboring tribe warriors fell in love with the same maiden. In a jealous rage, they fought over her while in this lake and the lake's phantom took her as a sacrifice. None of them were ever seen again."

"Ooh. That's scary. Why do you like Mukwonago so much if it's haunted? I wouldn't want to live here." Brianna seemed clearly affected by the tale.

"I don't think about it much, Bri. I've lived here all my life, and I've never seen a ghost or the phantom. But they are great stories to tell people who've never been here before. I just wanted to take you to one of the places I would hang out when I was a kid. I would ride my bike here with my best friend, Cat, and we would pack a lunch, fish off this pier, and read books until it was time to get back to her place for dinner."

"It must've been nice to have a best friend to hang out with," Benji said, almost forlorn.

"It was. She made life bearable."

"Do you miss her?" Riley asked.

"I do. But good news! She's coming back home for a visit next month. I can't wait! We like to go to the state fair together, the medieval faire, and if I'm lucky, maybe we can squeeze in a girls' sleepover. But she's got a husband and twins, so I'm not so sure that will work out. I hope we can get together so she can meet you all." Dillion took note. Not only did he need her dad's blessing, but he would have to get approval from the best friend as well. *Oh well, I guess I have a little bit of time to hold onto the rings. Better not reset them until the best friend approval is finalized.* Dillion thought to himself.

They hopped in the SUV one more time to go a little further down Main Street to a barn welcoming guests to the farmers market. Once parked, Aurelie showed them inside, through the maze of farm fresh jams, coffees, fruits, and vegetables, which led them to the deli and bakery counter. Aurelie knew exactly what she wanted and gave everyone a pie to take up to the counter. After depositing the pies in the SUV, they hopped into one of the electric train cars that would take them from Mukwonago to the neighboring village of East Troy. The conductor shared several interesting facts about the electronic railroad such as how the Village of East Troy brought the electric railroad to their community so that the electric company would be required to have electricity available to the businesses and the residents of East Troy. Dillion was almost put to sleep by the monotonous swaying of the train car, but the constant questions that Benji asked of Aurelie and the conductor kept him from closing his eyes. Still, Dillion found the experience quite soothing after walking all over Mukwonago for the past few hours. He appreciated the opportunity to sit down for a while.

When they reached the train station, Aurelie hopped off and pointed out the old-fashioned ice cream shop just a few steps away. The teenage waitstaff was dressed in turn of the century knickers with suspenders and matching caps. Dillion and his brood were enthralled at the menagerie of items that adorned the walls and dark stained wooden shelves, display cases, and tables. The menu had a large variety of specialty sundaes and Dillion honed in on one he hadn't had since he was a teenager.

"I'd like a hot tin roof sundae and a cherry cola."

When their order arrived, he realized his mistake. Each ice cream order was in a large sundae glass and the sodas and root beers were in large glasses as well. There would be a sugar overload and emotional explosions, he was convinced.

"Aurelie, I'm going to apologize before anything happens. This is way more sugar than they ever get at home." She laughed and patted his arm.

"No worries. I know what I got us into. If they can hold onto their sugar squirrelies for a bit, we can go swimming at my parents' house before dinner." She then leaned over and whispered into his ear, "And if you are good, I got my mom and dad to watch the kids after dinner so that you and I can have a date night. They are going to make an outdoor movie theater; the kids can watch the movie in their PJs from the tent and can fall asleep when they get tired."

"You think of everything, don't you?"

"I'm a high school band teacher. I know a few things about kids." Dillion laughed and decided to just enjoy the moment. He saw that Bri had a chocolate mustache and wiped it off her, but beyond that, he didn't let himself overthink anything. When all were sufficiently stuffed with ice cream and soda, they walked back to the train station and hopped the next one back to the farm store.

By the time they pulled into the Beres' driveway, Dillion was about to pull out his hair. All three kids were talking incessantly.

CANOODLING ALWAYS & FOREVER

Aurelie was a trooper and kept her calm the entire trip. When the doors opened, the Clark children ran with hands flailing toward their tent to change into their swimsuits. Aurelie joined them in a sporty number that made her look like she was on a professional sand volleyball team. Dillion wondered just how many swimsuits she owned and how he'd enjoy watching her strut around on the beach in every one of them.

After dinner, Dillion worked his efficiency magic to get all three children showered and into PJs before he hit the shower and put on a fresh pair of jean shorts and a white, short sleeve, collar shirt. He checked on the kids one more time and thanked Dr. and Mrs. Beres for watching them, before Aurelie came down in a lemon-yellow sundress and wedge sandals.

"Wow. I feel like I'm underdressed. You look amazing." Dillion said, not taking his eyes off her.

"Thanks. You look great. Listen, can you help me pack up two lawn chairs into my SUV? I've got to get a few items to bring with us. Dillion did as she asked and when she caught up with him, he noticed she was carrying a small picnic basket, and an insulated wine case. "Where are you taking me tonight?"

"You and I are going back to Mukwonago. There is one place I didn't take you, Phantom Junction, on the banks of the Mukwonago River. There is a big band concert playing there tonight and I thought you might enjoy it." Dillion couldn't help himself; he was so impressed with how she seemed to think of everything that he scooped her up and kissed her full on the mouth.

"Have I told you how beautiful you are tonight?"

"I think you just did. Thank you."

"Have I told you how much I love you today?"

"As a matter of fact, I don't believe you have." Her smile reached her sparkling green eyes.

"Aurelie Beres, you are the most beautiful, fun woman I know. And I am so in love with you."

This time, she kissed him full on the mouth and messed up his hair for good measure. "Dillion Clark, I adore your family, and I love you more than I've ever loved anyone."

They got into the SUV and held hands while she drove the short distance to Phantom Junction, where a crowd was already forming on the lawn. Dillion took the pocket lawn chairs while Aurelie grabbed the picnic basket and wine cooler. They were early enough to find a spot under a shade tree to help block the early evening sun rays and perhaps lend itself to a cool evening breeze. When the chairs were set up, they formed a little table between them that could hold a small charcuterie board which Aurelie lined with a variety of cheeses, artisan crackers, and a bunch of red grapes. Next, she poured both a glass of chilled Wildflower White wine from Pieper Porch Winery. Dillion took a sip and commented, "This is a really good wine. Perfect for a summer night. Where did you get it?"

"Oh, it's a local winery right here in town. On weekends they also do wine tastings. Maybe the next time you're in town we can stop by and make an afternoon of it."

"This weekend isn't even over and you're planning our next date?"

"Of course. Seeing how well everyone is getting along, I think we'll have lots of dates in our future." His heart was full, and it took everything to hold onto his secret and not blurt it out before the music began. Instead, he focused on holding her hand and bringing it to his mouth for a soft kiss.

As the band played all the standard favorites such as "Don't Sit Under the Apple Tree," by the Andrews Sisters, "Chattanooga Choo Choo," by Glenn Miller, and Dillion's personal favorite, "What a Wonderful World," by Louis Armstrong, he was taken away to a time when these songs played on a console record player his grandparents owned. He reminisced about their early Sunday dinners after church with the music playing in the background. The melodies took him back to a time that had been tucked away in his memory bank. Smothered by more recent memories that were so painful he had moved his own family out of state to be away from them.

But tonight, the memories weren't there to suck the life out of him. They were there as old friends. Reminding Dillion of the fun and joyful, simple moments in his life. The songs rekindled feelings of what it was like to be a child who focused on the present and who had just found his best friend in the little girl next door, Corinne. When "What a Wonderful World," began to play, he grabbed Aurelie's hand and led her to the grassy patch in front of them to hold her. To dance with her. To reconcile his feelings for the two women he loved enough to ask for their hands in marriage. And then a tear rolled down his cheek.

Chapter Twenty-Seven

"Are you sure that Grace and Gordon won't scare him? They can be a bit of a handful," Cat questioned her best friend.

"Honestly, Kitty Cat, I swear. He spent the entire Fourth of July weekend hanging out with all the crazy Beres and Clark kids. I don't know how he'll react to the horses, but they're fenced in so I don't think they will be a problem," Aurelie replied.

"Okay, you can bring him and what about that guy you're dating. What's his name? Dillion? Is he coming with you so we can meet him?"

"No, not today. Just me and Mumford. He's back in Minocqua helping cover another priest's vacation."

Aurelie heard a man's voice in the background, "Does he know that there is an initiation into this club? I had to sing on stage at a church festival for my initiation," Damon said.

"That's right! I have to come up with something just as devious," Cat commented.

"Not too devious, I hope. He is a priest, you know. He has connections. You don't want to piss him off," Aurelie chided. "Anyway, I'll be there in an hour. Do you want me to bring anything?"

"How about your guitar? The kids are all about music and dancing these days. If you've got 'Wheels on the Bus' in your repertoire, you'll be golden. They can't hear that song enough."

When she pulled into the driveway, Aurelie felt the flutterings in her belly. She hadn't seen her best friend and her family for what seemed like forever. Though they phoned, texted, and video chatted regularly, nothing replaced seeing each other in person. Taking a deep breath, she turned to Mumford and gave him a little talk. "Okay big guy, I need you to make a good first impression. Now I brought your dinosaur stuffy and snood to help you if you get too anxious. But it would be great if you could be on your best behavior today with the twins and any farm animals that we run into." Mumford cocked his head as if he were listening to her and gave her a slobbery kiss when she was done as if to say that he understood.

Aurelie grabbed the leash, doggy bag, and slung her guitar over her shoulder. When she reached the covered porch, the front door opened, and Cat came rushing down the stairs with her arms opened wide. Aurelie's eyes started to mist as she prepared for the bear hug that was coming her way. "You made it! God, it's so great to see you! I've missed you!" Cat exclaimed, barely breathing between sentences.

"it's incredible to see you too, Kitty Cat. I've missed you," Aurelie said as she hugged her right back. When they stepped back, Aurelie introduced her best friend to her best guy.

"Well, hello there, Mumford. Have you been taking good care of Aurelie for me?" Mumford tilted his head and then jumped up to put his paws on her shoulders to give Cat her own sloppy dog kiss. "Ugh!"

"Shit! Sorry! Mumford, bad dog! Sit!" Aurelie commanded.

"Oh, don't get mad at him. I just wasn't expecting it, is all. He's fine. He's just happy to meet me, aren't you, boy?" Cat bent over and scratched Mumford behind the ears, which as any good dog owner knows, is a sweet spot. Mumford rolled over and begged to have her scratch his belly.

"Cat, is it all right if I let the twins loose? I can barely hold them anymore." Aurelie looked up and saw Damon and the twins on the porch. Though he was the size of a lumberjack, Grace and Gordon were squirming so much that it looked like he was losing the battle to keep them contained. He had a look of utter concentration on his face as he meticulously took each step down the porch stairs to solid ground. Once reached, the twins wriggled out of his strong hold and bolted toward their guests as fast as toddlers can go.

Aurelie couldn't stop smiling and laughing while watching them with their wobbly gates. Listening to their jibber jabber tugged at her heart strings. Once they got to their final destination, Cat's arms, they screamed in unison. As curious as they were about their guests, they were even more wary. The twins hugged Cat's legs and hid behind her as they eyed the curious beast in front of them. Aurelie commanded Mumford to lay down and encouraged the red-headed siblings to meet him. As Mumford had done before, he had the sense to lay quietly, except for his heavy panting, and let the children come to him. Which they always did. Aurelie talked in low, quiet tones while petting his back. Cat held Grace and Gordon's hands and slowly brought their chubby fingers to the large black nose for Mumford to sniff. Once all were comfortable, the twins leaned in to give him a double hug, which brought a smile to the mammoth dog's face.

"Well, who do we have here?" Damon and Mia, Cat and Damon's black lab, came to join the group. Damon bent down and gave Aurelie a huge hug and kiss. "It's so good to see you, Aurelie. I've missed you too."

"Thanks, Damon. I've missed you. And of course, Mia, I can't forget you either," said Aurelie and she bent down to scratch Mia behind the ears and accept her dog kiss. "Mia, I'd like you to meet Mumford. Mumford, you need to play nice and gentle. Miss Mia isn't as big, and she's a lot older than you. Be careful." The dogs sniffed each other with tails wagging. At any point if Aurelie felt he was getting too rough, she still had him on his leash and would reel him in.

"You know, with as big as he is, Aur, he seems to sense others' abilities. I wonder if dogs can be empaths?" Cat inquired.

Damon responded, "Dogs are highly sensitive animals, just like horses. That's why they are so good as therapy animals and service dogs."

"Well, if they are just like horses, maybe you can perform acupuncture on him to see if it lessens his anxiety over loud noises?" Aurelie inquired, half-jokingly. "Then maybe I wouldn't have to haul his dinosaur stuffy and snood everywhere we go."

"That's an interesting idea, Aur. I'll have to get back to you on that. He is the size of a small horse."

"Let's get her stuff in the house and grab her a drink. I hope you don't mind, but I made a pitcher of lemonade vodka slushies for us. Damon's on kid duty today and I ain't driving anywhere. I plan on having myself a hell'uv'a good time with my best friend."

"Then let's get this party started!" They headed into the home that was handcrafted by Damon and his family many years ago. It still had that masculine feel to it, thought Aurelie, but she did notice a framed print here, a vase there, and tons of toys to keep the twins occupied.

"I hope you brought a swimsuit, Aur, because Dillion put up a water slide in the backyard for the twins to enjoy. It's going to be a hot one today so I think we may all have to have a turn."

"You didn't tell me to bring one. You'll have to lend me one of yours."

"Aww, bless your heart. You think you can fill out one of my swimsuits with your flat chest."

"Ouch. I'll have you know that as I've matured, so have my boobs. I'm no longer an A cup. I went up to a B. Bitch."

Damon heard the b-word and chimed in. "Hey Aur, watch your words. We have not one, but two parrots and they have a knack at picking up only the words we don't want them to use."

"Got it. If I can take a guess, I think you were the first one to learn that lesson. Am I right?"

"Cat chewed me out for a week. She had taken the twins with her to the grocery store and then they started screaming 'fudge' and 'fudge you.' They almost got her kicked out of the store."

"Yeah, and Damon almost got kicked out of the house."

"Almost?"

"I had a few nights on the couch."

Aurelie snort-giggled at Damon's confession. Then she took a sip of her drink and gave herself a brain freeze. "Shi … I mean sugar!"

"That's it," Cat said, "That's the ticket."

"Sweetie, you're dating yourself. No one says that anymore," Damon commented.

"Schmoopsie, it's girls' night-in tonight. You don't get to tease me, or it's the couch again for you."

Damon sighed, "I hate it when you call me that. You're right. I promised you a girls' night. So don't worry. I've got the kids, the dogs, and dinner."

"Come on, kids. Let's get our swimsuits on. Who wants to get messy?" Grace and Gordon squealed in delight and followed Damon up the stairs and into their bedroom to get changed.

"While he gets the kids ready, follow me to our room and let's see if I've got anything your big boobs can fit into." Aurelie laughed loudly and followed Cat to the master bedroom. Cat found her a simple, black one-piece swimsuit while she dressed in a navy one-piece.

Taking their drinks to the backyard deck, the women enjoyed catching up while watching the dogs try to drink from the water squirting over the edges of the plastic water slide as Damon was showing Grace and Gordon how to slide on their belly.

"So, tell me all about the Fourth of July. I know you said it went well, but I want details. Are you still a born-again virgin? Did you canoodle? I've got to live vicariously through you. Having twins sounded like a great idea at the time, but they really screw up your sex life."

"You crack me up, Cat. First you were upset because you couldn't have kids. Then you were upset because you got pregnant by the love of your life when it wasn't," she put the next word in air quotes, "'convenient.' You marry the guy, you get your dream job, and a two-fer with the kids and you still complain? What's wrong with you?"

Cat was laughing at Aurelie being overly dramatic, but she knew it rang true. "Okay, okay. I'm the bi … witch here. I honestly can't complain. I do have everything I want, it's just when I'm in the thick of it all, it can be a bit overwhelming and exhausting. I swear that my idea of a perfect vacation now would be to get a room, order room service so I can sleep and eat whenever I want. For however long I want."

Aurelie howled at her friend's confession. "That's just precious."

"Seriously, tell me about the hot priest and how you are making out in the back of church, or he's feeling you up at the Beres' dinner table. I do have needs that aren't being met. You can be my real-life romance novel."

"You are pathetic. But I'll cave. Most of the time we were with the whole fam or with his kids. There wasn't much alone time. But when we were getting ready for the fireworks, the kids were getting sparklers from my mom and there was some hot sexual tension release that had to do with a popsicle, his mouth, and my neck."

"Oh boy, this sounds good. Spill."

"I didn't mean to, but I had a popsicle that was dripping, and I was trying to get all the drips before they got on my hand and clothes. Dillion saw what I was doing and thought I was purposefully giving him a virtual blow job. That made him very, very excited, if you know what I mean."

"Ooh, this is great. Keep going,"

"When I realized what I was doing to him with just the popsicle, I may have embellished a tad. Then he put me in front of him, I suppose to hide his 'interest' in my popsicle licking. Except he turned the tables and began kissing, nibbling, and blowing on my neck. It was so erotic and intense that I didn't care about that popsicle any longer. I just wanted him to continue. I swear if his kids hadn't figured out where we were, I would have let him have a home run. He could have run all the bases."

"Whoa, that's hot. Speaking of, I feel very hot. I need to cool down. Wanna join me in a little slippery fun? Family fun, of course," Cat offered.

"Of course!"

The afternoon continued with the women acting like teenage girls and the rest of the group joining in when they could. When the twins went down for a nap, Damon started the grill and volunteered to get the rest of the dinner assembled. Cat led the dogs and Aurelie down to the paddock to check on her favorite horse, Butters. The gelding was a very proud, and strong-willed Palomino that had bonded with Cat that first time she came to the MacGregor horse farm. Aurelie was always amazed that Butters could be at the farthest corner of the paddock, yet when Cat was within the vicinity, he'd stop what he was doing to come and see her. He and Mia already had an understanding, but Aurelie wasn't sure how he would react to Mumford or vise-versa.

Aurelie kept Mumford's lead close to her as Cat supplied the introductions. When it came time for the two males to meet, Aurelie held her breath but found it wasn't necessary. Both seemed to be curious but kept a respectable distance. Neither made sudden movements to scare the other. "Interesting," Cat said.

"Why's that?" Aurelie questioned.

"It seems that Butters has accepted Mumford as part of our family unit."

"Maybe he's mellowed with age."

"Nope. One of Damon's brothers stopped shortly after we arrived, and Butters made it known that he wasn't welcome."

"Well then, thank you, Butters, for welcoming us into your family," Aurelie reached out and petted his soft nose while Butter's whinnied his pleasure."

The two friends meandered around the farm, stopping when something interesting was in their path. When they got to the creek, they took off their sandals and waded in the water while the dogs jumped right in and splashed around.

"You know, if it hadn't been for this creek and the crane with the broken wing, I would never have had this semi-perfect life," Cat contemplated.

"Well, I see it as serendipity. You and Damon were already in the universe's plan. This creek and the crane were the set up," Aurelie replied.

"Huh, good point, Aur." After Cat paused, she turned to her friend with a curious gaze. "Is that what you think about you and Dillion? Serendipity? Do you think you two are in some big cosmic plan?"

Aurelie looked a bit perplexed, then she pondered the questions Cat posed, while swinging her feet in the refreshing water. "I haven't thought about it like that. I'm more of a spontaneous, go with the flow kind of girl. But now that you brought it up, I think there is a cosmic connection. Like I had to make the changes in my life before I would meet Dillion. He's so opposite of me and yet, he feels like ..." now it was Aurelie's turn to pause, and she scrutinized her emotions. "Let me try to explain it with an analogy."

"Okay, go for it."

It's like he brings the lyrics to my melody. And together, we are creating a musical masterpiece."

Cat nodded and touched her best friend on the forearm. "That's beautiful, Aur. I can tell you really love this guy."

"Thanks, I do love him. I wasn't sure if it would ever happen for me. You know, like my parents. Like you and Damon. I didn't think I was worthy of love you know?"

"Oh, but Aur, you are. You always have been. If I wasn't into guys, I would have married you in a heartbeat."

"Ditto," Aurelie laced her hand with Cat's and gave it a squeeze.

"So, are you thinking of marrying him?"

"Wow, you're getting deep, Kitty Cat." She let go of her friend's hand to stand up in the creek and splash some water on her arms, legs, and run it through her hair. "I haven't shared this with anyone yet, but I do. I know we've only known each other for about a month, but these feelings I have for him are so intense. And his kids, too. I have this unconditional bond with Benji. He's different, you know? An underdog. A lost boy. He reminds me of you and me.

You with the super smarts and me trying to make just one friend so I wouldn't be so all alone. It's like I'm drawn to them. Riley had to grow up so young, too young, to help her dad take care of the house and the younger ones. I feel compelled to tell her she can take that heavy weight off her shoulders, give it to me, and go outside and play; be a kid again. Then there's little Brianna. She never knew her mom. She was only a few years old when her mom died. I can tell she wants me to fill that void. Anytime we play pretend, she's always casting me as the Mommy. She's pretending to build a family. How sad is that?" Aurelie's feelings were coming to the surface stronger than she expected. It felt like she was screaming at Cat to try and help her understand what she was feeling.

Cat got up from the shoreline and stepped into the creek to be toe-to-toe with her best friend. She reached out and pushed a glistening curl off Aurelie's forehead and then let her own hand touch Aurelie's shoulder. "That's an awful lot for anyone to take on, Aur. I can see this family means an awful lot to you. But I have to ask you a very tough question now. Just remember it's coming from a place of love."

"Hit me."

"Is what you are feeling actual love, or is it that you see a young, broken family who is in need, and you want to fix them?"

Aurelie's eyes began to shimmer with unshed tears. "I understand. You want to make sure I'm not trying to heal the whole family—as if I have the Florence Nightingale Syndrome."

"Yes," Cat almost whispered.

"I can't say that you're wrong for certain. But when I met Dillion and we had that accidental touch at the table, it felt like an electrical current was running through me. Every time he is in the vicinity of me, I can sense him. I can have my back to him, and I still know it when he enters a room. It's like an energy shift, the room has a charge in it, and I just want to get closer to the source. But it's multi-faceted, somehow. As if the excitement I feel being drawn to him has a counterpart. When I reach him, and after that first spark, there is a comfort to feeling him. Being near him. He calms me.

I'm content." Aurelie shook her head to try to make her thoughts clearer. "Am I making any sense?"

"Perfect sense. You are totally, emphatically, irrevocably, in love, my friend. Congratulations."

Aurelie released her tears as her best friend confirmed her own suspicions. They hugged, uninterrupted until the two dogs wanted to get in on the action, taking them off guard and off balance. They fell into the creek unceremoniously and laughed while Mia and Mumford thought they had stumbled upon a new game and were trying to give them numerous kisses while sitting on their owners' laps. The girls half-heartedly tried to get their four-footed friends off them while hysterically laughing. Then they heard Damon ringing the antique triangle to alert them that dinner was ready.

When the foursome arrived at the house, Damon disconnected the hose from the water slide and motioned that they all had to rinse off the creek-bed muck before stepping into the house. The twins were watching "Paw Patrol" and barely acknowledged the women entering the house. Aurelie followed Cat upstairs and took her clothes into the spare bathroom to take a quick shower while Cat was doing the same in the master bath.

"Man, Damon, if I had realized what a great cook you are earlier, Cat would have had stiff competition."

The ginger giant threw back his head and gave out a hearty laugh. Aurelie loved it when he smiled, because his crystal blue eyes sparkled, his dimples came out in full force, just like the deep timbre of his chortle. "Thanks, Aur, I might take you up on that the next time I get myself kicked to the curb by my lovely wife." Aurelie ate everything on her plate with fervor. The grilled beer brat with sauerkraut on a toasted pretzel bun reminded her of her first *not-a-date date* with Dillion. She ate two cobs of corn slathered on real butter and kosher salt. Damon served a warmed slice of Cat's *damn fine apple pie*, her signature dessert, with a scoop of vanilla ice cream melting on top.

Aurelie's eyes rolled into the back of her head when she took that first bite. "Jesus, Cat, I forgot how amazing your pie tastes. That's it guys, I'm moving in with you." That got a chuckle from the adults.

"I think we would become the talk of our conservative neighborhood. Not sure how they would feel about polygamy in their backyard," Damon shared.

"Well, what do you two think?" Aurelie asked Grace and Gordon, "Do you want Auntie Aur and Mumford to come to Montana and live with you?" The twins kicked their legs, waved their arms, and screeched in delight. They didn't seem to care that the food they had a moment ago in their hands was now on the floor and providing an evening snack for the two dogs. In between screeches and laughing herself, Aurelie finally had time to breathe. "Okay, okay, we'll work on your parents. How about we show them a snippet of what it would feel like to have us live with you? Why don't I get you two out of your highchairs and upstairs for a bath and jammie time?"

Aurelie followed through on her promise to care for her godchildren while her friends cleaned up the kitchen and had a little time alone in front of a bonfire, sipping on Irish whiskey. When she finally joined them, she had her acoustic guitar and both dogs following her. She plopped down on the empty Adirondack chair and began strumming a slow, simple melody. Mumford had his snood on and his dino stuffy in his mouth before he "harrumphed" and laid down next to her. Mia circled once and laid down next to Cat with a sigh. A slight grin reached Aurelie's face. She never felt like a third wheel with Cat and Damon. This day, this night, felt comfortable, familiar, as it should be.

They ended the night with songs sung around the campfire and the retelling of legendary stories from their past. By the time she loaded up her SUV, Aurelie felt a contentment and security in knowing that while her best friend had a life that was 21-hours away, they still had that unique connection that neither time nor geography could break them up. Both she and Mumford fell into deep slumber when their bodies finally hit their own mattresses.

"Are you sure you don't want to sleep at my place this weekend? I am confident that Mrs. Romansky will be fine with it. She's never minded before," Aurelie asked Dillion.

"I've thought about this a lot, Aur. Honestly, I don't think I could control myself if I slept at your apartment. I wouldn't ever let you out until it was time for me to leave to go back home."

Aurelie felt a tingling in all the right places and smiled a sultry grin before responding on the phone. "Alright. You've made a very, very good case. Cat and Dillion are picking up fish fry dinners from ZaZing and bringing them over. Would you mind picking up some Spotted Cow? They will be here in an hour."

"Can do. See you soon. Love you."

"Love you, too," Aurelie felt the tingles going away and replacing that physical response was a warmth that came over her like a wave. She cherished the way just saying those words to him and receiving them from him made her feel.

She took Mumford for a quick walk around Washington Avenue Park and a few of the residential streets that make up the Pearl and Grand Avenue historical district around the Mukwonago Community Library. Just as they arrived back to her flat, she saw the pick-up truck pull into the driveway and a minivan parked on the street.

"Dinner's here!" Damon belted out. She gave her friends each a warm hug before she saw the person she was most excited to see.

"Damon and Cat, I'd like you to meet Dillion Clark."

Dillion reached out his empty hand for an expected introductory handshake and instead, Damon grabbed him in for a bro-like bear hug. Then Cat reached in and hugged him with the kindness of a friend. When it was her turn, she could feel eyes on her, so she kept it simple. She kissed Dillion lightly on the lips and gave him a tender hug before whispering in his hear, "I've missed you."

He squeezed her back and replied, "I've missed you more," before deepening the squeeze.

"Okay, okay, we get it. You too like each other. A LOT. Get a room later. Now it's time to eat before dinner gets cold and the beer gets warm," Damon commanded.

When they got upstairs, Aurelie fed Mumford while the guys moved the kitchen table and chairs out onto the metal porch. Cat grabbed the dinner fixings from the kitchen and put the beer and ice into a metal party bucket that was on a stand in the corner of the deck. She eyed a bunch of wildflowers in a mason jar that Aurelie had on the dining table and brought it outside to adorn the kitchen table. Though it was a tight squeeze, they all fit around the vintage, wooden table topped with a yellow and white gingham tablecloth, that brought out the cornflower blue forget-me-nots, bright orange tiger lilies, and the powder pink and blue bachelor buttons adorning the table.

When everyone was seated, Damon was the first to talk. "So, Dillion, do you want to say grace or do we fend for ourselves?"

Dillion looked a little shell shocked at first and then grabbed his beer and lifted it, "How about a toast, instead?" Damon nodded his approval as he lifted his own beverage and the women followed suit.

"Here's to building relationships. Old and new. May ours continue to grow and flourish for many years to come." Aurelie smiled, thinking that Dillion just bested Damon in this unannounced test of Dillion's worthiness to join the family.

The foursome enjoyed the rest of the meal with stories regaled from the past, parenting foibles, and many other topics that found themselves into the conversation. Cat looked at her phone and then stood up. "Uh oh. We'd better get a move-on if we still want to get to Friday Night Live on time. It's already 6:30 p.m. They started already."

Damon reached his arms around his wife's waist and pulled her onto his lap. "That's my wife. You can take her out for date night, but you can't take the schedule out of her."

"Hey, I'll have you know, I was a stickler about being on time before I ever became a parent, mister." Cat lightly slapped him on his chest and then kissed him on his lips. "Let's get going. I haven't been to see live music that isn't part of a toddler play group in so long. I'm itching to go dancing."

The two couples piled into Damon's pick-up and drove the 10 miles down the road to the public parking lot on the Fox River. Once they got out, they took one of the wrought iron bridges across the river to the first stage in front of the Salty Toad. A three-man band, The Stephen Hull Experience, had the crowd on their feet. The lead singer and guitarist would belt out a song lyric and respond with the sultry, soulful, sad cry from his electric guitar. The rhythm of the bass guitar had Aurelie's foot tapping until the drummer played a sophisticated, complex solo that stopped her foot from tapping and mesmerized her mind. They listened for a few more songs, Dillion found his space behind her with his hands around her waist. During the leisurely guitar licks, she would meld into him, closing her eyes to see the music in her mind as vibrant colors, moving in an intricate dance. When they picked up the pace, her body responded by tapping her toes, swaying, snapping her fingers, just wanting to be a physical part of the music.

Stephen explained that the next set was to celebrate one of his heroes, Percy Mayfield, as Percy had both been born and died in the month of August. Stephen asked if anyone in the audience remembered any of Percy's songs. Aurelie's hand rose up like a student who knows the answer to the teacher's question. "Please Send Me Someone to Love," and then she started to sing the chorus. Stephen motioned for her to join him on stage. The emotional excitement she experienced being back on stage was there, and Aurelie felt right in that moment. She harmonized effortlessly with the lead singer and matched his soulful expression with her mournful crooning. She fit the part, too, in her retro 1950's daisy lace-up halter with shamrock green, high-waist shorts adorned with mother of pearl buttons angling off of the side pockets. Aurelie fell effortlessly into the rhythm of the music and the band, and the crowd continued to encourage the spontaneous collaboration. When the set was done, Stephen encouraged everyone to give a round of applause to Aurelie and then shared that the band was taking a short break.

When she got back to Dillion, he hugged her with new enthusiasm and kissed her hard. "That was amazing! You were incredible! I am so impressed that you can do that." She hugged him back but was too verklempt with excitement to respond with words, so she increased the intensity of the hug.

Cat tapped Aurelie's bare shoulder. "Come on, superstar, let's see who else is here."

In front of Martha Merrell's Books & Toys, they found a swing band. Cat was already bouncing to the beat when she reached out her hand to Dillion. "Come on, this is your initiation into the club. Let's see how well you can dance." Dillion looked at Aurelie and she shrugged her shoulders, leaving him at the mercy of her bestie.

Aurelie already knew Cat could do the lindy hop and was enjoying watching her loose auburn curls bouncing to the beat while her yellow and purple mum patterned key-hole swing dress swayed to the music. Aurelie had no clue if Dillion could dance at all much less keep up with Cat, but she became awe-struck at how he was leading Cat in a series of intricate moves, twirling her in an out of his arms. "Damn, that boy can dance. Look at them out there!" Damon commented. "Did you know?"

"Nope. Not at all. I'm just as impressed as you are." She switched her focus to the man who held her heart and was currently holding her best friend. She clapped in beat while watching his boat shoes bouncing and stepping as if he was drifting on a cloud. Then let out a laugh as his blue polo shirt untucked itself from his jean shorts. When the song was done, Aurelie screamed and clapped for the couple while Damon let out a whistle that almost blew out her ear drums.

When the dancing couple returned to their respective partners, Aurelie laid a big kiss on Dillion while Damon swept his wife off her feet and then dipped her for a dramatic kiss. "Well," Damon began, "I guess this means you're in. Congratulations, Dillion, you've passed initiation. Welcome to the family." Damon pulled Dillion in for a bro-hug and slapped him on the back. "But you've got to tell me, how the hell did you learn to dance like that? You're a priest, right? I didn't know priests could dance?"

Dillion caught his breath, "Well, it's simple, really. When you live in a small town and your parents run the church and all its events," he took another big breath and accepted a bottle of water Aurelie offered him from the street vendor. "It's like a requirement to learn how to dance with all of the church ladies. I can't do the running man, or the Dougie, but play a waltz or the lindy and I can hold my own."

"Man, that was fun!" exclaimed Cat. "I haven't danced like that since; I can't even remember. Dillion, you're awesome." Cat reached for her dancing partner and gave him a heartfelt hug and kissed his cheek.

The foursome continued to mosey between the music stages, stopping to listen or dance to the ones that caught their interest. By 9 p.m., the bands were winding down, the group found themselves near the gelato shop and stood in the long line to grab a tasty treat to end the night. They found an empty wrought iron bench on the river and sat down to quietly enjoy their gelato and the slight breeze that had stirred up since the sun went behind the buildings.

"So, what made you want to become a priest?" Cat inquired.

"Well, God has always been a foundation in my family, and I always knew I wanted to be one, just like my dad."

"Can priests marry outside of their faith? Or does their partner have to convert?" Damon asked.

"Jesus! You are embarrassing me! You just met him and thought it would be appropriate to ask him about interfaith marriage? Seriously??" Aurelie felt her ears get red to match the color of her lipstick. She felt Dillion put his hand on her knee and give it a squeeze.

"It's okay, Aur. Honestly. I don't mind. They are your friends, and they love you. They are just making sure that I'm good enough for you," and then he kissed her cheek. "It's alright. I'm in this for the long haul."

Once all Cat and Damon's questions were asked and answered and the gelato eaten, the foursome walked back to the truck and drove silently to Aurelie's flat. Damon and Cat stayed in the truck to say their goodbyes and Dillion followed Aurelie up the stairs.

She grabbed two beers out of the melting ice bucket and motioned for them to move inside to the couch. She could hear Mumford snoring soundly in his room. She kicked off her wedge sandals and sat with her legs tucked under her hips. Dillion followed her to the couch, put his free arm around her bringing her to lay onto him while he took a deep drink from his bottle.

"Well, what do you think? Of my friends?" Aurelie braced for his answer.

"Honestly, I am wondering why I was so nervous in the first place. They're great. I can see why they are so important to you. They love you to death. Very protective, yet they also want to make sure you're happy. That I can make you happy." He paused. "Aur, do you think I could make you happy?"

She almost choked on the beer she just drank as she realized his question to her. "You already do, Dillion. I don't see that changing any time soon," she said as she snuggled into his torso a little more.

"What about the kids. Do you see yourself as a parent? Could you see yourself as a parent to someone else's kids? Mine?"

She thought carefully and then answered, "Dillion. I fell in love with your kids before I acknowledged to myself that I love you. I know that I won't be perfect, and I don't want to replace their own mother, but I think we can come to some understanding that we all can live with. As for my own kids? Having kids with you?" For this, she felt it was important to look him straight in the eyes. She shifted her position and sat up, straddling him so she could see directly into his silver-flecked blue eyes.

"Dillion, I can't wait to have kids with you. I love your kids. I love you. I come from a big family, and I always thought that if I could find someone to love me, that I'd want to have children with him. I think we'd make beautiful babies. Don't you?"

He smiled and caressed her cheek with his thumb. "Yes, Aur, I think we would make beautiful children together. As long as they have your eyes and mouth. They could have my nose, though. I have a better nose." She giggled and kissed the tip of it. That slight movement had something shift beneath her. His attentions were starting to swing from her face to other parts of her body, and she was aware of it. Aurelie took both of their bottles and carefully placed them over his head and onto the side table.

That movement was a test, it was purposeful as she let her hips slide over him and her breasts move into the vicinity of his face. He didn't pause instead he kissed each of her breasts through the sheer fabric while his arms shifted so he could grab her ass and press her into him. Aurelie let a moan out. It had been so long since a man pleasured her, and she wanted to see how far he would go. How far she would let it go. Her hands found his hair and wrapped her fingers into his waves, released them and lightly scratched his scalp, feeling him release at the sheer pleasure of this unexpectedly arousing sensation.

In response, his hands left their resting place as he reciprocated with his nails scratching her back from her hips to her strapless bra. Aurelie arched her back as if she were a cat and let out a soft mewling sound to show her contentment. He struggled a moment with the hooks, but with a little of her help, the hooks released, and she began to move her hips in a rhythm that excited him and left her wanting more. Forgetting her promise to herself. Letting herself ride the erotic wave that was taking over, she expertly shed her top and lace bra, and sat up to see his response. And it pleased her.

Dillion pulled her forward so that his mouth could accept one of her breasts into it while the other was being stroked with his hand. Aurelie arched her back to bring her further into his mouth while she pressed and glided over his growing cock. When he released her, she found an intensity that wouldn't be denied. She wanted him. To see him. To feel his skin on hers. Aurelie pulled off his shirt before giving such a heated kiss that she could hear his breath hitch. She broke the embrace to journey down his neck and chest with searing grazes and long licks, stopping at each nipple to lightly nip each and suck them into her mouth to be played by her expert tongue. She could tell she was driving him to the point where he would lose control and join her in this erogenous rhythm they were building toward a titillating conclusion. When she got to the waist of his jeans, she noticed his eyes closed, his breathing heavy as she was increasingly aroused at the rise and fall of his taut stomach. She wanted to see the rest of him. Instinctively she grabbed the waist of his jean shorts and began undressing him. Dillion's natural reaction was to lift his hips to encourage the act. Once she had him free, she shimmied off his shorts and then stood up so she could take off her own. Turning around so that her backside was to him, she performed a slow and seductive striptease, while she wiggled out of her shorts. Purposefully bending over in a playful manner so he could see how the lace thong hugged her cheeks and slid between her legs as if inviting him to come and find out what titillating treasure was waiting for him.

Dillion shot up and put a hand on himself and began to squeeze and move it up and down. "You are incredible." He said in a husky voice. This pleased her very much and began to move her own hand so that she could easily slip a finger in between her legs and show him how much she wanted him.

"Do you want me, Dillion?" Now?" She asked him in a throaty voice.

"Yes!" Was his guttural reply. "I want you right now!" As his hand moved faster and faster, her finger matched his speed and she could feel that familiar arousal and wanted to finish with him. Now. Somehow, she found the wisdom to ask the most important question of the night.

"Did you bring any condoms with you?" She dripped her question with as much sensuality as possible.

"What?" His eyes now glassy with impending release. "What? Condoms?" She was ready to touch him. Put it on him and ride him until they both peaked. But then she saw something change in his eyes. His hand stopped moving. "Oh shit. Dammit. God damn it. I'm sorry. So sorry." Dillion sat up then put his hands through his hair. His eyes were no longer lustful. They were panic stricken.

Aurelie stopped giving herself pleasure and stood up. Not one to be ashamed of her body. She stood still in front of him, breathing heavily, while her body was calming down, her nipples were still in hardened peaks. The energy shift in the room had calmed most of Aurelie's emotions, but it hadn't yet reached her breasts, which were still waiting in anticipation. "What's wrong? Did I move too fast? Did something not feel right?"

"God no. Hell no. Oh Jesus, Aurelie. You are the sexiest woman I've ever met. I didn't think you'd want to. I thought you wanted to wait; I mean. That's why I booked a hotel room." Dillion sighed and put his hands through his hair. "That's why I didn't even think to buy condoms. I'm so naive. So stupid. Embarrassed."

Aurelie was a bit confused, so she sat on the recliner across from the sofa. "You aren't stupid, Dillion. Why are you embarrassed? Did we do anything that made you uncomfortable? Haven't you made out before?"

"Yes and no. I've only been with one other woman, and we waited until we got married. Oh man, I shouldn't be talking about her while I'm with you. I'm so sorry, Aur. I don't know how to do this."

"Do what?"

"Talk to you about this without talking about Corinne. I don't know how to have sex with a woman who can practically get me to orgasm with one look. I feel like such a teenage boy. I should get dressed. I should go. I'm so embarrassed. I'm so sorry. So sorry."

Aurelie took a deep breath and tried not to be angry. This was complicated for him. For her, too, if she was honest. They needed to figure their way to one another.

"There is nothing to be embarrassed about or to be sorry about. I get it that we have two completely different sexual experiences. That doesn't mean that one is better than another. That there is anything to be embarrassed about. What do you mean about how I look at you? Don't you enjoy the way I look at you?"

"Very much. Too much." He sighed and looked up at her with her head cocked to the side, intent on what he was going to say next. "Okay, talk about embarrassing."

"That's enough of that talk. This is a judgment-free zone, Dillion. Nothing is an embarrassment. We need to learn from each other. Not judge each other. Explain what you mean."

"Okay, remember when we first kissed, and I got an erection just by kissing you?"

"Yes, I remember. It was wonderful."

"Yes, well. It became an issue for me."

"How so?"

"Every time I even thought of you a little bit, I would get hard and in my line of work and being a single dad, I just can't walk around with an erection all the time. And I was terrified to be on a date with you and then accidentally … "

She could tell he was having difficulty talking about what was happening to him physically, so she nodded in understanding and then sat next to him on the couch, so he didn't have to look at her if it was uncomfortable for him. "I get it. But that hasn't happened. You've been able to control yourself. So why are you embarrassed?"

"It's because of how I manage to control it." He looked at her and then put his hand on his penis again.

"Oh. Ooh. Before the first date?"

"Yes, and every date."

"Really?" She smiled slightly, feeling her feminine power being engaged in the conversation.

"Really."

"Well, I'm flattered. I can honestly say that I've never had anyone go to that effort for me. Impressive."

"You don't think less of me? Like I'm less of a man than you've had before?"

"Listen to me, Dillion Clark, you are more of a man than any other guy I've ever been with. Just being able to have this conversation shows me how much more mature you are. And sexy. Very, very sexy." She looked quizzically at him.

"What? It looks like you have a question for me. What is it?"

"Well, where do you do it? I mean you have three kids, and you work in a church. Where does it happen?"

He chuckled. She could tell he was starting to relax. Trust in her. Trust in this very intimate conversation. "In the shower. It's part of my getting ready for our date routine."

"Smart. Very efficient. No messy clean up." This time he laughed out loud.

"Yeah. I thought of that, too." Then he got all serious again. "Look, I know that there are other 'ways' to have sex. But Corinne and I were young. We were each other's firsts. We enjoyed making love, but we only did it one way, with me on top. If I'm honest, I was relieved to hear you say that you were a born-again virgin, so that it helped take some of the pressure off. That's why I didn't buy any condoms before this trip. I didn't think I'd need them. I thought you'd want to continue on your born-again virgin journey. Plus, I've never bought them. Never used them. Corinne and I didn't use birth control."

"Is birth control a 'no-no' for you? Is it against the church law or something?"

"Oh no. Nothing like that. It's just we waited until we were married to have sex. Then since we'd known each other for so long and had a steady job/income, we wanted to start our family right away. As an only child, she wanted a big family. We never even thought about birth control." Dillion leaned forward, putting his elbows on his knees and then began again. "But now, I also need to think about my children. What having an intimate relationship while dating would mean for them. They understand that mommies and daddies sleep together in the same room and same bed. But what do I tell them about having a girlfriend sleep over? What if something happens and we break up?"

Aurelie shifted and looked at him quizzically. "You think we'll break up?"

He put his hand on hers. "No. I don't know. I mean, ugh. How can I explain this?" He shifted so that they were sitting across from each other, holding her hands in his. "I want to be with you for as long as you'll have me, Aur. That's the honest-to-God truth. But realistically, I am a parent of three young children who already have experienced one traumatic loss in their lives. I have to be protective of them as well. I just don't see that making love with you before a commitment is made is going to work for me."

"Okay, so where does that leave us? What are you thinking?"

"Well, what if you come up north next weekend and you and Mumford stay at the house. Platonically, of course. You can have my bed and I will sleep on the couch. Let's see what it's like to be a family for a weekend. See if you still want to be with me. A part of my family, after you experience living with us for a whole weekend."

Aurelie squeezed his hands and kissed him lightly on his lips. "Sounds like a plan. But if you're too nervous about keeping our distance at my place, how can you be sure you can keep your distance in your own home?"

"That's a no-brainer. I've got three kids who don't miss a thing. They will be watching us like hawks." Aurelie could feel his gaze shift from her face to her breasts. "I'm sorry, Aur, but I've gotta go now. The next time I see you, I need you to have many more clothes on or … " He kissed her sweetly at first, but then his tongue forced itself into her mouth while his hands began to massage her breasts. She let out a pleasurable sound and he quickly pulled back. "Now. Gotta go NOW."

Initially, she was a bit miffed, but then she smiled. She felt a powerful energy move through her knowing she had such a strong impact on him and his control. But she also respected his situation. After he left her, she lay down on her bed with one hand under her head and the other left to journey over the places where he had seared her with his mouth, teeth, tongue, and hands. When her fingers found where her latent pleasure laid, she closed her eyes and drew in a deep breath as she finished what he started.

Chapter Twenty-Eight

On the drive up to Minocqua, Aurelie called Cat to keep her occupied during the four and a half hour trip. "So, you're telling me you two still haven't had sex yet?" Cat asked.

"That's what I'm sayin,'" Aurelie replied.

"But he's hot! And I can say that, because I'm a happily married woman who has no intention of cheating. Well, Aur, I have to admit it. You have it bad."

"Have what bad?"

"You were a sexual machine before Dillion. You wouldn't even wait two hours to have sex with a guy and now you've been with him for a little over two months and still you're a born-again virgin. You are in love with him, bad."

"Cat, come on. You're a parent. You tell me. If, God forbid, something happened to you, do you think that Damon would go about and bring women home and have sex with them under your roof? With your children still living at home?"

"Well, he'd better not, or I would haunt him and those sluts for the rest of their days." They both laughed.

"Seriously, Cat."

"In all seriousness, if something happened to me, I would want him to find happiness again and if that would mean he'd find another woman to love, who would love our children, that would be okay with me."

"But, what about the sex thing? Do you think Damon would have sex with the woman before marriage? With the kids living at home still?"

"Hmm. I think it's complicated. I think he'd really have to like her before he'd let her near the kids. I'm very uncomfortable talking about this since I am very much alive, but putting it into perspective, I get what he is doing. I can respect it. But how are you handling it?"

"How I've been handling it for two years now. Batteries." That got them both to howl in laughter which woke up Mumford from his car nap. Aurelie reached over to scratch his head before he yawned and lay his head back down.

"Cat, I'm almost there. Thanks for listening."

"Hey, before we hang up, when's your final gig?"

"Next weekend. At the state fair. Will you guys be able to make it?"

"Wouldn't miss it for the world, Aur. I got you."

"Love you, Kitty Cat."

"Love you, too, Aur. Say 'hi' to Dillion for me."

"Will do."

Aurelie's red SUV sparkled in the late afternoon sun as she pulled into the driveway of the simple ranch home that would be her home-away-from home for the weekend. Brianna was the first to bust through the screen door and her siblings followed. Mumford practically jumped off his seat and couldn't wait to get outside to stretch his long legs and visit his friends. Aurelie was greeted with a group hug before they turned their attentions to Mumford. "Where's your dad?" she asked.

Riley replied, "Oh, he had to go to the hospital to deliver last rites to one of the parishioners. He said we could help you get settled in." Aurelie nodded. A bit disappointed, but understandable.

"Dad said we have to help you unpack the car," Benji said.

"That'd be great. Thank you." Everyone took something inside. She felt a little bit weird putting her things in Dillion's bedroom, especially when he wasn't there. *But*, Aurelie thought to herself, *this gives me a chance to get a feel for what it would be like to be here with the kids. Alone.* With everything put away, Aurelie suggested that they all take Mumford for a walk to help him stretch his legs, and hers. Benji asked if he could hold Mumford's leash while Riley led the group onto the hiking trail nearest their backyard.

When they returned, Dillion still wasn't back, so Aurelie decided to start dinner. "What did you guys plan to have for supper tonight?"

Brianna answered, "Pasketti and meatballs." Aurelie smiled to herself. She loved hearing the mispronounced names of things from little ones.

"Okay, let's help your dad out and start getting dinner ready." Putting her teaching skills into play, Aurelie had everyone take on a task. Benji fed Mumford his dinner and took him outside to do his duty. Bri set the table while Riley helped Aurelie locate everything in the small but efficient kitchen and even cut up the fixings for salad. Aurelie got so engrossed in making the meal, she didn't hear the door open. But she sure felt the energy shift when he entered the room. Keeping her back to him, she anticipated his touch before he even got to her. But once his strong hands enveloped her waist and she felt him nuzzle her neck, she leaned into him and smiled.

"Sorry I'm late," Dillion whispered in her ear in a way that gave her the shivers.

"It's okay."

"I know this sounds sexist, but it felt so good to come home and smell dinner cooking and see a beautiful woman in the kitchen, as if she belongs here."

"Well, it is sexist, but considering you've been at the hospital all afternoon with a dying patient, I'll give you a break." She turned around and without even thinking about it, she reached up to give him a kiss hello.

"Eww! Gross! No kissing in the kitchen!" Benji announced as he and Mumford returned from being outside.

Dillion pulled away a bit and mouthed the word, "See?" Then he turned to Benji, "Well, I'm going to kiss you in the kitchen," and placed one on Benji's forehead. That got Brianna's attention and she ran over to get hers which landed on her cheek. Riley was a little more patient and waited until she could give her dad a hug and kiss him on his cheek. "Now that I've kissed everyone in the kitchen, I think it's time for me to get out of my work clothes and into something more comfortable."

At the dinner table, the young family joined hands and gave thanks for the food on the table, their family, and friends. Much of the dinner conversation came from the Clark kids who were trying to impress Aurelie and their dad with the day's events. "Daddy," Brianna asked, "Can we have s'mores for dessert?"

"S'mores sound perfect. How about you all clean up the kitchen while Aur helps me get the bonfire started? Does that sound okay?"

"Aurelie," Riley began in a more mature voice than Brianna, "can you bring out your guitar so we can sing campfire songs, too?"

"Absolutely," Thanks for the cleanup, kids. I'll see you outside," Aurelie said.

"Come with me, help me find some kindling wood to start the fire," Dillion asked as he grabbed Aurelie's hand and dragged her into the opening of the woods. He pressed her backside into the trunk of an ancient oak tree and began ravishing her mouth. She responded by wrapping her arms around his neck and wrapping her legs around his hips. When he took a moment to breathe, his words came in a passionate whisper. "Damn, I've missed you so much. Aur. It's been agony, and then work got in the way. I wanted so badly to be here when you arrived. Sorry." He buried his face in her neck and held her close.

"So, how many 'showers' have you had this week?" Being coy but knowing he understood what she meant by 'showers'.

"Too many to count," he replied, which got her chuckling. "You?"

She took the opportunity to press herself into him to make her point. "Too many to count." They both heard the patio door open, so Aurelie released her legs and they leaned their foreheads together to catch their breath.

"Aur?"

"Yeah?"

"No pressure, but I am really, really hoping that this weekend with the kids works out."

"Me too."

"Because I don't know how much longer I can wait to make love with you." She smiled, lifted her head, and opened her mouth to suck lightly on his full lower lip, which encouraged him to open his mouth and let their tongues intertwine, even though their bodies could not.

"Dad! Aur! Where are you? Where's the fire?" Riley called out.

They released their embrace and Dillion replied, "Sorry! We're in the woods looking for kindling."

When they arrived at the entrance to the backyard with only a few sticks in their hands, Riley looked like a disappointed parent. "Dad, did you forget? You had us picking up sticks this week so we could have a kindling pile all ready for when Aurelie visited."

Aurelie grinned and elbowed him. "Sorry Riley. I forgot. I'll go ahead and start the fire."

After an evening filled with good food, funny stories, campfire songs and s'mores, the kids went inside to get ready for bed. Aurelie followed to put Mumford to bed next to her in Dillion's room, while Dillion put away the s'mores fixin's before he kissed his children goodnight. "The kids are asking for you to say good night to them."

She smiled and nodded, starting with the youngest. "Good night, Bri. Thanks for a great first night here."

"Aurelie?"

"Yes, sweetie?"

"I like you being here. It feels like home." Aurelie's heart skipped a beat, and her eyes felt a mistiness come over them.

"I like being here, too, Bri. Good night." She kissed Bri on her forehead and walked into Benji's room.

"I hear you wanted me to say goodnight to you?"

"Yeah, and to ask you a question."

"Sure. What's up?"

"Would it be okay if Mumford spent the night in my room?" Aurelie sat on the edge of his bed.

"That's a good question. I don't mind, but I'm not sure about Mumford. He's pretty attached to me. How about we give him the choice and he gets to decide?"

"That's fair." Aurelie went to get the giant dog and showed him to Benji's room. He brought his dinosaur stuffy with him, looked at Aurelie and then Benji, found a place on the floor next to the bed and laid down. Aurelie went to get him his travel bed which he was happy to use.

Riley was last and had just finished her prayers. "Thanks for helping me make dinner tonight and finding out what's what around here, Riley."

"I'm glad you came. You make my dad very happy. We have lots of fun when you're around."

"That's quite a compliment," Aurelie commented.

"It's true."

"Thank you."

"Aurelie, can I ask you a question?"

"Sure."

"Do you love my dad?"

A bit taken aback but impressed with Riley's maturity. "Yes. Yes I do, Riley. I do love your dad."

"That's good because I can tell he loves you, too. Very much."

Aurelie smiled, "Is that your question? Ready for bed now?"

"Just one more,"

"Shoot."

"Do you love us? Us kids?"

Aurelie hugged her and moved a curl from her face. "Yes, Riley, I do love you. All of you."

"Good, 'cause we love you, too. Night, Aurelie."

"Night Riley." Aurelie stood up and walked out of the room. Aurelie took a deep breath and headed for the kitchen. She needed a drink. Dillion was already there with a glass of red wine for her and led her back out to the firepit where the blaze they had before was more like a slow, glowing flame.

Dillion lay down on a padded lounger and motioned for Aurelie to lay on him.

"So, how did it go?" he asked.

"It went well."

"Really? No hard questions? No whining to stay up a little longer?"

"No whining, but I did have some important questions to answer. Not difficult."

"Huh. Can I ask you what they were?"

"Well, Riley asked if I loved you and if I loved them."

"What'd you say?"

"I said 'yes' of course."

"Good answer." He kissed the top of her head. "Now, the question is if you'll still say that after a full weekend of us."

"Hey, I may be small, but I'm tough. I can handle it."

The new couple lay like that, sipping wine, watching the low flames turn into glowing embers until the stars came out. Until their eyelids began to flutter and it was time to go to their respective beds. Dillion kissed her in such a sweet and delicate way, she took that sensation to bed with her. Dreaming of what it might feel like to have him kiss her like that every evening for the rest of their lives.

Chapter Twenty-Nine

"I don't want the butt piece! Don't give me the butt, Ri!"

"Bri, you know what daddy says, we can't waste food. You'll eat the butt piece."

"That's not fair! You eat it! I'm not a butt, you're a butt!"

Aurelie woke up to the sound of the girls screaming at each other. Nothing she hadn't experienced before, but it was usually her sisters and her yelling at each other at the top of their lungs for some mundane reason. She sat up in bed and felt out of sorts. *Coffee.* She said to herself. *Need coffee.*

At least she was aware enough that she had to get some clothes on before going into public spaces. She pulled on a pair of jean shorts and an old T-shirt before venturing into the kitchen. By the time she got there, Dillion, looking a bit sleepy himself, had gotten a handle on the situation. Apparently, this morning's argument was about the end of a loaf of bread being used for toast. He made each girl have an end with PB&J. Benji didn't want any part of it and made himself some instant oatmeal. Aurelie could smell the freshly brewed coffee and beelined straight for it.

She eked out, "Morning," to anyone who was within earshot.

"Morning," came back to her as a cacophony.

"How'd you sleep?" Dillion asked.

"Good. Thanks. Thanks again for letting me use your bed," Aurelie replied. "How about you? You okay on the couch?"

"Yeah. I slept just fine."

Benji added, "Dad'll be okay on the couch. He slept on the couch for almost a whole year after Mom died." Then went back nonchalantly to eating his oatmeal. Aurelie paused before she took another sip of her coffee, pondering what Benji had just said.

Changing the subject, she asked brightly, "So, what's on today's agenda?"

"Well, there's some kind of berry festival in Eagle River. I thought we could check it out and then back here for dinner."

"Sounds great. Is it okay if I take a quick shower?"

"Don't you want any breakfast?"

"No thanks. I think I ate a little bit too much last night." Then with a bit of sarcasm, "Plus, I only like to eat the bread butts for my breakfast toast, and there doesn't seem to be any left." The girls looked sheepishly between them while Dillion smiled and gave her a 'good one' nod before he took a sip of his coffee.

"Benji, how did it go with Mumford last night? Was everything okay?"

"Yup. Although he snores. But it was okay. I let him climb into bed with me and nudged him every time he snored. It all worked out okay."

After breakfast, they loaded up into the minivan and drove the 30 minutes to Eagle River. Another quintessential up north community built around water. Bald eagles carved out of wood adorn the main highway through town. The river itself was bustling with people in their bass boats, families on pontoons, and others paddling through in their kayaks and canoes. Eagle River's main street was a little smaller than Minocqua and a bit campier. Souvenir, moccasin, and T-shirt shops had a steady stream of customers roaming in and out of them. An old-fashioned candy store with the taffy machine rotating the sweet, sticky treat in the window enticed both young and old customers to come in and pick up a box to enjoy with family or for the long trip home.

They found parking, not too far from the fairgrounds. Dillion smiled as he held Brianna's small hand on one side and Aurelie's on the other. The blended group spent the afternoon weaving in and out of vendor booths, sampling snacks for sale, and enjoying people-watching. Aurelie smiled when she saw a local man providing the musical entertainment with a wireless mic and a souped up karaoke machine. But to Bri and Riley, it was time to dance. Aurelie joined them for a song or two before Dillion motioned that it was time to go and get ready for dinner.

The kids fell asleep on the way home while Aurelie and Dillion held hands. Aurelie closed her eyes a few times, taking in the warm, sweet breeze smelling of sunshine and pine trees that is quintessential up north. When they arrived at the ranch home, she could hear Mumford barking inside the house, a nervous bark that led Aurelie to say, "I'd better go in first and let him know it's okay. I should probably take him for a walk, too. Then I can help with dinner."

"Go ahead and do what you've gotta do with Mumford. The kids and I will take care of dinner tonight. We've got this." She smiled and kissed him lightly on the mouth in case anyone was watching.

"It's okay big guy. It's Momma coming in to take you for a walk." When she entered the house, she opened the bedroom door to see her scared dog wearing his dinosaur snood, panting quickly with his dino stuffy close by. But as soon as he recognized who it was, his face turned into a smile before picking up the stuffy to show her, as his butt wiggled with his tail wagging in synchrony. She carefully removed the stuffy and the snood before attaching his leash to his collar.

When she got to the kitchen, the kids and Dillion were working hard to get dinner ready. Dillion turned around and she smiled when she saw he was wearing an apron that said, "Best Dad" on it. "Dinner will be ready in about an hour and a half," Dillion said. "Enjoy your walk. Take your phone in case you get turned around out there."

Aurelie streamed music from her summer playlist. She didn't want to deal with Mumford's anxiety, so she decided to take Mid Lake Road, a local thoroughfare that tourists don't usually use. It is a meandering road with no markings but is sheltered by towering pine trees and has lake views throughout. When Cat would invite Aurelie to join her family on one of their up north vacations, the two friends would oftentimes chat about what it might be like to live in one of the mansions on Minocqua Lake or spent weekends in one of the cozy lake cottages dotting the shorelines. But today it was just her and Mumford. When they'd traveled the distance between Hwy 47 and the back entrance to the bustling summer town, she stopped at the gas station to grab a couple of waters for her and her companion. She found an empty park bench facing the lake for the two of them to rest and watch the menagerie of boats, skiers, fishermen, and swimmers enjoy all the lake had to offer. "So, what would you think about living here, Mumford? Could you see yourself happy here?" He cocked his head with one of his ears sticking straight up while the other one flapped down. Then, when it was clear she wasn't going to talk any more, he lay his large head on her lap and sighed, waiting for her to scratch behind his ears. When all the water was gone, they headed to the Clark home, again walking the road less traveled.

When they arrived at the house, she could smell a delicious aroma coming from the grill and it got her stomach growling. She heard all the commotion in the backyard, so that's where she headed. A picnic table was covered in a simple blue and white gingham tablecloth with a mason jar of sunflowers set in the middle. Simple white dishes and mason jar glasses were placed around the table.

The girls had changed into sundresses and the boys had on Hawaiian shirts and khaki shorts. "Impressive, Clark family. I guess I should change."

Benji came over, took Mumford's leash from her, and said, "I'll take care of Mumford while you change." Then he sniffed around her. "You should take a shower first. You stink."

"Benji!" Dillion exclaimed. "That's rude. Apologize."

"I'm sorry, Aurelie. But Dad, she does smell. And she's sweaty."

Aurelie laughed. "It's okay, Benji, I know I need a shower. I'll make it quick. Looks like dinner is almost on the table." She handed over the leash to Benji and beelined to the bedroom to grab her toiletries and her red halter sundress that she planned to wear to church the next morning.

Feeling refreshed after the shower and checking once more in the mirror to make sure she looked decent with her damp curls, she swiped on a little red lipstick, slipped on her leather flip flops and headed outside. Dillion had a pair of tiki torch Bluetooth speakers playing smooth jazz instrumentals in the background. Benji pulled out the lawn chair at the end of the table for Aurelie to sit. Everything was super elegant for a cookout, she thought to herself. It felt "off," but in a good way. Then she saw the whole grilled chicken on the stand with the beer can up its butt. "Beer can chicken. I haven't had that in a long time. Looks great, Dillion! I can't wait. I'm starving after that walk."

"It's one of my specialties. Why don't we say grace so we can all eat." Everyone bowed their heads and held hands while Dillion expressed thanks for the food and the people at the table.

Then Brianna chimed in, "And God bless Aurelie. Let her say 'yes' to marrying us!" It took a moment to sink in. Then Aurelie lifted her head and looked at the terror on Dillion's face, the anger on Benji's and Riley's.

"What?" she squeaked out. "What did you say?"

This time it was Benji who said, "Way to go, Bri! You ruined the surprise! Dad was supposed to ask her not you!"

Then Bri looked around and tears started to well up in her eyes, but she fought back. "I didn't do anything! I didn't ruin the surprise! I didn't ask her nothin'!" Then all three kids were arguing about what had happened and then Dillion finally came to.

"That's enough kids. Enough!"

"Dillion, what did she say? What's going on?"

He cleared his throat, moved his chair back and walked to Aurelie. Dillion took both of her hands in his and led her to stand up. "Oh Aur. I'm so sorry, it wasn't supposed to be like this. But I guess it helps you get a real feel for this family."

"Like what? What's going on, Dillion? I don't understand."

Dillion took a deep breath and began his semi-rehearsed speech. "Aurelie, I was just going through the motions living a life after Corinne died. I knew I had to hang on for our children, but there was no life, no energy in anything I did." He squeezed her hands thoughtfully. "Then I met you, and it was like an electric charge shot through me. You with your high octane energy, so full of color and life. I just had to be a part of it. I knew you were special right from that first time we accidentally touched. I didn't want to admit it at first, but after a while, I knew I loved you from that first look. That first incidental touch. And the way you are with my children. How they bonded with you from the get-go. It's like it's meant to be." She felt something important was about to happen, and yet was still befuddled about the whole thing. Until she felt him move. Until he pulled a small white box out of his pocket and knelt down on one knee.

"Aurelie. I love you with my entire being. You've taught me that I can love again, I can be a whole person. You've accepted me and my children into your life, and we accept you into ours, unconditionally." Aurelie stopped breathing and tears began to form, obscuring the world around her. The only thing that was anchoring her to this moment was the sound of Dillion's voice as he asked her his question, "Aurelie Beres, will you give me the honor of being my wife? Will you marry me and my children?" At the end of his speech, he opened the little white box, which looked a little worse for the wear, and saw the most incredible emerald and diamond ring she'd ever seen in her life.

This was it. This is why she was compelled to turn her life around. So she could have this moment. This future. With Dillion. With his children. She finally had what she'd always wanted right in front of her. All she had to do was answer him.

"Yes. Yes, Dillion, I will marry you and your family." She got out in between sobs. Aurelie held out her left hand and he placed the symbol of their promised future together on her finger. When he stood up, she saw he had tears in his eyes as well and they kissed. A kiss that sealed the vow they had just made that their lives, their futures were intertwined forever and always.

PART FOUR: THIS HIGGLEDY-PIGGLEDY LIFE

Chapter Thirty

Cat and Aurelie were having a late morning date at one of their favorite coffee shops, Espresso Love Coffee in downtown Mukwonago. Occupying one half of a turn-of-the-century building on Rochester Street, its tall ceilings and dark wooden furnishings gave it warmth as if it were the tangible equivalent of an Americano.

"Let me see your ring again. Gorgeous. Simply gorgeous! How could a priest afford something like this? Does he have a wealthy uncle or something?" Cat inquired.

"I don't think so. Well, his brother is doing well in the Chicago real estate market, but he didn't buy him the ring. It's actually an heirloom from my dad's side of the family."

"But it looks Celtic. I thought your family was French Canadian?"

"It is. We are." Twisting it with her other hand Aurelie continued. "His family comes from Scotland and Ireland. When he was at my parents' house on the Fourth of July, he asked for my dad's blessing and my dad gave him the ring to give to me. Dillion said my dad told him it was okay to redesign it, so Dillion and his brother found a guy who was able to change it into this."

"It's so cool. I haven't seen anything like it. Do you know if it has any special meaning?"

"Yes, the jeweler included a bit of the history of the Celtic knot. It's called the Serch Bythol, and it is the symbol of everlasting love. So, this is the first part, and the wedding band will bring the second part of the knot together. It's said that the parts, intricately intertwined, represent two people joined together forever in body, mind, and spirit."

"Amazing! And so thoughtful. You've got yourself a great guy, Aur. I am so damned happy for you!" Cat reached for her friend across the table and kissed her full on the mouth.

"What are the wedding plans? Are you going to move to Minocqua, or is he looking for another parish closer to here?"

Aurelie reached over and took Cat's hands in hers. "Well, first I have a question for you Mrs. Catrina MacGregor. Will you be my matron of honor?"

Cat screamed in excitement as the coffee shop customers turned to see the commotion. "Yes! Yes! Yes! Wait, when are you having the wedding? Next summer?"

"Well, a little bit sooner than that."

"How soon?"

"October."

"That's like only a month away! Are you crazy? Why so fast, you're not pregnant are you? Aren't you still a born-again virgin?"

"I know it's only six weeks away, but we don't want to wait. This long-distance thing is taking its toll and besides, you know I thrive on spontaneity."

"Mmhmm," Cat squinted at her best friend, "And …"

"Alright, also it's because we are waiting to have sex until we're married. It'll be simpler for the kids. They understand parents sleep in the same bed."

"And …"

"You are such a pest, Cat." In a hushed tone she continued, "And we are horny as hell. I'm afraid I'm going to explode if we wait much longer."

"There's my bestie. I knew she was in there somewhere."

"Shut up. Now, finish your chai so we can go shopping."

"Ooh, what are we shopping for?"

"We're meeting my mother and shopping for wedding dresses."

"Yeah! I can't wait!"

Six weeks later, almost to the day, Aurelie was standing in her parent's bedroom while her mother and best friend were helping her with the final touches. Aurelie delicately stepped into her off the shoulder, lace, mermaid gown while her attendants helped her into the long sleeves and zippered up the back. Then they carefully placed the headpiece over her pin curls. The pattern of the headpiece was a crown of intricately designed alternating curls and fern leaves made from crystals with a simple waist length veil trailing off the back.

When she took a step back to see herself in the full-length mirror, she was astonished. "Is this really me? Is this really happening?" She said out loud.

"Oui, Mon Cheri, it is you as your most beautiful self." Bea stood next to her daughter in a navy full length dress with a lace bodice, crystal pin on the side, and taffeta skirt.

"Thank you, Momma. I love you."

"I love you more." The mother of the bride hugged her youngest daughter on her wedding day.

"Okay, Bereses, I can't take much more of this emotional stuff, or I'll have to redo my makeup!" Cat said in a shaky voice.

"Come here, Kitty Cat. Let me see you." Her best friend was wearing a burnt orange lace mermaid off the shoulder bridesmaid dress, a perfect complement to the other two dresses. At that moment, Aurelie acknowledged she had the two most important women in her life at her side, as they always were.

She heard a knock on the door. "Mon Cheri, it's time." The voice was unmistakably her father's.

"Come on in, Dad." The door opened and her dashing father looked picture perfect in his navy tux. He smiled and put his hand on his heart.

"Aurelie, you are the most beautiful bride, except for your mother, of course."

"Of course," she smiled and went to him with her hands reaching out to take his. "Thank you, Dad. You are very handsome in that tux."

He smiled and kissed her hand. He looked over at his wife and said, "Bea, you are breathtaking. I would marry you all over again." She walked toward her husband and kissed him on his cheek while whispering some secret message of love in his ear before she took her place at the patio doors waiting for her son, Felix, to escort her to her seat.

"Uh oh, almost forgot!" Cat said. She turned around and found Aurelie's bridal bouquet. A rustic mixture of orange and navy roses, burgundy Gerber daisies, thistle, and eucalyptus created by the owner of the Americana Flower Station. "See you at the alter!"

"Ready?" Antoine asked as they stood in the doorway of the bedroom.

"Absolutely." He smiled, tucked her arm into his and walked his baby girl to the draped tulle adorning the patio doors.

In front of her were Brianna and Riley in matching lace and taffeta burgundy junior bridesmaid dresses holding smaller versions of her own bridal bouquet. Next were Gordon and Grace, her god children, as her flower girl and ring bearer. Gordon was sporting a navy suit, and Grace was in a white lace top with a burnt orange tulle skirt, the perfect colors to accent their ginger curls.

When the violins began playing the prelude, she closed her eyes and breathed deeply. This is what she wanted, and it was going to be perfect. She couldn't wait to become Mrs. Aurelie Clark. The walk down the aisle was a blur. She was getting everything she wanted. A simple fall, outdoor wedding at her family home. Having the kind of love that her parents and her best friend had. Having a family. Of course, it was a blended family, but who cares? She felt truly blessed in this moment. When she looked up, staged between two stately oak trees was an arch of tulle and sprays of the wedding flowers matching her bouquet. In front of that were the new men in her life. Benji, her soon to be son and current groomsman, her soon to be brother-in-law, Roger, and father-in-law who was presiding at the wedding and the love of her life, Dillion Clark. Dressed smartly in his navy tux, which, if she were honest was the real reason, she chose navy in the wedding palette. Dillion's eyes just popped in navy. They burned a path into her soul. This was it.

Chapter Thirty-One

Dillion was hyper focused. He was so proud of how his children were handling today. They were just as excited as he was. Aurelie changed him. Changed them. They all had an anticipation for what lie ahead. Benji looked so mature and dapper in his navy suit. Even his hair seemed to be under a bit more control than usual. Then he watched his daughters come down the aisle and his eyes started to mist. When did they get so grown up? So beautiful. He smiled at them as they walked toward him and then took their places on the bride's side of the aisle.

But when the music changed, and all the guests stood up he knew. Just knew that she was there, even though he couldn't see her quite yet. Beyond the sea of autumn colors, he saw a flash of white. He looked up at this vision of an angel coming toward him. An angel with emerald eyes and crimson lips. He couldn't think of anything else. Only her and how much he wanted to be with her. Make her his. She was the reason he felt whole again. He never wanted to be without that feeling again. And when her father offered her hand to Dillion and he accepted it, a warmth washed over him with such intensity, it almost knocked him over. When they reached the altar, he leaned over and let her know, "You are exquisite. You look like an angel."

She smiled and squeezed his arm. "Thank you. You are gorgeous in that tux." He wasn't expecting her to say anything to him. The way she said it also had a hint of sensuality to it. But he couldn't do anything about that now. He wanted to be present.

It wasn't as if he were just going through the motions. But he felt like he was going in and out of different levels of consciousness throughout the ceremony. When Benji and Bri gave the readings, he listened with his whole heart. When he and Aurelie gave their vows and rings to each other, he was present for that. When Riley stood by his father's side to present communion, he was there. The ceremony was almost over, and he was ready to get this party started, except his dad said something that he didn't expect. Something he realized he had to pay attention to.

"Before I make the celebratory announcement we've all been waiting for, the bride would like to invite Riley, Benji, and Brianna to join her and Dillion at the altar." This wasn't something they practiced or even talked about. Dillion was perplexed, but the look on his father's face told a different story. That his dad was in on this secret.

Aurelie spoke directly to the children, but loud enough for all the guests to hear as well. "The night of our engagement, Bri accidentally asked if I would say yes to marrying all of you. That stuck with me. I know that I will never replace your mother, and I don't want to. But Bri is absolutely right. I'm not just marrying your dad; I'm marrying all of you. So, I've asked your grandma and grandpa and Uncle Roger to help me with this next part. Roger, can you please bring me the rings?"

The best man moved from his station and brought out a green velvet drawstring bag from his pocket. He carefully placed five Trinity Knot rings on the open Bible that his father had in front of the wedding party. Aurelie began, "You'll notice that all five rings have the same Celtic design on them. It's the Trinity Knot, which is the symbol of family. These are our family wedding rings that we will all wear on our right hand as a symbol of our new family's love, honor, and respect for one another. When I give you your ring repeat after me, 'With this ring, I thee wed.'"

Aurelie started with the youngest, Brianna, and with each vow, Dillion became more and more emotional. The tears were flowing, streaming down his face and he was shaking. By the time Aurelie got to him, his brother had to help him stand. He barely got out the words with a whisper, but knew it was important for his children and his new wife, their new mother, to hear him make that commitment with them.

"By the power vested in me and by the State of Wisconsin, I now pronounce you husband, wife and family! You may kiss your bride!" Dillion couldn't wait any longer, he reached for Aurelie and brought her into a lung-crushing embrace. Then they reached down and made sure they kissed each of their children. When the processional began to play, the newly announced Clark family walked down the aisle as one.

Hearing the cheers and clapping of the guests, Dillion's crying jag began to dissipate, and pure joy enveloped him. He was ready to celebrate and have fun with his new family and friends. He didn't want to let go of Aurelie's hand, but people were crowding around to congratulate the new couple. He could not stop smiling, which was good because he was being summoned to the wooden archway that adorned the pier to begin the photo session. He understood that there would be days and maybe even weeks devoted to deciding on wedding photos, but Dillion recognized that no photo would capture Aurelie's essence this day. She was ethereal.

Chapter Thirty-Two

The wedding banquet was a farm to table feast. Roasted pork, mini red potatoes, artisan country white bread slathered in apple butter, roasted acorn squash slices drizzled with maple syrup, steamed green beans wrapped in bacon. The wedding cake was a compromise between his kids and his mother. She wanted something traditional. They wanted donuts. The baker took that crazy idea and turned it into a gastrointestinal masterpiece, an apple cider donut cake with mini donuts and eucalyptus adorning the three-tiered cake. The tables were dressed in wonderful thrift store finds of linen tablecloths and mismatched China and crystal. As the sun was setting, the outdoor bistro lights fitted with Edison bulbs lit the deck while hundreds of fairy lights shimmered in and out of the tulle and flower spray decorations.

Dillion couldn't remember the last time he had felt this happy. He couldn't believe how well his kids were behaving, even with all the mini donuts that they consumed. Oh well, in just a few more hours, he wouldn't have to worry about his kids. He and Aurelie would be leaving on their honeymoon, and the grandparents would have to deal with the sugar rush and crash.

Aurelie got the band back together for their final hurrah to play at their wedding and he was thrilled. Dillion was concerned that she would regret giving up so much of her life to be with him in his. But what he didn't know was that she had practiced with them to sing him a special song. "Dillion, when I first heard this song a few years ago, I thought it was interesting and I stored it away in my memory. Didn't think it was quite the right song for The Hot

Rockin' Horns. But then I met you, and I just knew that this song would fit somehow. I've asked my friends, here, to help me play it for you. Dillion Clark, this is my wedding gift to you. I love you!" Then she nodded to the band, and they started to play Brandi Carlile's haunting song, "The Story":

All of these lines across my face
Tell you the story of who I am
So many stories of where I've been
And how I got to where I am
But these stories don't mean anything
When you've got no one to tell them to
It's true…I was made for you

As Aurelie serenaded Dillion with the first verse, he started to tear up, thinking of what a tragic journey he had been on and how that grueling trek of illness, death, and grief somehow brought him to her. He cracked a smile and chuckled as she belted out the next two verses like the rock star she was.

I climbed across the mountain tops
Swam all across the ocean blue
I crossed all the lines and I broke all the rules
But baby I broke them all for you
Because even when I was flat broke
You made me feel like a million bucks
You do
I was made for you
You see the smile that's on my mouth
It's hiding the words that don't come out
And all of my friends who think that I'm blessed
They don't know my head is a mess
No, they don't know who I really am

And they don't know what I've been through like you do
And I was made for you …

Then Dillion's heart melted as Aurelie sung the final lyrics expressing how their lives make sense because they were made for each other.

All of these lines across my face
Tell you the story of who I am
So many stories of where I've been
And how I got to where I am
But these stories don't mean anything
When you've got no one to tell them to
It's true …I was made for you

When the song was done, Dillion practically leapt onto the stage, swept Aurelie into his arms, dipping her while kissing her with all the emotion he could give.

"Whoa, Dillion, you took my breath away. I guess you liked the song?" Aurelie asked in almost a whisper.

"You mended my heart. Thank you for the beautiful song. Thank you for being my wife. Thank you for loving me and my kids."

This time, it was Aurelie whose eyes misted, and she held him in such a bear hug that it was difficult to breathe. When she released him, she looked at him with her piercing green eyes and asked, "Wanna get outta here?" Ending her question with a sassy smirk.

Dillion felt the stirrings coming on and he knew exactly what she meant. "Absolutely."

After a whirlwind of goodbyes, putting their traveling gear in the minivan, they were off to spend their first night as a couple in a historical inn, just outside of Old World Wisconsin. The next evening, they would be taking their flight out of Chicago to Dublin for a 10-day honeymoon in Ireland.

When they arrived at the inn, the outdoor lights highlighted the stark white columns adorning the covered porch. The smell of a hardwood fire wafted from the chimneys. The female innkeeper welcomed and guided them to their romantic suite on the second floor. Dillion's anticipation for their wedding night began to wane as he heard the creaking of the floorboards with every step that landed on the oak staircase. *Great. Now everyone is going to hear us.* Dillion thought to himself. But when she opened the door, his frame of mind changed with the warmth and ambiance of the room. A low burning fire was crackling in the fireplace. Golden shapes danced on the lace curtains adorning the windows overlooking the Kettle Moraine forest. The deep, rich oak furnishings included a queen-size sleigh bed and an upholstered fainting couch and side chairs. The ensuite bathroom included a standalone shower as well as a two-person whirlpool bath. There were candles lit on side tables and in the bathroom. A large bouquet of flowers from the wedding were set beside a silver bucket filled with ice and champagne.

"If there is anything else you need, just let us know. The number is by the phone on the desk. We serve breakfast until 10:00 a.m. down in the dining room. But, if you'd like, just ring us and we'd be happy to deliver it to your room. Congratulations, Mr. and Mrs. Clark." The innkeeper smiled and closed the door behind her.

The newlyweds looked around the room and then at each other with an adolescent awkwardness about them. "I'll just put our luggage in the closet to get it out of the way," Dillion offered.

"Uh, yeah. Okay. Um, would you like some champagne?" Aurelie asked. Dillion thought he heard a little shakiness in her voice.

"Oh. Sure. Sounds great." When she offered him a flute, he took it from her hand, letting his fingers linger on her ring finger and her wedding band.

"Here's to us. The new Mr. and Mrs. Clark," Aurelie toasted. He took a deep drink of the sparkling golden liquid, hoping it would calm the nerves that came out of nowhere. But when he looked up at her, in front of the fireplace, he was in awe of the aureate aura that enveloped Aurelie in her form-fitted lace wedding dress and the shimmers flickering off her crystal headpiece.

He put down his glass and took hers as well. Next, he brought her hand to his mouth and brushed his lips against her knuckles and her ring. He heard her release a sigh and when he looked up, her eyes were closed but her red lips remained open. Nerves aside, he had to make love to her mouth right at that moment. He pulled her to him, placing his hands on either side of her face, drawing her closer still, until her lips were just a breath away. Using his tongue, Dillion outlined her crimson lips and ended with suckling her lower lip. That made her open her mouth further and press her body into his. She opened her mouth willingly and followed up with her tongue, begging to begin its intimate dance with his.

When they pulled apart to take a breath, he could feel her intense eyes penetrating into his soul. She pushed him ever so slightly away so she would be able to take off his jacket, undo his tie, and begin unbuttoning his shirt. Dillion couldn't tell if the shivers he felt were because of the anticipation of making love to his new wife, or sheer panic of not meeting her expectations as a lover. His desire for her was intensifying with every loose button. With every kiss, nip and lick Aurelie placed on his chest.

After his shirt lay on the floor, Dillion took the moment to ponder if he should begin to undress her. She guessed as much and turned around so he would have easy access to the zipper lying beneath the row of buttons lining her body from her shoulders to her hips. Instead, in a surprise move, Dillion reached up and ever so delicately began taking the hairpins out of her crystal crown, one at a time, placing them on a round table nearest them. When the last one was out, he deftly placed the headpiece on the table. Keeping her back to him, Dillion began massaging her head, spending particular time with circular massage motions where the crown and the pins had been moments before. He smiled hearing the soft mewling Aurelie was expressing and decided to add another technique that he perfected during Fourth of July fireworks. Using his hands, he skillfully tilted her head away from him so he could have access to her long, outstretched neck. Dillion faintly kissed every inch of it with the sensitivity of a feather. When he got to her ear, he whispered, "You look like a sexual goddess in that dress. But

I can't wait any longer. I want you. Now … " which he punctuated by sucking her earlobe into his mouth. The noise she made next made him wonder if she had already climaxed. Instead, she took her arms and reached behind him to squeeze his ass.

"Well," she said in a sensual voice, "you haven't seen what's under it yet." Curious, Dillion backed up so he could unzip her dress and what he found underneath stopped his heart and brought him to a level of hardness he had never experienced before. Aurelie adeptly stepped out of the dress, leaving it pool on the floor, turned around so he could see that she was wearing a white embroidered crop bustier and matching lace thong.

He pulled his hands through his hair, eyes wide open and expressed, "You are so damn hot!"

She laughed and walked closer to him. "I didn't think you were allowed to swear like that?" she asked coyly.

"What we do behind closed doors is our personal business. Plus, the way you look, Aurelie, damn it. It's warranted." He reached for her but this time, she held him off.

"Now it's my turn. What do you have hiding underneath those navy pants, I wonder?" Dillion felt those electric tingles that he had the first time they accidentally touched at the cancer event. She methodically loosened his belt, button, and unzipped the pants and just left them open like that for a moment, as she looked at his muscles inadvertently flexing for her, all of his muscles. "My, my. Mr. Clark, you are the sexiest priest I have ever met." With that statement, she shimmied his pants to the floor and paid significant attention to his matching navy silk boxers. "Silk boxers. You dressed to impress. Wow." She ran her hands up and down them until she stopped at the waistline.

"Wait," he held her hands in place. "Let me touch you now." She released his waist and let his hands explore each detail of the bustier, bending down to kiss each nipple through the lace. Then he turned her around and bent down to place hot, searing kisses on each of her cheeks. Though he was physically ready to consummate their marriage, his mind started having second thoughts. He pulled away and walked toward the glowing embers of the fire.

"What's wrong, Dillion?" She walked over to look into his face.

"Nothing's 'wrong.' It's just. I don't know how to say this."

"Say what?"

"It's embarrassing."

"Okay. As embarrassing as masturbating before our dates?" That got Dillion to laugh.

"Maybe not."

"Then it can't be that bad. Tell me."

"It's just a confidence thing. What if I don't meet your expectations? What if I don't please you?"

"Dillion, it's been two years since I've had sex with a man. I'm pretty nervous myself. I am afraid I'm not going to remember how to do this well." She took his hand and led him to the bed.

"Make love to me, Dillion. Show me how to make love to you." She began to unhook the fasteners for the bustier, while he pushed off his silk boxers. All that was left was her lace thong which she encouraged him to peel off.

She lay down on the soft bed and pulled him on top of her. His heart was racing as he maneuvered to find the sweet spot, which was wet, warm, and inviting. He slid inside of her which made them both groan in pleasure. He kissed her as if sucking her life force into his. He felt her hips grinding into him, and instinct took over. They found their rhythm which didn't take long to get up to speed. It excited him how vocal she was. It enticed him as the speed and intensity came to its pinnacle. An explosion of physical and emotional release between them as they climaxed together emancipated his doubts. Dillion smiled as he thought to himself, *this is going to be epic.*

After Dillion caught his breath, he leaned his forehead against Aurelie's, before saying, "Aurelie Clark, I love you." He saw her smile before she replied.

"I love you, Dillion Clark." She kissed him gently on his lips before speaking again, "And for the record, you have nothing to worry about. That was fantastic."

Dillion couldn't help himself. The little machismo he had increased his confidence two-fold and made him smile. "Well, that was my best and only move. Next time, you'll have to teach me a few new tricks that you enjoy." He carefully lifted himself off her and lay on his side totally amazed that he not only was gifted a second chance at love but he was now married to the sexiest woman alive. It felt too good to be true. Even if it wasn't, it didn't matter. Dillion was done playing it safe—always being the good guy and learning to be patient. He was going to ride this out as long as God offered it to him. He may be a nice, spiritual man during the day, but at night, he was going to enjoy learning how to be a bad ass to please his own, personal siren.

"Well, Dillion, I'll let you have a little bit of a break before I teach you a new trick." She rolled over on her side to face him and smiled. It was the kind of smile that reached her eyes and let him know that she was satiated, for now. He couldn't help himself. It had been more than two years since he made love to a beautiful woman and he didn't want to stop looking at her, touching her. He started by taking one of her loose curls and twisting it around his finger. Then he outlined her face and dragged his finger down her neck before landing on one of her taut nipples that was still sensitive from their love making moments ago. Aurelie's breath caught when he gave it a little pinch. *I'm going to touch every inch of this woman and memorize the places that excite her.* Next thing he noticed was she took one of her hands and began softly and adeptly moving from his temple to his mouth, down to his chest and pinched his nipple. It surprised him and yet it stirred something in him as well. However, he knew he needed to rest a bit before his first sex lesson. When she placed her hand on his abdomen, his muscles rippled in the anticipation of where she was headed, he knew he had to stop her, for now. Lifting her wandering hand to his lips he kissed each fingertip and landed one in her palm. "Being inside you was the first thing I couldn't wait to do when we got married."

"And the second?" She asked with a husky voice.

"The second is what I'm going to do with you right now." He gently turned her over on her other side, pulling her back into his front before wrapping his arms around her and kissing her tousled curls.

"Spooning?"

"Spooning."

"Huh, I've never spooned before."

He smiled and before drifting off to sleep he said to himself, *I just taught her a love lesson.*

Dillion was having one of those erotic dreams. He was back in college and scantily clad coeds were taking turns pleasing him. However, this particular dream was causing him to feel very real sensations. It took him a moment to sort out that wonderful space between his dream world and reality. Usually, he wanted to stay in the dream world as long as possible. Except this time, his body was being encouraged to behave as if it were a teen body having its first wet dream. He opened his eyes in an attempt to get a handle on the stirrings that woke him out of a deep sleep. What he found was even better than what was in his dream. There was his naked wife stroking him with one hand and touching herself with the other. He was in awe of what he saw. She must have gotten to the right moment, because next she straddled him before slowly lowering her very wet and excited body onto his rock hard one. It was a good thing he was still a bit drowsy, because with one swift movement, it could have been all over for him. She began to grind her hips into his while touching her own nipples in ecstasy. Her eyes were closed at first. Then she opened them and pulled his hands from the bed and put them on her breasts. It added to the level of excitement that she was taking the reins. Now the movement changed. She began gyrating in slow circles that had him going in and out of her. It was maddening. Dillion wanted the intensity to increase. He wanted to release into her. He took his hands and reached around to her ass and grabbed hard, pressuring her into a rhythm that he now controlled. Her eyes opened and he saw flashes of wickedness in hers as she shifted so that her hands were on either side of his head and she began pumping and grinding at a sinful pace. He knew he was losing degrees of control every time she pushed him deeper inside of her until he couldn't hold on any longer. His hips lifted off the bed as he screamed her name in passion, while feeling her contract around him in her own release.

Aurelie lay on top of him while he gently glided his fingers over her bare back. "Mmm. That feels good," she moaned.

"Not as good as what you just did to me." He felt her chuckle.

"That was sex lesson number one. Spontaneous sex."

"I thought I was having a dirty dream with sexy co-eds. Then I woke up and saw you touching yourself and feeling you touching me, and I was a goner."

"You did well my sexual apprentice. Now let's get a few more hours of sleep before we wake up for realsies."

Dillion kissed the top of her head before she slid off him. This time, she spooned him. And he smiled.

Chapter Thirty-Three

Dillion woke up to the delicious aromas of freshly brewed coffee and the spicy scent of cinnamon. Perhaps a cinnamon streusel coffee cake or cinnamon buns? His stomach made an audacious growl, waking up Aurelie. "What the hell was that?" she grumbled.

"Sorry, that was my stomach growling. My body isn't used to all this exercise," he grinned recalling the two strenuous workouts they had during the night. "It needs food."

"I need coffee."

"Did I marry a woman who isn't a morning person?"

"Just get me the coffee. I need a few more minutes," Aurelie pulled the pillow over her head, making Dillion laugh.

"Yes, dear." He located his overnight bag and rustled through it to find a pair of jeans and a T-shirt. He walked downstairs to discover the innkeeper putting together a breakfast tray for them. After some small talk, he brought up the tray and placed it on the round table so he could pour Aurelie a cup of that coffee she was desperately waiting for.

They enjoyed a breakfast of a substantial slice of egg casserole which had cheddar cheese, bacon, and onion in it, cups of fresh berries with whipped cream, and warm cinnamon streusel coffee cake slices. Dillion felt like he was in paradise. He married a beautiful and sensual woman, made love to her all night long, and woke up to this heavenly breakfast.

"I'm stuffed," Aurelie stated. "That was the best breakfast I think I've ever had."

"I have to agree. Can we keep her? You know, like Alice stayed with the Brady Bunch?"

"I think she may be a tad out of our budget. Unless Episcopal priests make a lot more money than they let on." Changing topics, "Can we try out that whirlpool bathtub before we leave?" Aurelie asked. "I'm going to miss sinking into my apartment's clawfoot tub. This one looks like it could be a close second."

"I tell you what, since you are still gloriously naked, and I have some clothing on, why don't you start it and I'll take these dirty dishes downstairs."

"Leave the coffee here, though. I don't think one cup was enough."

"Deal. By the way, while we're on our honeymoon, I am looking forward to having naked breakfast with you every morning."

She smiled and kissed him lightly on the lips. "That can be arranged. Wait a second. When the honeymoon is over, no naked breakfast? How come?"

"Kids. Remember?"

"Oh yeah. I almost forgot. Well, let's make the best of it while we can." She kissed him one more time and casually walked into the bathroom and started the bathwater.

By the time Dillion returned, Aurelie was already up to her chin in bubbles. He dropped his clothes on the floor and carefully climbed into the bath, opposite her. He was surprised at how much room they had to share. She grabbed a large sponge and poured liquid soap onto it. She moved toward Dillion and began to wash him, with bubbles and water slushing over his body. It was titillating, and yet tender. When she was done washing him, he returned the favor, savoring the intimacy of the moment. Then they just lay there, Aurelie resting her backside on his front, letting the jets pulsate against their muscles while the white noise from the jets lulled the newlyweds almost to a meditative state before the water cooled and it was time to check out of their room.

A few hours later, they arrived at O'Hare Airport to board a plane to Dublin, Ireland and to start their honeymoon. Dillion couldn't wait to see what sexual lessons his wife would have in store for him on the Emerald Isle.

The next morning, they landed on the tarmac on the outskirts of Ireland's capital city. Neither of them slept well on the plane, so they were a bit out of it when they disembarked. Luckily, the signage was in English, and they followed the crowd to get their luggage and to hail a cab. They heard horror stories from family and friends who attempted to drive in the largest city on the island. About an hour after landing, they arrived in front of their vacation luxury apartment overlooking Trinity College. Dillion couldn't tell if the tingling feelings he had were from exhaustion or being so close to the legendary Old Library's long room which houses literary masterpieces such as *The Book of Kells*. He knew that he'd see it soon enough during their walking tour of the college the next day.

Aurelie was the first to enter through the brightly painted kelly-green door and into the crisp, white hallway leading them into a modern twist of the old Irish townhome. Dillion followed her down the few steps that took them onto hardwood floors leading them to a white and silver galley kitchen. It overlooked the sitting room which was adorned with a large bay window and a beautiful view of the college campus. Off to the left was the efficient bathroom and a guest room with two twin beds. At the end of the hall was the master bedroom ensuite with sliding patio doors opening onto a small balcony that was fitted with a metal bistro table and two chairs.

"Wow, Dillion. Look at this! We have our own balcony."

"I'll see it in a minute. I just want to gawk at the view from this massive window for a few more minutes. Oh man, did you see we have a fireplace? This is amazing!"

Then he heard water rushing from the bathroom. "Not as amazing as this shower. Come here, Dillion. Let's christen this place and take a shower together. Don't you want to get out of your traveling clothes?"

His ears perked up and so did something else. All of a sudden it didn't matter that he was steps away from the most celebrated national treasure in Ireland. His wife was beckoning him to be with her in the shower. *The Book of Kells* would have to wait.

Dillion walked into the white marble bathroom and saw Aurelie's clothes piled up in the corner and her naked body behind the clear glass door of the shower. It took him only a few seconds to disrobe and walk in behind her. The steam and the hot water felt good on his skin, but she felt better. Being in the shower before him, she was already slick from the water running down her lean body. Turning herself around, she reached up, locked her arms around his neck and pulled him down for a long, lingering kiss, while her slippery, slender form slid up and down and around, his arousal increasing in intensity. He knew what her intention was but was naïve about how they would get there.

When Aurelie pulled away from the kiss, she found the body wash which she squeezed into the palm of her hand. Then she began massaging it on his chest, gliding down to his belly, before slithering her nimble fingers around him. At first, Dillion caught his breath in shock. But the rhythm of the motion and the intensity of the sensation took over and he closed his eyes before leaning his back onto the cooler marble wall. He was seeing colors behind his lids, with each shift in her holding and stroking pattern. "Do you like this?" Aurelie purred. Dillion was struck mum and could only groan his pleasure. "Good. Now it's your turn. Do me." He came to when he recognized she stopped touching him and was attempting cognitive recognition as to what she wanted. He must have looked like a deer in headlights because she smiled and giggled before moving him so they could trade places.

Aurelie put her hands on his shoulders while she carefully stepped so that her back was to the wall. Next, she looked deep into his eyes and said, "Give me your hand," which he did complacently. Aurelie took his middle finger and sucked it deep into her throat before taking it from her mouth and putting it into her. He found being inside her with his finger to be exciting and yet he was also nervous. He didn't want to hurt her. Dillion wanted to give her pleasure, hopefully at a level near to the ecstasy he just enjoyed.

Dillion carefully inserted his finger and heard her groan, "More," he deepened his penetration and felt her contract around it. He slowly pulled it out and then pushed it back inside her, wet and swollen. It was erotic and nerve racking at the same time. She began to wiggle before giving him another direction. Aurelie grabbed his finger and maneuvered it until Dillion could feel the tiny bud at her opening. "That's it," she moaned. Between her hips grinding and her soft mewls, he began to shift his titillating tactic to provide her with intensifying pleasure. Realizing that his own anxieties around underperforming were dissipating with every guttural sound his hedonistic wife was making; the intensity of his arousal was beginning to take over. His finger inside of her was no longer an option. He needed to be inside her. Now.

Though he was a novice in all things erotica, he let his imagination show him the way. Dillion lifted Aurelie so that her legs wrapped around his waist, and he glided into her warm wetness before letting his body's animalistic instinct take over. Dillion thrust into her with an intensity he couldn't control. It was manic. He was far beyond being concerned about his technique, at this moment he was driven to take her to the pinnacle point where reality and the dream realm blend together until he exploded into her like a willow firework. At his release he was thrilled to feel Aurelie's contractions match his and heard her own guttural release. Dillion couldn't help himself, he grinned. It may not have been perfect, but he managed to satisfy his very experienced wife with his very inexperienced lovemaking. A moment or two later, they uncoupled and quickly finished the rest of their shower before collapsing, damp, and naked onto the bed for a well-deserved nap.

Dillion could have slept the day away, except that he heard a gurgling and couldn't decipher if it was his stomach or Aurelie's. Slowly opening his eyes, he could tell that the midday sun had arrived and was streaming in through their patio doors. Aurelie began to wake as well, and he smiled when she patted her flat stomach. "I worked up a huge appetite, Dillion. Do you think we can get dressed and find something substantial to eat? I'm starving."

"I was just thinking the same thing. Let's get dressed and see what we can find." Around the corner from their apartment was a traditional Irish bar that served pub food. Aurelie ordered a ham and cheese toastie on sourdough, while Dillion got a slow roasted beef, cheddar, and horseradish sandwich on brown bread. They washed down the sandwiches with perfectly poured pints. After their sexual and hunger needs had been satiated, they decided to meander the streets of downtown Dublin. If Dillion were here on his own or with the kids, he would have likely had an itinerary and mapped out all the top tourist sites that Dublin has to offer. Instead, he was with Aurelie who didn't care for such things. Her free spirit encouraged her to amble around town and see where this or that winding path would lead them. Since they had no set plan or schedule to meet, Dillion was letting go and following Aurelie's zigzag pattern.

They found themselves crossing the Ha'penny Bridge over the River Liffey, in front of the infamous red Temple Bar where they went inside and ordered Irish whiskey. Then they strolled into the Avoca Wool Shop & Café for some browsing. Aurelie found their pre-cooked fare to be the perfect way to end the day by "cooking" at the apartment. They bought a small shepherd's pie, maple and grain parsnips, and carrots and a German Riesling. For dessert they couldn't agree, so Dillion picked out a rustic apple tart and Aurelie got a salted caramel chocolate brownie.

Back at the apartment, Dillion offered to warm up the dinner, while Aurelie lit the fire and found a streaming music station. They ate and spoke about all the interesting things and people they had seen during the day and talked about their plans for tomorrow. The newlyweds took their wine to the blue-gray plush sofa across from the fireplace and relaxed with Aurelie snuggling into the crevice of Dillion's arm. It was a perfect ending to a spontaneous day. He didn't know if the spontaneity could last once they got back home, it could lead to chaos and mass destruction. But here in Ireland, it was perfect.

After all the wine was drunk and desserts shared, Aurelie yawned. "I am getting tired again. I think I'm gonna get ready for bed."

"You go right ahead. I'll clean up first and meet you in there." He gave her a soft, but lingering kiss before heading to the kitchen with the empty plates and glasses.

When everything was put away and the fireplace turned off, Dillion made his way to the back bedroom. Even with the nap in the morning, he still was exhausted. He thought about the schedule for the next day, they had the walking tour of the college after lunch and then Aurelie booked them a haunted double decker bus ride after dinner. The good news was that they could sleep in before the schedule started.

As he entered the bedroom, he noticed candles were lit around the room and lying on top of the bed wearing a lusty face and a barely-there green and black lace, crotchless, backless teddy was Aurelie. He didn't need any words or additional signs as to what was on her mind. He was a ready and willing student. Dillion stripped and crawled into bed and on top of her. Letting the friction from the embroidered lace add a layer of rasping between his skin and hers. It would have been frustrating if it wasn't so hot. He couldn't wait for tonight's lesson.

Aurelie slowly and methodically made love to his mouth while gently rubbing her body against the lace and Dillion's heated skin. Then she lifted his head and pushed it down between her legs. "Lick me," she commanded. Dillion was nervous, but he trusted her to lead him to her pleasure points. He shifted the lace between her legs and thought about how he would lick an ice cream cone. It worked. He paid attention to her sighing and her hip movements to know where to place his tongue, how slow or fast and when she was getting ready to peak, he led himself into her quickly so that they could enjoy the explosive ride together.

Afterward, Aurelie lay with her head on his chest as they used their free hands to gently caress each other. Dillion could feel himself drift off to sleep, and it was the perfect ending to an unstructured day.

Chapter Thirty-Four

The smell of strong coffee roused Dillion from his deep sleep. The sun was streaming through the patio curtain, and he could see the shadow of his lovely bride sipping on her coffee while sitting at the bistro table. He wrapped himself up in the quilt from the bed and walked out onto the patio and breathed in the crisp autumn air before lightly kissing Aurelie on her crumb-cluttered lips. "Mornin,'" he mumbled.

"Morning. I woke up starving, so I got dressed and found a little coffee shop that also serves breakfast sandwiches and pastries. They are yummy! I brought back enough to share."

"Sounds great. You must have had a pastry with honey."

"How'd you know? It was so fluffy and sweet. It had an almond filling, toasted almonds and honey drizzled on top. So good!"

"I tasted the honey on your lips." He smiled and brought the hot coffee to his lips. "This is good coffee. Thanks, Aur, for breakfast." Dillion picked up an egg and cheese sandwich to eat with his coffee and ate the other almond pastry. "Looks like it's going to be a sunshiny day ahead."

After clearing away breakfast, Aurelie joined Dillion for a shower. *This is my new favorite tradition,* Dillion thought to himself as he lathered lavender bath wash over Aurelie's perky breasts.

On the streets of Dublin, the hustle and bustle of the businessmen and women were abound. Once they arrived on the Trinity College campus, the hustle and bustle was still evident, but instead of cars, double decker busses, and suited adults with brief cases and umbrellas, there were hordes of students wearing jeans and hoodies with backpacks instead of brief cases and riding bikes instead of inside mini cars and double decker busses.

Dillion became noticeably more excited the closer they got to campus. "What's with you? You're acting like a teenage girl?" Aurelie teased.

"I can't help it, Aur. Coming here has been a dream of mine since I knew I was going to be a priest. I am so excited to finally be able to view *The Book of Kells* in person!"

"You keep saying that, but I don't know what it is, exactly."

"Well, it is a lavishly decorated manuscript of the gospels written and decorated in gold leaf that's more than 1,000 years old."

"Whoa. That's impressive. But why is seeing it in person so important to you?"

"I don't know how to describe it, exactly. But it feels like I'm on a pilgrimage to see an artifact from the beginning of Christianity in my ancestral home. It feels important. Does that make sense?"

"I sort of understand. It's like if we went to London and walked across Abbey Road, recreating the Beatles album cover, I would expect to feel something transcendent during the experience."

"Exactly. I don't know how it will make me feel to be that up close to this important religious relic, but the anticipation has got me all giddy, as you said, like a schoolgirl." Aurelie grabbed his hand and squeezed.

"Then let's get going. We don't want to be late to our date with the most famous book in Ireland."

Aurelie and Dillion joined the group gathered around a young, sprightly woman with bouncy red hair and freckles on her nose dressed in a Trinity College rain jacket. "Welcome to Trinity College, everyone," she greeted in her Gaelic lilt. "My name is Saoirse, and I'll be your guide today. Trinity College was founded by charter of Queen Elizabeth I in 1592 …" Dillion attempted to listen to their well-versed tour guide, but he couldn't pay attention to her when all his senses were tingling looking out onto the campus and seeing the centuries old stone buildings and thinking about all of the history and prolific advancements in literature that occurred behind these walls.

"As we enter the Old Library, built between 1712 and 1732, it is the oldest surviving building on campus. Since 1801, the library has the right to claim a free copy of all British and Irish publications. By 1850, the shelves were completely filled with books and so in 1860, the roof was raised to form what we currently see in the Long Room as a barrel-vaulted ceiling and gallery bookcases. The Long Room is almost 65 meters long and houses 200,000 of the Library's oldest books."

Dillion stopped breathing as he entered The Long Room. He was in complete awe of the majesty of the dark wooden room adorned with marble busts of the most influential philosophical, political, and prolific writers in the world, such as Sir Isaac Newton, Homer, and William Shakespeare. Aurelie left his side to stand and marvel in front of Ireland's oldest surviving harp, which is said to be from the 1500's.

"Follow me, please to the next room to see *The Book of Kells*. They just turned the pages, so you are one of the first people to see these pages this year."

Dillion couldn't contain himself, "How often do they turn the pages?"

"Every three months," Saoirse's lilt made the word "three" sound like "tree" and it got a smirk from Aurelie. Dillion felt a warmth envelope him when looking at the delicate, intricate designs and the decorative calligraphy. He felt his spirit fill with absolute certainty that he was supposed to be here. As if it renewed his calling to the priesthood. Dillion felt closer to God in this moment, in front of this ninth century document authored by Irish monks than he did during his own ordination ceremony. Tears began to well up in his eyes, so much so that he had to step away so as to not drip tears onto the glass protective case over the missives.

The rest of the day was spent meandering in and out of storefronts, pubs, and talking about what they'd seen. After a dinner of bangers and mash, they walked to their double decker tour bus, for the haunted tour. The windows were adorned in blood red velvet curtains and the three tour guides, or story tellers, offered guests a nuanced history lesson with a macabre sense of humor. They learned about Dracula's Dublin origins, haunted houses, and famous haunted steps on Dublin's oldest street. Finally, culminating with a visit to St. Kevin's Graveyard to provide a body-snatching lesson enlisting Aurelie as a young victim and awarding her a T-shirt for her bravery. Exhausted by the time they arrived at their rental, Aurelie and Dillion sat in front of the fireplace, each sipping Irish whiskey while Dillion finger combed through Aurelie's curls, lulling her to sleep on his lap.

The next morning, they picked up their rental car and headed south into the Wicklow Mountains where a renovated stone cottage was waiting for them to enjoy. They arrived at the cottage during a break in the weather so they could peruse the gardens, and grassy meadows surrounding it. The cottage itself was a simple whitewashed plaster with a metal roof, but inside, it was a dream for Dillion. The far walls were made of now, graying stone pitched to partner with golden wooden trusses, and tongue and groove ceiling. Overstuffed chairs and a loveseat were comfortably stationed in front of a small wood stove. A rounded archway led to the single bathroom with a shower and the bedroom housing a queen bed and a skylight overhead bringing in a plethora of natural light. The minimalist kitchen was perfect for warming up simple suppers. Chunky afghans were artistically thrown around the cottage offering warmth and comfort even during the most miserable weather.

After the long drive, and a check on the weather, they decided to go for a hike in the Wicklow Mountains National Park, the largest and only national park on the east coast of Ireland. Dillion didn't know much about the flora and fauna of the area, but he was completely enamored with all the different shades of greenery and the sheer magnitude of flowering shrubs that adorned the hiking paths.

Arriving back at the stone cottage, they were too tired to make a large meal, so they took turns in the shower and putting together an evening meal of meats, cheeses, fruits, bread, butter, and artisan bread along with a bottle of wine to take out to the grassy meadow on the top of their mountain oasis so they could eat while watching the sun set over the mountain range.

Dillion, wearing lounge pants and long sleeve shirt, felt equally comfortable and emotional lying on his back on the soft grass with Aurelie, in a linen long-sleeve shift laying in his arms with one of the chunky afghans over the top of them. It may have been the full contentment he felt after a comfort food feast. Or the love and serenity he felt for his new wife and the intimacy they shared. But he recognized that this night was the first time he was seeing a true Irish gloaming and it was awe inspiring. The sky was a soft spectacle of gentle heather with hushed tones of blue, rose blush, and lavender. Dillion was verklempt with all of these powerful feelings rushing into his soul. He must have made a sound, because Aurelie lifted her head from the crevice of his shoulder and began caressing him with feather-like kisses on his eyes, cheeks, and lips. "I'll love you forever, Dillion," she whispered.

Aurelie's affirmation shifted his sleepy contentment to an immediate need to be inside her. Dillion pushed down his lounge pants and pulled her on top of him. Silently, they began their rhythm of lovemaking, slowly and in small circles until his sensations intensified. He placed his hands on her breasts and kept his eyes open to watch the fascinating way his muse's emerald-green eyes would cloud as his penetration deepened, reaching for the pinnacle state where they'd both climax. He could now tell when that moment would be and focused his own energy on joining her. They shuttered, not from the cold that was beginning to creep in as the sun was going down, but from the utter liberation felt during their united release.

That night, they lay quietly under a down comforter, looking up at the star-filled sky through the skylight until sleep overtook them.

The next morning, Dillion was a bit disturbed. "Hey, Aur, can you come here for a moment?"

"I'm kinda busy right now. Can it wait?"

"Not really. Seriously, I need your help. Can what you are doing wait?"

"I'm writing postcards. I thought you were going to the bathroom. What do you need?"

"I need you to check my ass."

"I've seen it. It's gorgeous."

"Seriously."

"I take your ass very seriously. It's gorgeous."

"Ugh. Seriously, Aur, I need you to check it. I think I have something on it and I can't see it or reach it. Can you just come here?"

"Fine." Dillion didn't know what it was, but he had leaned back to scratch and felt something on his buttock that shouldn't be there. But it was in that awkward position that he could sort of see it and feel it, but he couldn't get to it.

"Um, it looks like a tick."

"A tick? In Ireland? On my ass? What the hell! Get it off!"

"I'll try, but I didn't pack any tweezers. I'll have to try to get it with just my fingernails. Hold on. I think I ... almost ... have it." Just then, he felt a scratch and then a release but something else he couldn't quite figure out.

"Did you get it?"

"Oh God."

"What? Is it gone? What?"

"It ... it"

"Is it out? What's wrong?"

"Oh God, move, Dillion. Move! I'm gonna be sick."

He knew that voice so he moved to the side so she could get to the toilet and sure enough, she was right. This time, he had to be there to help her. Lightly rubbing her back while she heaved, and then grabbing a washcloth to run under cold water to apply to her face, it was like muscle memory for all the times he'd been there for Corinne when she was sick.

"How are you feeling now?" he asked after she'd accepted the cold washcloth.

"A little better. Thanks. Sorry about that."

"No worries. What happened though? What made you sick?"

"The tick, when I was trying to scratch it off of your butt, it exploded and it went into my mouth and I just started to gag and, well, you saw the rest."

"Oh, Aur. I'm so sorry. Can I help you anymore?"

"No. I'm fine. Honestly. Let me just brush my teeth, tongue, and wash my face and hair again and I'll be fine."

They spent the rest of the day being lazy, with on and off rainstorms and not sure if Aurelie's stomach would settle enough to do any touring, it seemed best to lounge around.

The next morning, they packed up and traveled to Waterford to tour the crystal factory. As a memento, Dillion bought Aurelie a crystal vase with a tulip beveled mouth-rim and a Celtic knot etching in the body that the engraver confirmed symbolized family. The engraver signed the foot of the vase and etched their wedding date on the opposite side of his signature. Aurelie picked out crystal snowflake and angel ornaments to give as thank you gifts to their mothers for staying with the kids and Mumford during their honeymoon.

They drove the short distance to their next cottage, nestled in the Knockmealdowns, Galtee mountains & the Comeraghs. This cottage sported a king-sized bed, a unique amenity for any Irish rental. The walls were whitewashed inside and out, complimenting the brandished dark exposed beams and rafters of the ceiling. Though Dillion wasn't a big fan of the teal cupboards in the kitchen, Aurelie loved their funky feel.

The owners of the farm arranged for Aurelie and Dillion to have a trail ride through the mountains before a picnic of Irish coffee and biscuits beside the lake for afternoon tea.

That night, Dillion was so sore from the trail ride that Aurelie suggested they give each other massages in front of the fireplace. It felt both relaxing and sensual at the same time. She used essential massage oils with scents of orange and peppermint. He was a bit surprised that she turned it up a notch by rolling him over onto his back so that she could massage his neck, shoulders, chest, abdomen, and his growing need. Even though she had been touching him there daily, by adding massage oils to her routine, it was proving to be difficult for him to contain his exhilaration for her new technique. It was time to change things up, so he could make sure she had time to enjoy her own massage.

Dillion pulled away her hands and non-verbally communicated to her that it was his turn to massage her. She lay on her back first while Dillion poured an ample amount of massage oil into his hands. He began with her neck and watched her go limp as he released tension from her trap muscles. Next, he moved in circular motions to her shoulders and her breasts, paying close attention to her nipples. Rolling them between his finger and thumb until she moaned and began to move as if to position him to be inside of her. But Dillion knew that there was more pleasure he could give her, enhance their intimacy before he claimed her. He moved to her abdomen and her hips before sliding a finger inside of her and finding her nub to caress simultaneously. He smiled as he felt her lift her hips up to meet his hand and cry out to him. "Oh God, Dillion. Oh yes! Shit, I want you now. Please." He knew it was an ego thing, but he couldn't help it. He was enjoying her begging for him, but he still had more to do.

His finger left her in pleasurable agony as he moved to her thighs and released the tightened muscles from gripping the horse's sides all afternoon. Next, he moved to her calves and her feet, releasing the tension in her instep and within each toe.

It was then he motioned her to roll over on her stomach. Just looking at her perfectly toned ass was making him hard again. Dillion poured more oil onto his palms and began the whole process all over again beginning at her neck, working her shoulders, having his thumbs straddle her spine while his legs were straddling her. When he got to her ass, he lifted himself up to get into a better position.

However, Aurelie had different plans. She scooted out from under him and lifted herself onto all fours. Dillion was confused.

"I want you now, Dillion Clark. I want you to take me from behind." Dillion was flummoxed. He had no clue what to do, how to enter her without hurting her. She sensed his hesitation and shifted position so that she looked like a cat stretching, while taking her free hand to insert her finger where she wanted him to go.

"Seriously? Won't I hurt you?"

"Yes, I'm very serious. No, you won't hurt me. This is my favorite position. Take me. Now."

Dillion's nerves moved over for his new urge, an animalistic impulse to seize her from behind. He slowly entered her where she showed him and felt a whole new set of sensations around him. She was tighter and yet, with massage oils slickening his hardness, it was a smooth ride gliding inside her.

"Deeper. I want to feel you deep inside me." He slowly continued his journey so that the tip of him felt like it was touching her throat. But when he went as far as he could go, she backed up a bit more and he was in heaven. "Oh God, yes. That's it. Mmm. That feels so good. Now take me. Take me hard!"

Dillion couldn't think. Instinct took over and he grabbed her hips and rocked her world. He couldn't tell if it was her screaming or him yelling "YES! YES! YES!" as they came together in pure hedonistic ecstasy. Dillion was exhausted as he fell on top of Aurelie after their climax. He kissed her neck as he asked, "Aurelie, what the hell are you doing to me? You're making an animal out of me. That was amazing! I didn't know it could feel like this."

She gave a husky chortle, "I'm your lover. Your instructor in the sexual arts. You just got yourself an A+ on this assignment."

This time, Dillion chuckled hoarsely. "Well, I would have done better in school if I had instructors like you and assignments like this." He rolled off her and onto his side so that he could kiss her lovingly on the mouth, then lightly suckled each nipple before landing a kiss between her legs.

"Oh, oh boy, I'm way too sensitive down there right now. Just lay next to me, please. I need to catch my breath."

"As you wish," Dillion kissed her again between her legs, each nipple and her mouth before laying down with her by his side in the fire's glow. Could life get better than this?

Chapter Thirty-Five

Trading dinner for a sexual massage session the night before, the newlyweds opted for a full farm-fresh breakfast at the farmhouse with the owners. They had Irish tea with cream and sugar, crispy toast with marmalade, Irish bacon and sausages, fried potatoes, eggs, grilled tomatoes, and baked beans. They also opted for a big breakfast because they had at least a four-hour drive to their next stop, Doolin.

When planning the trip, Aurelie requested they stop in Doolin because it is known as a global music hub. Once, when her parents were vacationing in Ireland, her mom told her there were just as many pubs as recording studios in this small town and there were no ATM's. They had to go to a nearby town to get some cash.

The west coast of Ireland is some of the most beautiful country Dillion had ever seen. The waves from the Atlantic Ocean welcomed surfers from all over as locals fish off the edges of cliffs as high as 700 feet from sea level! When they arrived at the cottage, Aurelie was like a little girl, shrieking in excitement. "Oh Dillion! It's perfect. Look at the bright red gate and door against all that white washing. It's like a traditional cabin but with attitude. I can't wait to see what it looks like inside." Dillion barely parked at the end of the gravel drive before Aurelie flew out of the car, opened the red painted gate. "Jesus! Dillion, honey, you've got to see this! It's like our own secret garden in here. It is so quaint and beautiful. Come here!"

Dillion decided to leave their luggage for the moment as his wife was practically hysterical with excitement. He walked up to the knee-high stone wall that separated the cottage from the road and through the red iron gate. Aurelie grabbed his hand and began pointing out the varieties of flowering plants that welcomed them in a wide range of colors and sizes: sunny, scarlet rose blooms, vivid violet butterfly bushes, hens, and chicks peeking in between crevices of the rock wall, while various varieties of violets and violas spilled over rounded pots and weathered wooden barrels. "I can't wait to see the inside," Aurelie exclaimed as she unlocked the door. What she found inside fed her enthusiasm.

The red door was an old-fashioned Dutch door that when opened from the inside, could have the bottom stay shut while the top of the door could let in the fragrant fresh air of the gardens and the seaside. To the left was an efficient kitchen with natural pine cupboards and a white porcelain farm sink below a four-paneled window looking out into the backyard and the cliffs. A weathered hutch was brought to life as the host to a full set of China in a cheerful floral pattern. It was apparent that a stonecutter had crafted the fireplace wall from the same gray stones that made up the outside wall. The ancient hearth, which likely saw hundreds of years of peat fires, now held a cast iron wood stove. Nearby sat a single red plaid chair adorned with a chunky off-white throw, with its high back near a simple window in which the midday sun was casting its rays onto the chair's warm fabric. Placed in the corner, was an acoustic traveling guitar and a bodhrán, a traditional Irish hand drum.

Across from the stone fireplace was a simple pine coffee table stained similar in color to the hardwood floors throughout the cottage. A currant-colored oriental rug adorned the floor between the table and the ruby-colored sofa which was placed dead-center of the single, white-washed plaster wall. On either side of the wall were pine doors, one led to the bathroom while the other led to the bedroom that offered a queen-sized bed overlooking the backyard garden. The barrel ceilings throughout the cottage were accented with brandished, exposed beams.

After their four-hour drive, Dillion smiled to himself because his new bride read his mind. They made sweet, simple love on their bed before taking a well-deserved afternoon nap. Aurelie's growling stomach woke Dillion up from a deep sleep. "I'm hungry. Do we have anything left to eat?" she asked.

"Um. I don't think so. But we passed several pubs in town. Why don't we freshen up and grab some pub food?"

"Perfect. And don't let me forget to bring the guitar, you know, in case they have a jam session tonight."

The night air was a bit cooler, so Dillion changed into a gray long sleeved shirt and his fleece. Aurelie wore a green long-sleeved shirt, down vest, and a green tweed herringbone Irish cap to cover her untamed curls. "Hey, I thought you bought that hat for your dad?"

"Well, these curls won't behave, he's not here and I'm sure not gonna tell him. Are you?"

Dillion laughed, tousled her crazy ebony curls before flipping the hat on backwards and kissing her lovingly on the mouth. "I'm not going to tattle on his favorite daughter. I just got into this family. I need to stay in his good graces a little longer." Aurelie swung the guitar over her shoulder and held Dillion's hand while they walked down the stony path toward Doolin's town central. With a population of only about 500, Doolin is a darling little village mid-point along the Wild Atlantic Way, that offers visitors easy access to the Cliffs of Mohr, the Aran Islands, and a myriad of pubs and recording studios where a global musical collective come to play and enjoy traditional Irish music. They ended their stroll at the entrance of Gus O'Connor's Pub which has been serving visitors and welcoming musicians since 1832. The Clark's entered the two story stone tavern through its black and gold old-style entrance and were met with a warm Irish hello from the hostess who led them passed the stone hearth to a table near the makeshift stage. A young lass took their order for two pints, a crock of fresh Atlantic mussels cooked in a wine and garlic sauce and served with brown bread.

"I see yer holdin' a guitar. Planning on playin' tonight?" she asked of Aurelie with her Irish lilt.

"I'm a little nervous, but I'd like to. How does it work? Do I have to sign up or something?"

"Nah. You just go on up when you're good and ready. It's still a little early, but it looks like a few of ta regulars are headin' up tere now." Dillion saw a young man with a bodhrán and a silver-haired gentleman in a tweed Irish cap bring his tin whistle and grab a bar stool to sit on while playing into the microphone. Dillion could tell Aurelie was just itching to get up there and play.

"Go on, Aur, what are you waiting for?"

"Oh, I don't know, a little liquid courage maybe? I don't know any Irish songs. I don't want to screw it up." Just then, the lass brought their pints.

"Still here, are ya? Well, maybe a pint'll do ya good. It's just Gus and his grandson, Rory, playing around. They would'na mind a pretty lass like yourself join' 'em."

Aurelie took a large drink and then asked, "What is the song they're playing?"

"Tisn't any song, at all. It's craic."

"Excuse me?"

"You haven't heard of 'craic'?"

"I don't think so."

"Well, it's just having fun. Enjoying, celebrating, playing around. What Gus and Rory are doing is just craic."

Aurelie nodded, "Oh, I get it now. Thanks."

"Go on up tere and show 'em what you've got." The Irish barmaid smiled, twirled, and left the table. Aurelie took another deep drink before getting up.

"Wish me luck." She kissed Dillion before she left.

"Nope. Wishing you craic."

"Is that how you're supposed to use it in a sentence?" She giggled.

"I don't have a clue. Give'm hell, Aur!"

Aurelie left the table with guitar in hand. At the end of the last "song," she asked the musicians if she could join and they welcomed her on stage. Dillion could see they were walking her through their next piece and he decided to grab his phone to take a video to share with the kids back home. Home. He couldn't believe he'd been away from his kids for almost 10 days, the longest he'd been away from them ever. He got a guilt punch in the gut, but then he heard Aurelie and her new friends begin a song, or whatever it was. In the middle of it, a young woman with long blonde hair joined them as she played violin. Dillion forgot to be sad as a new emotion enveloped him. It was pride. His young bride was up on a global stage, entertaining a pub full of locals, tourists, and musicians and she was keeping up with the best of them.

When their food was delivered, Dillion waved to get her attention and she left the stage to a crowd of cheers. Her cheeks were rosy and the gold flecks in her emerald eyes sparkled in excitement. "Aur, you were amazing up there! How'd it feel?"

"God, I miss playing in front of an audience. It was fantastic! The guys were so nice, gave me a quick lesson on the chords they were gonna play and then it was off to the races. I just followed their lead. Did you see that violinist?"

"Yes, I did," he managed to get in while he spooned mussels into a shallow bowl.

"She's from South Africa! Can you imagine?"

"Unbelievable. You guys were so good, I took a few videos to share with the fam back home. You'll be a celebrity in Minocqua."

"Yeah, yeah. Minocqua. Huh. That's coming up. Our honeymoon is almost over, isn't it?"

"Yup. Just a few more days and then we fly back and start our new life together with the kids."

"Whoa. It's not like we didn't talk about them, or find things that reminded me of them, but now it's so close."

"I know. I felt the same way when I thought about taking the video. This is the longest I've been away from them. Ever."

"Oh, Dillion. I'm so sorry. I'm being insensitive. How are you doing? Missing them, of course. Wanna talk about it?"

"Honestly, I did have a guilty gut moment. And then I saw you performing and the food came, and I realized that I want to enjoy this alone time with you, and I don't want to waste it. Because when we get home, I can't guarantee how much alone time we're gonna get. It'll be instant family for you. I really hope you don't freak out and leave me because we're too much to deal with."

Aurelie put down her spoon and pulled his face close to hers. He could feel her eyes piercing into his to make her point. "Dillion Clark. I have been a high school band teacher for almost 10 years. That's hundreds of horny, hormonal, high schoolers that I had to manage and attempt to get legible music out of on a daily basis. If I can handle that crazy crew, I can sure as hell manage three measly little preacher's kids and a giant dog." She kissed him hard on the mouth before going back to her mussels and brown bread. When their server came back to take the dirty dishes, they had decided on trying out the decadent dessert menu. Dillion went rogue and wanted to try Eton Mess, a meringue and raspberry dish while Aurelie went for the gusto and ordered a Bailey's cheesecake.

The newlyweds spent the evening refreshing their drinks, Aurelie periodically jumping up to play a few songs, and then together attempting an Irish jig or two, and slow dancing. When the pub pushed everyone out, Dillion and Aurelie hit the cold Atlantic air with shock. It helped them become a bit more aware of their surroundings, but they did find themselves swaying into rock walls and back onto the road until Aurelie spotted the little red cottage gate.

As they entered the quaint cottage, clothes began to fly and fall into a trail of sorts leading to the bedroom. When they reached the bed, Aurelie took the lead and pushed Dillion onto his back before mounting him. Dillion couldn't tell if the room was spinning because he was drunk or because of the force his wife was using to kiss and ride him into sexual frenzy. He joined her in an orgasmic howling that left them limp and exhausted. He fell asleep to her soft snores as she lay on his torso.

The next morning he woke up to brown bread, butter, marmalade, and strong coffee presented to him on a tea tray. "Good morning, husband. I found a few things in the pantry to help make some semblance of a breakfast."

"Mmmorning, wife. What's this? Breakfast in bed? Did I give another A+ performance last night?"

Laughing, Aurelie responded, "Yes, and the fact that you encouraged me to get up on that stage and play. Honestly, that was the most special moment of my musical career, Dillion. You have no idea how much that meant to me."

"Well, after your 'performance' in bed last night, I think we're even." He laughed at his own joke before reaching for the coffee and taking a bite of the fresh bread and jam.

When they arrived at the ferry later that morning, the wind was cold and strong while the skies were full of dark gray clouds. It was their last full day in Doolin before they took the drive to Shannon where their plane would depart in 72 hours. Thirty-five minutes of rough seas on the ferry and Aurelie was looking a bit pale.

"You okay?"

"I'll be fine once I'm off this ferry and onto land. I'm a little seasick."

They departed onto Inishmore, the largest of the Aran Islands and the home of the Aran Sweater Market. They wore their fleece lined rain jackets and hiking boots to prepare for the weather but were not prepared for the strong fish stench that permeated every breath they took outdoors. He could see that Aurelie was fading fast, so Dillion recommended they stop and warm up in one of the restaurants on the island. He ordered coffee for himself and a chamomile tea for Aurelie along with a warm loaf of brown bread, butter, and some homemade marmalade.

Once warmed and fed, Aurelie perked up, so they headed out to the Aran Sweater Market, famous for their handcrafted fisherman's sweaters not only for their intricate designs but because they are made with wool that withstands water to keep the wearer warm and dry. They found sweaters for themselves and one for each of the kids. Dillion was hoping to get a family photo in the backyard with the matching sweaters. He wanted to surprise Aurelie with a large, framed print to give to her for Christmas to help her feel more at home in the ranch house.

After shopping, they still had several hours to fill before the ferry would be back to pick them up, so they decided to walk around the island. Though it was still cold, wet and the smell of fish was constant, Aurelie seemed to be managing it better by midday. They followed the unmarked roads and the short stone walls that made a maze of the island. Sometimes their path led to something surprising like a herd of sheep, or a stone church. Other times, it felt like they were going in circles. Dillion didn't care, he was just enjoying spending this day with his new wife and talking about anything that came into their minds.

When the ferry finally arrived, Aurelie's hands were so cold that no amount of holding them was making any difference. Dillion found a bench inside the ferry to try to get her warmed up. It sounded like a great idea, but instead it just made her feel worse. The choppy seas had the little boat rocking every which way. Aurelie couldn't keep it together any longer, sprang up and focused on making it to a railing so she could throw up. Which she did. A lot. Though the ferry was full, there seemed to be a wide berth between the Clarks and the rest of the travelers.

Once they arrived in the little red cottage, Dillion helped Aurelie with all of her wet clothes and made sure she could get into the shower. Then he tended to a fire in the wood stove before making some hot chamomile tea and toast for a makeshift dinner.

All wrapped up in the chunky throw while sipping tea on the red sofa, Aurelie spoke. "Oh Dillion, I'm so sorry I ruined today for us. I didn't want to get sick."

"It's okay, honey. Honestly. It wouldn't be a family vacation without a fight or someone getting sick. Hey, we made it this long. I'd say our honeymoon was a complete success."

"You are so good to me. I don't know what I ever did to deserve someone like you. I hope you stick around. I'm feeling kinda spoiled."

By the next morning, Aurelie was feeling much better but a bit weak. Dillion was the doting husband; it was almost like muscle memory for all those times he had to take care of Corinne during her cancer journey.

Their trip to Shannon was uneventful, but just in case, they stayed put in their hotel room and used the time to leisurely organize and pack. Their flight to Chicago was also uneventful, except for a bit of turbulence over the ocean. Though Aurelie didn't get sick, she didn't look well either. Dillion made the spontaneous decision to grab a hotel room close to the airport to let Aurelie's stomach settle and for both of them to get one last good night's sleep.

The hotel room did the trick and Aurelie was ready to get back on the road the next morning. They arrived at Aurelie's childhood home to see her parents one last time and to drop off the thank you gifts for her parents. The sky was a radiant robin's egg blue this day, and Dillion could smell autumn in the air. Dr. and Mrs. Beres were out the door before Aurelie and Dillion were out of the car. "Oh Mon Cheri! How was it? We've missed you. The children missed you. Did you have a great time? How long can you stay? I'm sure you've got to go to get up north before it gets dark. How are you?" Bea rattled off her list of questions and comments without even a breath in between. Dillion had to laugh.

"Dillion, how are you? How was your trip?" Antoine reached out to give Dillion a handshake and hug.

"It was amazing. It was better than I had built it up in my mind. I hope someday we can go back there and bring the kids." He was going to say more but he heard something that stopped him cold in his tracks.

"My sweet Aurelie, you are not ill. You're pregnant. Congratulations, Mon Cheri!"

"W-what?" Aurelie stuttered, stupefied.

"All Beres women have to do is just blink, and they get pregnant. I can see it on you. You are glowing. Congratulations to both of you. You will be a wonderful mother, Aurelie. You were made for this. Welcome to the next chapter of your life, Mon Cheri. Motherhood."

Chapter Thirty-Six

"Does it show anything yet?" Aurelie could hear Dillion talking through the bathroom door in her old apartment.

"Not yet. I just peed on the stick. It'll take a few minutes." What the hell was happening to her? Aurelie's head was spinning. She never had regular periods, but with all the sex she'd had, she had never once gotten pregnant. Then she went without sex for two years and BAM! She's fertile Myrtle? Well, technically, she still wasn't sure if she was pregnant. But there was a chance she was. She and Dillion were so excited to be together. It was their honeymoon for Christ sake! They were supposed to be spontaneous. And they were so many times that Aurelie lost count.

"How about now?" Dillion asked. Aurelie looked down at the stick and stared. Her breath caught and her stomach did a little flip. She slowly opened the door, still looking at the stick until she felt Dillion's omnipresence in front of her. She could actually feel his anxious energy, and it was making her all jittery. She looked up at him and realized she couldn't speak, so she just shook her head *yes* and showed him the stick results.

"Oh my God. Oh God. Jesus. We're gonna have a baby. Aur, you're going to have a baby!" As Aurelie was trying to process everything, she heard Dillion's voice permeate her fugal state. She gazed at him with her eyes wide as a Big Eyes painting by Margaret Keane. Dillion's own were brimming with tears, which was confusing at first because she wasn't sure if they were tears of joy or fear. But then he came into her space and enveloped her with one of his magical hugs. The kind of hug that pushes everything outside of its protective bubble and just allows them to be present in their love.

"I'm pregnant," Aurelie whispered. "I'm really pregnant."

"Yes, yes you are, Aur. I love you so much. So much." Dillion pulled back and kissed her full on the mouth. The tingles she felt earlier in her stomach shifted into tingles of another sort and into different places. But she was not ready for THAT right now. When he realized she was still in shock, Dillion slowly pulled away and took her to sit on the old green sofa in the front room. "Here you go. I'm sorry, you probably need to sit down right now. How do you feel? Are you okay?"

Aurelie took a moment to assess her environment and what had just happened. "I think I wanna lay down for a few moments." She slowly got off the old couch and lay on the worn carpet. Dillion followed her lead and lay on his side next to her. They both placed a hand on her flat belly and simply lay still. Aurelie didn't know what to say at first, but then she found comfort in not saying anything. She examined the apartment she'd been living in for the past two years. It still appeared the same in the way that it had the same paint job, carpeting, curtains, and furniture, but it was different because all of her things weren't in it any longer. The final items were in the back of the vehicle ready to go to her new home, with her new family, in Minocqua.

During the plane and car ride to her parent's home, she used that time to begin processing the fact that she was now an official stepmother to Dillion's children and a priest's wife. So much responsibility in such a short time. But that is what she wanted. Her heart knew what it wanted, and she was still spontaneous enough to follow it. But this pregnancy was a whole other ballgame. They hadn't really talked about when to expand the family. Of course, she always thought she'd be a mom someday and her own mother was right. Beres women got pregnant with a change in the weather, the blink of an eye, a suggestive look. *Well,* Aurelie thought to herself, *I never liked playing by the rules. I have always been spontaneous. This is just that. At a higher level. I can do this. I will do this. We will* do this. *Together.* At that moment, Aurelie squeezed Dillion's hand, looked into his eyes that went from joyful to concern.

"We're gonna have a baby, Dillion."

He paused and cautiously responded, "Yes."

"I'm so blessed. Thank you, Dillion. I love you." She rolled to her side, lifted her head to meet his and kissed him warmly. A kiss that expressed her ultimate joy and love for their family and this baby.

"No, I'm the one who's blessed, Aurelie. Thank you for coming into my life. I didn't realize I could ever feel this alive again. And now you are carrying our baby. A child we can bring into this world together. I am SO lucky that you chose me to be your husband. So lucky. He embraced her with the essence of eternal gratitude. Then he bent down to kiss her belly. "Hello little one. You are one very lucky baby. You see, you are going to have the best mommy in the entire world to care for and love you."

They spent a few more moments on the floor before they heard the familiar footfalls of Aurelie's favorite landlord, Mrs. Romansky. "Knock, knock! Is it okay to come inside? I have a little something for you."

Aurelie and Dillion stood up and straightened out their clothes. "Sure thing, Mrs. Romansky. I think we're finished here anyways. Aurelie quickly shoved the pregnancy stick in her pocket and walked over to the bathroom to grab the remaining evidence of what they bought at the corner drug store.

The door opened and there she was in an orange turtleneck and a green sweatshirt that had all her grandkids' names embroidered on pumpkins. She was carrying a plate of her famous snickerdoodle cookies that smelled like they'd just come out of the oven. "Thought with all the traveling you've been doing these past few days you might like a little snack for the final trek home." She smiled, but Aurelie could tell that the smile didn't quite reach her eyes. With the intense emotions she was experiencing, Aurelie's own eyes began to mist as she reached out for the cookies to place them on the kitchen table before drawing in the four foot nothing lady who'd meant so much to her these past few years. Aurelie knew in her heart that she wouldn't have found Dillion and married him, with a clear path to a positive and exciting future, without the tough love Mrs. Romansky doled out to get her off of her self-destructive path.

"Thank you, Mrs. Romansky. Thank you so much. I'm going to miss you and this place. You were so good to me and to Mumford." Aurelie could tell that the wise woman she was hugging was crying and trying to get her own self-control back again.

"Oh hush. I didn't do hardly anything. You both were good for me. Kept me on my toes." Aurelie felt the intensity of the hug grow again. "I'm going to miss you, too. Maybe the next time you come into town to visit your family, you can find a moment to stop by and say 'hi.' I'll make sure I have a fresh plate of cookies for you and your kiddos."

When their hug was released, Dillion went in for his and thanked her also. Aurelie did one more check in all the closets and under the furniture, in the refrigerator, and the pantry before handing over the apartment key for the last time. She knew it was the right thing to do, but this place held so many memories of her and Cat, Mumford, and Dillion. She adulted in this space. It was a safe place to make mistakes, take chances. Grow up. Even if she never came back here, she'd remember how it felt to have her morning coffee at the kitchen table with the sun's rays filtered through the curtains, soaking up to her neck in bubbles in the clawfoot tub, or that scratchy bumpy, lumpy sofa that was probably as old as Mrs. Romansky herself. It didn't matter. It would continue to have a special place in her heart. She left the little upper flat with one last thought. *I wonder if this new home will be just as supportive and forgiving of my mistakes?*

The four and a half hour ride "home" ran the gamut of reminiscing of their wedding day, the honeymoon, the pregnancy, and what to say to the kids. When to tell them and everyone else in the family for that matter. Aurelie already knew the first person she was going to share this important news with. Cat!

It was already dark in the north woods when Dillion and Aurelie arrived at the simple ranch home that would be the center of their universe moving forward. "So, we agree not to say anything until Christmas. Right?" Dillion confirmed.

"Right. It's way too soon. I will call the clinic to see if I can get an appointment this week to confirm."

"Right. It's just that my mom has a sixth sense about this stuff. She always knew when I was lying. I'm scared of her," Aurelie laughed and kissed him quickly.

"I get it. Your mom kinda scares me, too."

They opened the door to the house and found Mumford and the children in the living room watching *Hocus Pocus* in their jammies and wearing dinosaur snoods on their heads. All the nerves left and raucous laughter took its place.

"Do we have the right house, Aur? I didn't know that a family of dinosaurs moved into our neighborhood while we were gone." Just then, all heads shifted to the backdoor to see Dillion and Aurelie coming through the entryway.

"Daddy! Aurelie! You're home!" Is what Aurelie thought they said, but it was very jumbled and was also garbled due to a giant dog's excited bark-talk. Before she knew what hit her, three little dinosaur people and one large dino-dog came at them in a fervor to get their undivided attention. When Mumford slammed into her, it took her breath away for a moment. Dillion, surrounded by his own dino-babies, went into protective mode and pushed Mumford away.

"Bad dog! You're gonna hurt Aurelie. Are you okay, Aur?"

"I'm fine." She saw the hurt on her fur baby's face and moved to get to him and give him love and attention. "It's okay, Mumford. Mommy's okay. You must be gentle with people. You forget how big you are." She got a sloppy kiss in return. "Yes, pup, I missed you too."

"Did you miss us too, Aurelie?" Brianna asked. "We missed you."

"Absolutely! In fact, all the way up here, I was telling your dad how excited I was to see all of you again." Bri shifted her hug to Aurelie, and the older children followed suit.

"How was Ireland? Did you go to the library at Trinity College? I can't wait until I'm old enough to go there. I hope I can go to school there and read all those old books," Riley shared.

"It was amazing. Your dad was practically drooling when we were touring it. I had to pry him away from *The Book of Kells* before they called security on us. I was afraid he was going to break into the glass case to bring it home." That got a laugh.

"Dad, were you really going to steal a book?" Benji looked very concerned but kind of hysterical because he also looked like the most studious dinosaur ever, with his oversized black framed glasses.

Just then, Dillion's mother appeared with a basket of laundry in her arms. Aurelie noted that the matriarch of the Clark family didn't look harried or tired in any way. She looked to be in complete control. "Who stole a book?" she inquired in a stern voice.

"No one, Mom. Aurelie was just joking about me and how excited I was to see *The Book of Kells.* Can I take that for you?"

"Oh, I see. Thanks, but I've got this Dillion. You two have stuff to bring into the house. You have enough to do." She shifted her focus to the children, "Alright my little dinosaurs, let your parents get their things into the house. Give them some room and then help them put stuff away."

"Oh Mrs. Clark, we've just got a few items to bring in tonight. It's so late, we thought we'd lock up the car and unload it tomorrow morning."

Rose Clare gave a half smile and nodded, but before leaving the room, she said, "That sounds like a good plan. And Aurelie?"

"Yes?" Aurelie could feel fear begin to register, not knowing what was going to be said next.

"We're family, now, dear. You can call me Rose Clare."

"Oh. Really? Okay. Thank you, Rose." A bit of the fear was still in her voice when she responded to her new mother-in-law.

"Rose Clare. And you are welcome. No need for formality. Especially when we live in caves to stay safe from dinosaurs." She smiled and gave a wink. Aurelie wasn't sure if it was a "joking" wink or "don't screw up" wink.

"Speaking of dinosaurs, where'd you all get those dinosaur hats?" Dillion asked.

"Grandma. She made them so Mumford would feel like he is part of the family," Benji answered.

"Thanks, Mom. Great idea."

She put down the basket to reach inside of it. Bringing out two items to give to Dillion and Aurelie, "You're welcome and these dinosaur snoods are for the two of you. Welcome home." This time, she smiled and giggled as she presented the newlyweds with their gifts.

Several moments later, all of the Clark family members were wearing their snoods and sitting down in various places in the living room gawking over their presents from the Emerald Isle. Rose Clare twirled her crystal angel up toward the light to see it sparkle. The kids put on their Aran sweaters over their pajamas as Dillion and Aurelie sat on the couch enjoying the experience.

"What do we call you now?" Benji asked out of the clear air.

"What do you mean? You can still call me Aurelie."

"Well, you aren't just Aurelie any longer. You are also our mom because our mom died," Benji replied.

"I don't know, Benji. Honestly, I hadn't thought about it. You already have a mother, so I just assumed you'd continue to call me Aurelie. What did you have in mind?"

That seemed to stump him, but then Riley chimed in. "True, you aren't our real mom, but we haven't had her in a long time. You are our new mom, now. How about something like, Momma Aurelie?"

"That's too much." Brianna decided. "Can we shorten it?"

"Good idea," Aurelie said contemplatively. "Well, my best friend, Cat, nicknamed me Aur. Can we use that somehow?"

"Momma Aur," Brianna said reflectively. Each of her siblings tried saying it as well. As if to get a feel for it. Looking at her siblings,

Brianna decided for the group, "Yep. That's it. Momma Aur. It's perfect." She walked up to Aurelie, hugged her, kissed her cheek, and whispered, "I love you, Momma Aur." The older children did the same. Aurelie was so filled with emotion, she started to cry. The dino-family leaned in for a family hug before the dino-children left to go to bed. Mumford followed Benji into his room. Dillion and Aurelie walked into each bedroom, gently pulled off the snoods, stayed for bedtime prayers, stories, and goodnight kisses.

Rose Clare brought up an air mattress and set it up in Brianna's room before saying good night to the young couple, leaving them alone for the first time in their home.

Exhausted from the day's traveling and news, they opted to go to bed early as well. There would be a lot to do in the next few days to get Aurelie's things organized, get acclimated to the new work/school schedule, and whatever things needed to be done for Aurelie's pregnancy. Aurelie climbed under the covers naked. Dillion jumped up and locked the bedroom door before shedding his boxers and joining her in their bed. Aurelie made a mental note to wear pajamas to bed or lock the door. Before she could think any further, Dillion had moved to be on top of her. Showering her with tender caresses like dew drops falling on delicate flower petals. Aurelie closed her eyes as she immersed herself in the sensory experience. Kisses fell on her forehead, each eyelid, the tip of her nose, her lips, chin, neck. Next, he used his tongue to outline her jawline and lightly bit the space where her neck met her shoulders.

Aurelie shifted so that she opened her legs for him, so he would continue his kissing journey down to her perky breasts, being careful to address each nipple with equal attention from his mouth. Moving slowly down her torso with his tongue, Aurelie felt the need grow in her loins. She lifted her hips to encourage him to enter her. Instead, he stopped at her stomach, kissed it, and laid his head on her womb. She was so moved by this intimate action that Aurelie opened her eyes, took her hands, and began to finger comb his hair. They lay like that for so long, Aurelie's sensual reaction had dissipated and another feeling, or emotion that she didn't have a word for, took its place. She closed her eyes and let the rhythm of her fingers lull her to an almost sleepy state. That is until Dillion moved ever so slightly to shift his face so that his mouth was now on her. Kissing her, while nudging her legs to open wider for him.

Aurelie responded immediately and began to express her enjoyment with her own motions and moaning. Dillion stopped for a moment, which frustrated her. *Why did he have to start and then stop?*

"Shhh. We have to be quiet now. We've got ears everywhere." *Oh. I get it.* Aurelie thought to herself. She nodded in acceptance and used her hands to encourage her paramour to continue his love language journey on her, in her.

His lips parted as he parted her lips, and his tongue danced its way into her erogenous zone. She knew her climax was coming soon, so she dragged a pillow over her face for that exquisite moment building up inside her. Dillion pulled the pillow from her face as he entered her. Slowly, he began his rhythmic drive into her wet, inflamed sacred gate. He looked deep into her eyes with an intensity from which she couldn't break away. Aurelie followed his rhythm, which quickened to a shattering pinnacle with his mouth devouring hers so her climax was buffered in the power of his kiss.

The next day was a bustling of getting Rose Clare packed and on the road to her own home, unpacking the car, finding places for Aurelie's things, and a voicemail for the doctor's office. It was chaotic, but Aurelie was pleasantly surprised at how helpful and cooperative the children were being. "Don't get used to this, Aur," Dillion warned. "They are still on their best behavior. Once this newness wears off, it won't be this easy. I promise."

"What? These angels?" She laughed and pulled him into a kiss that was witnessed by the kids who all responded by gagging and covering their eyes. The next day would be back to school and back to work, leaving Aurelie to get acclimated to her new environment.

A few days later, Aurelie left the doctor's office in euphoria. Her first errand was to the pharmacy to pick up prenatal vitamins, but before that, Aurelie went to the church to share the good news with Dillion. She shut the door behind her once she entered his office. "Just a minute, please," he muttered while his head was down, reviewing some paperwork. When he looked up, she couldn't keep the news from him.

"Dillion, we're going to have a baby," she confirmed. Dillion practically leapt over his desk and into her arms. He lifted her up and swung her around before landing an adoring kiss on her mouth.

"Oh Aurelie. I am so happy. I love you so much! I can't believe it. It's a gift from God." He embraced her again and hugged her.

"This isn't immaculate conception, Dillion. I think this gift came from you," he laughed.

"I suppose you're right. But you are a gift to me. From God. I do believe that's true." He hugged her again before breaking away and leading her to the small sofa in his office.

"So, can they tell how far along you are?"

"Dillion, that's a silly question. We've been married for less than a month. Their best guess is that I'm three weeks pregnant, but we have to wait a month before the first ultrasound to confirm. I made the appointment for the first week in December."

"Text it to me so I can make sure I'm there. I don't want to miss seeing our baby for the first time."

"Dillion, do you still think we can tell our families I'm pregnant at Christmas?"

"That would be an awesome Christmas gift, wouldn't it?"

"I thought so."

The phone rang and someone knocked on his door. "Sorry, Aur, but I have to get back to work. I think my next appointment is here."

"No worries. I'll see you when you get home tonight. Love you."

"Love you, too." Then he reached down and kissed her pregnant belly.

Aurelie had so much excited energy within her, she couldn't wait to share her news.

"Where are you?"

"I'm in the car waiting to pick up the kids from school. Can you talk?"

"Yeah, the twins are at preschool for a bit longer and Damon's at an appointment. What's up? How's married life?"

"Well, it's been pretty great, actually. Better than I ever thought it could be."

"The sex is that good or is it because you waited two years and were about to explode?"

"Geez, you're talking to a priest's wife, you know. Isn't that a bit crass?"

"Oh please. I'm talking to my best friend. This is bland considering how you used to talk to me about your sex life."

"Fair enough, Cat. But I didn't call you about my sex life. Wait, I take that back. It's kinda sorta about my sex life."

"Just get to the point, will you already? Give me the juicy details, because with the twins running us ragged and our two jobs, our foreplay lately is getting under the flannel sheets and snoring."

"Geez, Cat. Trying to make me jealous?"

"Sorry. I thought you were calling to rub my nose in erotic stories about all the canoodling you were doing on your honeymoon."

"I could do that or …"

"Or what?"

"Or tell you that all that canoodling we did got me pregnant. We're going to have a baby."

"Oh Shit! Oh Shit! Seriously? You're preggers?"

"Seriously."

"Congratulations, Aur! I am so happy for you and Dillion. Damn it. I hate being so far away from you for these moments. I wish I could give you a hug and celebrate with you." Aurelie's heart pained her in that instant.

"Me too. You were the first person I wanted to tell when we found out. But we aren't planning on telling anyone until Christmas. Then

I'll be at the 12-week point and should be safe from anything bad happening to the baby."

"I feel honored. I would have killed you if you'd kept this from me for three whole months. Wait a minute. You're not telling your folks till Christmas?"

"Sort of."

"What does that mean?"

"Well, when we got to my parents' house to pick up the wedding gifts, the first thing out of my mother's mouth was that I was glowing, and she knew I was pregnant."

"Damn that woman has a sixth sense about that. She could have been a doctor, too, you know."

"I know. I know. She reminded me that Beres women get pregnant on the first try. So, my guess is that we got pregnant on our wedding night."

"Well, well, well. You have a superpower. Better be very careful with that superpower, my friend or you'll have more kids than the Duggars."

"Fair point. Listen, school's let out so I gotta go. Don't tell anyone about this, okay? I don't want the word to get out before we're ready to tell anyone. Especially the kids."

"Can I at least tell Damon?"

"Sure. Tell him I say 'hi' and give a hug and kiss to the twins for me. Tell them Auntie Aur misses them."

"Will do. And Aur?"

"Yeah?"

"Congratulations, again. You'll be a fantastic mom."

"Thanks, Cat. It means a lot. I miss you."

"I miss you, too. And I'll plan our summer vacation for July so we can see you and the baby."

"You'd better!"

The Clark kids piled into the SUV and were chattering away about their day at school, vying for Aurelie's attention via increasing volume and dramatic storytelling.

"Whoa! Everyone, I can't understand anything you're saying because you are all talking at the same time. Is everyone buckled in?" Nods from the back seats confirmed they were all belted and Aurelie pulled out onto the road to go home. It would be a hard secret not to share with the kids, but she also didn't want them to feel slighted or afraid that she wouldn't love them as much as the child she was carrying.

"Okay, since it's a nice afternoon and I've been running errands all day, why don't we all take a break and give Mumford a nice walk?" Dropping their bookbags in their respective rooms, they ran through the backdoor where Aurelie was waiting with Mumford. They began their walk/hike from their yard and into the woods that surrounded their home. Aurelie felt contentment being in nature, with the cool crisp air in her face and the crunch of fallen leaves under foot. Reminiscent of the days when she was a child, she started singing and the kids joined in. Because they were in the middle of the woods, no one cared that a scared big dog was howling with them. Once back at the house, Aurelie began dinner while the children started their homework and Mumford took a nap. By the time Dillion came home, sticky chicken was on the table with rice and steamed green beans adorned with slivered almonds.

Dillion reached down to give each family member a kiss before he sat down. "Wow. This looks amazing, Aur. Let's give God and Aur thanks for this wonderful meal." He reached out to grab hands with his family and led a gratitude prayer. Aurelie thought to herself, *This is what I've been missing. A family of my own.* The cacophony of the day's events was hard to follow, but it really didn't matter. Everyone felt heard at some point.

Riley and Benji helped clear the table, while Aurelie drew a bath for Bri, who took sticky chicken to a whole new level. Her clothes were stained with the red sticky chicken sauce, so Aurelie took them immediately downstairs to the laundry to pre-treat the stains. A wave of nausea hit her, and she bent over the stationary tub to throw up. She took a few extra moments to get herself together when she heard Benji come downstairs to begin his piano lesson. When Aurelie brought her things into the house, her electric keyboard was moved into the semi-furnished part of the basement.

"Hey Momma Aur, what are you doing over by the sink?"

"Oh, hey Benji. I just needed a moment after cleaning up Bri's mess."

He looked quizzically at her. "That bad, huh?"

"Yeah, that bad. I'll be okay. Honest. Go ahead and practice. I'll be upstairs if you get stuck, okay?"

"Uh huh." She could tell his eyes were still on her as she slowly went up the stairs.

By Sunday, they had found a routine that seemed to work, for the most part. Aurelie still made mistakes, but the kids and Dillion tried to be understanding. Bri didn't get into a tizzy when her braids didn't match. Riley seemed to be a little peeved that Aurelie was now the woman of the house and was always there to point out when she did something wrong. But Benji and Mumford had a second sense around her. Like they knew something was different, except they couldn't figure it out. And then there was Dillion. Warm, delicious Dillion. Attentive to her needs when he wasn't at work. Their bedroom was his sanctuary. He shed his suit and his fatherly responsibilities at the door. They switched their joint shower time from morning to evening to coincide with the kids' bedtimes, so they could make love with their pleasure sounds buffered by the sounds from the water spray and the vent fan and at low risk for being interrupted.

Saturday night, Aurelie shed her days' clothes and joined Dillion for a steamy shower. She relished his tender touch as he lathered her in a spiced vanilla body wash, massaging her breasts before lifting her up against the tile wall so she could wrap her long legs around his waist and open herself up to him. Encouraging him to enter her and push himself into her deeper and deeper with every thrust of his hips. When her body shuddered, he joined her and expressed his release, "Oh God, Aur! Oh Shit!" She couldn't help it. It was a proud moment. She turned this docile, fairly inexperienced priest into a virile lover. When he was in their bedroom or in their bathroom, he was hers. Totally and completely. Everywhere else, she had to share him. But in this space, she was his priority. He became her man, and she was his woman, his sexual muse. It was blissful and a new level of intimacy that she had never experienced before. She loved it. Craved it.

Sunday morning was a bustle of activity. Dillion was out the door practically at sunrise, leaving Aurelie to attend to the dog, children, and find something appropriate to wear now that she would be front and center at the church service. Earlier in the week, she lucked out at one of the local thrift stores and found several vintage dresses in her size. She was able to braid Bri's fine hair into two equal length braids and found yellow bows to match her yellow romper. Benji was in his standard long-sleeved striped shirt with an open collar, as he hated the feeling of anything tight on his neck. Riley opted for a simple olive floral hi-low dress with long sleeves trimmed in large ruffles to match the ruffle on the tea length skirt. She pulled her long locks back in a matching olive headband. Aurelie walked out of the house wearing a three quarter length sleeve black and yellow vintage a-lined cocktail dress with full skirt. The collar was off center, rounded on one end pulling to a point at the other with a yellow and black polka dot underlay collar highlighting it. The torso was fitted with classic black buttons leading to each hip. The full skirt had a split in it that showcased more of the yellow and black polka dot fabric matching the collar. She finished the look with bright red lipstick and a pair of classic black pumps.

When they arrived in the lobby of the church, she could tell all eyes were on her and the kids. Several members of the parish came up to congratulate her on her recent nuptials and offered help with everything from meal prep, grocery shopping, babysitting, and all things church related. She felt his presence behind her before she saw him. Her body was all kinds of tingles remembering last night's lovemaking shower session.

"Mrs. Clark," he whispered in her ear, and it nearly knocked her off her heels. She smiled, turned around right into a warm hug from the sexiest priest she'd ever seen. "You look amazing in that dress. You're making it very difficult for me to concentrate on my job this morning."

She pulled away and replied, "I'm so glad you like my dress." Just then, Riley authoritatively pulled her away and motioned that they needed to lead the congregation into the church to sit down for the service. Riley made sure she was sitting right next to Aurelie to help her follow along with the mass bulletin. At least with the music, Aurelie could follow easily and felt confident in singing aloud with the choir and even singing in harmony, which boosted her self-confidence.

After mass, the accolades continued during *donuts for Jesus*. By 1 p.m. parishioners filtered out of the cozy field stone church and back to their regular lives. Aurelie ushered the Clark kids into the SUV while Dillion tied up some loose ends before joining his young family back home. It was the perfect day to work outside in the yard, doing fall clean-up. Cutting back flowering bushes, raking, and burning leaves, changing out the screen door for the glass door. Bri helped Aurelie put up Thanksgiving decorations on the windows while a beef roast was simmering in the slow cooker.

Once the kids were in bed, Dillion led his beautiful wife to their shower sanctuary, where he showed her just how much he liked her new dress. The next morning, Aurelie was finding it hard to get out of bed. Her stomach was more upset than usual, and she just couldn't seem to wake up. Dillion let her sleep in while he got the kids off to school and took care of Mumford. "Today's not a good day, Aur?"

"Mmm, hmm. I feel like I got run over by a freight train."

"Well, I took care of everything this morning. Stay in bed as long as you want to. Everything is taken care of until this afternoon. Don't worry about dinner. I'll take care of it." He kissed the top of her head before leaving for work.

Aurelie attempted to go back to sleep, but she just couldn't get comfortable. She thought about eating something, but that just made her feel worse. So much so, that she rushed to the toilet and retched.

There was a little relief to getting it out of her system, but she still didn't feel quite right. *Maybe a nice bath would help*, she thought to herself. Aurelie began the water for the bath while she brushed her teeth and splashed some cold water on her face. After stripping off her PJs she lowered herself into the clear, warm water and closed her eyes. *This feels better.* She began to relax and closed her eyes to take in the moment. Then something shifted. She felt the cramping before she saw her bath water change color from clear to a rusty red color. "Oh shit. Shit. Shit. No. No! No! Please no!" Aurelie said out loud as she bolted out of the bloody bathwater before she found herself on the toilet. "No, no. God no. Please don't let this happen. Please." She was louder now, and the sobbing began. So loud that it frightened Mumford who nosed his way into the bathroom to check on her. He licked away the tears that were constantly falling while she wailed in surprise, in grief, in pain. When the cramping subsided and Mumford dried all her tears, she found the strength to stand up and look into the toilet, where a mass of something like the consistency of brown coffee grounds was floating. It didn't look like a baby. But she felt it like the loss of one. Empty. She felt so empty inside. She knew what she had to do.

"Hello, this is Aurelie Clark. I think I had a miscarriage. Yes. About four or five weeks. Uh huh. Okay. I'll leave now. Thank you."

She called Dillion's cell, and it went to voicemail. Not wanting to leave something like this on a voicemail, she opted to text him to call her. They connected as she pulled into the hospital parking lot. "What's up? Feeling any better?"

"No. Listen, after you left," it stuck in her throat. It was one thing to admit it to the doctor, but quite another to admit it to Dillion. Sweet, loving Dillion who was so excited about this pregnancy. It broke her heart, but she had to get it out. "I think I had a miscarriage, Dillion. I think I lost the baby."

"What?" She heard the terror in his voice, and it crushed her. She felt like a failure.

"I'm at the hospital now. I'm meeting the doctor at her office."

"I'll be right there."

Fifteen minutes later, they were in the doctor's office where it was confirmed that Aurelie had miscarried. "I'm so sorry, Aurelie, I know this is difficult for you to hear, but you did experience a first trimester miscarriage. During the exam I didn't see any evidence that we will need to do a D&C."

"D&C?" Dillion asked.

"Dilatation and curettage, or D&C, is the use of surgical suction to clean out all of the extra tissue that hasn't already been eliminated through the miscarriage. You will likely bleed for the next seven days or so, like a normal period."

"Isn't that what they use for an abortion?"

"It is the same procedure, but in Aurelie's case, it isn't to abort the baby, as the miscarriage already occurred. It is used to protect the mother's health moving forward. If fetal tissue is left in the mother's body too long, it can become infected and impair any future pregnancies and can even cause the mother's death."

All this talk just made Aurelie feel worse. Words like abortion, impaired, infected, death, were of no comfort to her now. She wanted to hear words like, healthy, baby, and congratulations.

"So, what's next?"

"Well, Aurelie, you should take it easy for a week or so, and let me know if the bleeding changes into something worse than a heavy period, or you develop a fever, or anything else that is out of the ordinary."

A few months ago, she wouldn't have even asked this question, but it was heavy on her mind. "Doc, when is it safe to try again? How long do we have to wait before having sex again?" She could feel Dillion looking at her in shock, but she didn't care. Yes, it was a surprise that she was pregnant so soon, but that feeling, that need to be a mother was now as strong of a desire as she had ever experienced before. She desperately wanted to have a baby. Dillion's baby. She wanted to be a mother.

"In most cases, you can try again after your bleeding stops, as long as intercourse isn't painful or you have any other concerns; you can start right away. But, and I can't stress this enough, Aurelie, you've experienced a loss today. Take time to grieve. But physically, you can try again in less than two weeks."

Dillion followed her home and lay down next to her on their bed, Mumford lying on the floor next to her side of the bed. Dillion stroked her short, curly hair and rubbed her empty womb. They shared an ugly cry together before he spoke. "I'm so sorry this happened to you, Aur. So sorry."

That struck her as odd, "Us," she replied.

"What?"

"Us. This miscarriage happened to us."

"You are so right. I'm sorry. That was insensitive of me."

"I'm just going to take a nap before I go to get the kids from school. There's nothing more you can do for me. Why don't you go back to work?"

"I'm not going back to work today. I've got everything covered. I'm sticking around to take care of everything here while you rest."

Too exhausted emotionally and physically, Aurelie just nodded and fell into a restless sleep until Dillion brought the kids home from school. She knew she had to get up. Maybe being with the kids would help her get out of her funk. Keeping busy could be a good thing.

"Aurelie is not feeling well today. She went to the doctor and was told to take it easy for the next week or so, so we all need to help out around the house a bit more than we have been. Okay?"

Benji just stared at her almost protectively, just like the way Mumford was sticking to her side. "Is it because you threw up the other day?"

Not knowing what to say that wouldn't give it all away she responded, "Yes, Benji. That's when I knew I was getting sick. But I promise. I'll be back to myself in no time."

Aurelie's first venture out into the world was for Sunday service. This time she wore a simple burnt orange floral T-shirt dress with a burnt orange cardigan. When she and the kids arrived at church,

Dillion was right there to lightly hug her and welcome the family before going back to his congregational duties. As usual, Riley was at Aurelie's side. This time, she controlled her critical voice and offered her help in a more nurturing voice to help Aurelie follow the service. Aurelie didn't harmonize during the songs, but she did sing them. During a moment of silence, she contemplated if God was punishing her for all the mistakes she had made up to this point in her life. When it was time for the Prayers of Intercessions, she silently prayed for her unborn child and the chance to have another.

During *donuts for Jesus* Aurelie was engaged with a small group of young parish women when she was struck by an insensitive remark, "Oh, I'm sorry, Aurelie, carrying on so much about being exhausted all the time. Since you've never been pregnant and all." In reference to how tired the young woman was as she was into her third trimester.

Another of the women boldly asked, "So, when are you and Father Clark planning on adding to your family?" A stake thrust into her own heart wouldn't have hurt her as much as that question did in that moment.

"Well, we've only been married a short time. We're focused on the family life we have right now," she said. However, her inner voice said something completely different. *Listen you insensitive bitch. I just lost a baby. Fuck off.*

Dillion found Aurelie and asked to speak with her, while taking her to the side. "I'm sorry to do this to you, Aur, but one of my long-time parishioners is actively dying and his family wants me to be there with him. I don't know how long I'll be. Will you be okay with the kids alone?"

What choice do I have? She thought to herself. It wasn't his fault. He had no clue what those women were saying to her, and she felt childish bringing it up, so instead, she said, "Of course, Dillion. I'll be fine. The kids will be fine. I'll see you when you get home." Dillion gave her a peck on the cheek and headed off to his car. Aurelie called on the kids to pile into the SUV for the quick drive home.

In the driveway, she realized that she was still angry and upset and didn't want to take it out on the kids. When they got inside, she asked, "Listen, I think I'd like to take Mumford for a short walk, to see if I'm really feeling better. Do you think you could be in the house, alone for a little bit? I promise I won't be long."

The girls were fine with the idea and seemed to be excited about being able to be in the house without supervision. But Benji was concerned. "I think I should come along just in case you don't feel well, or Mumford starts pulling." Aurelie didn't fight it.

After dropping her church clothes on the floor, she put on some comfortable gray sweatpants, a T-shirt, and an oversized hoodie, changing out her heels for hiking boots. Benji switched into his own sweats and hoodie and joined her in the backyard leading to the trail.

It was kind of a gray day, which was perfect for Aurelie's mood that was brewing. At first, she wanted to be annoyed at having an eight-year-old babysit her, but as they started out, she realized that there was something comfortable about him walking by her side. Benji didn't say a word but did reach out to hold her hand. Mumford was on his best behavior as well. It was as if both of her boys were innately aware of her need for quiet, and they both felt very protective of her as well.

Once they got back to the house, Benji went downstairs to practice his piano lesson while Aurelie went to check on the girls. Riley was in her room reading, but she didn't find Brianna in hers. "Hey Riley, where's Bri?"

"I dunno. I thought she was in her room playing with her dolls. She said something about having a tea party."

Aurelie went past her room and stopped. There was a light coming from the bathroom. "Bri, honey, where are you?"

"I'm in here." Aurelie was a bit nervous about what she was about to see. When she turned the corner to peek into the bathroom, she was stupefied. Standing in her black heels, barely wearing her floral dress, was Bri. Bri who also had Aurelie's favorite lipstick all over her face and looked like she was planning to add even more.

"Oh Bri, what did you do? What are you doing?"

"I wanted to look pretty, just like you Momma Aur. Don't I look pretty?" Aurelie wanted to be angry, but instead she started to laugh. Something that had been foreign to her since the miscarriage. The bigger kids were curious as to what made her laugh, so they came in to see for themselves and began to laugh as well.

"Oh, sweetie, I'm at a loss for words."

"Is Daddy home? Can I show him how pretty I am?"

"No, Bri, not just yet. How about I snap a picture for him before you step out of my clothes and take your bath?" She took a photo before stripping the five-year-old of her own clothes and helping her wash off all the red lipstick.

Dillion didn't come home until after the whole house was in bed. She felt his exhausted body spoon hers. "I hope your day was better than mine," he spoke.

"There's leftovers in the fridge if you're hungry. And everything here went just fine. I promised Bri I'd show you a photo of her after I got home from a walk." She reached over to the side table and picked up her phone to show him.

"Holy cow!"

"I know, right?"

"What possessed her to do that?"

"She said she wanted to look pretty, like me, and that I needed to take a picture to show you. So you could see how pretty she was."

"That's an understatement."

"How are you doing?"

"Mostly exhausted. Having to work an almost 20-hour day is rough. But as death calls go, this one was a good death. Mitch was ready to be with his late wife in heaven. Their kids were all able to make it back to say goodbye to him. It just took a lot longer than we all expected."

"I'm glad, and I'm sorry. Not sure what I'm supposed to say in these situations."

"Just knowing you're here to come home to is all I need right now. I'm going to grab a bite and meet you in bed."

"'Kay," Aurelie said softly before she closed her eyes and rolled over.

The next morning, after the kids were at school, Aurelie felt compelled to take Mumford for a long walk in the crisp autumn air. This time, she decided to walk along the residential streets, and she made up a guessing game as to who might be living there. During this leisurely meandering, her phone rang, she picked it up and sighed, not wanting to talk to the person on the other line, but knowing she had to.

"Hey Mom. What's up?"

"Hello Mon Cheri, I've been waiting patiently to hear if I was right. But you haven't reached out at all. What's going on? Are you pregnant?"

Aurelie realized she had walked them to the lakefront where she found an empty bench on which she sat before answering. Her stomach was in knots and even though there was a chill in the air, she felt flush. "Sorry, but I am still trying to process everything myself, Mom. You were right. I was pregnant."

"I knew it!" Bea said enthusiastically. "Wait a moment, you said 'was pregnant.' Didn't you?"

Aurelie could feel the tears welling up in her eyes again and her voice caught in her throat. She tried to speak. "Yes, Momma, I was pregnant, but I lost it. I lost the baby."

"Oh, my sweet Aurelie. My poor baby. I am so sorry. I wish I was there to comfort you. Do you want me to come up to be with you? Help out?"

Aurelie felt comforted a bit just by her mother's offer. "Thanks, Mom, but I'm handling it okay. Dillion has been great. We told the kids I was sick, so I needed to rest for the week and they were pretty good about it. That reminds me, I've got to send you a photo of Bri playing dress up in my clothes and lipstick. The lipstick is dead, but the photo is priceless."

"Oh, alright. But then we are coming for Thanksgiving. I'm changing plans. Your brother and sisters can get along just fine without us."

"Mom, you don't have to do that. We'll be okay on our own."

"Don't you want me to be there for you?"

The tears began to stream down her cheek. Aurelie did want her mom. She would understand the mean comments from the parishioners, she always had a way to make Aurelie feel better without being overly protective.

"Of course I do. It's just that I know how important Thanksgiving dinner is at your house for everyone. I don't want to ruin everyone else's Thanksgiving because I'm sad."

"Mon Cheri, it hurts me that you have been in such pain and haven't told me about it. I'm your mother, and I want to be there for you and Dillion. Period. I'm getting off the phone now so I can arrange a room for your father and me. We'll see you soon. I love you, Aurelie."

"Love you too, Mom. And thanks. Can't wait to see you and Dad."

After she hung up, the tears came more freely. She was trying hard not to ugly cry. Mumford sensed her sadness. He crawled up onto the bench and lay across her lap so she could bury her face into his fur and sob, while muffling the sounds of her grief.

The Monday of Thanksgiving week, she heard their car roll into the driveway. Butterflies filled her stomach. She was nervous. Aurelie didn't know what to expect. Trepidation filled her. She wanted to show off her new home and how well she was taking care of everything, but she also wanted to just lay her head on her mother's lap while she would finger comb Aurelie's hair to lull her to sleep.

The knock on the back door almost startled Aurelie, even though she knew it was coming. Mumford began to bark, sensing new people. "Shh. It's okay, Mumford, it's my Mom and Dad. No need to bark."

Opening the door, Aurelie was overthinking how she would greet her parents but glad she was home alone so she didn't have to put on a front for the kids or Dillion. She thought a simple *hi* would do. But didn't expect the wave of pent-up emotions to hit her like a storm surge. Aurelie barely opened the door and got out a "Hey there," before her parents were in front of her and the ugly crying began. Aurelie fell limp into her parent's arms as they enveloped her with all the love and support they came to offer. Aurelie really wanted this first visit to her home with her family to be so different. The kind where the new wife/mother presents a show-and-tell for her guests to impress them. Instead, she collapsed with grief consuming her once again.

The beautiful thing about her parents, though, was that they loved her unconditionally. As much as Aurelie wanted to show them how much she'd improved at something, or learned something new, it seemed she was more often coming to them with a problem, or after she made a mistake, to share her failure with them. Aurelie was so tired of failure. And that is what finally left her body when the tears slowed. In this non-judgmental space she didn't feel like a failure. Aurelie felt loved.

Mumford broke into the love fest, not wanting to be left out, which made Aurelie smile and almost tip over. "Okay, big guy, come on into the family hug." He gave her a big, sloppy kiss, which made her laugh.

Many moments later, they were taking Mumford for a walk on the woodland trail, so her parents could stretch their legs after a long drive. Selfishly, Aurelie thought walking could shift her focus onto Mumford and release some of the anxiety of sharing her story of loss.

"Aur, you've been through a lot these past months. How are you and Dillion managing? Do you need help?" Antoine asked

"We're doing okay. I was going to look for a job, but it's been such a whirlwind just trying to get settled and with the baby and miscarriage and all. There hasn't been a moment. You know? I used to wonder, Mom, why you didn't work, but I get it. With three kids to take care of and a husband whose work can take on a life of its own, I'm not sure where I'd find the time. It's so hard to keep up. One minute everything is in order and the next, it's piles of laundry, homework, the dog needs a walk, Dillion's on a death call, and it starts all over again the next day.

"I think that Riley and Benji would be okay if I worked out of the home. But Bri is only five. As you saw in the photo, she can't be left alone too long." That got a laugh from her parents.

"Well, you've been through a great deal in a very short time. I had years to build our family. It didn't hit me all at once," Bea confirmed.

When they got to the point Aurelie usually turned around to head home, she stopped. "You know, I really didn't know if I wanted you to come at all." She could see the hurt in their eyes, so she tried to explain.

"It's just that I wanted your first visit here to be when I could show off everything—how great it's all going. What a good wife and mother I am. Instead, you came to the door, and I was a sloppy mess. I felt the loss all over again, and I just didn't want to disappoint you. I'm so tired of letting you both down."

This time it was her father who spoke directly to her. "Aurelie, you've never been nor ever will be a disappointment to me or your mother. Your mother had a miscarriage before we had you, and it was devastating. But then she was pregnant with you, and we saw it as a gift. Because of that loss, we felt so blessed that we were given another opportunity to have a child. You taught us so much. We are very grateful for you. Don't ever forget that." He leaned over, hugged her, and kissed the top of her head.

"I, I didn't know. How come you never said anything about losing a baby before?" Aurelie asked in surprise.

"It's not something to discuss with your kids, especially when they are young; I lost it in the first trimester, just like you." Bea looked wistfully into the bare trees as she recalled that barren feeling so many years ago.

"Do you still grieve for that baby? Does it ever go away?"

"Mon Cheri, I don't know if that grief ever leaves you completely. There could be a song or something else that brings that pregnancy, that loss to the forefront again. For me, it's most often the calendar. I'll look at the date and think about how old the baby would have been if it lived. But it doesn't hurt as much as it did at first. Besides," Bea gave her daughter a side hug, "you kept us on our toes. We didn't have much time to be thinking about the past with you and your antics." That made Aurelie smile.

"Yes, you gave us the most important parenting lesson of all," Antoine said.

"What was that Dad?"

"To embrace our higgledy-piggledy life."

"What does that mean?"

"It's a phrase that I learned during one of my travels to England. It means that life is messy. Convoluted. It isn't perfect. Don't fight it. Celebrate the chaos."

"Huh, so I taught you guys something?"

Bea laughed, "Every single day."

Thanksgiving Day saw the little ranch house bustling with activity. Aurelie knew she should be sad, but she felt a ray of happiness breaking through the darkness of the past few weeks. Dillion was out on the back porch grilling the turkey. After Benji set the table, he and her dad were in his room going through a pile of medical and science books that Dr. Beres brought with them for Benji to read. Her mom was teaching the girls how to make orange cranberry sauce, while Aurelie was making sweet potato casserole with some Canadian maple syrup that her parents brought with them as a housewarming gift.

Dillion snuck in behind Aurelie, put his arms around her waist and nuzzled her neck. "How's it going in here?"

"Everything is looking good and almost done. How's the turkey?"

"Almost to temperature. I'd say another 30 minutes and we're ready to eat."

"Perfect." He kissed her neck and hugged her before showering his girls with praise and kisses on his way back to the turkey. Aurelie smiled. It would have been special to celebrate Thanksgiving and their baby, but this was a close second. She still missed the feeling of something growing inside her, but she was no longer devastated. Seeing her parents again warmed her heart and gave her a sense of comfort that no one else could have given her. With all she put them through, she knew their love for her was limitless. Even though she and Dillion committed to their own love, it was still new and at times, unfamiliar. Like a brand new fawn trying to walk for the first time.

"Turkey's ready!" Dillion announced as he carried in the main dish to be served. Aurelie closed her eyes and took a deep breath to savor the aroma of the grilled turkey. *Smells like bacon.* She thought to herself. The kids scrambled to their places as her parents found their seats on the opposite side of the table. "Let us pray," Dillion began as he took hold of one of each Benji and Riley's hands. "Lord, we thank you for this generous feast you've put before us and for the family that is with us and those who are with us in spirit," Aurelie felt her heart ache and instantaneously felt her mother squeeze her hand. "Amen." Hands released and before anyone could reach for a brown and serve roll or a slice of turkey, her father raised his wine glass.

"If I may, I'd like to propose a toast." Dillion nodded and encouraged the kids to raise their sparkling grape juice glasses as well. "Bea and I would like to thank you for welcoming us into your home and joining you for your first Thanksgiving together as a family. May there be many years of celebrations around this table. Holidays and otherwise. Sante!"

With the excited chatter and homemade holiday feast, Aurelie felt the happiest she'd felt since the miscarriage. She recognized that there would always be a place in her heart for their unborn baby, but on this occasion, Aurelie was beginning to feel hope. She caught Dillion's eye and smiled. He looked genuinely touched and mouthed the words, "I love you," before grabbing his wine glass and raising it in the air to her.

Chapter Thirty-Seven

"Aur, the kids are in the car already."

"We have time for a quickie. Tell them we're finishing laundry. They won't care."

Dillion was conflicted. On the one hand he had a day off, and he promised the kids a day of Christmas shopping in the city, Wausau. On the other, Aurelie wanted to have sex with him. A quickie. In the laundry room. NOW. Both of his heads were vying for position. He already knew which one was going to win. After having sex daily for a month, it had been almost a month since the last time. Since the miscarriage. He didn't want to press her for his own selfish needs. But now that she was primed and ready to go ... well, it was damn hard to have his parenting head overturn his carnal head.

He walked to the minivan and already knew what he was going to say with a tad of guilt, "You kids warm enough in here?" He got three head nods, and not one of them was really paying any attention. Benji was reading a book in the back seat with Mumford lying on his lap. Riley started a movie for her and Brianna to watch during the car ride. "Listen, Momma Aur and I are just finishing up the laundry, so we have one less thing to do when we get back tonight."

Dillion shut the door to the minivan and practically ran into the house where he found his wanton wife already half undressed and touching herself while sitting atop the washing machine. He went rigid and his jeans were uncomfortable. "Sorry, I couldn't wait. Oooh, this feels almost like a vibrator. Better get over here before I finish by myself." Instinct took over after he shut the door. Dillion dropped his jeans to the floor and reached Aurelie in one stride. Removing her hand, he sucked off all her juices before sliding her to the edge of the vibrating machine so he could let his tongue finish the job.

It didn't take long. "Yes! Yes! Oh God, Dillion! Now! I want you now!" That was all he needed. He pulled her off the washing machine and turned her around so her tight ass was right in front of him. He entered her from behind carefully, not wanting to hurt her. But when he heard her guttural moaning, he knew he could release the beast. If she wanted a quickie, she was getting him fast and hard. Putting his hands on her hips, he entered her as deep as she would allow him. She was soft, swollen, and easily enveloped him. Dillion lost all conscious effort to be anything but a sensual being at that moment. He thrust in and out of her like a firing piston. It felt so raw and right. The rhythm kept getting faster and faster until finally he exploded into her. Releasing all the pent up sadness, guilt, anger, frustration, and leaving euphoria in its wake.

Dillion collapsed on top of Aurelie who fell onto of a pile of towels to be washed. His hedonistic instincts satiated; his concerned nature returned. "Did I hurt you? Are you okay?" Dillion asked.

"It was exactly what I needed. The way you took charge. You were amazing. You were an animal!"

Dillion smirked, feeling very smug and a bit snarky. "Literally." Kissing the nape of her neck, he lifted himself off her and pulled his jeans back up. Aurelie pulled down her sweater, found her fleece leggings and slid into them. He smiled seeing that the sparkle had come back into her beautiful emerald eyes. Once they were both dressed, Aurelie reached out to him and pulled him into a deep embrace. He missed the feel of her tongue in his mouth and the little humming noises she made when she kissed him. His erotic muse was back. Finally. "Why don't you get in the van. I'll just throw this load of towels into the wash so it kinda looks like we were doing laundry," he offered.

After dropping off Mumford at Ruth Luther's, they were on the way to the big city. Wausau, about an hour and a half south of Minocqua, felt like the big city because it was home to almost 40,000 people, it had a bus line, and more than one street of stores. Wausau was nestled between the Wisconsin River and the fourth highest point in the state, Rib Mountain.

The Clark family began their shopping trip in the oldest bookstore in the state, Janke Bookstore, built in 1874. Aurelie found the children's book section where she intended to pick out a few picture books for her youngest nieces and nephews. The girls dragged Dillion into a plethora of stuffed animals. Benji, usually interested in all things dinosaur-related, science, and lately, medicine, found himself pulled toward the local history book section. They went in and out of boutique stores in the river district and on Third Street. Aurelie encouraged them to follow her into a shop where they learned how to make evergreen wreaths. All the Clark kids got very excited when they drove past the children's museum. Dillion felt it was a solid investment to get them to play hard before the long ride home, so he parked the car and paid the admission while Aurelie, just as excited as the kids, headed into the museum to play.

A few hours later, Dillion pulled into their driveway with three groggy children and a very large, very hungry dog. Inside, Dillion's job was to make sure packages were placed in the storage room in the basement. Aurelie made a simple dinner of sloppy joes, Bri fed Mumford while Riley and Benji began bringing up the Christmas decorations because tomorrow, after church, they were going to get their Christmas tree and begin decorating for the holidays.

During church service, while everyone else was reading from *The Book of Common Prayer*, Aurelie was silently praying that Dillion wouldn't get pulled away from their first Christmas tree and decorating day as a family. At home, the Clark kids and Aurelie got changed into their winter wear when she heard Mumford barking and the backdoor open. "Who's ready to pick out our first family Christmas tree?" Aurelie snuggled into her hat and scarf to hide her smile. God must have granted her this small favor. She looked up at the ceiling and mouthed *"Thank you."*

"Momma Aur, I like this one! I want this one!" Bri begged.

Aurelie looked at the eight-foot tall blue spruce on the Christmas tree farm. "Oh sweetie, that's too big for our house. It won't fit." The little girl pouted, held onto Aurelie's hand until the next best tree was found.

"This is it," Benji confirmed. "Here's our Christmas tree, a balsam fir."

"Well, it's a good height alright," Dillion said. "Why this one, Benji?"

"Because, after Christmas, I can use the resin to mount specimens onto my microscope slides, like they did in the early days."

"Huh, I didn't know that," Aurelie said.

"I read it in one of those historic books in the bookstore."

"So, we boys like this tree, what about the girls? Is this our Christmas tree?" Dillion asked.

There was a resounding "Yeah!" from the female family members, so Dillion grabbed ahold of his saw and began the process of cutting down the tree.

At home, the boys and Riley worked together to bring the tree inside and set it up in the stand in front of the family room window. Aurelie and Bri worked at getting mugs of hot chocolate ready with the right number of mini marshmallows. Aur also put on some Christmas music to further embrace the holiday spirit.

Dillion's heart was about to burst; he was so happy. He wasn't sure he'd ever fully enjoy Christmas again, but with Aurelie, there was a new, invigorating energy that just filled the space she was in and it filled his heart. Though he was the expert lights guy, he only worked to get the top half of the tree strung with the multi-colored lights and then Benji took over for the bottom half. Benji was just as meticulous, if not more so than Dillion had been. Next Aurelie brought the silver garland over and had the girls follow her, carefully holding the garland behind so as not to get it stuck on needles before it was placed. Then it was a free-for-all as they went searching for ornaments that had special meaning while singing, sometimes at the top of their lungs. This brought Mumford into the celebratory chaos with his own howling until Dillion made Benji find the dinosaur snood to keep Mumford calm and from howling any more.

Dillion was feeling full of the Christmas spirit watching his children excitedly accepting ornaments from Aurelie to place on the tree. Looking at her engaging all three without even a scuffle, he felt another level of love grow inside of him as he observed the next scene unfold. "And what about this lovely ornament? Any stories go with this one?" Aurelie inquired. All of them stopped and stared. Benji walked up to touch it first, but it was Riley who spoke.

"Momma made that. The last Christmas she was with us." Riley fingered the red ribbon and then carefully held the oval wood slice with live bark edges. She stared at the gold silhouette scene of the Virgin Mary, baby Jesus, and Joseph, printed onto the bare wood background. "She was very sick but wanted to give us one last Christmas present, so Grandpa took a slice from one of the trimmed branches of the tree out back and Grandma helped Momma with the ribbon and found a nativity rubber stamp for her to use." Dillion's breath caught and tears welled up in his eyes. He remembered.

Aurelie cleared her throat, clearly full of emotion herself. "Well then, this one needs an extra special place on the tree. Why don't you, Riley, pick a spot and have Benji and Bri help you hang it?" Riely looked very seriously all over the tree and decided on a spot right in the heart of the tree, front and center. Benji gently carried the ornament as he walked it over to the tree, holding Brianna's hand until they were directly in front of it. He carefully handed it to Brianna to hold while he lifted her, so she was eye-level with the perfect spot for the precious present from their mother. Dillion walked over to Aurelie and held her tight while whispering in her ear, "Thank you. I love you so much." She hugged him right back.

Dillion released his wife when Benji asked, "Momma Aur, what about you? Don't you have a special ornament?"

"As a matter of fact, I do." She reached into an old shoe box filled with crumpled newspaper and pulled out a pink satin globe, about the size of a softball, decorated in pearl and gold beads with a pink tassel pinned to the bottom.

"What makes this ornament so special?" Brianna asked curiously.

"Well, when I was about your age, Bri, I didn't have very many friends. As a matter of fact, I only had one true one, and she made this for me. She told me that if I needed a friend and she couldn't be there for me, that I should hang it somewhere where I could lay underneath it and spin it. It has special powers, she said, to let her know I needed her."

Benji spoke up. "Was that Cat?"

"Yep."

"Does it still work?"

Aurelie smiled, "Let's find out." She stepped over to the tree and found a spot deep inside the center of it to hang the pink ornament and set it to spin. She waved the whole family to join her laying underneath the tree to watch it spin in the myriad of color lights glistening off silver garland strands and glass ornaments. "Best friend magic is some of the most powerful magic out there. Mix it with Christmas magic and …" Once they all had their fill, they sat up carefully and Aurelie saw she had a message light on her phone. Cat left a text asking for a chat tomorrow.

When the tree was fully decorated, Brianna carefully selected the manger scene which was her special gift from her Mom and had been on their Christmas tree ever since she could remember. It was tradition that the plastic miniature manger would be the last ornament hung, so Dillion picked her up and lifted her to place Bri selected.

While the older children put up the Christmas stockings over the fireplace, Dillion found the Advent calendar and put it out on a side table. He opened the first drawer and the children gathered around to hear him read off the first chore of the Christmas season, "Put up the Christmas tree and the stockings for St. Nick."

After a simple dinner of chicken and wild rice soup, they took a family photo, wearing their Irish sweaters in front of the Christmas tree. Mumford wore an Irish scarf to blend in. "Hey Daddy, can we do a silly photo, too?" Brianna asked.

"A silly one, huh?"

"Yeah. How 'bout with all our dinosaur snoods on?" she asked. Dillion couldn't help but laugh, he almost said 'no,' but then he looked into the eyes of his wife and saw that twinkle again. This time he knew it meant that she was game for being silly. A few minutes later, the family was all in front of the Christmas tree, wearing their Irish sweaters AND dinosaur snoods. Dillion thought to himself that this was going to be the best Christmas ever.

After a very busy day, the Clark family sat on the couch and lay on the floor to watch the first Christmas movie of the season, "Merry Christmas Charlie Brown," before the children headed off into their respective rooms to get ready for bedtime stories and prayers.

Dillion took Mumford outside for his final potty time before bed and saw snowflakes floating in the backyard spotlight, like miniature ballet dancers. Inside, he went to give kisses to each of his children and tried to take it all in. They made memories today and tonight. Good ones. He hoped that with Aurelie in their lives, they'd have many more good memories than bad ones moving forward.

After stuffing each stocking with St. Nick treats, Dillion walked into the bedroom and noticed an ambiance of romance had saturated the space. Lights were off, but flickering candles were scattered throughout. Barry White was playing from wireless speakers, and he noticed something shimmering in the doorframe between the bathroom and bedroom. Making sure that the bedroom door was shut and locked, he let his eyes acclimate to the low, soft light. Then he saw her, and his mouth dropped wide open.

"Happy St. Nick's Eve, Dillion," Aurelie purred. He was dumbfounded and hard at the same time. She looked like the December centerfold in Playboy. Her ebony curls were shining as if freshly washed. Aurelie had taken a moment to put on dramatic jade eye shadow and darker eye liner that embraced her cat-like features. Then his eyes dropped to her crimson lips looking as if she had just licked them, which stirred something inside Dillion.

But what did him in. What made him feel like a 13-year-old pimply teenager who was terrified of ejaculating in his pants was what she was wearing or barely wearing.

Over her left shoulder was a wide crimson satin strap that met with two triangles of the satin fabric barely covering her breasts but formed the top of a large bow. From the center of the bow that was formed between her breasts, two long ribbons flowed freely over her glistening skin. Then there was the piece de resistance, the crimson ribbon that began at the bow's center, hugged her body, and slipped between her legs. To add to the shear torture, she was wearing six inch high, strappy red stiletto heels. Aurelie shifted so that one arm was over her head, resting on the doorframe while the other was sliding up and down the center satin ribbon teasing him as it slipped between her long limbs.

"Oh man, Aur. Damn, you are so hot! Where did you get that? You know what, I don't care. I need you now." He reached for her, and she smiled the smile of a siren who knows she's got you.

"Not yet, darlin'. There's still a little bit more to your present. Get comfortable on the bed. I have something for you." Dillion did as he was told. He wasn't about to screw this up by doing something stupid. He felt like a virgin going to a brothel to learn lovemaking from a master.

The music changed to Journey's "Lovin', Touchin', Squeezin'" and the room came alive with a sensual dance that had Dillion mesmerized. Aurelie's lyrical body was using the door frame almost like a pole for a striptease dance, rubbing her backside up and down, then straddling the door frame between her legs and rubbing herself while singing along with Steve Perry in a throaty, deep voice. Then she strutted to the middle of the room where she began to tease Dillion by rubbing her breasts and shifting the bow so that her nipples would peak out of the slippery fabric. When she turned around, he could see that the teddy had skinny spaghetti straps trailing down her back and ending in a G-string.

Dillion had lost all control. He unzipped his jeans and pushed them off so he could grab hold of himself and provide a bit of relief from the tension her private dance had given him. However, Aurelie wasn't having it and brought her sexual dance to the bedside before she straddled him and began rubbing and gyrating on top of him. With her hot, glistening body on top of his, he realized something else. She was wearing something slippery with a spicy aroma. He took a deep breath. She was exciting all of his senses into a frenzy. Aurelie whispered into his ear, "It's musk massage oil. Do you like it?" Before she nipped his earlobe.

Dillion freed his arms, took hold of her face and pulled it to his in desperation. It felt as if he were running out of air and the only way he would survive was to take hers. He opened his mouth to accept hers and ravished it. It was blind lust at this point. Her erotica surprise turned him from a passionate priest and family man into a fanatical lover. Though Dillion loved Aurelie's lithe body and enjoyed every moment he could lay naked against it, this satin bow teddy was a titillating treat. He slid his finger between her legs and shifted the satin ribbon to the side before sliding into her, furthering his ecstasy. Aurelie took control of setting the rhythm of their lovemaking. Grinding and rocking back and forth in a frenzy until the ultimate rapture was released.

Afterward, Aurelie lay on top of him and looked into his eyes, her own now smudged, and asked, "So, how did you like your present?"

Dillion tried to laugh, but even though she was light, she was laying on top of his chest which made his laugh turn into more of a cough before she rolled off him in concern. He turned onto his side to look straight into those gold-flecked emerald eyes that intoxicated him and confirmed, "There is no comparison. This was the best St. Nick's gift I've ever had." He moved in to kiss her softly on her smeared crimson lips. "I'm not sure I can even get you anything to match this."

"Well, there is still some massage oil left. I wouldn't mind a total body massage as my gift from you."

Dillion grinned, touched his forehead to hers and said, "As you wish," and walked into the bathroom to grab the bottle of massage oil to begin his St. Nick gift to his vixen wife.

Chapter Thirty-Eight

The next morning, after the stockings had been emptied, the kids were off to school, Dillion heard Aurelie on the phone with her best friend, Cat. He understood that they needed privacy, and he needed to get to his office. He kissed Aurelie on the cheek, said "hi" to Cat through the phone before leaving for work. He could only guess as to how the phone call would impact his wife's mood for the rest of the day. Luckily, he was kept very busy until he could finally leave, well after his children were in bed.

This time, when he entered their bedroom, it was no longer set up like a boudoir. Aurelie was lying in bed, sans make up and crimson bow, wearing a simple gray nightshirt. It looked like her eyes were a little swollen and red, as if she were crying. After taking off his collared shirt and dress pants, he lay on top of the covers, placed soft kisses on each eyelid and whispered, "hi."

"Hi," she softly replied.

"Wanna talk about it, or would you like me to do something for you?"

"Both," she sighed. Dillion slid under the covers and gently pulled Aurelie onto his chest before kissing the top of her head.

"Cat called today to let me know about their plans to come home for Christmas." While she paused, Dillion began to finger comb her messy curls. "She asked how I was feeling and if we had found out the sex of the baby yet."

"Oh. No."

"Yup." Dillion kissed her head again and hugged her before moving his hand to her back to rub it.

"So, she didn't know."

"Nope. At first, I didn't want to tell her because I was in such pain. I didn't want to tell anyone. And then I kinda put it out of my mind. Forgot about it on some level. Then after Thanksgiving, I was in a better place and didn't want to do anything that would make me sad again."

"How did she react?"

"She was hurt. Very hurt. Moving toward anger, but then she realized that I started to cry and then we cried together for the longest time."

"How did that feel? How did the call end?"

"Well, if I'm honest, I was mad at her for making me sad again. But then I realized it wasn't her fault. Then when we both began to cry together, it was another way to let go. I thought I had left all that anger and sadness behind me, but there must be some left and she helped me let some of that go."

"So," Dillion began, not sure what he should say next, if anything at all.

"So, it looks like there are a few dates that may work during the kids' Christmas break when I can take them down to my parents and see Cat. That is, if you are okay with that."

"Let me know the dates and I can see if I can arrange my schedule to join you."

"It isn't necessary, but it would be great if you can make it." Aurelie yawned and her eyes fluttered.

"Hey, you've had a tough day, and I just got home. Why don't you get some rest while I make a quick dinner before I go to bed? Would that be okay?" Aurelie yawned and nodded before snuggling down into the comforter.

Dillion carefully closed the door and checked in on each of the kids, gently placing a kiss on their heads and one on Mumford's as he lay at the foot of Benji's bed. He grabbed some leftover chicken and wild rice to microwave as well as a glass of milk. Sad memories don't evaporate, they just slink into the quiet corners of our minds until something brings them back to the forefront. The goal then, isn't to eliminate them, but to acknowledge they exist and create boundaries so they will not hurt as often and as deeply as they had initially.

The rest of December was a whirlwind for Dillion. Not only did he have his regular duties at the parish, but with the Christmas season, there was a ton more to do. Luckily, Aurelie had volunteered to help out with the Christmas pageant and recital, so Dillion didn't have to step into that craziness.

"Hey there little brother. Looks like I'm going to be in the neighborhood in the next few days. One of my clients wants to close on a lake home next week, so he can fly his whole family up for the holidays. Are you up for some company?"

"Roger, it's so great to hear from you! Of course, I'd love to see you. I will make it happen. Aur and the kids will be thrilled you're coming. We can set you up on the couch, we've got extra blankets and stuff."

"Thanks, but no thanks, Dillion. With the commission I'm getting from this sale, I may be able to rent out the whole hotel just for us to celebrate. I'll keep you posted on my ETA."

The week before Christmas, Roger arrived at the Clark home with early Christmas gifts for the kids and a bottle of Dom Perignon for the adults. "Good to see you, Roger, and thank you for this. Wow. I hope it goes with ham, asparagus, and au gratin potatoes," Aurelie expressed.

"Perfect. It's best paired with something a little on the salty side." Aurelie laughed and reached out for a hug.

"Make yourself comfortable. Dinner will be ready in about an hour."

The Clark kids peppered their uncle with tons of exciting news about school, the play, and recital. The adults caught up on the basics since the wedding. Then when it was time for dinner, Roger opened the chilled champagne while Aurelie placed crystal flutes in front of everyone's place setting and poured sparking grape juice in the kid's flutes.

"Momma Aur, why do we get to use your special glasses?" Brianna inquired, looking a bit concerned about being able to handle the fancy glassware.

"It's because Uncle Roger wants us to celebrate with him. He just sold one of the mansions on the lake."

"Oh!"

Dillion held up his flute to give a toast, "To my brother. Congratulations on a successful career, and a successful house sale. Thank you for wanting to share your good fortune with me and my family. Sláinte!"

"Sláinte!" The family cheered before carefully clinking their crystal flutes and drinking the golden bubbly liquid.

After dinner, Aurelie encouraged the brothers to go back to the hotel and spend some alone time together while the kids caught up on homework and she prepared for the next day's after school activities.

They drove separately to the lakeside resort, and when Roger opened the door to his king loft suite, Dillion's mouth dropped. "Holy shit! This whole place is for you? It's bigger than my house!"

Laughing, Roger replied, "I admit, I did splurge. Part of it is because I can afford it, but the other part is my early Christmas gift to you and Aur."

"Huh?"

"I'm staying an extra day so I can take the kids off your hands for a night, and they can stay here with me. I will pump them full of greasy, fried foods, sugar, and soda and then take them to the waterpark. I'll be the best damn uncle they've ever had."

"Sounds like you're the best damn brother there ever was! Thank you!"

"Want a beer? I picked up some local microbrews that I can't get in Chicago."

"Yes, please."

Dillion sat on the overstuffed chair and took a long drag from his bottle while Roger turned on the fireplace and lay on the overstuffed matching sofa. "So, little bro, how's married life treating you?"

"It's been a wild ride so far."

"Well, you did decide to embrace spontaneity and get married after only three months of dating. What'd you expect?"

Dillion stared into the flames and took another drink before he answered. "I don't know what I was expecting. But I didn't believe I could feel things again. Emotions like love, happiness … "

"And …"

"Lust."

"Okay, now we're getting somewhere." Roger sat forward with his elbows on his knees and looked at Dillion with curiosity. "Spill."

Dillion, feeling flushed, wasn't sure how far down this road he wanted to go, but Roger had always been there for him. His best friend, really. He needed to share with someone who didn't always see him as a pillar in the community, their priest. "Don't look to me to share all the nitty-gritty details of my sex life, but I do want to tell someone how mind-blowing it is." He finished with a shitty grin.

"Whoa. Seriously?"

"Seriously."

"Dude, you've got to give me something."

This time, Dillion took a drink and looked forlorn into the flames. "Well, Corinne was my first and I was hers. It was beautiful making love to Corinne in a simplistic way. No frills. Just love."

Roger nodded, took a drink and said, "I get that. But what about Aurelie? How was it getting back in the saddle after being celibate for more than two years? Any issues?"

"Shit, Roger, you're embarrassing me. Wanna come into the bedroom and take notes?"

"No thanks. I'm pretty confident in that department already. Besides, seriously, I wanna hear why it's different. What makes it different? Is it just sex with you? Or do you love her?"

Dillion gave Roger a piercing look. "Of course, I love her, damn it! I wouldn't have married her otherwise. It's just different. So very different than what I had with Corinne."

"Sorry, man. I didn't mean it like that. I just know that my dick can have a mind of its own, and it can be very difficult to think straight and make good decisions when he is in control."

"I get it. And I did think about that as well. But it isn't just sex and lust with Aur. It's so much more. I was dead inside. I wanted to die with Corinne. I forced myself to keep going for the kids, but I didn't have any feelings left. Didn't think I would ever feel anything ever again. I was just going through the motions of 'life' for the kids. It was like I was in a black and white movie. But then Aurelie shows up and she has all this energy around her. I saw colors creeping into my sight again. She found a way into Benji's being that only Corinne had been able to reach. She saved him, Roger. I'm convinced of it."

"Go on," Roger encouraged before bringing his beer bottle to his lips.

"I believe that the girls would have come away from all this just fine, but Benji was spiraling downward, and I couldn't reach him, his teachers couldn't, and I didn't have a clue what to do for him. Then Aur shows up and teaches him a few notes on a piano, and suddenly my boy looks alive again. Next, she brings into our lives this spastic giant dog who absolutely adores her and Benji. He lets my girls paint his nails, play tea party, and listen to Benji read to him from science books for hours on end."

"Aurelie doesn't make us choose her over Corinne's memory. We were putting up the Christmas tree and that wooden ornament that Mom and Dad helped Corinne make before she died. You remember that?" Roger nodded. "Well, she encouraged the kids to put it in a special spot on the tree."

"Oh yeah, I saw it, right in front?" Dillion nodded as tears started to well up.

"Yep. Then she had her own special ornament and apparently her tradition is to spin it and then lay down underneath the tree to watch it spin. So, here we are, the whole family, and that big bulky dog, lying under the tree watching the lights blinking and that ornament spin. If anyone walked in on us at that time, they would have thought we were nuts. But it was a truly magical moment. I fell more in love with her right then."

Roger reached over and slapped Dillion's knee. "That's great, Dillion. I'm happy for you and glad that she's given you your reason to live again. But what about the S.E.X.?"

Dillion chuckled and leaned back with a grin on his face. "It's mind-blowing."

"Now that's what I want to hear. Tell me more."

"I've always wondered about those stories where kings and noblemen would send their virgin sons to brothels to learn the ways of having sex with a woman, so they'd know what to do when they got one of their own. Well, being with Aur is like having my own private love guru. Sometimes it's soft, sweet, simple. Other times it's quick and dirty. Then there are those times where it's like she knows my deepest, most lustful fantasies, and she brings them to life."

"Wow. Intense. Good for you, bro. You deserve this. Hell, with all the sex you all are having, I'm surprised you guys aren't expecting yet." Roger said jokingly, laughing as he reached for his bottle. Then he saw a sadness move over Dillion.

"We were. I mean. We did. But then … " He finished his bottle and walked it over to the kitchen to dispose of it before he grabbed another.

"Dillion, I'm so sorry. I was just joking around. I didn't know. No one said anything. Why didn't you say anything?"

Popping the top of his second beer, Dillion walked back to the fireplace and stood in front of it before answering. "It all happened so quickly, Rog. Honestly, we weren't planning it. We were just enjoying our honeymoon without any thought of protection or wanting to add to our family. But when we got to her parents' house, her mom said something like Aur was 'glowing' or something like that. So, before we left Mukwonago, she bought a pregnancy test, and it was positive. No sooner did she get it confirmed by the doctor … then she had a miscarriage. It was devastating. To be that elated and then that distraught. We hadn't told anyone yet. Not even the kids. We just explained that Aur had to go to the doctor because she was sick and needed to stay in bed to get better."

"Oh man. You could have called me Dillion. I would have been there for you, brother. I will always be there for you. Just let me know." Roger stood up to join Dillion at the fireplace and gave him a strongman hug.

"Tonight, Aurelie seemed to be in good spirits. How is she now? How are you doing now? How long before you can try again? Do you want to try to get pregnant?"

"Thanks, Rog. I appreciate your offer and your concern. She is doing much better. We both are. Her parents came for Thanksgiving and right after they left, she accosted me in the laundry room and since then, it's been amazing sex almost every day."

"No shit?" Roger's mouth dropped wide open.

"No shit." Dillion smirked and took a long drink from his beer.

"Well, damn it, little brother. It sounds like I may need to get sex advice from you. Don't get me wrong, I certainly am not hurting for 'companionship' but not every day. You still didn't answer my question about having more kids. Is that in the cards? Do you want to?"

Dillion moved away from the fire and watched a fresh snowfall from the window. "I didn't even think about having more kids before Aur was pregnant. Now, I don't know how to explain it, but I feel an innate urge to make at least one baby with her. She's great with my kids. She loves them dearly. But there is something, like a yearning, for me to want to share a pregnancy and child with Aurelie. I want it. She deserves it. I know it doesn't make sense. None of this does. I don't think I'm explaining myself correctly." Pouring the rest of his beer down the sink, "I'm not used to drinking during the week, Roger. I think the champagne and beer mix is making me all muddled. Mind if I grab one of your iced coffees to clear my head a bit before I drive home?"

"Go right ahead, lightweight. And, hey, I've got two extra beds and a sleeper sofa here, so if you don't feel safe driving home, stay here. I'll call Aurelie and let her know."

Chapter Thirty-Nine

The next day after school, Roger was waiting for the school bus with Mumford and the kids' overnight bags already packed and in his car. They squealed with excitement and barely said goodbye to Dillion and Aurelie before jumping into their uncle's vehicle.

Dillion looked into Aurelie's eyes, and they almost sprinted inside their home. Excited to be alone. He put Mumford into Benji's room with a chewy before meeting Aurelie in the kitchen as she was starting dinner. "Stop." He commanded as he moved his hands underneath her sweater and found that she wasn't wearing a bra. *Bonus,* Dillion thought to himself.

"Stop what? Mmm. That feels good. Don't stop that. Doing that."

Dillion nuzzled into her neck. "Stop making dinner. I'll order in." He bit her earlobe. "After."

"Ooh. Okay." She sighed. Then added, "After what?" Dillion couldn't believe his boldness, but he quickly unbuttoned and unzipped her jeans, then used his teeth to drag her lace thong down to her ankles.

"Spread 'em for me, Aur. Go on. I'm gonna take you right here in the kitchen. Right now." He could feel her shiver as she kicked off her garments before spreading her long, lean legs as he commanded. "Good girl," he mumbled as he grabbed her waist to get her into position. As Dillion unbuttoned his own pants and pushed down everything with one hand, he began fingering her with the other. "Oh baby, are you ready for me?"

While gyrating her ass and pushing it toward him she spoke in an almost agonized voice, "Yes. I want you. Now!"

Dillion smiled. "What's the magic word?" He teased.

"PLEASE!"

Dillion couldn't wait any longer. He took his time, carefully entering her and closed his eyes. Letting all of his senses enjoy the moment when ecstasy began. She was warm, wet, and swollen, surrounding him. It was exquisitely sensual and painful to be taking it so slow. He wanted it to last. They had all night and into the next morning to make love. He didn't want to rush it. But then she pushed toward him, deepening his penetration and taxing his willpower. Next, Aurelie began gyrating again and he couldn't stop himself. If she wanted it hard and fast, that's what she was getting. Dillion increased the intensity and the rhythm. He could feel his body slapping against her and held onto her hips for dear life. Without anyone in the house to hear them, they peaked and screamed in unison. Shuddering in the complete release. Enjoying their hedonism.

"Dillion, that was impressive," Aurelie said later as they picked up their strewn clothes.

"You liked that, did you?" he asked bemused.

"You took charge of me right here in the kitchen. I don't think we've ever done it in the kitchen before." She kissed him softly and tussled his hair.

"We haven't been alone in the whole house before. Besides, I think it is a tradition to make love in every room of the house."

"Well, I don't think I could make love in the kids' bedrooms, but if it's a tradition, I'm ready and willing to have sex with you everywhere else. But first, I'm starving. Pizza? Chinese? Fish fry?"

"Pizza." Dillion went to Benji's bedroom to let Mumford out and feed him dinner. "I'll order the pizza before taking Mumford for a quick walk. And you, my love, why don't you change into something more comfortable? Surprise me."

"I better hold off until the delivery guy leaves, or you might have some competition." He laughed, then kissed Aurelie full on the lips before bundling up and walking out into the winter wonderland.

When Dillion returned, the pizza delivery person was pulling out of the driveway. *Perfect timing,* Dillion thought. After taking off his snowy outerwear, Dillion found the steaming pizza on the counter by some paper plates and an open bottle of red wine. Mumford was glad to grab his dino stuffy and rest on Benji's bed. "Aur, we're back. Where are you?"

"I'm in the bedroom changing into something more comfortable. I've got something for you to change into also." He stepped in and found she was wearing a black silk, button-down nightshirt, and there was a pair of matching black silk pants lying on the bed. "Since we're living on a priest's salary, I thought it would be more economical and more fun to share pajamas." He smiled and already felt his blood getting hotter taking in her tousled curls and looking as provocative as a centerfold model in her new black silk pajama top.

"Thank you for being so thoughtful and economical, wife." Dillion took off his clothes and stood in front of her, naked. Dillion took a moment and stared at Aurelie in awe at this natural beauty who just oozed sexuality. He got hard gazing at her and began to rub himself. Aurelie walked over and released his hand before she knelt in front of him to finish with her expert mouth what he had started. Dillion closed his eyes and enjoyed the erogenous intimacy.

A little while later, they sat on the couch with the fireplace crackling and the only lights on were the twinkling colored lights from the Christmas tree. "Sorry the pizza got cold," Aurelie apologized.

"No worries, Aur. You more than made up for it with my early Christmas present. Besides, who doesn't love cold pizza and red wine?" Dillion asked before taking a bite of the pepperoni pizza and then a sip of Chianti.

"True. I just realized I don't think we have anything for dessert," Aurelie stated.

Dillion thought for a second and smiled. "I think I know just the thing for my sweet tooth."

He walked into the kitchen, opened the refrigerator and grabbed "dessert" before leading her to the floor, prying her legs open, and unbuttoning her silk top. Shadow flames were dancing over her silky skin. Being near the fireplace would keep her warm while he teased her with something cold. "Close your eyes," he whispered. She lifted her eyebrow but did as she was told. Dillion squeezed a small dollop of canned whipped cream on her nose and licked it off. "Stick out your tongue," he ordered, and her little pink tongue came out of her crimson lips so he could place the sweet cream on its tip, which he sucked off before devouring her mouth with his. Dillion lightly licked her neck until he reached her perky breasts which he covered in cream. Slowly, methodically lapping up the cool sweetness and nipping at her taught peaks until he made her moan in pleasure.

He continued licking her down her torso before reaching her pleasure point. He placed an ample amount of cream on her to lick and suck off until she screamed his name and shuddered. Dillion was very pleased with himself. The student was becoming the master. He slid inside her while staring deeply into her eyes where golden flames were flickering. Aurelie took her fingers and while he was buried deep inside her, she scraped her fingernails slowly down the length of his back. The added sensation sent shivers down his spine and increased his need to release inside her, which he promptly did while he testified, "Oh God, Aurelie. Oh God!" He succumbed to his need for gratification before falling flaccid on top of her.

"I love making love to you, Aur," Dillion confirmed once he regained a semblance of presence.

"Mmm. I love making love to you, Dillion Clark. Who knew that priests are so passionate?"

"Well, that's the pot calling the kettle black. Who knew that band teachers are hedonistic?"

"Uh, duh. I was the lead singer in a rock band. I'm all about debauchery." They both began to giggle which made Dillion realize that he was a bit heavy on Aurelie's body, so he started to roll off, but it was tricky as she was so sticky.

"Gross," Aurelie said, "I think it's time for a quickie."

"Oh, babe, I'd love to, but I need to rest a bit longer before I can be up and at 'em again."

No, silly! A quick shower. I need to wash off all this leftover whipped cream."

"Oops. Sorry about that."

"Don't be sorry, Dillion. It was erotic, exciting, and fun. Don't ever apologize for spicing up our sex life. I just need to clean up, that's all. Come with me." She led him to their bathroom. Found some candles and lit them around the room before leading Dillion under the hot water. He noticed she was getting ready to wash up when he stopped her, grabbed the washcloth and soap, which he worked into a lather. Then, Dillion prolifically lathered his lover while peppering her with soft, short pecks and long, lingering ones. This was love making of a different order. The intimacy was titillating, intense, emitting waves of emotions that had no words to describe the impact his movements were having on his lover or on himself.

Dillion's cadence in the shower was matched when he dried Aurelie and then applied her favorite lotion, making sure to massage it into every nook and cranny, in between her toes and fingers, rubbing it into her lower back, kneading it into her calves. Aurelie returned the favor in which Dillion felt equally pampered and aroused.

Back in their respective PJs, Dillion made popcorn, while Aurelie chose a Hallmark Christmas movie. They sat on the couch, covered in a plush throw, eating popcorn, and enjoying a romantic comedy. They turned it into a drinking game with another glass of wine. Aurelie found a Hallmark Christmas movie bingo card while they were in Wausau and brought it out so that every time a character does something that's on the card, like bump into her love interest around a corner, or wear high heels while in the country, or kiss, they take a drink.

Well past their usual bedtime, Aurelie fell asleep on top of Dillion, with the plush throw wrapped around them and the flickering fireplace offering the afterglow of a night well lived.

Chapter Forty

Christmas Eve Dillion woke up to his children fighting over who had more orange juice in their glass. Aurelie was still snuggled under the covers and while he wanted to stay there, with her, he knew that the orange juice could escalate into WWIII. "Okay everyone. Pipe down. Momma Aur is still sleeping, so what the heck is going on out here?"

All of the Clark kids were vying for position with their voices. Dillion could tell that today could be a total disaster if he didn't get a handle on it. "How about I make sure all the juice is even? Then I want you all to clean up the kitchen and get dressed. Be on your best behavior so that Santa doesn't give you coal because you've been fighting."

The rest of the day Dillion tried to keep the kids occupied enough that they got their extra energy out in positive ways like having a snowball fight and building a snow fort. He noticed Aurelie moving a little slower today, but she had taken on a lot of extra stuff with the Christmas play and the recital. Tonight, all would be over, and the only thing left between him, and a week's vacation was his Christmas Day mass.

Rarely did Dillion get a chance to sit in the church pews and just be a guest in church. On Christmas Eve, though, he found it a privilege. He could just be "Dad" for a few moments while his children showed off in their respective Christmas activities. First up was the Christmas play where Riley was the Christmas angel narrator and Brianna was in the angel choir. Then it was time for the recital. Dillion was most nervous about this, as Benji tended to overreact if something wasn't going his way, wasn't perfect. Benji knew his piece, "O Holy Night," backwards and forwards, at home. However, Dillion was concerned that the added pressure of playing in front of an audience would be too much for him. He saw Aurelie in her red, velvet wrap dress whisper in Benji's ear before she sat down next to Dillion and squeezed his hand. Then it was Benji's turn.

Benji took a deep breath, closed his eyes, and began playing a melody that ebbed and flowed, taking Dillion's breath away. Silent tears slid down his cheeks as Dillion watched his son, who usually struggled to show emotion, totally immerse himself into the piece. When the last note was played, Dillion was the first person to stand up and clap. He noticed that Aurelie had also been crying and they hugged each other while Benji stood up, bowed to the audience, and watched while the entire congregation gave him a standing ovation. Dillion couldn't get over how mature his son looked at that moment. Yes, his hair still had a cowlick or two, but with his black hair, black framed glasses, black suit, white shirt, and red tie, he looked like a young man. Dillion's heart ached a bit with the realization that his boy was growing up.

All three kids received accolades from the audience as well as Aurelie. Dillion was so proud of his young family. He couldn't wait to get everyone home and start their own Christmas festivities.

"How does this work again?" Aurelie whispered in Dillion's ear.

"You 'forget' your purse or phone and go back inside to secretly put Santa's presents under the tree, nibble on a few cookies and drink some milk. I'll wait in the car with the kids and then we go look at Christmas lights for a bit and then voilà! Santa came while we were gone. Works every time." Dillion looked at his wife, who seemed tired and looked a bit pale. "You okay, Aur? Are you feeling alright?"

"Yeah, yeah. I'm okay. I just don't want to be the one to screw up Santa Claus for the kids."

"You won't. They love you. Sometimes more than me. More times they love you more than me if I'm honest. But if you're tired, why don't you stay behind and rest your eyes? I'll take Mumford and the kids to look at the lights. Just turn on the porch light when you're finished so I know it's safe to come home."

"That sounds good. I can handle that." Aurelie kissed him lightly on the lips and helped the kids open their candy canes, the first ones off the tree, for their ride. Mumford picked up his candy cane stuffy and jumped in the front seat while Benji and the girls filled up the back.

Dillion knew the drill as did the kids. No candy canes come off the tree until Christmas Eve. Then each person can take just one off the tree to eat while looking at Christmas lights. He found a radio station playing all the standards and backed out of the driveway with a car full of Christmas carols being sung and howled with at the highest decibels possible. Thirty minutes and a massive headache later, Dillion turned into the driveway saying a quick prayer of gratitude that the singing/screaming was over. Now it was time for the sugar rush from plates of cookies and mugs of hot cocoa and chaotic present opening. He was hoping Aurelie would be ready for it.

Of course, Bri was the first one inside, "Santa was here! He brought presents! Momma Aur! Santa was here! Did you meet him?"

Aurelie did a great job of pretending to be sleeping on the couch in her flannel PJs. "Huh? What did I miss?"

"Momma Aur! Santa was here! You missed him," Bri excitedly shared again.

"Bri, honey, let Momma Aur wake up a bit. I tell you all what. Why don't we all get into our PJs and then we can meet back here to open presents." Dillion smiled at the audible sigh from his kids, but they shrugged off their coats and boots before changing into their sleepwear. Dillion sat next to Aurelie and gently ran his fingers through her slightly messy curls. "Feeling any better?"

"Yeah. I guess this priest wife stuff takes a bunch out of me. I'm usually like the Energizer Bunny, but today just hit me like a truck. Thanks for letting me stay back and rest." In a whisper she continued, "I hope I found everything."

He kissed her forehead. "I'm sure you did just fine. I'm gonna go and change into my PJs. Do you think you can get the cookies and cocoa ready? It's going to be a long night."

"I can handle it. Besides, they can't start without me."

Christmas morning, Dillion's alarm went off at 6:30 a.m. He really wanted to shut it off and turn over, but this was one morning he couldn't do that. He did, however, stay a few minutes longer snuggled up to Aurelie, thanking God for all the blessings he'd come to have in the past year. He kissed the back of her head and scooted out from under the flannel sheets into a cooler room. After a quick shave and brushing his teeth, Dillion quietly put on his black clergy attire and walked out into the kitchen to grab a travel mug full of freshly brewed coffee. Soon his family would be up and getting into their brand new Christmas dress clothes for mass, but right now, the house was still. It was perfect.

At church, he wished a Merry Christmas to the few volunteers who would be helping with this morning's mass before he went back to his office to change into his Christmas clergy robes. Out in the vestibule, Dillion's congregation began to file in. Mostly older couples, but some young families were there, also. He could hear the choir practicing down the hall and a few moments before mass would start, he saw Aurelie and their family walking toward him in their Christmas dress clothes.

Brianna was wearing a long-sleeved red sequined dress with a red satin waist bow. Benji was wearing his new suit with a green plaid bowtie. Riley wore a red and green plaid skirt with a red satin bow at the waist and a fitted black long sleeve top with a sweetheart neckline. And then there was Aurelie. His beautiful bride. She never ceased to amaze him. The dress he bought her for Christmas fit her perfectly. It was a green long-sleeved, double-breasted coat dress with a green and red tartan bodice and side slit cut outs. The dress went perfectly with her emerald eyes and her crimson lips. He walked over and hugged and kissed each of them. When he got to Aurelie he whispered, "You look amazing," she smiled that mega-watt smile of hers, and he could barely remember that he had to work.

When it came time for his homily, Dillion walked up to the podium, looked out into the pews, and began. "This Christmas, I would like to take a few moments to talk about what Christmas means to me. As a child it was all about the presents. When I was a young man, it was about spending it with my family and my girlfriend who later became my wife. It was also about this time that I devoted my life to God and studied the scriptures so that I could share the good word with others on this special day. Then it was the look on my children's faces when they opened their first Christmas presents and learned of the magic of Christmas spirit and Santa Claus. But then I had several Christmases that weren't so special or magical. They were hard. So difficult I didn't want to get out of bed. I forced myself to move forward and find a way to make it special for my kids. I muddled through."

"This year, however, I feel as if I understand what the first family felt. After a very hard and long journey, Mary and Joseph had to rely on others to help them get through the difficult stuff. But it was worth it. She gave birth to God's only son, Jesus, and he brought new hope and light into the world. That's how I feel about my family this morning. It was a hard and long journey, emotionally, for us to get here. But it was worth it. Having Aurelie in my life, in our lives, has brought us hope and light. I thank God every single day for bringing her into my life, our lives. She has been the absolute best Christmas gift for me and our children. So today, I want to leave you with this. I hope and pray that you each find God's hope and light to bring into your own spirit, your home, your family. Amen."

That night, lying in bed after an amorous couple's shower, Aurelie and Dillion were facing each other and just being present in the moment. "Aur, you've got a twinkle in your eye tonight. What's going on?"

"Well, I was trying to see if I could keep it a secret until New Year's, but I suck at keeping secrets from you. So … " she turned around and reached into the drawer of her side table. She pulled out a long jewelry box with a shiny green bow. "Merry Christmas, Dillion."

He looked at her quizzically and opened the box. He pulled out the long plastic stick and looked at the lines printed out in the center of the stick. "You're pregnant?"

"No, WE'RE pregnant." Dillion couldn't control his emotions. Tears sprung through and he kissed her full on the mouth. It truly was the best Christmas ever!

Dillion and Aurelie agreed not to tell ANYONE this time, until the first trimester was over. This was probably the most difficult secret to keep ever, especially since they went to visit with her parents, her best friend, and then his family in Illinois, all the week between Christmas and New Year's. After the holidays, Aurelie and Dillion went to her first prenatal appointment to confirm the pregnancy and find out what, if anything, they had to do differently from the last time. Dillion felt relieved when the OB said, "Honestly, Aurelie is in great health and the miscarriage was likely a fluke. I don't see anything to be concerned about. But to be on the safe side, reduce stressors where you can, no heavy lifting. Make sure you take your prenatal vitamins and let me know, ASAP if something doesn't feel right."

Besides being a bit tired, Aurelie was not as nauseated as with the first pregnancy, so Dillion felt that it was a good sign. He and the kids took care of all the shoveling, and he forced Aurelie to wear Yak Tracks anytime she took Mumford out for a walk to help reduce the risk of a fall.

During their private times, he found himself rubbing her stomach, talking to, and kissing it. He noticed that she stopped wearing jeans and was forever wearing leggings and sweatshirts and baggy sweaters. He enjoyed watching her breasts grow and though she said they hurt, they were tender, she still allowed him to lightly kiss them on occasion.

The week of Easter, both Aurelie and Dillion were excited. They agreed to tell their families while visiting during Easter/spring break, since she was 12 weeks along and had no complications. On Easter morning after church, the kids and Mumford went on an Easter egg hunt around the house. When they regrouped, there were gift bags in front of each of them, including Mumford.

"What's this?" Benji asked.

"Open it and see," Dillion replied. They all dug into their respective bags and Aurelie helped Mumford with his. Each one picked up a T-shirt.

"Big brother, again!" Benji read aloud and looked a bit shocked.

"Big sister, again!" Riley read and smiled.

"I can't read! What's mine say?" Bri demanded. Riley helped her out by whispering it to her. "Oh! Mine says, 'Big sister, finally!'"

Then Aurelie held up a T-shirt for Mumford and read it aloud, "And you my fur baby, yours says, 'Big brother, finally!'" Mumford only understood that he was getting special attention and his tail thumped loudly on the floor.

"So," Riley inquired, "Does this mean you're having a baby, Momma Aur?"

"Yes, it does, sweet girl. We're having a baby!" Dillion's heart felt like it was going to explode like a firecracker. Tears welled in his eyes. Happy tears. As his family all scrambled to change out of their Easter clothes and put on their new T-shirts. Aurelie helped put Mumford's T-shirt on and the family had a spontaneous dance party in the family room.

"Hey daddy?" Bri asked.

"Yes, Bri?"

"Do we have to wait until tomorrow to tell anyone? Can't we go to Grandma and Grandpa Beres' today? Keeping secrets is hard for me." His littlest looked up at him with her sad, puppy eyes, and he was a goner. Really, they were almost all packed anyway. He didn't want to wait any longer either. Dillion looked over at Aurelie who shrugged as if to say, *why not?*

"Well, let's take a family vote." All the hands went up and two paws (with Aurelie's help). "That's it! Pack up the car!" In about an hour, the Clark's were going over the river (Wisconsin River) and through the woods to grandmother's house they went.

Just in time for Easter dinner, the Clark family jumped out of the car and practically ran, shedding jackets to show off their new T-shirts and share the exciting news. Dillion was in a happy mood, but Aurelie was elated. Celebratory chaos ensued as members of the Beres family jumped up to offer their congratulations to his family. That night, snuggled in their sleeping bags Aurelie whispered, "Dillion, you awake?"

"Yep. What's up?"

"Just wanted to thank you."

"Thank me for what?"

"Thank you for letting us be spontaneous and share the baby news with my family today. It means a lot. Really."

"You don't need to thank me. Our family voted; you need to thank the kids too." He heard her husky chuckle and he wished they were alone and not sharing the loft with three kids and a very large, snoring dog.

"I want to thank you because, well, it's silly and a little immature. Never mind." That piqued his curiosity.

"What? Tell me. I promise I won't laugh or think you're childish. Spill."

"Well, when I was growing up, all the celebrations seemed to be for my sisters and my brother. You know they all got, like straight As through school, so we celebrated their scholarships, awards, Magna cum whatever. Then they all got engaged, married, and had kids while I was still acting like Peter Pan, never wanting to grow up."

"Okay, I'm still not getting it. So … "

"So, since I've met you, I've been able to celebrate my new boyfriend, my engagement, wedding, and this pregnancy in this house. With all my family around me. I finally feel like one of them. Like I'm no longer the ugly duckling. Thank you for helping me belong." Dillion reached out of his sleeping bag and pressed his hand to her cheek.

"Oh, Aur. You've always belonged here. I'll tell you a secret, your dad told me that you were always his favorite. But even more importantly, you belong here," and he found her hand and pressed it against his chest where his heart was beating.

The next morning, he found Aurelie on a video call with her friend, Cat, in Montana. He heard the screeching all through the house, even though she was on the call in her dad's office. "Well, I guess that's taken care of," Bea said as she gave Dillion a hot cup of coffee.

"I guess so. Thanks for the coffee."

"You are welcome, Dillion."

"Hey Bea?"

"Yes?"

"When are girls old enough not to screech when they talk to each other?"

"Never, Mon Cheri."

"Is it wrong for me to hope for another boy?" His mother-in-law kissed his cheek and laughed before she left him alone to wake up.

They piled into the SUV the next morning, wearing their newly washed "big brother/big sister" T-shirts, to drive the couple of hours to Dillion's parents' Illinois home. While he was happy to be seeing his parents again, he was really looking forward to seeing Roger. He hadn't seen him since their "bro to bro" talk before Christmas. When they pulled into the driveway, chaos ensued again as the Clark kids ran from the car and into the house where Dillion grew up, to be greeted with hugs, kisses, and tears of joy at the good news. Roger grabbed Dillion in a bear hug and whispered in his ear, "I'm so happy for you, little brother. I know how much this one means to you." Dillion couldn't help himself. He tightened the hug in appreciation.

The rest of the day was spent catching up with his parents and Roger. Rose Clare made the traditional ham and au gratin potatoes, green beans, and fresh baked rolls. The meal was a basic, home cooked meal, but it reminded Dillion of a simpler time. Before Corinne was sick. Before she died. Before his heart broke and he didn't know how to live without her in their house, this town.

"Mom, Dad, tomorrow, do you think I could leave the kids with you for the afternoon?"

"Do you have to ask? Why? What's up?" Rose Clare asked.

"I want to show Aurelie around town tomorrow. I think I'm ready." She stared into his eyes and nodded. He thought he caught a glimpse of a tear before she moved her head away.

"That sounds like a great idea."

To break the serious mood, Roger came up to Dillion with a baseball and two mitts. "How 'bout we teach these kids about pickle in the middle?"

The next morning, they all said goodbye to Roger who had to leave to show a condo that afternoon. Dillion grabbed Mumford's leash in one hand and Aurelie's in the other. It was a beautiful early spring morning. The trees had buds that were ready to burst, but not quite yet, and the grass had pockets of green dispersed between splotches of brown. It was still cool enough to wear layers outside in the morning. It was a quiet walk. A comfortable walk. An important walk.

The first stop was in front of the elementary school. With everyone on break, they had access to the swings and sat down to swing while letting Mumford sniff around. "So, this is where the great Dillion Clark went to school?"

He laughed, "I don't know that I'd say 'great,' but yes, this is where I went to school with Roger and Corinne."

She smiled and pumped her legs to begin to swing. "Tell me about it. What were you like?"

"Well, we knew everyone in our town, so we knew everyone in school. I was average, but so was everyone else, except for Roger. He was great at everything. At school we didn't hang out or anything. I was the preacher's kid, but I didn't really get picked on. I was just there. Then Corinne came along, and we started to hang out. We went everywhere together. That's why I had to move. She was on this playground. At church, in the grocery store, at the candy counter, everywhere." He noticed Aurelie stopped pumping her legs and slowed down to touch her feet to the ground.

"And now?" she asked, staring at him in concern.

"Now it's different. A good different. All because of you, Aur. That's why I wanted to bring you here. Show you my hometown. See where I hung out. Be here with you. In a way to prove to myself that those memories, her ghost, if you believe in that, won't hurt me anymore. Can't hurt me. I can enjoy this place again. I can share it with you, and it doesn't hurt. Does that make any sense?"

Aurelie got up. Slid her lean legs between him and the rubber swing seat to sit on his lap facing him. "I'm glad." She smiled, kissed him lightly on the lips, and encouraged him to join her in a couple's swing. The cool air as they swung higher felt as if it was christening Dillion into his new life. A life free of grieving Corinne in this place. A life with new memories with his new wife. A new beginning.

The next day they traveled back home to Minocqua with the excitement exhausted, but a blissful calm took its place. They ordered pizza when they got home so they could have "dinner and a movie." *Life doesn't get much better than this*, Dillion thought to himself.

The rest of Easter/spring break was spent spring cleaning, getting ready for Sunday's mass, and school. After the kids went to bed, they cleaned up the dirty dishes and went over the calendar for the next week. "Oh, and I have to call the doctor's office to set up my next appointment. Do you think you can make this one?"

"Honey, I will make it. I promise."

He kissed her with a confidence that led to stirrings that they hadn't been able to act upon for almost a whole week. She led him into their bath where she stripped herself bare, and he stood in awe. Her flat belly had a roundness to it, and her small but perky breasts were plump, she had a glow—an ethereal light that transformed her. He was afraid to touch her, to tarnish that aura surrounding her. But Aurelie took his hand and began taking off his clothes with purpose. If this goddess wanted him, then who was he to deny her?

Dillion followed her into the shower. Tenderly kissed each of her breasts and her growing belly, before she lifted his face up to hers and forced her tongue into his mouth with a passionate thirst that had to be quenched. He rose to the challenge and lifted her up so that her hips were aligned with his. She wrapped her legs around his waist before he pressed her against the tile and ground into her, following her every moan, deepening his penetration with every scratch she laid upon his back, quickening his rhythm as she begged him, "Faster, faster!" And the release was pure ecstasy.

Hours later, lying in bed, his phone rang. He tried not to wake his sleeping wife as he carefully left their bed and prepared his body and his mind for the last rights he would be proclaiming in less than an hour.

"Morning, Babe," Aurelie called to him as she handed him a tumbler of hot coffee. "Another late night, early morning call?"

"Yeah, the third one in a week and a half. I'd better get the vestry on task to recruit younger parishioners. I can't keep up this pace," Dillion shared before a loud yawn escaped him.

"Well, I believe that deaths come in threes, so you should be done for now. Hey, listen, if you're too tired to meet me at the clinic today for the ultrasound, I'll understand."

Dillion perked up. Not sure if it was the coffee or what she said. "No, I'm not missing it. I promised. I'll be there. What time? Do we need to get someone to watch the kids?"

"Nope. It's at 11. Maybe afterwards we can grab a bite to eat? Call it an early lunch?"

"Perfect. See you then."

A few hours and several cups of coffee later, Dillion arrived at the clinic and found his wife already prepped and on the table for her ultrasound.

"Hello Mr. and Mrs. Clark. I'm your ultrasound technician this morning. I'm going to take some pictures of your baby to see how well it is growing and then the doctor will be in to see you, and you can ask her any questions you may have at that time. Do you have any questions for me?"

They both shook their heads, and the technician began to squeeze the cold gel onto Aurelie's protruding belly. Dillion was always in awe of these appointments. It was as if the ultrasound brought the baby into his realm of reality. Before the pictures, the baby was more theoretical, but to see it moving and everything, the ultrasound gave him a sense of awe. The best part was hearing a baby's heartbeat; thub dub, thub dub, thub dub.

"Good morning Aurelie, how are you feeling these days?" The doctor had been a dairy farmer's daughter who decided to go to medical school instead of veterinary school. She was very stoic in stature, but she had kind eyes and a warm bedside manner.

"Still a bit tired, but overall, I feel great."

"Any spotting or cramping?"

"Nope."

"Any concerns or questions before I take a look at your little nectarine?"

"Excuse me?" Dillion asked.

"Oh, sorry, at 14 weeks, your baby should be the size of a nectarine."

"Oh, got it," Dillion chuckled. But that was the last time he felt like laughing in that appointment.

The doctor kept going over to the same places and stopping. Then took a few still shots. And a few more. Just the way in which she was moving, he could feel his stomach drop.

"Great job, Aurelie. Here, let me wipe this gooey gel off you, and you can go ahead and get dressed. The technician will bring you back to my office, and we'll go over everything there," she said with a smile, but not a real smile.

Aurelie dressed quietly and grabbed Dillion's hand. The technician gave them another smile, but Dillion recognized that the smile didn't reach her eyes. When they reached the doctor's office, the technician practically ran away. The doctor began, "Aurelie,

Dillion, during today's ultrasound, I was looking for specific growth measures to make sure that your baby is coming along and is healthy."

She turned on a monitor and faced it towards Aurelie and Dillion. "On the left here, you can see what a normal baby looks like at 14 weeks, and on the right is your baby." Dillion looked at both photos and saw that the one on the left was the size of a nectarine, the one on the right, their baby was significantly smaller than a nectarine. More like a small apricot.

"Is it possible that you've miscalculated how long Aur's been pregnant?" Dillion said hopefully.

"That is possible, Dillion, but then I heard the heartbeat, and I am so sorry to say this to you, but it is very weak."

"But I don't understand, you heard a heartbeat? I heard a heartbeat. Our baby has a heartbeat. We heard it." Dillion was feeling anxious now. He didn't want to believe what she was telling him. Them. He looked over at Aurelie, and she was in shock.

"Yes, Dillion, there is a heartbeat, but as I said, it is very weak. Another concern I have is that your baby hasn't grown as much as we expect a baby to grow by this time. I'm so sorry, I know how much you really wanted to have this baby. I am afraid that this baby will not survive."

Aurelie found her voice. Faintly she asked, "Was it anything I did wrong? Didn't I take care of myself? The baby?"

The doctor took a hold of Aurelie's free hand. "No Aurelie. You've been a great mom to your baby. Up to this point, your baby was doing well. It was healthy. Sometimes you do everything right and the baby still doesn't make it. I'm so sorry, Aur, but this is one of those times."

Dillion had a sick feeling, but he had to know. "Doctor, were you able to see the sex of the baby? Do you know if it is a boy or a girl?"

"Yes, Dillion I did. It's a boy."

He felt a crushing pain in his chest. It was his fault. God was punishing him for wishing for a boy. He would never forgive himself for using his special relationship with God to ask for a baby boy. He knew better than to ask God for something that selfish. He counseled people all day long about making that mistake. How would he be able to face Aurelie?

A few days later, Aurelie woke Dillion up in the early morning to take her to the emergency room. She had lost their son. Dillion was convinced that God was punishing him.

Chapter Forty-One

Aurelie was going through the motions, as she had for the past few months. Get up, make sure the kids were out of bed and ready for the school bus, and then take Mumford for his morning walk. She used to change up the scenery, but since the miscarriage, Aurelie felt the most comfortable on the state forest trail near their home. She felt that being in the middle of the thick forest cover offered her protection from the cruelty that seemed to be attracted to her since she married Dillion.

He offered for them to go to counseling together, but the counseling he offered was through his church, in front of his God. Right now, she wasn't sure she even believed in God anymore. No one could tell her why she lost two babies. If another parishioner offered the not at all helpful, "It's God's plan," she may commit murder. But if one of them offered she should do something different like lay like a starfish for 36 weeks, drink green tea, and eat kale chips every day, or some other weird ass shit that would remove all the toxins and protect her baby until it was ready to be born, she'd consider doing it.

Dillion was focusing on his religion to get him through this awful, all-consuming grief. One Sunday in late spring, Aurelie told Dillion that in no uncertain terms, "I am not going to pray to your God to heal me. Heal us. If he is so glorious, Dillion, so perfect, then tell me why he chose not to let our two babies live? How do their deaths fit into His plan?"

Dillion couldn't find the words. He just left. Later, in bed, she did leave a little opening, "Look, I am still hurting, and I took it out on you. I'm sorry about that. But please understand, your God and your beliefs aren't working for me right now. I will continue to go to church with the family and bow my head during prayer, but that's all I can offer. Please don't ask me for more than that. I am too angry and hurt." He kissed her on her forehead, nodded, and with his arms around her, she fell into a restless sleep.

After this miscarriage, Riley's criticisms of Aurelie's mistakes lulled and she offered to help out in any way she could. Which Aurelie appreciated as Bri still needed someone to watch over her and sometimes Aurelie just needed to be alone.

The only people who seemed to be any comfort to Aurelie were Benji and Cat. And Mumford. Cat called or texted almost every day since the emergency room visit. Mumford had been sleeping in Aurelie and Dillion's room since the miscarriage and stuck close to her. She even gave him permission to snuggle up to her on the couch, and when Dillion was working late or on a death call, Mumford was allowed on the bed to comfort her. Benji seemed to be in tune with her need for stillness and quiet, except for when they worked on his piano lessons. She even started playing the piano for herself these days, after Benji's encouragement. "You know Momma Aur, you don't have to talk about your feelings if you don't want to. But remember what you taught me?"

"What's that?" she asked in a monotone.

"That music is a window to your heart. Why don't you play music for yourself again? Maybe it will help you release all the bad, angry, and sad things you are feeling. Maybe you'll want to start listening to music with a higher vibration frequency, which will attract more positive energy to you, so good things will come to you."

She smirked as she remembered that TED Talk and how Benji had been engrossed in reading about vibration frequencies and their healing powers. Aurelie took his advice and walked into her church. Talked to her god. In the middle of the forest, where she brought the tools of her communion, her traveling guitar, and Mumford's dinosaur snood.

Aurelie played sorrowful melodies into the trees while their blooming leaves absorbed her pain, hate, sadness, anger, and everything she put out into their vast world, one note at a time. Sometimes she put words to her music. Sometimes she screamed. Mostly, though, when she exhausted herself, she felt cleansed. Within her church, confessing her rage to her god, Aurelie felt absolution of her wrath, her passionate proclamations, and the offer of emotional emancipation. Liberating her from any guilt of her feelings.

After a week or so, her song style shifted. It wasn't so furious it was more like a smooth jazz set. Instead of everything looking and feeling brooding, dark, depressive, she began feeling a sliver of peaceful calm. She was playing in that higher frequency arena that Benji talked about. When she gazed into the forest, she no longer saw the starkness of the barren trees, the gray and brown trunks, branches, and stems. She noticed the tiniest specks of color. A sage green leaf, a crop of white crocus with golden centers, and the unfurling of fern leaves that were basking in a small stream of sunlight. Then, as if by magic, a beam of sunlight warmed Aurelie's face. She closed her eyes as she bent her head back to capture the full effect of the sun on her skin. She felt heard. She felt comforted. She felt, for the first time in months, like smiling. A genuine smile. It was as if mother nature accepted her imperfect self, her ire, her despondence, and showed Aurelie that she was still loved. She was worthy of love. "Come on, Mumford. It's time to go home," Aurelie concluded.

Back at the house, she looked inside the pantry to figure out what she wanted to make for dinner. Everything looked bland, boring. Plus, she'd been serving the same five or six dishes for the past two months. Probably everyone was tired of the same old things but were too afraid to complain. Closing the pantry door, she glanced in the corner and saw something that triggered a memory. As a child, when she was feeling bad, her mom would make Aurelie a plate of poutine, a French Canadian classic. Of course, Bea would make the French fries and brown gravy from scratch, but Aurelie was just starting to get her positive feelings to stir, she didn't have the energy to go all out. So, she searched in the freezer and good news! She saw the red and yellow bag of frozen French fries. Closing the freezer door and opening the refrigerator, she took note that she didn't have any cheese curds. Finding a grocery memo pad and a pen, Aurelie began writing down the items she needed to pick up at the grocery store for tonight's dinner.

"Momma Aur, what's that?" Riley asked carefully, not wanting to upset her.

"It's poutine. It's all the stuff you like to eat, but just mixed together. There's French fries, cheese curds, and gravy. It's delicious. Try some."

Dillion saw this moment to lead the charge, "Mmm, looks great, Aur. Thanks for making dinner tonight. I'm gonna help myself to some after we pray." She felt his hand grab hers as she bowed her head and this time, she actually listened to his words, not just the timber in his voice. Perhaps she was beginning to heal?

It was a tougher sell to get Benji to try the poutine, but once the girls and Dillion expressed their delight at this new dish, Benji took one fry with the tiniest bit of gravy and a smidgen of cheese to take a bite. The Canadian bacon and pineapple pizza was an easier sell. The conversation around the dinner table was a bit more expressive than it had been, everyone walking on eggshells for months, not knowing what to say. But this evening's dinner was opening up towards a freer conversation. The kids were talking over each other to gain Aurelie's ear. It was a cacophony of comments, a higgledy-piggledy exchange, but it brought a smile to Aurelie's face.

"Momma Aur, what's for dessert?" Brianna inquired.

"Well, to complete this tour of French Canadian dishes, I thought we could have strawberry crepes with whipped cream. What do you think?" She knew that the kids loved pancakes, fresh strawberries, and whipped cream from the can (especially when she squirted some in their mouths). It was a no brainer. Aurelie reached into the freezer, grabbed a box of frozen crepes and microwaved all six, putting the last on a paper plate with the strawberries and cream for Mumford. He deserved the celebration treat just like the rest of them.

After dinner, Dillion and the kids cleaned up the kitchen while Aurelie took Mumford for his final walk of the day. This time, she didn't bring her guitar. She didn't head into the woods. This time, she chose a different path.

When she returned, the kids and Dillion were huddled together around the kitchen table. As soon as she entered the kitchen, their talking ceased, and they looked at her with those "deer in headlights" look. "What's going on?" she asked as she was hanging up Mumford's leash.

"Nothing," Dillion replied.

"Hmm. Doesn't look like nothing to me."

"Oh, look at the time! You kids need to get ready for bed. Tomorrow's the last day of school for the week. Let's make it a good one." Aurelie was surprised that there was no complaining, and instead they all fell into line to go do their bedtime tasks. When all three were nestled in their beds, and Mumford snoring soundly in Benji's room, the young couple walked out into the backyard where Dillion made a small bonfire in the firepit. Aurelie went back into the fridge to grab two Spotted Cows to enjoy on this cool, late spring evening.

"So … " she started.

"So … " he copied.

"What was that about? At the kitchen table?"

Dillion took a long drink before answering. "You're not gonna let this go, are you?"

"Nope."

"At the risk of ruining a great evening, I'll tell you. I don't know if you've thought about it at all, but this Sunday is Mother's Day." He stared at her trying to assess her response.

Aurelie stopped looking at him and instead moved her gaze into the fire before she took a drink from her bottle, "No, I guess I didn't realize it. Go on."

"Well, they were wondering what to do, with everything that has happened. They, I mean, we don't know what you want to do on Sunday, after church."

Aurelie gazed deeper into the fire and took another drink before looking at Dillion. "You mean the miscarriage. What to do on Mother's Day when we can't celebrate our baby making me a real mom. Is that what you mean?"

Dillion looked down at the ground. "Aur, I didn't mean it like that. The kids. I. I mean we think of you as a mom. I am so grateful for you in our lives. You are great with the kids, and they are doing so much better than when I was an only parent. They want to celebrate you, but none of us want to make you feel bad either."

Aurelie sighed, stared at Dillion, and reached across the armrest of her Adirondack chair to hold his hand. "I know. I know. I'm sorry I snapped. I didn't mean it. I'm sorry."

Dillion squeezed her hand. "I understand. I'm still trying to work through my grief as well, Aur. I'm struggling here. I don't know what you want to do. If we didn't have the kids, I'd say we just pretend it's like every other Sunday, but they want to do something. They are looking forward to not being the only kids in school who don't celebrate it."

"I know. I know. I'm just barely starting to feel anything other than sad and mad. How about something simple? Away from all the hype and other people, in case I break down or something."

"Okay, what are you thinking?"

After a long pause, she answered. "What about asking Ruth if we can have a picnic on her beach and go fishing for the afternoon?"

"I can text her. I know that she's left to spend the weekend with her daughter's family. I'm sure it will be fine. Let's not tell the kids anything until I get the go ahead from Ruth."

"Okay."

Sunday, Mother's Day, arose with a rose colored sky. Aurelie awoke to burnt scrambled eggs and toast with orange juice and milk on a tray brought to her in bed. "I made the toast!" Brianna announced proudly.

"I made the scrambled eggs," Riley said, "Sorry they burned. I forgot to spray the pan first." Aurelie smiled and then Benji added. "I fed Mumford and took him outside already."

"Thanks, guys. This is wonderful. I'm sure it will all taste great. Thank you." Aurelie kissed them each on the cheek before they left her to clean up.

Before leaving for church, Aurelie called her own mother to wish her a happy Mother's Day. "Mon Cheri, thank you for this. How are you feeling?"

"Honestly, Mom, earlier in the week I had an epiphany. No matter what bad things happen to me, to this family, it's not because I've done something bad, or I deserve it. But I'm not going to lie to you, I'm still not that happy, crazy, hopelessly optimistic person I was before the miscarriages."

"I do understand. But you can't let it define you either. What are your plans today?"

"Keeping it simple. After church we are going on a picnic at Loon Lake and doing some fishing."

"Sounds perfect. Oh oh, I hear grandkids screaming in the driveway. I'd better get going. Love you, Mon Cheri. Call anytime."

"Thanks, Mom. Happy Mother's Day to you. Love you."

As she promised Dillion before, on the outside, she wore the face of a pious Episcopalian priest's wife. On the inside, she was pretending she and Mumford were in the middle of the woods again. After church and at home, she wasn't allowed to pack or do anything. She just got into her comfortable, ratty jeans, T-shirt, and sweatshirt and waited in the car while Dillion and the kids did everything else.

At Loon Lake, they drank out of soda cans, munched on bags of potato chips, and bit into sandwiches smothered in peanut butter, slathered in jelly. And who doesn't love Oreos for dessert? After cleaning up the food mess, the kids went back into the SUV and brought out a shirt box covered in polka dot paper and a bright pink, shiny bow adorning the top.

Riley said, "I know you didn't want anything for Mother's Day, but we wanted to do something to show you how much we love you. How much you mean to us. Happy Mother's Day, Momma Aur."

Aurelie looked at all of them and saw the trepidation in their faces. She didn't want to disappoint them. She could tell this gift and her reaction to it would mean the world to them. But she was afraid that she couldn't act the way they wanted her to act. She took a deep breath and committed herself to fake it if she had to. When she opened the brightly covered box, she saw a note, sort of—more like a declaration or a certificate. She scanned it and saw that all three children signed the bottom in a very formal, like a contract, kind of way. She looked up quizzically.

Dillion spoke, "Read it out loud, please."

"We, Riley Clark, Benjamin Clark, and Brianna Clark, are formally asking you, Aurelie Clark, to be our adopted mother, now and forever." Aurelie's heart stopped. Her mouth gaped open. Tears formed in her eyes. "Is this what I think it is?"

Dillion responded. "The kids came to me and asked me if they could give you the gift of motherhood for Mother's Day. They know how much you wanted to have a baby of your own, but they love you too. They see you as the mother in their lives and asked me how to go about making you their mom, permanently. I reached out to a couple of people who know the process, it takes about a year, and they told me they'd be happy to help us move forward with your adoption of the kids. That is, if you want to."

Aurelie was speechless. Her heart started beating again, with a feeling she had forgotten she had the ability to feel. It was love. No longer a grieving love but a happy love.

Riley shared, "We prayed to our mommy up in heaven to ask her if it would be okay and then Daddy helped us make this certificate to give to you for Mother's Day."

Benji added, "Momma Aur, we know you've been really sad because your own baby didn't live long enough so you can be a momma here, but we love you. We want you to be our mommy here on Earth. Will you?"

Aurelie was flooded with emotions now. She was still mourning her own babies, but here were three children who already saw her as a mother. How could she say no to them? They were just as broken as she was. "Yes. Yes! Yes! I love you all so much!"

They all gathered in a family hug. Tears of joy and celebration were abundant. Mumford stopped looking for frogs long enough to join in the group hug. Then when everyone was calm again, they broke free and gathered their fishing gear into the boats and rowed out onto the clear, glass lake. The loons must have heard their celebration and joined in with their own special calls.

That evening, in their bed, Aurelie held the certificate to read and reread it, in awe of the maturity of the Clark children. Dillion crawled into bed with her. For the past months, they went to bed wearing comfortable T-shirts and boxer shorts. They hadn't had their daily sex showers. At first, there was the physical healing from the latest miscarriage, but the emotional healing was taking a toll on their marriage. This one was harder to come back from. But in the past week, they had made some strides. Aurelie didn't flinch when Dillion tried to kiss or hug her. She knew that hurt him, but it was involuntary. Now, she snuggled into him, holding the paper document as if it were a precious jewel.

"Mrs. Clark, how was your first Mother's Day?"

"It was a surprise. That's for sure. But a good surprise. Thank you, Dillion. I won't ever forget this one."

He kissed her forehead. Gently took the paper from her hands and placed it on top of his nightstand. "I am glad. We all are. Wasn't sure if it was a good idea or not at first, but the kids insisted it was what they wanted to do. I couldn't say no."

Aurelie lifted her head up, stared into his eyes, clouded with curiosity and concern. She slowly let a smile cross her face before lifting her lips to his in a soft, warm embrace. Aurelie wanted to kiss him but was unsure how she would feel when she actually did it. As with her other emotions, they were barely there. But they were there. She didn't flinch or back away when he kissed her back, even as he intensified the kiss. Aurelie, used to the flood of emotions and animalistic responses to Dillion's lovemaking prowess, felt something, but it was still masked as if there was a barrier between them and the flaring synapsis that physically occur with her husband's caresses. She didn't want to stay inside her head to overanalyze how she was reacting to him and his light touches. But she also didn't feel like initiating anything either. Instead, she let her lips respond to his lips. Her tongue felt his tongue. His body was moving over hers. When he entered her, there was a brief moment where she felt herself contract. But Dillion was responsive and stayed still while asking her, "Do you want me to stop?" She looked up into his concerned eyes and nodded "no." She wanted him inside her. She was in the moment of the rhythm he led and when he released, she relaxed.

A week later: "So, how do we go about with the adoption?" Aurelie asked Dillion.

"Well, Johanna's husband is a lawyer so I asked her if he could help us."

"Hmm. I was hoping we wouldn't be including the whole parish in our private lives. I hate the feeling that they are judging me." Aurelie sipped her wine as they were on date night at a local supper club on a nearby lake.

"I know, I know. But lawyers and their wives know how to keep secrets. If they don't, they could be in big trouble. Ted is a good man and a family lawyer. We need a family lawyer to walk us through the process, Aur."

Just then a young server delivered their relish tray, consisting of marinated olives, pepperoncini, spicy carrot slices, celery sticks, and petite dill pickles. "So, how long will this process take? I hear adoptions can take years." Aurelie inquired as she sampled the spicy carrots.

"Well, ours isn't as complicated as all that since I am the biological father, and their biological mother is deceased. There are still a lot of steps to be followed as it is a legal process, but he told me it could take anywhere from a year to 18 months. For us, he is expecting a year."

"So, what are the steps?"

"We work through an adoption agency, which Ted will recommend. Then the children are assigned guardian ad litem, who will speak for them, interview them, etc. Of course, there will be lots of paperwork, home visits, and who knows what else. But Ted has offered his services pro bono which will help us, financially."

"Wow. This is seriously a lot to think about."

"Are you thinking you might not want to go through the adoption?"

"No, of course not. I wouldn't have said 'yes' and then reneged on a promise. It's just that I'll be under so much scrutiny. I'm nervous that they'll find something in my past that will make them think I may not be a good parent. At least when you have your own, you don't have to go through this rigorous process to see if you're fit to be a parent."

"Aur," he grabbed her hands and caressed them. "Love, they know that no one is perfect. But look how the kids adore you. How much I adore you. Do you think that I could stay this parish's priest if I married someone who was a bad person? Do you think I would marry someone who didn't have my children's best interests in their heart?"

"No. I guess not," Aurelie replied.

"Enough of this serious talk for now. Let's get back to date night talk."

"That sounds great," Aurelie brought her wine glass up for a toast, which Dillion accepted and then she said, "So, what should we talk about on date night?"

Dillion took a sip of his wine and leaned over the candlelit table, "What are you wearing under that dress, Mrs. Clark?"

Date night ended with Dillion slowly, meticulously undressing Aurelie and kissing every exposed body part before laying her on their bed and making love to her. She was getting better at it.

Perhaps it was the wine, but she was more relaxed than the last time. Not so much that she had her own orgasm but enjoyed the fact that she was beginning to feel sensations again. The friction of their bodies moving together. His mouth and tongue caressing her body. But that barrier was still there. It was thinning and Aurelie was hopeful that it would go away so that she could be a full partner in their lovemaking. Just not yet.

The school year ended on a rainy day. All the outside, last day activities were canceled and Aurelie met the somber Clark kids at the bus. "What's with all the sad faces? I thought you'd all be crazy excited to start summer vacation?"

Brianna wined, "They cancelled all the fun stuff because we couldn't go outside in the rain."

"Huh. That's a bummer." Aurelie gazed at the maudlin group and felt her creative juices flowing. A bit of the old spontaneity came back. "I tell you what. Why don't you drop your school bags in your rooms and get into your swimsuits? I'm just going to run to the store for a minute."

About a half hour later, Aurelie came into the Clark home to see her family sitting in front of the television watching cartoons. "Get your butts off that couch! We've got some last day of school celebrating to do!"

The kids turned around and saw that Aurelie was pulling out a bag of water balloons and a water slide from another. "Bri, go get a laundry basket and Riley, start filling up the water balloons in the kitchen sink. Benji, set up the water slide in the back yard. I'm going to my room to change into my swimsuit."

"But Momma Aur, it's raining outside," Brianna said.

"Yes, love, it is. But we're going to get wet anyway, so why not play in the rain?" That got a raucous cheer from the Clark kids who were excited to start their summer vacation off with a splash.

Aurelie scrounged in her drawer to find a suit. She got her hands on a tankini that she wore last year, but it was a little snug. Perhaps all her moping had slowed down her metabolism. For good measure, she put on an old T-shirt to hide the muffin top she was now sporting.

Out in the rain, the kids perked up and Mumford wasn't quite sure what was going on but wanted to be part of it. He ran around, barking and was drinking from the sprinklers in the plastic slide. They played until thunder rolled in and Mumford was no longer barking in excitement, but in fear. Once inside and semi-dry, Aurelie fitted Mumford's dinosaur snood on his head and handed him his dino stuffy.

"Don't be scared, Mumford, Jesus and God are bowling up in heaven, is all. They're just playing a loud game. Nothin' to be afraid of. I'll come and sit by you, so you aren't scared anymore," Brianna said to comfort the giant dog.

Benji put in a superhero movie while Aurelie made some popcorn and brought sodas for everyone. It was a great way to end the school year and usher in summer vacation.

At bedtime, Brianna hugged Aurelie hard. "Bri, honey, you're choking me."

"I'm sorry, Momma Aur. It's just that it was such a fun day today. I wanted to thank you very much."

"I had fun, too. Thank you for the hug, sweetie."

"Love you, Momma Aur. Can't wait 'til you're our for-real mommy." Aurelie's breath caught, and a tear formed in her eye.

"Me too, Bri. Sweet dreams."

"Sweet dreams."

Back in her own bedroom, she considered her naked body in the mirror from all angles. She was a little bloated in the belly, but that was about it. It was too soon. Wasn't it? Dillion was coming home late tonight because he and Johanna were planning the cancer event for next weekend. She didn't think she should bother him just yet. They weren't having regular sex, but they were having it again. Aurelie lay in bed, apprehensive, rubbing her belly. Then her mind drifted back to that fateful day, almost a year ago when he thought she was the IT guy and she got lost in his dreamy eyes.

The next morning, she woke before Dillion and took a moment to watch him sleep. She smiled as she remembered that first electric touch, the clumsy conversation, his face when she strutted her stuff on stage in that leotard. She had an idea. Aurelie lightly kissed Dillion's forehead and rolled out of bed to see what the kids and Mumford were up to. Then, after a cup of coffee, she had a few phone calls to make.

While out for an afternoon hike with the family, she pulled Dillion back so she could catch his attention. She whispered in his ear, "Do you know what day it is tomorrow?"

"Sunday. Why?"

"No, silly, what special day is it tomorrow?"

"Sorry, Aur, but you've got me. What's tomorrow?"

"It's our anniversary."

Dillion looked quizzically at her, "It's June, we got married in October."

"I know, but it's the anniversary of the day we met. Our first date." Dillion stopped walking and looked deeply into Aurelie's eyes and then she saw the "aha" moment reach his eyes.

"Oh my God, you're right! I'm so sorry I didn't remember, Aur, I've been so busy planning for the cancer event that I just forgot. We should do something."

She kissed him lightly on the lips and felt a little of that electric tingle that was so prevalent early on in their relationship. "No worries. I've got it all covered. Ruth is going to babysit overnight tomorrow and let us stay in the little cabin to celebrate."

Dillion kissed her back, full of emotion. "Have I told you today that I love you?"

"Not yet," she smiled with a little giggle.

"Well, Mrs. Aurelie Clark, I do. I love you more and more every day. I don't deserve you." This time, Aurelie reached up to pull his head into a more passionate kiss. One that let him know she was starting to come back to him.

"Ugh. Gross! Come on guys, you're slowing us down," Benji complained.

Sunday mass ended and while Dillion and Aurelie packed the SUV, Ruth came up the drive, and the crowd went wild. She made homemade caramel corn for the sleepover, and that was enough for the Clark children to forget all about their parents.

Dillion drove to Otto's Beer and Brat Garden where they had their first date. They requested a table in the beer garden and ordered Bloody Mary's and Reuben sandwiches. "It looks a little different during the day, doesn't it? I kinda miss the twinkle lights and seeing the stars while we're eating," Aurelie commented after taking a bite of her spicy pickle spear.

"True," Dillion then grabbed both of Aurelie's hands in his. "But now I can just take in your beauty." He brushed his lips over her knuckles and squeezed. "Mrs. Clark, have I told you how absolutely stunning you look today in that dress? Is it new?"

Almost blushing, Aurelie grinned, "Thank you, Dillion. I do feel pretty in this dress. It's new to me. Found it at the thrift store." Aurelie was wearing a flowing floral, tea length dress with spaghetti straps, a heart neckline, and a ruffle off-the-shoulder sleeve.

"Well, it looks magnificent on you today. You look like you're glowing. It's so nice to see you so, please don't get upset, but you look like you again."

She took a sip before she responded, thoughtfully. "I'm not upset, Dillion. It's taking me a long while to start feeling like myself again. Today I feel like celebrating. Something I haven't felt since before."

"I know. I hate that our little family has experienced so much pain and suffering in such a short time. I don't understand it, but I'm trying to keep us moving forward."

"Well, it's been quite a ride so far. Even though I've always been a thrill-seeker, a lover of surprises and spontaneity, I wouldn't mind some calm and mundane in our lives for a bit."

"Ditto." Just then their sandwiches were delivered. Onion rye grilled golden brown, overflowing with shaved corned beef, crispy bacon, melted Swiss cheese, and sauerkraut served with German Pub sauce on the side.

After a comfortable lunch, they walked back to the SUV and drove the backroads to Loon Lake. The sun shone high in the robin egg colored sky. A light breeze rustled the leaves. They opened the cabin which looked just the same as it had for decades. The red water pump over porcelain sink. The totem pole towering over the main room sitting on the hand-carved hearth. The tattered green couch and rag rug on the well-worn hard wood floors. Aurelie pushed the pine doors open to the far side bedroom and saw that fresh sheets were already on the bed and a handful of early summer wildflowers were set in an old tin coffee pot atop the ancient wooden dresser.

"Oh look, Dillion, Ruth even found the time to make the bed and pick fresh flowers. She is such a wonderful lady. She reminds me of Mrs. Romansky."

Dillion came into the small space, putting his duffle bag at the foot of the bed. "Wow, she went above and beyond. We'll have to find a way to thank her. But first, I'd like to take a moment to thank you for setting all this up." Dillion pulled Aurelie into a hard embrace. She almost fell into him, losing her balance and ended up biting his lip on accident. "Ouch!"

She pulled away and looked at the damage. "Oh shit, Dillion. I'm so sorry! I didn't mean to bite you. You just surprised me, and I lost my balance and I … "

"You bit me. Look, it's okay. Honest. I'm not bleeding. Hey, it still ranks up there as one of the best dates I've ever been on." Dillion suggested, "Tell you what, why don't we walk down to the swimming beach and hang out there until dinner time?"

Holding hands, they walked silently down to the swimming beach. The sunlight and shade were playing peek-a-boo with each other on the walking path between the main house and the beach.

When Aurelie and Dillion arrived at the secluded space, they kicked off their shoes and sandals and tested the water with their toes. "It's still a little chilly, but I think we can get used to it." Dillion assessed. He noticed that Aurelie had a coquettish look in her eyes before she took his hand and pulled him, running full force into the cool lake water, fully clothed.

Aurelie dove into the water and let the droplets run over her face and body. "Holy shit Aur! That was a surprise. We still have our clothes on." She rose from the water, fully aware that the white background of the dress would be see-through, and he would be able to tell that she was not wearing a bra, or panties. His look of surprise changed quickly into desire. He had been so careful with her these months. Always making sure that he wasn't hurting her, scaring her, or forcing himself onto her. Today, Aurelie wanted to show him that she was ready to take the lead in their lovemaking.

Aurelie stalked him like a cheetah and when she reached him, she pulled his face to hers and forced her tongue into his mouth with a fierceness that took his breath away. Then she turned around, pressing her backside into his front, pulling his hands to feel her breasts and nipples protruding through the cotton fabric that was clinging to her body. Dillion's reaction was immediate. He nipped her neck and shoulders while his fingers fondled the hard peaks of her nipples. Aurelie's hips began to grind into him, and she felt his immediate reaction. Next, one of his hands left her breast and traveled down, between her legs, and he began rubbing her. The friction from his finger and the wet fabric was throwing her into a frenzy. But she wanted to last, so she turned around and pulled his shirt over his head. Licked the water droplets off his chest and let her tongue glide until her mouth felt the waistband of his jean shorts.

She frantically pulled and pushed his shorts down so she could see him and feel him in her mouth. Dillion's moans echoed throughout the virgin woods. She could tell he didn't want her to stop, but he was also losing his balance. He was ready for her. She was ready for him. Aurelie stood up, wrapped her arms around his neck and her legs around his hips and let him glide right into her. She couldn't help it, but her own guttural sounds escaped, and she didn't care who heard her. In this moment, she wasn't someone's mother. She wasn't the priest's wife. She wasn't a woman who lost two babies. She was a sexual being. Aroused to incoherency. Abandoned to her own wantonness. Aurelie felt the rhythm intensify and her willingness to reach her peak and scream her release.

It was freeing. It was exhausting. She allowed herself to feel again. To let her emotions and instincts rule her actions and it was exhilarating.

They broke their grip on one another to glide over to the raft where they would lay in their naked glory—letting the sun's rays dry them.

"That was amazing, Aur. I was hoping for, I mean, it would have been okay if we didn't, but I'm really glad we did."

"Did what?" she said coyly.

"Have mind blowing sex."

She chuckled. "It was pretty great."

Dillion rolled onto his side and kissed her warmly before saying, "Yes it was."

They lay like that, sometimes with their eyes closed. Sometimes just staring at each other and tracing each other's body with their fingers. When they got too warm, they would jump in the lake for a swim.

Aurelie felt herself begin to dose off when she felt Dillion jump off the raft and then slide her to the edge of the raft before lifting her legs over his shoulders. Then the warmth of his tongue tasted her. Long, slow licks. Quick teasing laps. But when he found her spot, she hung on for dear life. He took her on an existential journey that gave her a feeling of leaving her body. Dillion shifted her legs so that they were around his hips, and he entered her carefully. Finding no resistance, he drove deep into her, practically touching her soul so that when he felt her contract around him, they shared the moment together, in a bonded spiritual act of love.

That night, they grilled porterhouse steaks and aluminum pouches filled with butter, salt, sliced potatoes, and onions. It was served with a Chianti, a loaf of fresh Italian bread, and a tossed salad. For dessert, Aurelie packed strawberries and whipped cream for them to enjoy eating off one another, backlit by the fireplace.

At one point in the middle of the night, they managed to get into the queen-sized bed and snuggle under the covers. Aurelie lay on her side and stared lovingly at her sleeping husband. Moments like this were what she was hoping for when she accepted his proposal. They were few and far between these days, but when they did happen, it was magical. Did she want to break the magic moment now with a dose of reality? Or wait until they were at home with their family. Dillion stirred. "Hey, there. Was I snoring again?" he asked in a deep, morning voice.

"No. No snoring. I was just watching you sleep."

"Oh. Okay then. What time is it? Is it time to get back to the kids?"

"No, not just yet. But it is time for something else."

"Mmm, that sounds nice, but I think I have to wait a little bit longer before I can be fully operational again."

She smiled and giggled a bit, knowing what he meant. "No, silly. Not that. I need to tell you something, but I need you to open your eyes first."

His brow furrowed and his eyes squinted open. Cautiously he responded, "Okay."

"I think I may be pregnant."

His eyes went from caution to concern. "Seriously? Did you take a test?"

"Not yet, but I brought one with me. Honestly, I wasn't sure if I should do it alone or not. I didn't want to get your hopes up if I wasn't."

Dillion kissed her and looked deep into her eyes as if searching for the right answer. "Let's do this." He'd made his decision.

Aurelie reached over into her bag and pulled out the pregnancy test, slipped into her flip flops and walked out of the cabin and into the outhouse. She made sure she didn't read the results before reaching Dillion. By the time she entered the cabin, he was standing in the middle of the main room in trepidation. Aurelie reached him and said, "Let's look at it together at the count of three …"

When she peered down and saw the word "Pregnant" on the test stick, she was overjoyed. Dillion had tears in his eyes before he kissed her full on the mouth and then hugged her so she could barely breathe.

A few days later, Aurelie apprehensively sat across from a familiar face, "Hello Aurelie. How are you feeling today?" inquired the doctor.

"Good. A little excited and scared, though."

"I get it. Well, let's get right to it then. The good news is that our blood test confirms you are pregnant. Congratulations!"

"Thank you. But we've been down this road before," Aurelie cautiously confirmed.

"Yes, you have. You are considered a high risk pregnancy at this point. While all our tests show that everything looks normal for this early stage in the pregnancy, we recommend being cautious and restrict you to bedrest until the third trimester."

Aurelie's heart skipped a beat. "Excuse me? Bed rest for what five months? Six months? I can't do that. I have three children at home. It's summer break. They need me. I can't expect Dillion to take on everything while I just lay in bed all day. Plus, I'll go bat-shit crazy. No. Bed rest is not an option."

"I understand, Aurelie, I really do. But you've asked me to be honest with you, and I am. You seem to get pregnant very easily, but for whatever reason, the babies have miscarried. Staying on bed rest will reduce the risk of losing this baby."

"But it's not a guarantee. Correct? You can't guarantee that I won't lose this baby. Can you?"

"No, I can't."

"And you can't determine why the other babies didn't make it to term."

"Correct."

"So, you are making an educated guess."

"Yes."

"Look, doctor, if God wants me to have this baby, I will have this baby. But I cannot ask the children to sacrifice any more for me. I haven't been there enough for them. And they want me to adopt them. I have to be an active part of their lives. I'm sorry, but bed rest is not an option."

The doctor nodded her head and smiled. "I understand Aurelie. But it doesn't change the fact that you are still a high risk pregnancy, so this next option is non-negotiable. I am assigning a nurse navigator to you. She will check in with you every week by phone and you will see me monthly unless there are concerns that pop up and warrant more frequent monitoring."

"That's reasonable. Thank you for understanding, doctor. If it was a guarantee that this baby would make it, I would do whatever you asked of me. But I won't put these children through any more than I absolutely have to."

"Got it. I will do whatever I can to help you come to full-term and birth a healthy baby. Before you leave today, stop at the nurse's station to make your first appointment with the nurse navigator, get your prenatal vitamin prescription, and if everything goes well, I'll see you in a month. Congratulations, Aurelie." The doctor reached out her hand for a handshake, but Aurelie pulled her into a hug.

When Aurelie got into the SUV, she looked at the clock and saw she still had a small window of time before she had to pick up the kids from swim class, so she headed to the church.

Arriving at the church, she took a deep breath and walked in to hear Dillion in the sacristy practicing his homily. It was Pentecost this Sunday, and he was sharing his own rebirth within this Episcopal community and via Aurelie. She smiled as he hadn't seen her just yet. She could tell he was getting to the climax of his story when he saw her and stopped. "Aur, I'm sorry, I didn't see you there. Is everything okay?" He almost leapt from the podium and met her halfway down the main aisle. He held out his arms and grabbed her hands.

"The doctor said everything is just fine. I am considered a high-risk pregnancy and she assigned a nurse navigator to me who will check in with me every week, but other than that, everything else will be the same as before." Dillion drew her into a bear hug.

"This is such a blessing," he pulled away a moment to look into her eyes and she saw in his, a sparkle that hadn't been there in a long while. "Would you mind sitting with me as I say a prayer of thanksgiving?" She noticed he didn't ask her to join in the prayer and that made it easier for her to accept. They sat down on a nearby oak pew. Dillion took her hands in his and bent his head before she heard him say, "Lord, thank you for this miracle you have bestowed upon us. We are grateful for your love always and specifically for its manifestation as a brand new life forming inside of Aurelie. Please protect this baby until it is ready to be born. Amen." In conclusion, Dillion brought Aurelie's hands to his lips and kissed them before releasing them and gazing into her eyes. "Thank you, Aur. You are so brave. I love you so much."

His declaration brought tears. "I love you too, Dillion. So much." Their foreheads met and they stayed like that for a moment before she broke their solemn silence. "Dillion, do you think we should tell our parents this weekend? You know, while they're up here for the cancer event?"

He pulled away and contemplated while he gazed at her. "That's probably our best option. But I don't want to tell the kids just yet. I think we should wait until you are observably pregnant."

"Good idea. We can tell them after the kids are in bed."

Saturday was a rainy June day. Perfect for an all day, indoor cancer event. Dillion and Johanna were thrilled with the turnout, and Aurelie played the perfect host, helping people find their name tags, seats, workshops, etc. She was in rare form, she just oozed positivity and her parents noticed, but she promised Dillion they would wait until tonight.

"Okay, Aurelie, the kids are in bed, your father and I know you two are up to something. Spill it." Bea said.

The Clarks and the Beres all sat down around the kitchen table. Aurelie led the conversation since her parents directed her to answer them. "Well, I won't beat around the bush, this week Dillion and I found out I am pregnant. Again."

She saw the excitement and the apprehensive looks in their parents' faces. "I am happy for you both. A baby is a miracle and a blessing, to be sure. But for you, Aurelie, at this point, is it safe?" Father Clark asked.

"Thank you, Riley, we do see this baby as a blessing, and we have concerns. But I've gone to the doctor, she believes that I am about three weeks pregnant, and everything looks good so far. She's assigned a nurse navigator to me to check on my progress weekly, and I'll see the doctor monthly unless there are complications." She recognized that the group nodded in understanding, but the uneasy looks were still there.

Dillion spoke up. "Look, we wanted to quietly celebrate this wonderful news with you all. But we aren't ready to share this with the rest of the world, because Aur is a high-risk pregnancy with two miscarriages. We've decided not to tell the kids until she is really showing. So, we are asking you to celebrate with us, but quietly until we are ready to tell everyone else."

"We'll support you in whatever ways you need us to, Dillion. I hope you know that. How would you like us to quietly celebrate this pregnancy?" Rose Clare inquired.

"Well, tomorrow is Father's Day. We are hoping that you'll stay for an afternoon barbecue. The kids can set up lawn games, and we can just be together to celebrate both as a family. What'ya say?" Aurelie suggested.

Rose Clare spoke first. "We can check at the hotel and see if we can stay an extra night. We'd love to help you celebrate."

"I'll have my office clear my schedule for Monday, Aur. You can count on us," Antoine confirmed.

Father's Day was a sunny, warm day. The Clark kids were on their best behavior in church, having two priests in the family celebrating mass together. But when they got home, they behaved like squirrels on speed. It was hard to reign them in, but Rose Clare had the knack and helped them focus on getting the water slide set up in the backyard, badminton in the front yard, and four square on the driveway. Mumford was so excited, his tail never stopped wagging and he was always chasing one of the kids to be part of the party.

Bea helped Aurelie bring out all the fixin's for the burgers and brats that Dillion grilled up. There was also potato salad, fruit salad, pickles, and olives to enjoy. Since it was a special occasion, Aurelie brought out frosted mugs and poured maple root beer into everyone's glass.

After a lively lunch, Rose Clare announced that there was another game that was a team competition. "Alrighty, time to settle down and be serious. There is one final game that will crown the Father's Day king. Children, I want you each to grab a kitchen chair and bring it to the lawn. Aurelie, Bea, can you please help me get the equipment?" Everyone looked a bit surprised but followed orders.

Each woman brought outside a quart of ice cream and an ice cream scoop. Rose Clare also had a box of ice cream cones. "Now, I want all three dads to lay down behind a chair, with your head closest to the chair. Kids, you each pick a "dad" as your teammate and stand on the chair with an ice cream scoop. Ladies, place one cone in your husband's mouth and bring the ice cream over to their teammate. On my count, each child will try to get as many scoops of ice cream into the cone as they can before time runs out. I'm putting five minutes on the timer and GO!"

The next five minutes were absolutely crazy, messy, and hysterical. There was more ice cream on the dads' faces and shirts than landed in the cone. Aurelie was laughing so hard that she was crying and finding it hard to breathe. When the timer finally went off, it was team Riley that won with two scoops that made it into the cone. Rose Clare brought out a cheap, paper crown from a local burger place and placed it on her husband's head with as much fanfare as a backyard barbeque could muster.

That night, in bed, and after a thorough cleaning, Dillion joined Aurelie and said, "That is probably the best Father's Day I've ever had. Thank you." He kissed her warmly while placing his hand on her belly.

"Even though the kids and I didn't get you anything?"

Dillion bent down and kissed her stomach through her nightshirt. Then smiled. "Aur, you're already giving me the best Father's Day gift ever. A baby. Our baby. I love you so much." Aurelie felt him shift in the sheets and move up to kiss her with deep emotion. A mix of gratitude and adoration.

Chapter Forty-Two

The Fourth of July came quickly. Aurelie got permission from her doctor to leave Minocqua for the week to visit her family in Mukwonago. While she was down there, Cat and Damon would be visiting from Montana. While she was excited to see her family, if she were honest, Aurelie was most eager to see her best friend and godchildren again.

"Do we have everything in the car?" Dillion asked.

"YES!" The Clark children yelled back, already excited and agitated that they hadn't left yet.

The long trip to the Beres' home went pretty smoothly, by Clark standards. For Christmas this year, Aurelie's parents gave them a family tent, so all three kids and Mumford could fit comfortably in one tent while Aurelie and Dillion would continue the tradition of the adult Beres children and their spouses bunking in the upstairs loft.

Since they didn't know when they would see Aurelie's siblings again, Dillion and Aurelie agreed to let each couple know, privately, about the baby. If word got out to the kids, there would be hell to pay that they were not told first and foremost. Of course, her sisters and brother were all equally thrilled and concerned about the news. Aurelie bonded them to secrecy via the sacred pinky swear.

That Friday night, the Clarks and the MacGregors met in front of the Salty Toad where a retro jazz trio was playing outside for Friday Night Live. The twins were in a souped up wagon with mag wheels and a drink holder. Dillion commented, "Damon, man, that is awesome! Where did you get that?"

"Isn't it like a mini man-mobile? Cat whined a little when I brought it home, but the kids love it as much as I do. Got it back in Montana. Why, aren't your kids a bit too big for something like this?"

Dillion looked around and saw that all five kids were in different stages of enjoying the music. Aurelie spoke up, "Well, I wanted to tell you in person, but you have to keep it under wraps, Cat … "

"Oh my God! You're preggers, aren't you Aur? Seriously?" Aurelie nodded and her best friend grabbed her into a death grip filled with love and support.

"I. Can't. Breathe," Aurelie gasped.

"Oh, sorry!" Cat released her bestie and looked at her with tears in her eyes. "I am so happy for you, Aur. Honestly. We will have to have a check-in every day and if you need me more than that, just text or call. Damon can help out whenever. Right, babe?"

A little surprised, but tracking his wife's facial expression, "Umm, oh yeah. Absolutely. Whatever she said." Damon smiled and Dillion laughed before slapping him on the back.

"So that's the secret to a happy marriage?"

"You've got it. Just say 'yes' and nod a lot." Damon slapped Dillion back.

"Come on, let's celebrate!" Cat announced then saying loud enough for even the kids to hear, "Who's got their dancin' shoes on!" The twins screeched and raised their hands. Brianna and Riley followed suit. Benji just looked around and Aurelie could tell he was looking a little peeked.

"Benji," she said while motioning for him to come near her. "Don't worry, bud. No one is going to force you to dance. Just do what you're comfortable with, okay?" He nodded and a little more color came back to his face.

This particular Friday night, there were bands playing jazz, the blues, country, and 80's rock. While they gave every band a chance, the group ended up at the 80's rock stage. Benji found a space behind the keyboard player while everyone else found the makeshift dance space in front of the stage and began enjoying themselves. The adults were singing along to all the songs their parents used to play at home and in the car when they were just kids, hopping, jumping, and swinging their arms around.

During a break the lead singer came up to Aurelie and asked, "Excuse me, but I know I've seen you before. Were you in a band or something?"

She smiled and shook her head. "Yeah. It's been about a year since we were together, but yeah, I was the lead singer of The Hot Rockin' Horns."

Recognition dawned in his eyes, "Yes! That's it! I saw you all at state fair one year. You were smokin'. Why'd you stop?"

"Well," Dillion, looking a little jealous came up and put his arm around Aurelie, "I asked her to marry me." The older man's eyes looked back and forth between Dillion and Aurelie until recognition hit.

"Oh. Oh, well, congratulations, then!" He shook hands with the couple and then asked, "Say, what'd'ya think about joining us for a song or two? We've got a couple of songs that could be duets in our set."

Aurelie looked up at Dillion and he kissed her with a smile. "I'd love to. What were you thinking?" She asked as she followed the older man to the stage. The group gathered round as they came up with a game plan for two songs that she could join in on.

"We're back!" The lead singer yelled into the microphone. "And we have a special guest joining us for the beginning of this next set, Aurelie Beres, the lead singer of The Hot Rockin' Horns!" The crowd clapped kindly, but the MacGregors and Clarks whooped and hollered.

The familiar lead guitar came on for Meatloaf's "I'd Do Anything for Love," and led right into Ozzy Osbourne and Lita Ford's "If I Close My Eyes Forever." Aurelie felt as though no time had passed since she last performed on stage and enjoyed every minute of it. The response was so positive, the crowd had grown to twice the size it was earlier, and the applause were almost as loud as the guitars. With that reception, the band asked her to play one more. This time Aurelie chose a solo, Joan Jett's "I Love Rock N' Roll" and just belted the lyrics. She felt energized by the audience and the band; her whole body was buzzing as if an electrical current was running right through her.

When Aurelie was done, the audience was on their feet giving her a standing ovation. She gave the microphone back to the lead singer and thanked the band before joining her family. "Wow, Momma Aur! You crushed it! I didn't know you could sing like that. Like a star. A super star!" Brianna complimented.

"Momma Aur, you were amazing up there! I don't know those songs, but I couldn't help myself. I had to dance to them," Riley admitted.

"How did you do that? Weren't you afraid to get up in front of all these people and sing like that?" Benji asked.

Then the twins had to come in to say their piece, "Auntie Aur! Auntie Aur! You're a star!" They yelled in unison.

Dillion gave her that look. The same one he had when he first saw her at the festival. He pulled her in and this time, he dipped her before laying a very deep and erogenous kiss on her. When he pulled away and guided her back up, he said, "You are amazing, and sexy and I love you so much right now." Aurelie smiled and was filled up with the accolades of her fans and family.

A little after 8:00 p.m., the twins were showing signs of exhaustion and the group decided it was time to say goodbye.

The following weekend, the MacGregor's made it up north to spend a few days with "Auntie" Ruth before the long drive back to Montana. Dillion had to work, but Aurelie packed up a picnic and got the Clark kids in their swim gear and Mumford rode shotgun to Loon Lake.

The twins squealed in excitement to see their new best friends and the giant dog again. Damon invited Benji fishing while the girls helped the twins make sandcastles and practiced their swimming lessons back and forth to the raft. And Mumford? He was happy doing his favorite thing at the beach, searching for frogs.

That night, around a bonfire, the children were mesmerized by the yellow and orange flames. The loons had quieted down for the night, and the stars were thick in the sky. Damon was working his magic helping with roasting marshmallows while Ruth was the designated s'mores maker. Mumford lay by Benji snoring away.

"These past few days with you, Aur, have been wonderful. I really miss hanging out with you."

"Yeah, it's gonna really suck when you leave again. But the daily check-ins will help."

"Ugh. It's times like these that make me question moving out to Montana. But then again, I have a great job out there. We have made a wonderful life for us and the kids. Living on the mountain, well, I just can't replicate that in Wisconsin. But I do miss the fam and you," Cat confirmed.

"I'm not gonna lie. I could have really used a best friend at my beck and call a few times this past year. Okay, three years. But I moved too. If you and Damon stayed here, we'd still be four hours or so away from each other," Aurelie commented.

"True. True. But four hours is a long weekend. Twenty-plus hours is at least a week's vacation."

They slung their arms around each other. "Cat?" Aurelie asked.

"Hmm?"

"When are you leaving?"

"We thought we'd go with Auntie Ruth to church to see Dillion's service and enjoy *donuts for Jesus* before we head on out. The twins will be ready for their afternoon nap by then and we could get a solid couple of hours in before we have to stop for them and dinner.

"Ugh, this time is going so quickly. I hate saying goodbye," Aurelie whined.

"You are always welcome to visit us in Montana, you know," Cat offered.

"I know. It's just that Dillion took off so much time for our wedding and honeymoon last fall that he is still catching up. And I promised my doctor that after the Fourth of July, I was staying put in the Minocqua area."

"I know. I get it. It's just that it's hard for me too. I'm going to miss you, Aur."

"Ditto."

The next morning, the Clarks and the MacGregors sat in the front row of the little country church and were all on their best behavior. Later, the children were the first in line for *donuts for Jesus*. After a brief gathering, the goodbye hugs began and so did the goodbye tears.

During Aurelie and Cat's final embrace, Aurelie confessed, "Cat, I'm scared."

"I know you are, Aur. I would be, too. But I put together our text, call, and video chat schedule through February. If you need me to be here, I will make it happen. I promise."

"I love you." The tears flowing freely down Aurelie's face.

"I love you, too, Aur. God, I'm gonna miss you. So much." Then Cat's hiccups began. A sheer sign that she was verklempt.

"I'm going to miss you more. You'd better get out of here before I won't let you leave," Aurelie threatened.

With that, the best friends released their hug, and Cat joined her family in the truck before driving onto Highway 51 North to begin their trek home to Montana.

Aurelie was both emotionally and physically exhausted. She could tell that Dillion was tuned in and gathered the troops to drive home. "Hey kids, I feel a little left out since you all got to have a beach day yesterday with Momma Aur. How about a daddy and kids' afternoon? Why don't we take Mumford for a hike and then have a water balloon fight?"

The Clark kids' collective "YEAH!" was palpable to the tourists across the street who stopped and stared at the commotion. Aurelie mouthed, "Thank you," to Dillion who hugged her and kissed her forehead before getting into the SUV himself to begin the afternoon's festivities. At home, Aurelie lay on their bed and fell into a deep sleep.

Chapter Forty-Three

The rest of the summer was a blur for Aurelie; taking Brianna to drama camp, Benji to science camp, and Riley to bible camp (again), play dates, doctor appointments, check-ins with the nurse navigator, her parents, meetings with the lawyer, visits with the guardian ad litem, and Cat. She was grateful for staying busy, it kept her from being worried all the time, but she couldn't quite tell if she was exhausted because of the baby or her busy schedule. At least when September came, she'd have a few hours to herself while the kids were in school. She found early afternoon naps to be her favorite activity.

By October, she couldn't fit into her clothes anymore. She was shopping at the thrift store and the sales for larger sizes. She wasn't quite ready to buy maternity clothes yet. She didn't want to jinx it.

On a dinner date to celebrate their first year anniversary, Aurelie brought up the idea of telling the children about the baby. "Dillion, what do you think about telling the kids about the pregnancy soon? I'm running out of excuses as to why I had to get new clothes or why my old ones don't fit."

"Yeah, I was thinking the same thing. I don't want to pull out the T-shirts again. I think that might scare them."

"Well, what about a family Halloween costume?"

"You mean something that would tie into your pregnancy? What are you thinking?"

"I saw this dinosaur costume, and I thought it would be cute for all of us to be dinosaurs, including Mumford, and I could be carrying a giant dinosaur egg?" Aurelie pulled up the picture of the costumes on her phone to show him.

"That's hysterical. Let's do it."

That Halloween Eve, the Clark family went all out and celebrated their expanding family with their children first and then with the community. It was a Halloween to remember.

The first snowflakes of the season began to fall a few days later. Aurelie had a bag of groceries in each hand when she looked up to the gray clouds covering the sky and smiled. She didn't care that there was no sunshine, she welcomed the flakes as they hit her cheeks and nose. Feeling childlike at that moment she put the bags down on the ground, lifted her head once again and this time, opened her mouth and stuck out her tongue. The first few snowflakes melted quickly and reminded her of all the wonder and magic they held when she was young, carefree, and didn't have to worry about schedules, budgets, grocery shopping—you know, adult stuff.

When she had her fill, Aurelie reached down to pick up the bags, pushed her butt out to hit it against the open door of the SUV and relished the overwhelming warmth she felt all over. Especially between her legs.

Chapter Forty-Four

"Father Clark?" the executive assistant called into the conference room. No answer.

"Excuse me, Father Clark?" Dillion was trying hard to shoo her away. This was the finance committee meeting and it demanded all of his concentration right now.

"Dillion! It's your wife. It's an emergency." That got his attention. He was out of the room and the building before she even had the opportunity to give him the full message. He didn't need it. He knew. He already knew.

Aurelie had been glowing when he left her this morning. Now, on the examination table, she was ashen. Her early morning rosy cheeks were tear stained. His heart sank further than it had when he heard about the call. He went to her side and grabbed her hand in his and kissed her wedding ring before holding it to his heart.

"I am so sorry to tell you this, Aurelie and Dillion. You've done everything right, but sometimes it just isn't enough." The doctor said as she stood closer to the shell shocked couple.

Dillion, not wanting to be in the dark asked, "What happened? Is Aurelie alright? What happened to the baby?"

Aurelie blurted out in a hiccup sort of way and the tears began to flow again. "I was just so stupid! I was catching snowflakes on my tongue. Then I went to pick up the groceries from the ground and used my butt to close the car door. That's when it happened. It's all my fault!" Dillion was trying to comprehend what she was saying in between the hiccups, stops, and starts. When she confessed, he just took her face to his chest and kissed the top of her head.

The doctor interjected. "Aurelie, it is not your fault. You've done nothing wrong. Your water broke early. Too early. It happens. Listen to me, it is not your fault." The doctor held onto one of Aurelie's hands while she drilled home and said that Aurelie was not to blame.

"I'm sorry, doctor, can you please help me understand what is going on? Are we having the baby now?"

"Sorry, Dillion, I will start from the beginning. About 30 minutes ago, Aurelie called and let us know that her water broke. She drove herself to emergency, and I met her here. I just finished my clinical assessment. Aurelie has experienced what we call a preterm premature rupture of the membranes. In simple terms, her water broke too early. Your baby is only 20 weeks and weighs less than one pound and her heart is still beating."

"That's good, right? That's a good sign that her, wait, our baby is a girl?"

The doctor nodded. "Yes, I confirmed it with the ultrasound exam. Your baby is a girl."

Dillion felt a little bit of hope and guilt that they had decided not to know the sex of the baby until it was born. Hope because it gave him one more attachment to this living, heart beating being. Guilt, because it was clear that she would not survive, he wasn't very attached to having a baby daughter. They hadn't even picked out a name for her. But maybe that was God's plan all along. Not to get too attached.

"Unfortunately, Aurelie is not dilated, and she is not in labor. I am so sorry to have to tell you this, but no baby can live outside of the womb at 20 weeks, weighing less than a pound. Their brain and their lungs are not developed enough to survive."

Dillion's head and heart were pounding. His breathing was shallow. He was trying to support Aurelie, but he was devastated. They were going to lose another baby. A baby girl. Oh God. Not again. "Okay, so I'm lost. Aurelie has no more amniotic fluid to support the baby, but her body isn't going into labor. The baby's heart is still beating, but she won't survive. What are our options? What do we do now? Can we induce labor now?" The doctor's face dropped. Great. worse news. *What could be worse?* He thought to himself.

"Unfortunately, in the State of Wisconsin, I legally cannot induce labor on Aurelie due to the fact that your baby's heart is still beating."

"Okay, so we have to wait for our baby to die, in the womb, before you can induce labor?"

"Yes. In the State of Wisconsin," she emphasized, "that is the law."

Dillion nodded. He was comprehending a little better. Aurelie still looked shell shocked.

"Unfortunately, I have more bad news we have to discuss." Dillion's mouth went dry. The doctor continued, "As you know, Aurelie was already at high risk for this pregnancy. With her water breaking early and her body not going into labor automatically, she is at very high risk for infection, sepsis, and she could die."

Aurelie's eyes went wide. Dillion couldn't believe what he was hearing. Not only was he going to lose his baby girl, but he could also lose his wife? His Aurelie? Right then and there, he knew that he would do whatever it took to save Aurelie's life.

"So, let me get this straight," Dillion was starting to feel his anger rise up inside of him as he spoke. "If I understand what you are saying, our baby girl has no chance to live, regardless of what we decided to do. Correct?"

"Yes," the doctor replied.

"If we stay here, in Wisconsin, we have to wait until Aurelie goes into labor on her own or the baby's heartbeat stops on its own before we can deliver her. Correct?" Dillion knew he was reiterating everything the doctor said, but by breaking down the information into smaller chunks, it was imperative that he understood very clearly what was being said and what were their choices.

"If we stay here, in Wisconsin, and Aurelie doesn't go into labor very soon, she could get very sick and die. There is a real chance that she may die, and I would lose both my baby girl and my wife," his anger swiftly moved into being terrified as confirmed by the shaking of his voice.

The doctor practically whispered her answer, "Yes, Dillion. I am so very sorry to confirm that there is a very real chance you could lose both mom and baby."

Dillion strategically asked his next question. "If we stay in Wisconsin, correct?"

Awareness shown in the doctor's eyes. "Yes, if you stay in Wisconsin."

Now Dillion boldly asked his follow-up question. He knew what he was about to ask was risky, in more ways than one. But to save his wife's life, he was willing to make a deal with the devil if he had to. He'd already lost one young wife, and it damn near killed him. He was going to see this through. Whatever it took.

"What if we lived in, let's say, Illinois? Would that still be our only option?"

The doctor, very calculatedly, answered Dillion. "In the State of Illinois, if there is a fetal heartbeat but the baby's life is not viable, labor can be induced if the mother's life is in danger."

"Thank you, doctor. When can I take Aurelie home?"

The nurse gingerly assisted Aurelie out of the wheelchair, while Dillion waited in the minivan. He couldn't wait to get out of sight of this place. With one hand on the steering wheel, he held Aurelie's in the other. His head was spinning. As much as he wanted to leave Minocqua right now and drive straight through to Illinois, he had work and the kids to sort out. But his mind was made up. He wouldn't risk Aurelie's life. Period.

When they got into the driveway, they both sat there. Until Aurelie said something. "Dillion, I'm sorry. I'm so sorry," she wept. Seeing her like this broke his heart. He took his hand and began to brush tears from her face.

"Shh. Shh. Aur, it isn't your fault. It isn't anyone's fault. It just happened. We have to take care of you now. I love you. So much. I won't lose you, too." He pulled her hand to his lips and kissed it tenderly.

She stopped the heavy crying, but the tears were still traveling down her cheeks when she finally had the strength to talk again. "I just need to say this. Before the children come home." He nodded, listening with full intention. "I love all three of them with all of my heart. You know that, don't you?"

"Absolutely."

"But there is a part of me that was really excited about this baby. The opportunity to feel it grow inside of me. To hold it. I mean, her. To name her." She paused and he squeezed her hand. "I know that my life is at risk right now. It scares me shitless. But, what would be even worse, for me, is to not even have the *possibility* of holding our little girl, even if it is only a moment, while her heart would still be beating."

Dillion's tears broke through and started to stream down his face, blurring Aurelie as if she were an ethereal being fading from existence. But he held on to her, fingering her wedding ring as if it held some magical powers to help them through this dark time. To keep her safe with him.

"I guess what I am trying to say is, thank you for your willingness to drive to Illinois. To give me, us the slightest chance to meet our baby girl before she has to leave us." Dillion understood. While his priority was clear, he also wanted to take this chance, however slim, to meet his baby girl, alive.

Dillion leaned over the consul and rested his forehead to hers. They stayed like that listening to their silent tears drop and cover their entwined hands. Aurelie was the first to pull away. "Dillion?"

"Hmm?"

"What do we tell the kids? We just told them about the baby. They've only had a week with her."

"I'll have to tell them the truth. I'll help you inside and you go ahead and call Cat and your parents. I'll take care of everything else. The kids won't be home from school for a bit. Call me if you need me. For anything. But I'm going to need reach my parents and their hospital to see if they will take us."

Dillion worked with determination. He wasn't taking no for an answer and with his dad's help, found a physician who was willing to induce Aurelie the next day. He checked in on her and saw Mumford was right by Aurelie's side, laying his head on her lap, and she was talk crying on the phone. Dillion wanted to give her the space she needed, so he began packing for everyone and throwing everything into the back of the minivan. His assistant was arranging for someone to pick up the SUV at the hospital and bring it back to the house. He already called his bishop to give him the news and start the process of coverage for the week. His parents and Roger were preparing the house for the extra bodies.

In between phone calls and packing, Dillion heard the school bus pull up and the familiar voices and foot stomps coming up to the back door. Aurelie was lying on the couch with Mumford right by her side. His head and ears perked up but he didn't budge.

"Hi Daddy! Why are you home so early?" Riley could tell something was off.

"Hi sweetie. Why don't you all take off your snow stuff and meet us in the family room? We have something to tell you."

As was her new routine, Riley came over to Aurelie kissed her on her cheek, then kissed her belly before saying "hi" to the baby.

Dillion really didn't want to do this. It was as awful as when he had to tell them about Corinne. "We got some sad news today."

"What's wrong, Daddy?" Brianna scooted up to Mumford on his other side to receive his comfort.

"Well, our baby is going to heaven soon. Aurelie saw the doctor today and the fluid that keeps the baby safe and healthy inside, has leaked out. The baby can't survive inside Aurelie without the fluid and she is too small to live outside of Aurelie either."

"I don't understand, Daddy. I just talked to the baby in Aurelie's belly. She's there. I can feel her spirit in there."

"I know, Riley. I know. It's very hard to understand, while the baby's heart is still beating now, it will stop. We just don't know when that will happen. And that's the problem." Dillion could feel himself choked up again, but he had to get through this.

This time Benji spoke up. He was sitting on the floor, at Aurelie's feet. "What's the problem, Dad. What is it?"

This time Aurelie spoke. "The problem is, Benji, that if I don't have the baby very soon, I may get very sick. Very, very sick."

"You mean, you could die, too?" Benji asked, with fear palpably resonating in his voice.

"Yes, Benji. There is a very real possibility that I could die." The children clung to Aurelie as their tears began to stain their cheeks. Dillion was barely keeping it together. But just enough to get through the rest of the conversation.

"We have a chance. A very small chance to deliver our baby alive and save Aurelie's life. It's not a guarantee, but it is the best chance we have, and it means that we are all going to drive down to Illinois tonight and stay with Grandma and Grandpa Clark. Aurelie will be admitted to the hospital down there and be given medicine to help her go into labor and have the baby tomorrow." They all nodded. Then Benji spoke up again.

"Wait a minute. Did you say, 'her'? Is the baby a girl?" Benji asked.

Aurelie barely audibly confirmed, "Yes."

"She should have a name. Can we name her?" Riley thought logically. Dillion's eyes filled up, but he could still see the outline of Aurelie's head nodding *yes* in agreement.

Brianna spoke up quickly. "I think her name should be Angel. 'Cause she's gonna be an angel up in heaven, like Momma."

Aurelie found her voice, "That's a wonderful idea, Brianna. What about maybe something that is a girl's name but has 'angel' in it?"

Benji thought for a moment and then said, "What about Angelica? I have an Angelica in my class. That has angel in it."

"I know an Angelina. She was my friend in Big Rock," Riley offered.

"How about Angela?" Dillion suggested.

Aurelie dried her tears and spoke up. "Great ideas, everyone. I don't think I can choose. How about if you write them on a piece of paper and we pick one?" Which is exactly what happened.

The ride to Big Rock was very quiet. Everyone seemed to understand the seriousness of their situation and allowed Dillion to drive without distractions. Several hours later, they arrived in his parents' driveway. Physically and mentally exhausted.

Dillion lay awake, just staring at the ceiling. His troubled mind was running through all kinds of scenarios, making sleep an impossibility. He slid out from under the covers and walked into the kitchen, rummaging for something to eat, just for something to do. "Couldn't sleep, son?" His dad asked, looking as rumpled as Dillion.

"No. My mind keeps racing. Can't make it stop." Dillion found a box of cereal, while his dad brought out the milk from the refrigerator. They sat at the kitchen table with their bowls of cereal, reminiscent of earlier times, when Dillion was a child and couldn't sleep.

"Do you want to talk about it, or would you prefer to eat in silence?" Riley asked.

"Maybe talking through some of this might help," Dillion considered.

"Okay then, son, what do you want to talk about?"

"Do you think it is a sin what we are about to do? Am I going to be in trouble with the church? Could I lose my job?"

Riley paused to finish his spoonful of cereal then placed his hand on Dillion's arm. "What I think doesn't matter, Dillion. It is what is important to you and your family that counts. We believe life begins when the baby can survive on its own. However … " he paused.

"I know. I could lose parishioners over this. Hopefully, not enough to lose my job." Dillion looked into his father's eyes as his own were filling with tears, emotions rushing through him. "I can face losing my job, Dad. I cannot lose her. Aurelie. Like I lost Corinne. I will do whatever it takes to save her life. Period."

Riley squeezed Dillion's arm in solidarity. "I know, son. I will support you no matter what. Your mom, too. We love you. We empathize with what you're going through. However we can help, we are only a phone call away."

After finishing their bowls of cereal, Dillion reached out and hugged his dad fiercely. His emotional confession finally brought him the sleep that had evaded him earlier. He crept into his old bedroom, snuggled into Aurelie, and passed out.

Aurelie woke him with her rustling around the bedroom. "Sorry I woke you," she almost whispered. He could see the concern, fear, and sadness in her eyes. He wished he could take it all away, but he couldn't.

"No, don't be sorry. I need to get up and make sure the kids are getting ready."

Everyone congregated in the kitchen, where Dillion's dad led the family in prayer before Dillion drove Aurelie to the hospital. It was another quiet ride, he just needed to have enough focus to get them to the hospital safely.

When they arrived, Aurelie and Dillion were ushered into a private birthing suite where her labor and delivery nurse met them and talked them through the steps. Dillion assisted Aurelie in getting undressed and into her patient gown. He held her hand as the nurse inserted the IV while Dillion focused on being present. Whatever Aurelie needed, he would give her.

The contractions began very soon after the IV was dripping medicine into Aurelie's veins. Dillion was a pro at being the support during contractions, having been in that position three times before. He felt comforted by the fact, at least in this situation, he knew what to do, when to do it, and that he was being a help to Aurelie who was doing all the work. During the few breaks between contractions, he just sat in amazement at how brave his wife was. What courage it took for her to go through all the physical and emotional effort to labor and give birth to a baby, knowing the outcome.

The doctor came in to check on her and her baby's vitals until it was time for Aurelie to push. Dillion took a deep breath, closed his eyes, kissed Aurelie and whispered, "I love you," before praying to God to give them an opportunity to meet their daughter, alive, before they have to say goodbye to her, forever.

He heard Aurelie's moaning and screaming and accepted her hand-crushing grip. It was the least he could offer her. Then he heard what made his heart stop. "Last push, Aurelie." Would they be able to hold a live baby in a few moments? Or would the grieving begin immediately?

When the baby was delivered, he could tell by the way the team behaved that all his prayers, their efforts, were in vain. Then the crack in his heart deepened. "I want to hold her. Where's my baby? Is she alive? I want to hold her. Please!" He heard the desperation in Aurelie's voice, and it matched his own. Why couldn't they get even this prayer answered?

Without even cleaning her up, the care team quickly moved to lay the lifeless little body on top of Aurelie's chest. Dillion reached out to touch their baby girl. While she was still warm to the touch, her heart was no longer beating. The trauma of birth was just too much for her. Tears were flowing heavily and he had absolutely no words of comfort for his wife as he couldn't control his own grief. His own pain.

They huddled like the broken family they were for what seemed like an eternity, until the warmth left her tiny body. It was then that Aurelie finally accepted the offer to allow the nurses to take her, clean her up, and put her into some pink, preemie clothing. Also, around this time, Aurelie started to feel contractions again, this time to release the afterbirth.

While the team helped Aurelie clean up and change the bed linens and her gown, Dillion took those few moments to call his parents and hers. Bea and Antoine had been traveling from Mukwonago to Big Rock that morning. They would be there within the next hour. Rose Clare and Riley were getting the children ready to come to the hospital.

While Aurelie was finishing her clean up in the bathroom, one of the nurses came into the room with the tiniest pink bundle he had ever seen. She almost looked like a doll when the nurse offered for him to hold his daughter. He opened his arms and accepted her. She was bundled in a fuzzy pink blanket that opened to see her head covered in a pink handknitted cap. She looked like any of his other sleeping babies, except that her skin was more translucent. Paper thin, as he could see the miniscule blue veins running through her face and eyelids. Dillion bent his head to gently lay a kiss on her lips, as if he had the ability to breathe life into this petite being.

When Aurelie came out of the bathroom, she was helped back to her bed with crisp, fresh linens and pillows. She gingerly lay down and when she settled, Dillion carefully laid their daughter in her arms. He lay on the bed next to them and was that way until their families came.

Though their parents were sorrowful, it was his children. Especially his girls' grief crying that undid any semblance of decorum he had left. Riley and Bri were on either side of them and sobbed gut-wrenching tears. He held onto Brianna and let her cry on his lap. He had no words of comfort for her. He could only hold on to his daughter until she was ready to let go.

Aurelie offered Rose Clare the baby and she accepted her. He didn't remember seeing his mother cry except when Corinne passed, but she was crying now. And whispering a prayer. The girls clung to Aurelie while Benji was standing in a corner. Dillion couldn't make out what he was doing or feeling. He looked almost statuesque. That is, until Bea and Antoine came into the room. Then his son made a beeline to Antoine and was by his side the entire time.

His baby girl made the rounds with the grandparents. Dillion's dad was the last one to hold her and invited everyone to pray with him. After the prayer, he offered the baby back to Aurelie before he encouraged the entourage to leave. Dillion thought that perhaps Aurelie would want some private time with her parents, so he followed his family out of the room and to the hospital entrance. He hugged his children and his parents goodbye. This should have been a day of celebration and instead, it was something entirely different.

When he turned around and started the slow trek back to the birthing center, he noticed that he was walking past the chapel. Dillion ambled into the quiet space as if drawn to it. He sat in the last row of simple cushioned chairs and bowed his head with his hands folded in front of him. At first, he waited for calm serenity to wash over him. He was in God's house now; he was expecting divine intervention. But reality hit hard instead. He had devoted his entire life to God. Throughout this pregnancy he prayed. Prayers of the faithful. Prayers in communion with his followers, his family. Prayers in private. This morning, he begged. Pleaded. Prayed to his God. The God he thought he knew. The one he followed throughout his life. Surely all those hours in prayer, studying theology, in church, leading his flock, leading his family, would count for something. Allow his prayers to be answered. Instead of the calm and serenity he expected to feel, he felt his anger and confusion rising up. He looked up at the cross on the altar and the lighted stained glass window behind and began his rant.

"God, I have devoted my life to you. I thought that's what you wanted from me. I willingly sacrificed a traditional life to have one in service of you. I believed that is what I wanted. What you wanted. I've accepted that you took away my Corinne. I've accepted that you have a plan for our two unborn babies, and even this one. This precious little girl. All I asked is to have her heart beat a few moments for us to celebrate a life we made together." Dillion's voice rising as anger filled his veins.

"Why was that so much to ask? Why couldn't we have one minute? One lousy minute to hold a live baby in our arms and welcome her? Tell her that we love her? Before we had to give her up to you? Why couldn't you give us, me one minute after all the minutes, hours, years that I've devoted to you? What have I done that is so awful that you would refuse me this one, miniscule request?" Dillion demanded.

Dillion rose from his seat, stretching his arms as if he were nailed to a cross and wailed out in agony, "God, why have you forsaken me?" He stayed like that until his arms ached and this tears dried up. Dillion was hoping for a sign, symbol, something that would help him understand why his devoutness wasn't enough. Would never be enough.

Dropping his arms and his head, Dillion left the chapel feeling worse than when he walked in. He shuffled back to Aurelie's room where he found her and their baby alone. He wiped his eyes before going in and found his way back to her bed and lay beside her with one arm around her head and the other gently laying on their baby girl.

"She's perfect, Dillion. Isn't she?" Aurelie asked. Not waiting for a response, she said, "I checked. While she and I were alone. I just needed to see. She has 10 fingers and toes. Not a mark on her." Dillion kissed Aurelie's forehead. "You're not mad, I hope. That I did that, I mean."

His heart hurt when she asked if he was mad at her. For checking for a physical sign. "No, Aur. Absolutely not. I'm glad you did." He paused and then asked her a question. "Does it help?"

She paused then looked up into his eyes. "No. Not really. I just. I just needed to. That's all."

They lay like that for as long as they wanted. Aurelie holding their little angel and Dillion fawning over both of them.

Dillion could see the autumn sun, a bright orange ball in the crisp blue sky, begin its descension and that's when Aurelie said, "I'm ready. Call the nurse."

The next afternoon, when they drove up to his parent's home, there was no smidgeon of hope left. No prayer that hadn't been said. Dillion felt like a shell of himself. He walked around the vehicle to help Aurelie out and to walk with her into the house. His sanctuary as a child. But it didn't have that feeling now. Nothing did. He felt himself just going through the motions.

Inside, Rose Clare made homemade chili and offered them each a cup. They ate without interest, but because it was an expectation. The girls were trying not to swarm them but wanted to offer and receive many hugs. Benji was still standing as an outlier.

"Tomorrow morning, we will be driving back home. Make sure you have all your things packed up tonight except for your jammies and tomorrow's clothes. Okay?" The heads nodded. Mumford put his head on Aurelie's lap and left it there as she mindlessly spooned the chili up to her mouth without actually taking in any of its sustenance.

The next morning, Dillion was focused on getting the car packed up when Riley came up to him. "Daddy? I can't find Benji anywhere. He's not here." She was fretting and it scared him. He wasn't going to lose two children in 24 hours, he had to think. He stopped packing, investigated the bedroom where Benji had slept to see if there were any clues. And there it was, lying on the floor. He picked it up and had a hunch as to where his son would be.

A short drive to the familiar home and it was like traveling back in time. He inspected the backyard and saw a black spec under the branches of the old oak tree and walked toward it. He half thought that he would find Corinne baking cookies with the girls in the kitchen, but she wasn't there. He sighed as he readied himself to talk with his son whose grief was manifesting itself in a different way but was very real. "Hey, buddy. Wanna talk about it?"

Benji's bushy dark hair shook, but his finger wiped away a tear before it pushed up his black rimmed glasses.

"How'd you find me?"

"I saw this on the floor and I took a guess. I guessed right." Dillion handed Benji the photo of his mom pushing Benji on a tire swing from this very tree.

"I just thought," he sniffled. "I thought that since this is our special tree, she would be here. I could talk to her. Find out why she was gone and why my sister was gone, too."

Dillion nodded in understanding and asked, "Well, it sounds like a solid plan to me."

"Yeah, I thought so, but it didn't work. This stupid tree doesn't work. She told me it would. Mom said that this is our special tree and anytime I needed to feel her, to see her, think of our tree and she'd be there. But she's not. The baby's not. She lied. She's gone. The baby's gone. God … " he paused as if to contemplate the repercussions of his next statement.

"Go ahead, Benji, say what's on your mind. Get it out."

"I don't believe in God anymore. He doesn't make any sense. Not like science or math. He is fake. If he were real. If he could perform miracles, why didn't he perform miracles for you? Us? You are close to God, and he took away your wife and you and Momma Aur's babies. Why would he do that if he existed?"

Ouch. "I can understand that, Benji. I really do. They are your feelings, and you have a right to them." Dillion hugged his son before confessing where he had been and what he had done in the hospital chapel.

Benji looked up at his father with bloodshot eyes. "Really? You yelled at God?"

"You bet I did. I was angry. Still am. But I've got to be there for Aurelie. And for you and your sisters. I have to move forward and part of that means I've got to take us all back home. Are you ready to go home now, son? Or do you need some more time? Here with your special tree?"

Benji's breath hitched before he began to stand. "She's not here anyway. I might as well go."

Dillion patted Benji on his shoulder and walked him to the minivan. "Did you believe she'd be here, Dad? That God would be here?"

"Honestly, Benji, I hoped she would be. He would be. He certainly wasn't in the hospital chapel with me. At least I didn't feel him."

"Dad?"

"Yeah?"

"How are you going to continue being a priest? I mean after this. After God left you. Didn't answer your prayers."

Whoa. "Right now, Benji, I'm just focusing on getting us all home safely. I want to believe that God has a plan and that I don't understand it yet, but I can't think about that right now."

Benji let his dad hug him before they drove back to the Clark family home. Dillion thanked his parents and made sure that everybody was packed in and began the silent drive back up north. Quietly contemplating Benji's question and how he would move past, no, forward through this with his faith intact. With his family intact.

Chapter Forty-Five

Aurelie lay in bed pretending to be asleep. The truth was that she just wanted to have a moment to herself. The past few weeks were exhausting. Dillion, the kids, her parents, his parents, were all doting on her. Barely able to go to the bathroom on her own without someone checking on her to see if she was okay. She wasn't okay, damnit. Didn't know when or if *ever* she'd be okay again. The only one who seemed to get her was Cat. They talked almost every day and sometimes, in the middle of the night, which was a comfort. But no one or spiritual being helped her understand why she had lost this baby. Why did she have to go through the difficulty of labor and still could not hold a living, breathing baby at the end? Life was cruel. She didn't know why she deserved this cruelty. Was she really that bad before? So bad she had to be punished? That couldn't be it. There were plenty of horrific people in the world and they still got to live a life and not worry about consequences. Ugh. Every morning was like this. She'd wake up, pretend to be asleep and then all the gloom and doom came rushing into her thoughts. Not even giving herself a chance to wake up and just be.

"Momma Aur, you up?" Brianna asked as she came into the bedroom.

"Morning, Bri. Yes, I'm up."

"I had Daddy help me make you some coffee to help you wake up. You know since you've been so sleepy lately. Would you like some?"

"Sure. Thanks." Aurelie slowly slid up into a seated position. "Just let me get dressed first," she added, "privately, please."

Brianna nodded and shut the door on her way out. Aurelie could hear the chain of command echoing through the house. She found a long sweatshirt and fleece leggings and laid them on the bed. While she freshened up in the bathroom, she found herself rubbing her stomach and looking at herself. If only her water had broken this week instead of two weeks ago, her baby could have had a chance. Most women her age would be thrilled to have a flat belly. Aurelie, however, wasn't most women. Aurelie wanted her round belly back with her baby being nurtured inside of it. She ran her fingers through her short curls and threw on her clothes.

When she lumbered into the kitchen, all the activity came to a screeching halt while they all looked at her. Even Mumford. She felt simultaneously angry and awful. Why can't they just act normally like they all did before? "Morning, Aur. How'd you sleep?" Dillion asked before kissing her cheek.

"I don't know. Fine I guess." She took her first sip of the hot, black liquid that Brianna offered her. She momentarily wondered *if she could wish herself small enough, could she dive into it and let it suck her under?*

"Did you want anything to eat before I go into work? The kids have a half day today, and then they are off for the week. For Thanksgiving."

She thought hard about what he was saying, but she was in a fog. "Um, half day, Thanksgiving. Okay. No. No, I'm not hungry."

"They've been invited to go ice skating with the Donovan kids. Mrs. Donovan offered to take them after school and treat them to lunch, but she's asked if we can pick them up at the rink because they have a dentist appointment. I've got a meeting until 6 o'clock. Do you think you can handle picking them up at the rink at 4:00 p.m.? Or should I cancel?"

What was she going to do today? She didn't remember. Sure. What the hell. She could get herself up and out of the house to the skating rink by then. She nodded her head *yes* and allowed the family to give her goodbye hugs and kisses before the back door closed, leaving her with her thoughts.

Aurelie sat at the kitchen table and sipped her coffee. Mumford lay next to her on the floor. She caught a glimpse of the handmade calendar on the refrigerator with the comical turkey in place of Thanksgiving Day. Huh. Last year at this time, she was grieving her baby boy. This year, her baby girl. Her line of sight blurred as the tears welled up and her breath caught. She screamed at the top of her lungs and threw the ceramic coffee mug across the room where it smashed on the floor, scaring Mumford who ran into Benji's room for safety.

Just then, her phone rang, it was Cat. "Hey Aur, is this a good time? I had a feeling …"

"I. Can't. Do. This. Again. Ever." Aurelie's breath hitching between words.

"Oh honey, what happened?"

"I saw the calendar, remembered that I lost our baby boy last year and now our baby girl and … I smashed a coffee mug all over the kitchen floor."

"Is anyone hurt? Are you hurt?"

"No, just scared Mumford, is all. I'm home alone."

"Well, in that case …" Aurelie's curiosity was piqued during Cat's pregnant pause. "Let's smash some shit and scream. Put me on video. Let's do this." Aurelie grabbed a glass that didn't match anything and then a vase from the thrift store. She saw Cat throw a juice glass and then a plate. Aurelie let out a loud yawp as she found something else worthy of breaking into a million pieces. She wanted to see as many pieces as possible of broken shards of glass, ceramic, and pottery to represent the pieces of her heart that were broken and would never fit together again. Ever.

"Thank you, Cat," Aurelie said as the wave of relief from her release hit her.

"You're welcome, Aur. Anytime." They talked for a while longer, then Cat had to take care of the twins. Aurelie stood on a chair, then on top of the kitchen table to get an overview of her miscarriage masterpiece. She took her phone and snapped a photo of the cacophony of chaos that lay in disarray on the kitchen floor.

Aurelie felt a sense of calm flow through her. It's as if the act and the result were exactly what she needed. The sharp-edged fragments littering the linoleum represented how she felt in that moment in time. The rage incorporated in the making of the art was just as valid as the tranquility resulting from the exhaustion and the overhead view.

When it was decidedly the time to clean up, Aurelie methodically swept up the bits, slices, chunks, fragments, hunks, wedges, and dust and put them into an empty moving box. Then she found the roll of packing tape to meticulously shut it so as not to have a single molecule fall out and be lost. She drew a broken heart on top of the box before carefully sliding it onto a shelf in the basement.

After washing the floor, Aurelie found that she was hungry. Ravenous. She made a veggie omelet and set out to take Mumford for a hike. It was a crisp, autumn day with a sky the color of a robin's egg and a bright sun that forced Aurelie to put on her sunglasses. She finally had energy. She felt there was a slight sign of life.

They hiked into the woods. Took moments to sit and just *be*. The sun was beginning its early descent behind the trees. She smiled when she remembered the release she felt while making her art piece and something else. Something she hadn't had in a long time. Aurelie felt excited. She was excited to show the photo to Dillion. *I think he'll finally understand what I'm going through,* Aurelie thought to herself. The photo would show him what she wasn't capable of putting into words.

Dillion's minivan was in the driveway and he was on his phone, frantic when Aurelie arrived. She waved and when he caught sight of her, she saw concern turn into anger. "Where have you been?" he yelled.

"I took Mumford for a hike in the woods. Why are you home so early? Didn't you have a meeting or something?" She saw the kids starting to run towards her but stopped by Dillion and his directive to go back into the house and stay there. Aurelie was confused as she got closer to him.

"Yes, I had a meeting. A vestry meeting that I had to cancel because Mrs. Donovan called me upset because *you* hadn't picked up the kids from the rink and she was late to the dentist."

Aurelie was trying to comprehend what Dillion was saying. *Why was he so angry with her?* He'd never been this upset before. She wanted to explain and share her breakthrough, but the rage was seeping back into her veins and her thoughts.

"Well, why didn't anyone call me to remind me? I would have picked them up, but no one called me."

"We did. Dozens of times, but you left your phone at home. You can't be so irresponsible, Aur. Not as a parent. These kids depend on you. I depend on you. If you want to adopt them, you can't make this kind of mistake."

"Dillion, I'm sorry that I forgot to pick them up and forgot my phone. But you have no right to belittle me this way."

"Look, Aur, I can't keep picking up your slack. We have a lot on our plates right now. I have a lot going on at home, trying to take care of you and the kids and the house. At work, I'm dealing with a small group of very upset parishioners and then the adoption," Dillion complained.

"Shut up! Just shut up!" Aurelie yelled. She was done. So done. "I can't do this anymore. I've gotta get away from here. From *you*. I need a break."

"What are you talking about? Needing a break? I've been taking care of you since we came home. You haven't had to do anything. The kids and I have been walking on eggshells and trying to take care everything for you. All I asked you to do was to pick up the kids, and you couldn't even do that! You haven't had to do anything. We've been doing it all for you. So you wouldn't have to. So you could heal."

Aurelie exploded as if she had lava in her veins, "Enough! That's enough, Dillion! Stop making me out to be the bad guy here. I already feel like all of this is my fault. You have three kids, so we know it's not you. You've always wanted to be a priest, so, you know, you're practically perfect *and* you're holier than shit. I get it. I'm the bad one. I'm the worst. And I'm leaving. You don't have to worry about taking care of me anymore. I'm outta here," Aurelie confirmed.

Aurelie stormed past him and into the house. She stomped down the stairs to the basement to grab her suitcases and bring them upstairs to their room where she began to throw her clothes and toiletries into them.

Dillion followed her into the bedroom and shut the door. "What are you doing? You can't leave."

"The hell I can't."

"Aur, we're having a fight. We've been under a lot of stress. It happens. Let's just sit down and talk about this. Maybe it's time we get some counseling."

She continued to throw things into her bags. "You mean the kind of counseling that we can afford? With a priest or bishop? No thanks. I don't trust in your God right now and honestly, I'm not at all sure that I ever will. I can't live here right now, Dillion. I've got to go." He found her hand and held it still, encouraging her to sit across from him on their bed.

"Okay, I get it. Prayer isn't what you need right now. I can look into other counseling services for us." He started to beg.

She sighed. "It's not just that, Dillion. I feel suffocated here. You're telling me that everyone is on eggshells around me, but I feel that I can't take a breath without someone asking me what's wrong? Can they get something for me? I can't live like this anymore."

"I can see that, but we can move past this. It's just a rough patch is all it is. We can't fix this if you go away. We can do this together. As a family. I love you, Aurelie. Don't do this."

She looked into his fearful eyes and with conviction said, "It is not just a rough patch for me, Dillion. I am grieving the loss of our little girl. And today? I realized that last year, at this time, I was grieving the loss of our little boy, and our other little baby. I honestly don't know if I have it in me to be a parent right now. I don't know how long I will be grieving my three babies, and I won't be on some timeline for my grief." Rivers of tears were running down his stubbly cheek, and she wiped them before she went on. "In two days it'll be Thanksgiving and I can't think of anything I'm thankful for right now. Not without my babies. I can't pretend I'm okay. I don't want you or the kids to fawn all over me. I need space. I'm sorry, Dillion, but I'm leaving. Tonight."

"Aurelie, I love you. I know you love me … "

She let go of his hand and said something she thought she'd never say, "I don't know that I do." But it was what she needed to say, and he needed to hear to let her go.

Aurelie zipped up her bags and put them in the back of her SUV. The kids were a mess and she hugged them and kissed them but couldn't say anything. She motioned for Mumford to join her, but he didn't budge from Benji's side.

Driving down Highway 51, she was exactly where she wanted to be at that exact moment—alone. However, it didn't feel like she anticipated it would. Instead of being free and energized, she felt void and cold.

A few hours later, Aurelie found herself in a Podunk town across the Mississippi River. She secured a room at a budget hotel and found a bar across the street. She was slamming Jack and Cokes like no tomorrow when a guy in a tractor hat and flannel shirt sat next to her and offered to buy her next drink. She accepted.

"You're not from around here," he said as he took a glug from his beer.

"Nope," Aurelie answered before she downed half the glass.

"What'd ya doin' here, 'cept drinkin?"

"Drinkin's what I wanna do right now. Got a problem?" She couldn't tell exactly what he looked like as her vision was a bit fuzzy. However, he definitely didn't look like Dillion and that made him all the more attractive.

"No, mam. No problem at all. Just makin' conversation is all. Get this lovely lady another one. On me," tractor hat man said to the bartender.

In addition to the fuzzy feeling, Aurelie was enjoying the warmth growing inside of her, with each hit of the whiskey and soda. At the end of the bar, Aurelie noticed some movement and a young cowboy got on a stool with his acoustic guitar and began to sing. It was an upbeat honky-tonk song about a guy, beer, and his truck. Aurelie felt the beat move her, so she went out onto the makeshift dance floor and began to dance. Tractor hat guy followed her. When he got into her space, Aurelie let him hold her and twirl her, while she laughed and pretended she knew the words to the song. The whiskey was starting to make her spin, or was it how he was dancing with her? Tractor hat guy twirled Aurelie some more and was making her feel a bit off. Still, she didn't flinch when he pulled her close to him and put his hands on her ass. She could feel him grinding into her, but at this point she was so drunk that her brain couldn't figure out what to tell her body to do, how to move.

"Let's get outta here and someplace more, private," tractor hat guy said.

Aurelie felt her head nod, and he stopped dancing. He smiled down at her and led her off the dance floor. She was trying to comprehend what was going on, but, again, her brain was caught up in a whiskey haze and couldn't get her body to do what it wanted her to do. Instead, it just seemed easier to follow tractor hat guy because he seemed to know what he was doing. Just as they got to the door of the bar, a gust of ice cold wind came and whipped into Aurelie's face, shocking her. Woke her stomach as well. So much so that when tractor hat guy turned toward her and asked, "Something wrong?" She projectile vomited all over his flannel shirt, jeans, and work boots.

"You bitch! What the hell?"

Aurelie didn't know how she found the energy, but she ducked under his arm and ran as fast as she could into the hotel lobby and up the stairs to her room, only stopping when she was in front of the mirror over the sink. She couldn't tell if the cold sweat she broke into was because of her exertion or the alcohol, or both. But when she looked in the mirror, she didn't recognize herself. She was a car wreck. Her face was covered in sweat beads, vomit, and spittle. Her eyes were bloodshot, and her hair had chunks of vomit sticking to her matted curls. It had been years since she'd been this bad. She promised that she would never act that way again. Tonight, she almost broke that promise.

Clothes and all, Aurelie jumped into the shower and scrubbed herself so hard that it looked like she had road rash in some places. She wrapped herself in clean, dry towels, brushed her teeth, filled a glass with water and got on the phone. She knew who she needed to talk to and what she needed to say. "I'm on my way."

The next morning, she dried her clothes with the hairdryer before getting dressed and going down to the continental breakfast to grab a coffee and a muffin for the trip. It was going to be a long drive, but she relished the peace and quiet of the open road.

When she pulled into the driveway, her muscles finally relaxed. Aurelie put her head on the steering wheel and took a deep breath. It wasn't going to be easy, but she had to try and heal if she could ever move forward. Aurelie opened the door and looked up at a familiar face. "Welcome to Montana."

PART FIVE: OUT WEST

Chapter Forty-Six

"I can't believe she left me. Us. It's over." Dillion dragged his hand through his hair and then set his forehead on his arms. Roger reached over and put his arm on his little brother's shoulder.

"I can't believe it either. Maybe it's like she said, she just needed a break. To heal a bit before coming back. She's had a shitty past couple of years, losing three babies. Back-to-back. That's gotta be hard to come back from."

"Roger, she said she didn't love me anymore."

"I got nothin', bro. I don't know." He grabbed a shot glass and waved for the bartender to fill it with tequila before giving it to Dillion and then having another poured for himself.

"How could I screw this up so badly? Was I this bad with Corinne and didn't know it? Am I a terrible husband?"

"You and Corinne were great together. Her getting cancer was terrible but no one's fault. What you have with Aurelie is completely different. Aurelie is different. She's spontaneous, exciting, tons of energy. So, being hit back-to-back-to-back with loss, well, that would take any of us down. But to someone who's like a firecracker? You're right. She may not come back from this."

"I should go to her. Now that you and Mom and Dad are here, the kids are taken care of. I should drive out to Montana and bring her back."

"Dillion, it's good that she let you know she was safe, and she was there, but she made it very clear she needs space right now. I may not be the relationship guru, but I do know that when a woman tells you what she needs, she means it. Give her some space."

Dillion lifted the shot glass to his mouth and slammed another tequila down his throat. He welcomed the burn. He deserved it.

"Rog, I didn't want to lose her. Didn't want to lose another wife, so I went all out to make sure that she had the best chance at living, holding our baby girl, healing at home. But it wasn't enough. She told me I was suffocating her. We were all driving her away. The one thing I didn't want. The opposite of what I wanted. How did I screw up so bad?"

They both took another shot. "Maybe you held on too tight. She's a free spirit, kinda like those mustangs out west."

"I'm not like that. That's what I love best about her. She helps me get outta my head, you know? Get out of my box. She told me she loved how I kept her grounded. She always wanted a big family."

"What about you?"

"What?"

"Did you want a big family? Did you want to have more kids or were you doing it because Aurelie wanted kids?"

"It didn't matter to me at first. But then when she got pregnant the first time, I felt this rush. This need to make a baby with her. Before she left, she told me she was done. She's not going through with this again. That hurt me. Really hurt me. It's like I don't have a choice in the matter, you know?"

"Dillion, dude, she could have died this time. You don't want her to risk her life again, do you?"

"No, no, of course not. Why do you think I took her to Illinois? But it's the fact that she just made the decision for us. It wasn't even up for discussion. She shut it down. My opinion doesn't matter. I mean, we could try via a surrogate. It would still be our baby, just someone else carrying it, hopefully to full term. We could adopt. But she wanted to have a baby. Our baby. That's not going to happen. It's over."

Roger lifted his hand to get the bartender's attention for another round of shots. "What's going on at work? Dad told me you're having a bad time at church, too."

"Yeah, a bit of a hiccup, I guess." Dillion let the heat trickle down his throat. "I've got some parishioners and two vestry members who are 'morally' opposed to what we did by going to Illinois. They believe that we should have let the baby die naturally, even though Aurelie's life was at risk. They are trying to put together a petition to force my resignation."

"Jesus."

"Yeah."

"Can you lose your job over this?"

"According to Episcopal law, we didn't do anything wrong. The baby was going to die no matter what we did. But these members don't see it that way, and so they are trying to force a vote to get a new priest."

"Dammit. I'm sorry, Dillion. You are not getting a break."

"Well, my bishop is supporting me and helping me through this mess. If they get a majority of the parish to sign the petition, then I'll have to find a new job."

"If they don't get the signatures they need?"

"Well then, I'll get to keep my post, but I'll likely lose some parishioners and their tithing."

"What about the kids, how are they doing?"

"Mumford has been a huge help. He takes turns sleeping with each of them, and sometimes I'll come out in the morning and find them all sleeping on the family room floor together. Mom and Dad will be here through the holiday and then Aurelie's parents are driving up to help out as well. The kids and I did fine before, but Aurelie's leaving was such an emotional gut punch, we are all worried about them."

"Whatever I can do to help, if you need money to pay some bills, take the kids for a weekend getaway. Take you on a weekend getaway. You name it. I'm here for you, bro."

"You mean it?"

"Absolutely."

"Then can you write my sermon and go to mass for me on Sunday?"

"That's a hard no. Sorry."

Dillion and Roger took an Uber back to the house where the kids were already in their beds and tonight, Mumford was sleeping in Brianna's room and wearing a pink tutu. That dog was a saint.

Rose Clare was finishing prepping for Thanksgiving dinner while her husband was taking a phone call. "Are you sure? Oh, wait, he's just stepped in. Dillion? Dillion, it's your bishop on the phone."

Dillion's head was sloshing around, he wasn't in a good place to be talking with his boss but accepted the phone regardless. "Hello?" he managed.

"Yes? You're sure? I can't thank you enough. Yes, I'm grateful. Relieved. Thank you, sir."

Dillion hung up. "What did he say?" Riley asked.

"They wouldn't get enough signatures for the petition to be valid. The bishop had lots of parishioners contact him to see how they could help me. Support us. Johanna was one of them. He offered her an opportunity and she accepted."

Thursday morning, Rose Clare was already busy in the kitchen preparing the turkey when Dillion got out of bed. He smelled the familiar aroma of sage and cooked pork link sausages for the stuffing. His head was pounding, and his stomach was swirling. *Ugh, I don't know if I can stomach a big Thanksgiving dinner. I'm too old for this shit.* Dillion thought to himself. Still he managed to get into the shower, a cold one, to help wake up and to stop the pounding in his head or at least get it to a soft murmur. After brushing his teeth, he decided that he would just be casual. No hair product, no shaving. Just jeans and a long sleeved shirt. His mom would be disappointed, but he didn't really care. He didn't feel like being thankful right now, he just wanted to get through the day.

When he opened his bedroom door, Brianna came barreling in and her head almost gave him a gut punch. "Oomph," Dillion exhaled. "Morning, Bri. How'd you sleep?"

"Okay, I guess. How'd you sleep?"

"Okay, I guess. Is everyone else up?"

"Yup. Benji is downstairs 'playing' the piano. Sounds more like he's breaking it, but whatever. Grandma and Riley are in the kitchen and Grandpa is taking Mumford for a walk. I just needed a hug first." Dillion's heart fluttered a moment as he reached down and kissed the top of his youngest's head. He said a silent prayer that she would stay as sweet when she got older.

"Daddy?" she asked quietly.

"Hmm?"

"I miss Momma Aur. I was wondering if we could call her today? Would that be okay?" That little heart flutter just came crashing down into the pit of his sour stomach.

"I don't know, Bri. She was pretty clear she wanted some time away." He could feel his shirt getting wet and he knew his little girl's heart was breaking. "I tell you what, I'll text her to see if it would be okay."

"I guess that'll be okay. Thanks, Daddy."

The backdoor opened to a very excited and snowy dog and a frazzled grandpa. "Man, that dog can go! I might have to check into urgent care to see if my arm was pulled out of socket. I think I need a nap after that walk." Dillion's dad started to peel off his snowy outer layer and kick off his hiking boots as Riley offered him a hot mug of coffee. "Thanks, Love, grandpa was looking forward to this and a warm fire."

"Thanks for letting me sleep in. Is Roger here yet?"

"No, he texted to say he's running a little late. He'll be here before dinner's ready, though." His dad offered.

Dillion moved into the kitchen and grabbed the coffee pot to pour some liquid energy into his mug. "I bet," he said under his breath. Once the caffeine hit his system, the headache began to wane and he had enough energy to put on his boots and flannel jacket to go outside to grab some wood and kindling to build a fire.

Once the fire was roaring, Dillion looked around and saw everyone keeping busy, Brianna had Grandpa and Mumford in her room for an impromptu tea party, Riley and Grandma were making the stuffing and pumpkin pies in the kitchen, and Benji could be heard pounding out the theme song from *Jurassic Park*. It was time for him to check on Benji.

The basement was always a few degrees cooler than the main floor, but Benji didn't look like he cared. His brow was furrowed and he pounded out the cords. He wasn't even looking at the sheet music, he was playing the whole thing from memory. "Hey, buddy," Dillion calmly said while putting his hand on Benji's back. "Sounds great. But are you supposed to hit the keys that hard?"

"Momma Aur always says to let the music express your emotions. That's what I'm doing."

"I get that. Well, you're playing extremely well and with a lot of emotion."

"Thanks," Benji put his hands by his side and let his shaggy hair fall into his face.

"Dad?"

"Yeah?"

"Why did she leave? Did I do something wrong? Did you?"

"She's just really sad and mad right now. She needs to be in a different place so she can work through all her feelings without being so close to everything that reminds her of the babies."

"Will she come back?"

"I hope so."

"Dad?"

"Yes?" Dillion's heart aching was overtaking his headache at this point.

"You know you can work through your mad and sad feelings through music, too."

"Benji, I don't know how to play the piano."

"On the guitar. She left one of her guitars here. I'm sure she'd be okay with you playing it."

Dillion walked over to the acoustic guitar on the stand and picked it up, looking it over before strumming a chord. "Does it work?"

"Of course it works, you just played it."

"No. That's not what I meant. I mean, 'Does it work?' To get the mad and sad out."

"Well, if I'm honest, not all the time. But the more I do it, the better I feel. Plus, it keeps me from beating up on my sisters, or stupid kids at school, so I don't get into trouble as much." Benji smirked.

"Yeah, I can see that. Thanks, Benji. I'll give it a try."

When Roger finally came over, Dillion and the kids joined him and put their snow gear on to play football in the front yard. It wasn't real football as Mumford tackled both sides to get to the ball, but it gave everyone a brief reprieve from feeling sad and mad.

"Dinner's ready!" Rose Clare yelled out the back door and the snowy group came inside and shed their wet gear before joining the elder Clarks around the table. This Thanksgiving, Dillion's dad took over saying grace as Dillion's heart was nowhere near being ready to be thankful for anything. If Dillion were honest, he didn't even tune into what his dad was saying. He just followed the motions of the rest of the clan.

Rose Clare made an impressive table. Of course there was turkey and stuffing, but she made homemade mashed potatoes and gravy, a cranberry and orange relish, green beans almondine, and homemade dinner rolls with a cinnamon butter she picked up at a local farm. Dillion tried to eat, but either the tequila or his emotional turmoil negated his appetite.

After dinner, Dillion sent off the text to Aurelie. He waited in trepidation for her reply, which finally came right before the kid's bedtime. They each had a private conversation with her right before bed and then he took the phone to his bedroom and shut the door.

"Hey," he said warily.

"Hey," she said in reply.

"Thanks for talking with the kids, it meant a lot to them. To me." There was a long pause.

"Sorry it took me a while to reply before. I didn't know if I could do it."

"I understand."

"Do you?"

"Not really. But I'm trying to,"

"Thanks. Well, I should get going. I promised to help feed the horses tonight."

"Aurelie?"

"Yes?"

"I love you." A pregnant pause ensued before he heard …

"Good night, Dillion." He wanted to throw the phone across the room but thought better of it. When he appeared from the bedroom, he saw that his parents and brother had all left to go to their rental. His kids were asleep in their rooms, Mumford was with Benji tonight, so the house was eerily quiet except for the remnant embers from the fire.

Dillion walked down into the basement and grabbed the guitar, remembering what Benji had said hours earlier. Upstairs, he threw another log on and stoked it until the burnt orange flakes of fire sparked and lit the oak log. He lay on the floor with his back on the sofa and began strumming. Nothing specific, just a series of singular notes while tears stained his cheeks.

On Sunday, the whole Clark family went to church, Mumford included. He lay down at the children's feet and didn't budge unless they did. Dillion went up to the podium and spoke to his congregation. "As you are likely aware, my family and I have been dealing with some very difficult challenges. It has been said that God doesn't give you anything that you can't handle. Well, this time, I'm not sure I can. We can. You see, I've prayed and put my faith in God all my life. I've believed in the mantra that He has a plan. But recently, I lost my baby daughter and could have lost my wife, Aurelie, as well. This experience has broken us. I stand before you, today, angry with God. Therefore, I cannot, in good conscience, deliver the Word of God and explain its meaning. At this time, I am a lost sheep.

"But our congregation is also a family. Our spiritual family. I've learned that a member of our parish, Johanna Bradley, would like to share what the Word of God means to her. So, I will relinquish my space at the podium, in front of the altar, and sit with my family to hear the Word of God and pray with them and you. Pray for a better understanding of God's Word. Johanna … "

As Johanna was passing Dillion, she hugged him. He felt relief and sat by his family; Brianna moved to sit on his lap during the sermon. During the homily, all Dillion could think of was *God, oh God, why have you forsaken me?*

Chapter Forty-Seven

"It's been a week, are you going to call him?" Cat inquired of her best friend.

Aurelie was watching Cat brush Butters down after a ride. "What's the point, Cat? My mind hasn't changed. I can't be there, in that house, right now. Everything reminds me of loss, guilt, failure." Just then they heard Mia barking in the background and Damon's truck kicking up gravel on the driveway. But something was different. He was hauling a horse trailer.

"What'cha got there, hon?" Cat asked.

"Where are the kids?" Damon inquired.

"Aurelie put them down for an afternoon nap so I could take Butters out for a little ride before dinner."

"How are the trails?" Damon asked as he came around to give his wife a kiss over the fence, to Butters' disapproval. "Hey, buddy, she was mine first."

Cat chuckled. "Not bad. Snow covered, but we didn't run into any ice. Why? What's up?"

"I brought home a project from work." He sauntered back to his truck and opened the trailer. Cat and Aurelie were intrigued. Then they saw her.

Aurelie's heart dropped. She saw the picturesque painted pony with a distraught face. "What's wrong with her?"

Damon led the mare to the paddock, all the while whispering assurances to her.

"One of my clients picked her up at auction a couple of years ago. She's as bright as they come. She caught on really quick to ranch life. They were so pleased with her that they bred her, but her foal died. She's been this way ever since. The client said she's refusing to go back her to ranching duties. She's got to earn her keep or they're getting rid of her. I asked if I could bring her home to see if I could get her to move through her grief and willing to do her ranch work again. Aurelie felt compelled to go to the mare and reach out her hand. The mare bent her head down and moved forward so that Aurelie could pet her. Aurelie placed her forehead on the horse's nose, and they stayed that way for a moment. Cat mouthed "thank you" to her husband.

At dinner, Gordon and Grace were all excited to meet the new horse. Damon promised them they could see her but to be very careful not to spook her. As a family group they came out to the paddock and the mare warily came up to the fence. "Daddy, what's her name?" Grace asked.

"Her name is Angel," Damon replied.

Angel, hearing her name brought her nose up to Damon who welcomed her with a fresh apple slice. She used her lips to accept it from his flat hand. He gave slices to everyone else in the group as well. Gordon and Grace had fed horses many times in their young lives, so they were very comfortable letting Angel nibble the sweet treats from their chubby hands. Aurelie was the last one and when Angel was done with her treat, she leaned forward to have Aurelie pet her nose once again. "Aur, tomorrow I want to take her out onto the trails. I want you to ride her while I ride Butters."

"Damon, I don't mind pulling my weight around here, but I don't know very much about horses. I might screw something up and make her worse," Aurelie expressed with concern.

"I'll be right by you the whole time, Aur. I'm thinking that since you both have lost babies, you may be able to heal each other. She trusts me, but something is holding her back. I can't seem to get to it, but you might. Anyhow, it's worth a shot."

"Hey, Auntie Aur, Angel kinda looks like Mumford with all those spots," Gordon belted out.

Aurelie smiled. "You're right Gordy, except she has two blue eyes. Mumford only has one. But they are about the same size."

"Okay, everyone, let's give Angel a little space and time to get used to her new place. Butters, sweetie," Cat called out as the Palomino pranced over to his favorite person. "Butters, take care of Miss Angel, here. She's a special guest." Butters neighed before putting his nose into Cat's hands for some petting.

"Now that you're all full of horse spit, I think it's bath time," Damon called out.

"NO!" The twins whined.

"No whining or Auntie Aur won't sing you to sleep. Tomorrow you've got your last day of preschool for the week. Let's make it a good one," Cat said as they walked into the log home.

Aurelie sauntered into the walkout basement and toward the bathroom she'd been using for the past week. After washing up, she threw on an old, holey sweatshirt and pair of sweatpants. Grabbing her travel guitar, she walked upstairs and found her godchildren already in their jammies, impatiently waiting for their bedtime song.

"I got a new one to share with you all tonight." Two pair of bright blue eyes looked out from their comforters, and she began to strum the song that she had always hoped to share with her own babies, Kenny Loggins' "Return to Pooh Corner."

"Can you sing it again, Auntie Aur?"

"Not tonight, Gracie. Tomorrow's a school day."

"Okay. Love you, Auntie Aur." Aurelie bent over and kissed Grace on her forehead before reaching over on the other side of her to do the same to Gordon.

"Love you, Auntie Aur," Gordon said.

"Love you too, Gordy. See you both tomorrow."

After turning off their light and closing the door, she joined Cat and Damon in the great room, in front of a roaring fire with a glass of red wine. Snuggling under a chunky Afghan, she took a sip. "So, Damon. Be honest with me. Is this work project really for work? Or for me?" Aurelie inquired.

He grinned, and it made her smile to see his dimples through the red, scruffy beard. "It's a little bit of both if I'm honest. She really is having a hard time and while we will always be here for you, Aur, the truth is we don't know what you are going through. Are you willing to give it a try?"

Aurelie gazed into the fire. "I guess so. Nothing else seems to be working. I've been here a little over a week, and I still cry every day. I don't have any energy, and I don't know what to tell Dillion or the kids. That call on Thanksgiving almost sent me to the hospital. I could hear it in their little voices that I've hurt them deeply. And then Dillion says, 'I love you,' and I couldn't say it back. I felt like the worst, most evil person in the world, but I swear, I couldn't say it back." She got choked up and used the arm of her sleeve to wipe away the wetness that lie on her cheeks.

Cat moved over to her best friend's couch and laid Aurelie's head on her lap and started humming that tune her own mother would hum when Cat felt sick or sad. It didn't have any words, it was just a simple tune, "Hmm mmm. Hmm mmm. Hmm mmm. Hmm hmm, hmm hmm mmm." The humming and the stroking of the hair put Aurelie in a trance, and she fell asleep just like that.

The next morning, Cat took the twins into town for preschool, before she went to work at the university. Damon and Aurelie had the house and the day to themselves. Mia joined them outside to bring Butters and Angel into the barn to prepare them for a morning ride. Angel seemed a bit nervous, but Damon's calm demeanor soothed her to the point that Aurelie could begin to brush her and clean her hooves. Next, Damon carefully situated a pad and then a saddle on Angel and encouraged Aurelie to continue to pet her and talk calmly to Angel while he got Butters ready for their trail ride.

Once outside, Dillion led them into the outdoor arena to walk them around a few laps before testing Angel's comfort level with Aurelie on her back. "Now, don't show her you're nervous or it won't work. Aurelie nodded and did a few deep breathing exercises before reaching out and petting the mare. Then talking to her to let her know Aurelie's intention to ride her. Aurelie mounted the steps and hooked the ball of her left foot into the stirrup before bracing herself to lift off the step stool and straddle the saddle. She was not very smooth getting on, but Angel kept fairly calm through the whole ordeal.

Once in the saddle, Aurelie walked Angel a few times around until Damon felt confident that both the horse and its rider were ready for the trail. He led them from the arena past the front paddock and into a crop of trees on the far side of the property. The skies were a dove gray this morning. Aurelie got settled into the pattern of the horse's movements.

She was almost hypnotized by the swishing of the long, bushy tail, the clip-clop of the horseshoes on the ground, and the swaying of Angel's backside as she walked. Every few moments, Damon would look back to make sure the horse and rider were doing okay. Aurelie didn't know how much time had passed, as she was finding the whole experience to be putting her into a meditative space. As they left the grove of trees, there was a stream ahead and Damon motioned for Aurelie to dismount so the horses could have a cool drink.

Damon walked around Angel and spoke to her in whispers as his hands never left her hide. She let him touch her and move her away from the water and back toward Aurelie to finish their morning ride. This time, he had Aurelie take the lead so he could observe his patients from a different angle.

When they returned to the barn, he helped Aurelie with the reins and the saddle so she could brush Angel and give her a treat before releasing her into the paddock.

"You did really well, Aur. Angel seems to trust you. I think only one or two more assisted rides and then I can let you two loose on your own."

"Really? Aren't you afraid that I'll screw something up? Or hurt her?"

"As long as you don't try to jump her, I think you will do just fine. Look at her. Does she look as forlorn as she did yesterday?"

Aurelie gazed into the grassy area and watched Angel walking around with her head just a smidge higher than yesterday. "Not as bad."

"Do you think you could be okay for a little while? I've got to run some errands in town. Do you need me to pick you up anything?"

She thought for a moment and then said, "Yeah. Would you do me a favor and pick up a postcard? I think I'd like to write a quick note to Dillion and the kids about the trail ride." Damon nodded and walked up to his truck and drove onto the gravel drive toward the highway. Mia came bounding out of the barn, all disheveled in straw. Aurelie took one more look back at Angel before leading Mia into the house for a cleaning and to start the slow cooker for dinner.

To be honest, Aurelie didn't feel like eating or cooking. But she was staying there, free of charge, and for as long as she needed to, so it was only fair to help out where she could. Tonight's dinner was going to be a beef roast with onions, potatoes, and baby carrots. After throwing the frozen chuck roast into the pot, Aurelie cut up the smallish potatoes into cubes, quartered an onion, and tossed a few handfuls of baby carrots around the frozen meat. Then she reached into the spice cupboard and pulled out a package of dried onion soup mix and a package of au jus mix to sprinkle over the beef and veggies. Then she took a cup of water and poured that into the pot before covering it with a lid and setting the temperature to high.

Aurelie went back to her room on the lower level and took a hot shower. Being on the trail on this December morning had given her a chill. She wanted to warm up and wash off the horse smell. She turned on the water as hot as it would go and jumped under the stream. Her mind started to wander. Questioning, really. Why was it okay for her to be here around Gracie and Gordy but not in her own home with Riley, Benji, and Brianna? How much does Angel understand what happened to her own foal? Did she get to see her foal alive at all? Did they get to interact before it died? Why couldn't God give her one moment of holding her daughter alive? Why was that too much to ask? Why couldn't she stay pregnant? Could she ever go back? Could she ever love again? Would she be alone for the rest of her life?

All the questions kept percolating in her head like popping corn. It gave her a headache, and she was exhausted. Finding her old sweatshirt and sweatpants, Aurelie slid them on and then climbed into bed. Her final thought before sleep was a simple one, *I don't have any answers.*

Aurelie woke to Mia barking, the twins babbling, and Cat trying to get everyone into the house and ready for dinner. She was flummoxed as to how long she slept. Aurelie put on some fuzzy socks, ran her fingers through her still damp curls and walked up the stairs to join everyone for dinner.

Cat looked tired but was firing on all cylinders. "Gordon, please feed Mia her dinner. Grace, I need you to put silverware at everyone's plate. Dillion, honey, would you mind cutting up the roast and setting up the twins' plates? I need to get out of these dirty clothes."

"You heard your mom. Get your 'bitty butts in gear!" Damon commanded. Aurelie smirked at the scene unfolding in front of her. Then she was sad wondering *what Dillion and the kids were doing for dinner? How they were doing? How sad they must feel because she left? Ugh.* Aurelie just wanted to crawl back into bed and hide under the covers.

"Thanks for dinner, Aur, you're a savior. Work was ridiculous today. I swear, all the horses decided they were going on strike and the students just stood there like they'd never even seen a horse before. Damon, I think I might need more than one glass of wine tonight. Just warning you."

Aurelie stayed quiet as the cacophony played out around the kitchen table. "Alright, guys, it's Friday movie night, so hurry and get into your PJ's and then you can each pick out a Christmas movie."

"But Dad, we don't have a tree yet. How can we watch a Christmas movie without a Christmas tree?" Grace asked.

"The weather looks good for us to go and cut one down tomorrow." In unison the twins yipped in celebration.

Aurelie's heart sank. She felt worse now than when she was in the shower. She started to help with the clean up when Cat said, "No you don't. You cooked. I clean. You look worse than I do. Why don't you go back to bed? I'll come and check on you after the kids go to sleep."

"Maybe I just need a little fresh air. I'll go check on Angel, see how she's doing." Aurelie grabbed her winter gear and walked outside. It was crisp and the stars were crowding the sky. Impressive. When she got to the barn, she heard the shuffle of the horses and a few 'neighs' as her presence had them a little excited. She walked into the barn and saw Angel in the back corner of her stall. A bit unsure of her surroundings. This was the first night she was going to stay in a stall, but with the weather getting colder, it was safer for her inside.

"Hey, Angel, want company?" Aurelie asked in a hushed tone. Angel shifted and turned around to look Aurelie in the eye. The two females got close to each other and pressed their foreheads together. Aurelie could feel Angel's sadness coming off of her in waves as it met Aurelie's in the essence around them. Aurelie broke the bond and went to open the stall. "I'm coming in, girl." She found a brush and thought perhaps that monotonous activity would help calm her mind and it may help Angel as well, like when someone brushes your own hair. So, she brushed the painted pony in long strokes, humming and singing as she went along. It was calming the mare to the point that she lay down for her deep sleep. Aurelie felt compelled to sit next to her head and stroked it while she hummed that tune which Cat had hummed to Aurelie. After they lie like that for about an hour, Angel whinnied and stood up. Aurelie was getting cold and decided it was time to go indoors. She kissed the mare's nose before saying good night.

The next day, Cat and her family went to cut down the family Christmas tree, which Aurelie couldn't stomach. If she couldn't do it with her own family, she damn well wouldn't do it with another family altogether. Instead, she drove to town to help with the grocery shopping. While she was in Bozeman, she saw a gift shop, ran in, and bought a whole stack of postcards. It was difficult to think of talking to Dillion or the kids on the phone because she could hear the pain and sadness in their voices. But writing down her first riding experience with Angel was cathartic. She wanted to share it with Dillion and sending him the postcard felt good. So, she decided that every time she wanted to tell him or the kids something, she'd write it on a postcard.

When Aurelie returned to the house, the tree was in the family room and the decorating had begun. Not willing to decorate the tree, again, something she couldn't do with her own family, she offered to make the hot cocoa for the decorating team and afterwards, make everyone grilled cheese sandwiches and cream of tomato soup for an early dinner.

A few days later, Aurelie found her confidence in riding the painted pony. With Damon's approval, they would take the trails through the woods, and then when they got to a grassy meadow, sometimes Aurelie would let Angel trot. They were getting comfortable with each other. There was an unspoken language between the two females. The pain was still there. The loss would never go away, but they were finding something else. They were finding their resiliency. Together.

On Christmas Eve Aurelie was trepidatious. She wanted to hear Dillion's voice. But she wasn't ready to see him yet. Not at all ready to go back home. She texted Dillion, *Do you think it might be okay to have a phone call today or tomorrow? It's okay if you don't want to. I'll understand.*

He texted back, *I'd like that very much. How about tomorrow, after church? It's very chaotic today with the nativity play and recital. If you want to talk today, I will find a way to make it work.*

Aurelie sighed. She should be there. Helping with the costumes, making cookies, helping with all the preparations. She just wasn't feeling Christmas at all. She was lost. She was lonely, even though she wasn't alone. Nope, the better word was *empty*. She thought back to her last time in her own kitchen, breaking everything she could get her hands on. She was *broken* and *empty*. Somehow, she had to figure out how to go on.

"Hey Aur, you downstairs?" Cat called, and then Aurelie heard the steps.

"Are you getting ready for church? Are you joining us?" Cat was wearing her black dress coat with a bright red and black plaid winter hat, matching scarf and black gloves and boots.

Aurelie was wearing a red sweater and black leggings. Sitting cross legged on her bed. "Sorry, Cat, I just can't force myself to celebrate Christmas in a church. I'm still so angry with God, I'm afraid I'll scream out something bad like 'liar!' in front of the whole congregation and get you all banned for life."

"Yeah, maybe it's better you stay here." Cat tilted her head and looked deeply into Aurelie's green eyes. "This has got to be tough on you. Do you want me to stay here with you? We could break open the mulled wine and Christmas cookies early."

"No. You go with your family. I'll stay here. I, um …"

"Whatever you want to do, Aur,"

"Thanks, I just want to let you know I texted Dillion. We're gonna talk tomorrow. On the phone."

"Alright, then. We'll make sure you get time to yourself. Maybe when the twins pass out from their sugar and present high."

"Cat?"

"Yes?"

"Thanks. Thanks for everything. I don't know where I would have gone or what kind of trouble I would have gotten into if you weren't here for me."

Cat knelt by her bestie, took her hands, and kissed them. "Aur, I will do whatever it takes to help you through this hell that you're in."

Aurelie began to cry, and so did Cat. They hugged it out before Cat left to join her family.

After the truck left, Aurelie bundled up and walked out to the barn to check on Angel. The mare sensed Aurelie's presence and was already at the stall door waiting for an apple slice and Aurelie's forehead to rest on her nose. They stayed like that for a long while before Aurelie left to get Christmas Eve dinner started.

Out on the path between the barn and the house, Aurelie felt compelled to look up at the sky, where she saw the north star, burning brighter than the other stars in the dark sky. She stared at it a moment before she spoke, "If you are really there, God, I want you to hear what I have to say. I think it's really shitty that you let me get pregnant, get my hopes up to have a baby, *three* times, and then lose them. And my little girl? My sweet, innocent, little girl? Even when I knew she wouldn't make it, I prayed to you. I PRAYED TO YOU to let me hold her, just a moment so she would know I'm her momma. So that she could hear me say 'I love you,' before you took her. AND YOU COULDN'T EVEN GIVE THAT TO ME! WHY? What have I done that's so bad that you couldn't grant me that one wish? What kind of sadistic plan do you have for me? Where I can't be with my own babies?"

Exhausted from yelling into the vastness that is the Montana sky, she fell to her knees in a pile of snow. "Look, I am tired of being sad, mad, and crying all the time. I don't know what's next for me, but I know I can't stay here forever, and I'm not ready to go back to Dillion and the kids. Honestly, I don't know if they will ever forgive me for leaving them. I'm sick with guilt, but I don't know what to do. If you can't tell me why this all happened. What great plan you have for me. Then can you at least show me or give me a sign as to what I'm supposed to do now?" Just then, the north star looked like it twinkled for a moment. Aurelie held her breath. It wasn't exactly something that she could work with but it was a start. She felt heard.

Once inside, Aurelie started a fire and then got to work in the kitchen shredding last night's leftover chicken into a stock pot, adding wild rice, pine nuts, cranberries and chicken broth to the pot and set it to boil, before she set the table.

When the MacGregors came into the house, Mia was the first to greet them as they debundled. Damon and Cat were grateful that Aurelie made dinner and then afterward, they did the cleanup while Gordon and Grace slipped into their jammies.

Cat and Damon's Christmas tradition was to open one gift on Christmas Eve and then the rest on Christmas morning. "Auntie Aur, Auntie Aur! Please open our present tonight!" Gordon and Grace pleaded.

"I didn't think I had any presents under the tree. Are you sure you want me to open it tonight and not in the morning?"

"Now!" They treated the green and red wrapped box adorned with a gold bow with great care as they handed it to her.

When she opened it, underneath a bed of tissue paper lay a ceramic frame with a wallet-sized photo of Aurelie and the twins and on top of the frame was written, "World's Best Godmother." Aurelie's shattered heart made a small jump. Perhaps two slivers of her heart fused together at that moment.

"Oh Gordy, Gracie. This is so beautiful. I love it!" She carefully put the delicate frame ornament down before collecting the jiggly bodies in front of her and pulling them into a bear hug and accepting their kisses. "Thank you. I love you so much."

After the twins went to bed, the adults lie on the couch, sipping mulled wine and nibbling on Christmas cookies while watching "National Lampoon's Christmas Vacation." At bedtime, Aurelie assessed how she was feeling. She wasn't happy. But she wasn't sad. She thought to herself, *Calm? Content?* Neither quite fit, but it didn't matter. She was too tired to care.

Christmas morning came like a freight train. The twins were screeching at the top of their lungs while Mia's excited barking and nails clicking on the hardwood floors above Aurelie's room woke her in a fright. Aurelie dragged herself out of bed, slipped into her fuzzy socks, and robe to join the MacGregor family Christmas.

"Momma, Daddy, Auntie Aur's up! Can we open presents now? Please?" Grace pleaded.

"Give her a moment, Grace, maybe she wants to have a little breakfast and some coffee first." Cat replied while pouring a mug of the hot black liquid and handing it to Aurelie.

"I'm up. Awake is a different story, but I don't want to get in the way of opening presents." Aurelie took a deep sip and felt the warmth run down her throat as her mind drifted to another home, with other children opening the presents she carefully chose and wrapped all year long. A sadness washed through her and landed like a gut punch.

Wrapping paper and bows were thrown to the side as squeals of delight were expressed from Grace and Gordon. It didn't matter if they opened a box of new bed sheets, a doll, or toy, they were genuinely excited about everything. "Alright, now that you've opened all your gifts, it's time to pick up the mess and get some real clothes on," Damon instructed.

"Why don't you all go get dressed, and I'll clean up the paper explosion?" Aurelie offered. She grabbed a garbage bag from the pantry and began filling it when her phone rang. She recognized the number right away and headed downstairs.

"Hello?" she answered nervously.

"Hi," Dillion answered back, cautiously. "Um, Merry Christmas."

"Merry Christmas, Dillion. Thanks for calling."

"I wasn't sure if it was too early by you."

"No, perfect timing. I was just cleaning up the Christmas tornado so they all could get dressed. Were you able to find where I hid the presents?"

"Yeah. I think so. But I found a box downstairs that I don't remember. When I opened it, it was filled with…"

Aurelie almost forgot about it. Her heart sank a bit. "Broken glass and plates."

"Yeah. I'm really confused. Why didn't you just throw it away?"

Aurelie took a deep breath and shared her story. "It happened that morning, after you left and the kids went to school, then went to the rink. I had a breakthrough of sorts, no pun intended." She stopped for a moment as the scene in her head came back to her.

"I had so much anger inside of me, Dillion, it was eating me up and making us all miserable. I had to get it out. I grabbed old glasses, plates, vases, whatever we wouldn't miss, and I threw it down on the ground and screamed as loud as I could."

"Ah, that makes sense. And the broken heart written on the box?"

"After I was done, I cleaned everything up and put it in an empty box because every single piece, all that dust, represents how broken my heart feels. My heart is in so many pieces that it may never heal and be like it was."

"Wow, that is really powerful. I just wish you would have shared that with me instead of leaving. I probably would have joined you. It sounds cathartic."

"Oh Dillion, I wanted to show you. That's why my phone was on the kitchen table. I stood on top of the table and took a photo of the chaotic mess on the floor before I swept it all up. I took Mumford for a long walk to sort through all those feelings and when I was done, I wanted to share the photo and my feelings with you. I was hoping you'd be able to understand what I felt by looking at the picture. But then things didn't turn out as I planned."

"I blew up at you. I'm sorry, Aur. I really am. I was under so much stress at work and the kids at the rink, ugh. I didn't give you a moment to explain. I just kept yelling. Can you forgive me?"

Aurelie's heart did a little flip. He was getting it. Late, but they were starting to communicate. "Yes, Dillion. I can forgive you."

"Oh Aur, I miss you so much. The kids do too. Home just isn't the same without you. I miss sleeping next to you. The energy you bring to the house. Christmas isn't the same. When will you be coming home?"

Her heart sank again. She wasn't ready. It was still too soon. "Dillion, I'm still healing. Damon has this painted pony here. She lost her foal, and we've been bonding. Trying to help each other. I feel like I have made some progress. Her too. But I know she's not ready to go back to the ranch, and I don't want to go back to the house with that shame and anger. I don't want to take it out on you or the kids. And I can't promise that I won't. At least right now. I'm sorry. I can't be who you need me to be right now."

She heard him trying to stifle tears on the other end of the phone. Then he finally spoke. "I guess I thought with the postcards and the text that you wanted to talk. I suppose I got my hopes up that you wanted to come back home to us."

"I'm sorry, Dillion. I'm just not ready."

"Um, I should get off the phone now. The kids will wonder what I'm doing, and they'll want to talk with you. I guess it's too soon for that also."

She thought about it. It would be nice to hear their voices, but she couldn't take the guilt that would likely be there when she would tell them she wasn't coming home. "Yes. Too soon. Thanks for the call, Dillion. It was really nice to hear your voice and to talk some of this through." She paused as she listened to her heart and finally gave him the only Christmas gift that she could offer. "I love you, Dillion." She heard his breath catch.

"I love you, too, Aurelie."

Chapter Forty-Eight

January came to Montana with a blanket of snow and a bitter cold front to follow. Angel was always excited to see Aurelie and vice versa. The vast barren landscape was the visual depiction of Aurelie's feeling of losing a baby. It seemed to her to be a symbol for what she was going through. This day she was considering the symbiotic relationship between the winter scenery and the feelings she had about herself. It helped her realize that even after the most difficult winter, there will be spring. A time of rebirth. A time for hope. Aurelie shared these thoughts as she continued to write postcards to her family back home.

Damon was working with Angel to get her to trust him and prepare her for working with Cat on the specifics of cattle ranching. When they finally got a day above freezing, Cat rode Angel and Damon rode Butters deep into the mountains to test Angel's confidence in riding on rocky terrain. Cat and Aurelie began working Angel in the indoor arena practicing roping and tagging.

"Angel," Aurelie said as she was brushing down the mare after her practice ranching work one day, "you are doing great. Really great. I'm so proud of you." The bright blue eyes of the painted pony looked to be smiling at the compliment. "I guess what I'm trying to say is, if you can move on, I guess I can start taking baby steps to move forward as well. I really miss hearing the kids' voices, you know? Brianna has got this vivid imagination. I can see her doing something very creative when she's grown. Benji, he's so special. Kinda like you and me these past few months. Keeping everything inside yet he's curious about how the world works. He's so smart.

Brilliant, actually. Questions everything. But it's music that is his love language. With every note he plays, you can feel what he's feeling. Then there's Riley. So smart, but she has her daddy's heart. So warm and giving. She's mission-driven, that one. And so mature. I wonder, if she came out of the womb with an old soul or if it was out of necessity after her momma died?"

Aurelie put the brush down and grabbed an apple slice for Angel who neighed and then nibbled it gently from Aurelie's hand. When Angel was done eating the treat, Aurelie sat down on an overturned bucket and sighed, hard. "Oh Angel, I haven't talked to any of the children in so long. I'm such a chicken. I'm so afraid to hear anger in their voices, or worse, pain." Angel stepped closer to Aurelie and used her long neck and nose to coax Aurelie's head into her side and stayed that way while Aurelie began to sob uncontrollably. Angel stayed, providing comfort, until all the tears were shed. "Thank you," Aurelie whispered.

That night, at dinner, Damon had an announcement. "I talked with Chuck, from the ranch. I told him how good Angel has come along. He's gonna stop by tomorrow to see for himself. See if she'll trust him and is ready to go home." Aurelie nodded. She knew this day would come. She was going to miss Angel. A lot. But if Angel could push past her grief and start moving forward, perhaps it was her time to move a bit forward, too.

She texted Dillion the next morning, Sunday, "If it would be okay with you, I'm wondering if I could talk to the kids?" She knew he would be busy with church and everything, but she was a bit disappointed that she didn't hear from him at all that day. She was already a little blue because Chuck was pleased with Angel's progress and taking her back to the ranch. Aurelie gave Angel an entire apple, and then a big hug around the neck. "Thank you for saving me and giving me hope, Angel. I'll never forget you," then touching foreheads together, Angel neighed softly. Aurelie understood it to mean that Angel felt the same way.

To keep from crying and moping all day in her room, Aurelie worked in the barn, cleaning out Angel's stall and still had enough energy to clean out the other horses' stalls. By dinner, she smelled like shit, and was completely pooped out. Aurelie went back to her lower level suite and took a long, hot shower to clean off as much muck as possible and wash away the sad emotions she was feeling.

At dinner, it was a rule in the MacGregor house not to have phones with you at the dinner table. So after eating heartily, Aurelie went back downstairs to check and see if she missed a call or text from Dillion. She didn't. Suddenly, all she wanted to do was sleep. And so, she did.

It had been 24 hours since she had texted Dillion and still no answer. She had lost him. And her one chance at having a family. Any family. She pulled herself out of bed and put on an oversized green sweater and jeans. It was a bright, sunny morning in early February, the sun's rays were almost blinding her through the patio doors. It was time to go upstairs and face the day. Whatever was in store for her. Then she heard Mia's excited bark. The one she used when someone was driving up to the house. Yup, Aurelie could hear the gravel crackling under the tires.

Aurelie walked upstairs and realized that she'd slept so late that Cat and the twins were in town for work and preschool and Damon put a note on the counter that he was driving out to the ranch to see how Angel was acclimating. *Great. I'm hear all alone. It's probably someone running from the law.*

But something curious happened. She heard a sound that she hadn't heard in a long time. Another dog barking, but it was a deep, almost guttural bark. *Wait a second, it couldn't be. Could it?* Aurelie threw on her boots and winter jacket before opening the door to see a familiar minivan packed to the hilt with suitcases, three dazed children, an equally exhausted dad, and one extra-large dog.

"Thank God, we made it. Dad, can we get out of the car now?" Benji whined.

"Hey! Don't take the Lord's name in vain, Benji. Dad!" Riley corrected and then complained.

"Ugh! Mumford, stop wagging your tail. It's hitting me in the face. Dad!" Brianna cried.

She could see that Dillion was on his last ounce of patience. They must have started driving right after church. After he got her text.

"Okay, try not to kill each other. Carefully get out of the car. Mumford, I'm talking to you, buddy."

The doors to the minivan slid open and a very excited and spotted Great Dane came barreling toward Aurelie before jumping so he could put his feet on her shoulders and lick her face. Mia was maneuvering to get a sniff of Mumford's butt without getting trampled on. "Hey there big guy. So, you missed me? I've missed you. Okay. Okay! Enough, Mumford. Enough kisses. Down boy." He obeyed and then became very interested in Mia and the other animal smells.

The Clark kids were a little wobbly getting out of the car, but once they got their footing, they practically ran and enveloped Aurelie in a group hug. It felt so good to be the center of that kind of affection. Unconditional love. She kissed the tops of each of their heads.

"I missed you so much!" Bri said.

"I missed you more," Benji declared.

"I missed you the most," Riley confirmed.

"I missed you all so much. So much," Aurelie said as she kissed them all on their foreheads. Then she saw him, swaggering toward her. Nervously. With his hands in his pockets, his hair disheveled, and his eyes darting from hers to the ground and back to hers again.

"I'm sorry I didn't text you back."

The kids let Aurelie go and backed away so their father could get closer. "It's okay. This is better."

He stopped in front of her and stared into her emerald eyes, searching. "Is it? Honestly?"

"Yes," she almost whispered and reached out to run her fingers through his hair. Dillion grabbed her so tight she could barely breathe. They stayed like that. Weeping. Not saying a word. But their silence said so much. A release of the pain, anger, sadness, and fearfulness.

"Um, Daddy? Momma Aur? I gotta use the bathroom. Real bad," Brianna said as she tapped on their shoulders. Soon all three Clark kids had to go. Aurelie brought them into the house and called the dogs in as well.

"Are you all hungry? Did you eat any breakfast or anything?"

"We're fine."

Just then Benji called out, "Dad! That 'breakfast' at the sketchy hotel was garbage. A granola bar, milk carton, and a juice box."

"Okay, I'll see what we've got to work with. Why don't you grab the plates and silverware to set the table, Benji. I think we've got enough to make scrambled eggs with toast." Aurelie went to work on scrambling the eggs, while the kids sat at the table and Dillion poured out the milk and orange juice.

When breakfast was served, they all bowed their heads in prayer and Aurelie said a silent *thank you* as well. The kids babbled on about the long and horrible trip, but that they were excited to stay with wolves.

"What do you mean that you're staying with wolves?" Aurelie asked curiously.

"I reserved the guest house at the Howler's Inn. It's also a wolf sanctuary. I thought the kids would like it."

"Yeah! It's a log cabin like Grandma and Grandpa Beres live in!" Brianna exclaimed.

"Wow! Sounds amazing. I think I know that place. I believe..." Just then the door opened, and Damon walked in.

"What? A party at my house and no one invited me?" The kids laughed and got up to give Damon a hug. Dillion stood up and offered his hand.

"Sorry, Damon. It was kinda a spontaneous decision. I got us a place to stay, but they don't accept dogs. Would it be okay to keep Mumford here? With Aurelie?"

"Absolutely. Where are you staying?"

"Howler's Inn."

"Howler's is great. I've got some wonderful memories of that place," Damon said with a nostalgic look on his face and a twinkle in his bright blue eyes.

"How about after you're done eating, I'll give you kids a tour of this place. Would you like that?"

A resounding "YEAH!" came from the table. Soon all the eggs were eaten and the juice drunk. They scattered from the table and into their boots and coats. With the dogs in tow.

"Since you cooked, let me clean up," Dillion said.

After the kitchen was tidy, each took a mug of coffee and sat on the sofa. "I can't believe you're here!" Aurelie exclaimed.

"I hope you aren't angry. It's just I read your text and saw it as an opening."

She took a sip while still staring into his pale blue eyes, looking so worn and worried. She knew she'd done that to him.

"No. Not angry at all. When you didn't text back, I thought, I thought, I'd waited too long. You were done. Waiting for me."

"Aurelie," he said, grabbing her hand and giving it a squeeze. "I'm not done waiting for you. I promised you and G … " his eyes opened, in shock. Afraid that he'd gone too far. Aurelie sighed. She didn't want him to be fearful to talk to her openly. Honestly. Her doubts were clouding her excitement for having her family here, in Montana.

"Dillion. It's okay to say it. Here, I'll say it for you, 'God.'" She pulled her hand away and looked wistfully at Cat and Damon's wedding photo over the mantel and next to it, their family portrait. "I had a little 'come to Jesus' moment myself." Aurelie shared her experience on Christmas shouting at the sky and feeling calm afterward. "For this to work. If it's ever going to work, we can't be afraid to talk to each other about our feelings and what's important to us. In the moment, in the future. Whatever."

"Aurelie, you ARE important to me. So are the kids and God. It's like you all make up my personal trinity. I can't give up on any of you."

She sat back, deep into the cushions and looked up at the vaulted ceiling. "Dillion, I've wrestled with what's important to me for the past two years. I didn't know I wanted my own babies until I got pregnant that first time. Then, it consumed me. Like a heroin addiction almost. It clouded every decision I made. If I'm honest, somewhere, during that time, I stopped enjoying the pleasure of making love with you. I saw it as a means to an end, to become pregnant." She put her coffee down on a table and shifted so that she was sitting cross legged across from Dillion.

"Look. I know it should be our decision, but I have made the decision for myself, and if you can't be with me anymore because of it, I'll understand."

Dillion put his mug down and turned toward her, carefully. Cautiously. *Oh damn. I'm gonna cause him even more pain. Well, here it goes, and maybe any chance I have at saving this marriage.*

"When I do decide to go back to Minocqua, I plan on contacting the doctor to get my tubes tied. Dillion, I can't go through the roller coaster ride from hell any longer. I am done. So done."

Dillion took a deep breath, hung his head, and then reached out for her hands. "Aur. My Christmas present to you is that I got a vasectomy."

Tears filled Aurelie's eyes. He had been listening. He understood. Inside, her heart seemed to heal a few more broken pieces together. "Thank you," she whispered and then leaned in to kiss him lightly on the mouth. He accepted it and let her linger as long as she was comfortable doing so. Then, they rested their foreheads together. And that is where Damon and the Clark kids found them.

While Riley, Benji, and Brianna babbled on about all the cool things they saw, Aurelie noticed that Mumford had exhausted himself and had taken over Mia's bed, in front of the fireplace.

The morning ran into the afternoon. By the time Cat came home with the twins, the sun was going down. Aurelie made a quick pot of chili while the twins showed off their toys and rooms and the dogs gnawed on rawhides in front of the fire.

After a rip roaring dinner, the twins begged to have a sleepover with their "cousins," so Aurelie went out to the minivan with Dillion to bring in their suitcases. Cat and Damon had extra sleeping bags and pillows, a must for any Montana mountain home in case people got stranded. Outside, Aurelie looked up at the star-filled sky and saw the north star shining brightly, almost as a sign. "Say, Dillion?"

"Hmm?" was all he could offer as he was rifling through the pile that was their suitcases, to-do bags, snack bags, etc.

"Would it be okay? I mean, would you consider a sleep over at the Howler's?"

"Aur, I just got the kids' bags all sorted out. Really? You want everyone back there?"

She giggled, perhaps they still needed to work on their communication skills. "Sorry, what I meant to say was, is it okay if I wanted to have a sleepover with you at the Howler's?"

He dropped everything and stared at her. "Are you serious?"

"I think so," Aurelie replied with trepidation. Now she was reconsidering her offer. Then she looked into those eyes that held every good memory of what they've had together. What unconditional love, married love looks like, and she had her confidence back. "Yes. Please. If you'd like to. I don't want to push you out of your comfort zone."

Dillion reached over and crushed her in a kiss that had all her synapses going off like a pinball machine. When they pulled away, they each had a naughty grin on their face. Like two teenagers telling their parents they were sleeping over at a friend's house but really meeting up to have their own private sleepover.

They went back to the house with the suitcases and kissed everyone good night. When Aurelie hugged Cat, her bestie whispered in her ear, "We'll take good care of everyone here. Go ahead and 'sleep in.'"

Aurelie and Dillion walked back to the minivan and drove in silence to the Dutch-revival log cabin nestled into the Bridger Canyon on the other side of Bozeman. Though it was dark, they heard the wolves howling as they parked in front of the garage. Aurelie helped Dillion bring the bags from the minivan up the flight of stairs and into the guest house connected by a wooden walkway to the main house. There was a fire glowing in the fireplace, not only for ambiance, but it kept the living space warm and cozy. Under the windows that offered a panoramic view of the front fields and Bridger Mountains during day, was a mission-style futon with wildlife printed fabric that matched the side chair. A simple coffee table rounded out the room. To the right was a homey kitchen that could fit five people comfortably around the dining table. Down the hallway and to the right was a full bath and the first of two bedrooms with a queen bed. During the day, this room enjoyed the spectacular sunrise over the mountains.

Once inside, Aurelie's nerves took over. *Was it too soon to be with Dillion? After spending so much time apart?* "Hey, Aur, I brought a bottle of that wine that you like. Would you like me to open it?" Dillion showed her that he had a bottle of Cardinal Red, a rich berry and dark fruit wine, from Mukwonago's own Pieper Porch Winery.

"Yes, please." She wasn't thirsty but thought the wine would help ease her nerves. Dillion sat next to her on the futon, and they clinked glasses. "Cheers," Aurelie offered, a little jittery, before she took a sip.

Dillion noticed. "Aur, we don't have to make love tonight. We don't even have to sleep in the same bed. I just really want to be with you. I miss you. This … "

"Sorry, I didn't mean, I mean. I don't like teases. I don't want to be one. Especially not with you. It's just," Aurelie paused.

"There isn't anything to be sorry about, Aur. I swear. We can take this as slow as you want. You aren't a tease. I promise. I wasn't sure if I should bring this. Ugh, what I mean is that I have a gift for you. I think this is as good as a time to give it to you. Can you excuse me for a second?"

"Oh, Dillion, I've put you through so much and you still thought about getting me a present? I don't think I can handle it. Honest."

Dillion put his hand on her arm and looked into her concerned eyes. "It's not that kind of present, Aur. Honest. Besides, you've already given this one to me. Think of it as a regift. Of sorts." He smiled when her concern turned to one of being perplexed. Then Dillion got up and walked to the bedroom where he put his stuff. When he came out, he had an acoustic guitar. He sat in his spot on the couch to tune the guitar before speaking again.

"You gave me the gift of this song on our wedding day. It meant the world to me. At the time, it reminded me of all of the challenges we faced just to get to that moment, to celebrate us as a new couple. While you were gone, I played it over and over again and I think I got to be pretty good, if I do say so myself," he winked and smiled at her. Aurelie couldn't help but grin. "As I played it, this song began to unfold another layer of our story. Now when I hear Brandi Carlile sing 'The Story,' or when I strum it on the guitar, it's ours. The story of us."

Dillion began to strum the chords and then stopped, "Boy this is nerve-racking. I didn't think I'd be so nervous to play in front of you." This time, Aurelie laid her hand on his arm and gave it a light squeeze. "Alright. Here it goes … "

All of these lines across my face
Tell you the story of who I am
So many stories of where I've been
And how I got to where I am
But these stories don't mean anything
When you've got no one to tell them to
It's true … I was made for you
I climbed across the mountain tops
Swam all across the ocean blue
I crossed all the lines and I broke all the rules
But baby I broke them all for you
Because even when I was flat broke
You made me feel like a million bucks

CANOODLING ALWAYS & FOREVER

You do
I was made for you
You see the smile that's on my mouth
It's hiding the words that don't come out
And all of my friends who think that I'm blessed
They don't know my head is a mess
No, they don't know who I really am
And they don't know what I've been through like you do
And I was made for you ...
All of these lines across my face
Tell you the story of who I am
So many stories of where I've been
And how I got to where I am
But these stories don't mean anything
When you've got no one to tell them to
It's true ... I was made for you

Aurelie's wall around her heart came tumbling down with each verse, like the tears she was releasing. She saw all of the pleasure, pain, and loss they've been through together. It was emotively familiar. "Thank you, Dillion. That was absolutely perfect. What a special gift." She leaned over and lightly kissed his lips in gratitude.

She took a sip of wine and then looked into the fire. That song and this fire lessened the ache she felt in her core. The fire soothed her. It was mesmerizing seeing the flames flickering in red, burnt orange, and gold. Dillion just poured his soul into that song to share it with her. It was time she did the same for him.

"Remember when I told you I had that 'come to Jesus' moment?"

"Yes."

"Well, there's a bit more. If God has a plan for all of us. For me. Then why did three babies have to die? Why can't you and I make and keep our own babies? I still don't have an answer to that. I guess that is what all my anger has been about. After the grief, of course. I've been so angry because I don't understand. Dillion, what is the purpose of all this?"

She turned and looked at Dillion as she finished. He took a sip of his wine and then gave her the only words that made sense to him. He hoped it would be enough. "I don't know."

She did a half smile as did he. Then she lay on his front while they watched the fire turn into embers. "Dillion?" Aurelie asked nervously.

"Hmm?"

"Would it be okay if we slept in separate rooms tonight? I thought I could, but, um, I'm just not sure yet."

"Absolutely. Are you ready for bed now?"

"Yeah. I'm pretty tired. A lot happened today."

"A lot did. That drive almost did me in."

"Sorry."

"Nothing to be sorry about, Aur. I'd go wherever I needed to, to get to you. I hope you know that."

She felt a little more of her heart fuse together. "I do now."

"Let's go to bed."

"Okay."

Aurelie didn't bring anything sexy to Montana, nor did she bring anything romantic to the Guest House. She pulled off her green sweater and jeans and slid on her oversized pajama shirt and lounge pants and then a pair of fuzzy socks. She lay there and stared at the ceiling. Then she rolled to her side. Not feeling it, she rolled to the other side. She tried to hum herself to sleep when she heard snoring coming from the other bedroom. Dillion's room.

Dillion. The unassuming young Episcopal priest who she fell in love with the first time he touched her and shocked her. The man with the kindest eyes and a loving soul who would do absolutely anything for her and their kids. No matter how difficult it would be. Like letting her leave and stay away for two and a half months.

Like driving 18 hours just to answer a text, in person. Like having a vasectomy so she wouldn't have to worry about a miscarriage ever again. The man who agreed to sleep in different rooms after being separated for months and driving more than 1,100 miles to be with her.

Aurelie sat up in bed. She was an idiot. She made a promise to be with Dillion for better or worse. Richer or poorer. In sickness and in health. She was going to make good on her promise. Tonight. She kept the lights off but followed the muffled snoring of the man she had pledged her life to only two years prior. She slipped under the covers and snuggled up to him, which startled him. He snorted. "What? What's wrong?"

"Shh," Aurelie said and then placed her lips on his. Giving Dillion a kiss that started sweet and simple then turning on the heat by using her teeth to nip his lower lip. He responded by using his tongue to open her mouth and search hers out. Aurelie kept her eyes closed and let the experience waft over her. Soon Dillion was pulling off her shirt and pulling her on top of him so he could palm her breasts and squeeze her nipples until they went hard. She bent over so he could take each of her breasts into his mouth and work his magic.

Aurelie shifted so she could pull off his T-shirt and throw it on the floor. Next, Dillion carefully moved her to lay on her back so he could slide off her lounge pants. When she was freed, he pushed her legs wide, leaned into her so he could kiss and lick her to ecstasy. Aurelie arched her back and made a guttural sound as she began her climax. Dillion lifted his head, swiftly pulled down his own lounge pants and entered her speedily. He found her rocking rhythm and let her orgasmic spasm lead him into his own climax. Their lovemaking released so many insecurities, cautions, and left them feeling reborn. Right before Dillion freed himself, he kissed her with such tenderness that it made Aurelie's heart ache a moment. Then kissed her with a promise on his lips, whispering, "Aurelie Clark, I loved you from the first time I saw you. I love you today. I'll love you always and forever."

Chapter Forty-Nine

The next morning, they awoke to the wolves howling and another bright, sunny day in the mountains. After the rigorous lovemaking from the night before, they were starving. Dillion found a loaf of bread and put four slices in the toaster while Aurelie started the coffee pot. "I didn't pack for a vacation. I think there's peanut butter at the bottom of one of the bags and the jam should be in the cooler. Aurelie fished around and found the PB&J to slather on her toasted bread before handing the knife over to Dillion.

"Dillion?" She asked.

"Yeah?"

"How long were you and the kids planning to stay in Montana?"

"I dunno. However long it takes to get you to agree to come home with us, I guess."

"Seriously. It was a long drive for you all. If I said I want to start going home today, would you really do that?"

"Honestly, I would. It wouldn't be my first choice though. I had to prepay for at least two nights. I'd hate to waste it. But I'd do it. For you."

"How much did you pack for?"

"I don't know. I just told the kids to throw a bunch of clothes into their suitcases and get in the car. I think they'd like to hang out with the twins a bit and maybe see some of the sights in downtown Bozeman since we've never been."

"I just think that we may need some time to connect away from the house. A day or two?"

"Sounds perfect."

"I think it's time for one of our special showers. Don't you?"

"Again, sounds perfect."

They worked together to clean up the kitchen before stripping their pajamas and jumping into the shower. Aurelie forgot how soothing it was to have Dillion wash her hair and body. How exhilarating it was to have him touch her. This shower wasn't as spacious as the one back home, but it didn't take a lot of room for him to slide his fingers inside her or for her to lather him. Though the space was confined, she felt unconstrained and let her hands glide up and down his body while he skimmed her heated skin with his. Afterward, they toweled each other off and ended their sensual shower by slathering lotion over their exposed skin. When Dillion got to her buttocks, he slid his fingers inside of her and it made her shiver. She was surprised she could be aroused so quickly and that he was ready to be inside of her again. Aurelie bent over, holding onto the bathroom sink, giving Dillion ample access. He entered her slowly at first, enjoying how easy it was for him to glide inside her. She looked up in surprise, when she felt him touch her so deeply, it was like magic. That's when she saw him looking into the mirror at her reaction. It was carnal and possessive at the same time. His usually kind eyes appeared greedy. As if he was coveting her and possessing her with each thrust. Between that look and how deep he was driving into her, Aurelie was taken to a higher plane. It was intoxicating watching him watch her. She accepted every probe willingly as he plunged into her. Her body not only received him willingly, but warmly, with every thrust, every groan, she couldn't wait any longer. She pushed her backside into him encouraging him to increase his pace until she was about ready to black out with an orgasm that exploded as brightly as Fourth of July fireworks. Her climax was heightened by watching everything unfold in the mirror. Dillion's climax matched her intensity, and he fell on top of her in utter exhaustion.

"I can see why Damon has fond memories of this place," Dillion commented after they'd freshened up and dressed. Aurelie playfully slapped him on the butt as they walked down the stairs and into the minivan.

After a day of shopping in downtown Bozeman and touring the Museum of the Rockies, they went to a thrift store to pick up some swimwear and towels to use at Bozeman's hot springs. The kids were amazed that they could be swimming in 100 plus degree water while it was snowing outside. They stayed even after the sun set so Aurelie could show them how the stone walls erupted into flames and bright colored lights. Nothing like that in Minocqua. But Bozeman didn't have a snowshoe baseball team either.

For dinner, Damon grilled bison burgers, Cat made homemade French fries, and Aurelie had picked up some huckleberry ice cream in town for dessert. The Clark kids took a bath before another sleepover, and Aurelie and Dillion went back to the inn.

They made slow, passionate love on the floor in front of the fire before picking up and lying skin to skin in bed. "Did you ever think we'd be able to get back to enjoying sex again?" Aurelie asked as she gently skimmed her nails over Dillion's bare chest.

"I hoped so. I mean, hell, you trained me to be a sexual beast. I didn't want all that schooling to go to waste." Aurelie's guttural laugh got Dillion to laugh also and when it subsided, she lifted her head and kissed him softly on the mouth before looking deeply into his eyes to say, "Dillion Clark, I love you."

The next morning, Aurelie had an uneasiness about leaving. She was fearful about going back to Minocqua and being hit with all of the memories and bad feelings that had chased her out of the house months before. While Dillion was packing up both cars, she touched him and said, "Sorry, but I need a minute."

"Do you want me to come with you?" he asked, with concern.

"No. I'll be fine. I just need a minute." Aurelie walked over to the pasture, followed the wood fence until she got to the tree line and stood in front of a majestic pine, straight as an arrow pointed at the heavens. Something was still nagging her. It was the one thing that she still hadn't been able to resolve. Aurelie heard foot falls crunching in the snow behind her. She expected to see Dillion, but instead …

"Momma Aur. What'cha doin' out here? Don't you want to come home with us anymore?" Benji asked, his head cocked, pushing up his glasses.

"Of course, I do, Benji. It's just. Oh, I don't know. It's silly, I guess, but it feels like I'm still missing something. Something I was supposed to figure out while I've been here and I haven't been able to. Does that make sense?"

"Sure it does. You've got a hypothesis and you haven't found a theorem that proves it."

Aurelie laughed. Only Benji could turn her emotional struggle into a scientific experiment.

"Maybe if you share it, I can help. I'm pretty smart, you know."

"Benji, you are the smartest boy I know. But I'm not sure you can figure this one out."

"At least give me a chance to help. You always tell me that."

"Alright. Here's the thing." Aurelie stopped looking up at the tree and stared right at Benji. "If there is a God and He has a plan for me, what was the purpose for me to have the miscarriages? How does that help me become the person I'm supposed to be? Why did I have to lose those babies?"

Benji had a contemplative look on his face. His process began by staring deeply at Aurelie, then the tree, and then the sky. It made Aurelie curious. Then he spoke, thoughtfully. "My momma died of cancer and went to heaven leaving her three babies without a momma here on earth."

"Okay," Aurelie commented waiting to hear his conclusion.

"You lost your babies,"

"Uh huh," she still was perplexed and Benji looked a little frustrated that she wasn't getting it.

"We know that Momma had to go be with God in heaven, leaving us with no momma. Maybe he sent you to us to take care of her babies on earth while she's taking care of your babies in heaven?"

Aurelie stopped breathing. She could feel the jagged, imperfect stitching of her heart's fragmented pieces coming together in a twisty, crooked pattern. Once upon a time, her heart was perfectly shaped, smooth, healthy with a strong heartbeat. Then it became damaged, so damaged that Aurelie did not believe it could ever be mended. This day. After this child's revelation, her heart's pieces, scattered and in disrepair, mended together, like a crazy patchwork quilt.

She reached out and hugged Benji until he asked her to let him breathe. "Oh Benji, you are the smartest person I know. Thank you for this. You solved the mystery. I understand. It's so simple, and I couldn't see what was right there, right in front of me." She grabbed him again and kissed his floppy hair. "I love you, Benji. So much. You and your sisters are my purpose. I'm so glad you picked me to be your momma. I can't wait to adopt you and your sisters."

The day the Clark caravan arrived home was Valentine's Day. After unpacking, bathing, and putting on their jammies, Dillion whispered something to Brianna who got very animated. "Momma Aur! Sit down and close your eyes. We've got a surprise for you."

"Really? Oh, okay."

Dillion came from the basement and put the box with the broken heart drawn on top in front of Aurelie. "Okay, you can open your eyes now."

She looked at the box quizzically. When she opened it, "It's empty?" They all giggled.

"Exactly. Now close your eyes again." Dillion said. She complied. This time she could hear him going into their bedroom and sliding something on the floor. "Okay, now open your eyes again." Laying on the ground was a much larger box, wrapped in red paper with a silver bow on top.

Aurelie began ripping the paper, still no clue what was hiding underneath it. She opened the box slowly and she gasped. In front of her was every scrap, fragment, piece of smashed glass, dish, and vase. But now they were held together in cement made into two sides of a fractured heart. But in the middle were large pieces of every single postcard she had mailed to them. They were haphazardly suspended in clear resin and were holding together the two halves of the heart in a zig-zag pattern totally replicating, in art, what Aurelie felt her own looked like on the inside. "What? How? When? It's amazing!" Aurelie began sobbing. Happy crying but ugly crying nonetheless. When she calmed down Dillion explained.

"This was all Bri's idea. We all helped, of course. But Brianna was the mastermind."

Brianna looked very proud at that moment and explained. "When we were looking for the Christmas stuff, Daddy found this box and didn't understand what it was. So, when you talked to him on the phone and told him, I had the idea to make it like an art project and make it look like a real broken heart. Then your postcards kept coming so I put them in the middle, and Benji thought of the resin and we all helped make it as a surprise for you. For when you came back."

"This is the best present I've ever had. I love you all so much!" The Clarks came together for a group hug and ugly cry. But a happy one.

Chapter Fifty

On a warm, sunny Mother's Day afternoon, Dillion dug out a space in front of Aurelie's flower garden. With a little help from the kids, placed the mended heart art piece in the ground to be a showpiece for all to see. Aurelie ran inside and grabbed the adoption papers and had the kids hold them while standing behind the heart with her while Dillion took the photo.

Aurelie's journey to get to this point was filled with stops, starts, detours, and backtracking. But she found her purpose and learned that unconditional love is messy. Complicated. Resilient. Life is not about reaching a goal. It is about celebrating the journey along the way.

Epilogue

"Momma Aur, It's Riley. Can you hear me?" Aurelie's breathing was labored, and her eyesight was poor. She was so very tired. She couldn't remember a time that she had been this tired. But something was missing. Someone perhaps? She had to wait a bit longer. She was trying with all the energy her 90 year-old body could muster. Aurelie recognized Riley's voice, so she focused on getting her eyes open to sort out what Riley was trying to tell her. She was using her priestly voice. It must be important. When the scene cleared a bit, she saw that Riley was wearing her priest collar and black short sleeved shirt and pants. *Hmm, this must be very important.* Aurelie thought to herself.

She started to look around the room that had been her home for the past few days. A simple room, at the end of a hallway so she could look at the flowers and the birds outside her patio door. She thought she heard the word "hospice" the other day, but Aurelie couldn't quite comprehend what that meant. She saw some things she recognized. Framed photos. Her photos. The wedding photo that was always on the fireplace, the one of Riley when she was ordained. Next to that was a beautiful blonde woman in a burgundy couture dress holding something shiny. Focusing a little harder she saw the shiny thing was in the shape of a little man. Funny sort of thing to be holding. What was her name, though? The fog was rolling in again and she felt muddled. "Momma Aur, honey, Brianna's here to see you. Can you keep awake just a little bit longer?" Riley asked.

With her eyes closed, she could feel a drifting sort of energy, wanting to make her lighter. But then she took another strenuous breath and in wafted a familiar scent. Bringing her back in time when she was dressed in a classic black formal, sitting next to that beautiful woman in the photo. What was her name again? "Momma Aur? Momma Aur, it's me, Brianna. I just wanted to tell you how much I love you. You helped me gain the confidence to go for my dreams. Dreams I didn't even know I had. I am so grateful God brought you to us. You've been the best mom. I'm gonna miss you like crazy. Goodbye, Momma Aur. I love you to the moon and back." *The pretty lady, Brianna, bent down and kissed me on the cheek. I remember her now. I called her Bri. I was her momma. She fixed my broken heart.* With that, Aurelie opened her eyes and searched the room. There, on the little table was the photo of her standing in the middle between Brianna, Riley, and a young fellow in glasses. Who was he again? What was important in this moment was that she could see the heart made of broken pieces and brought together by a river of postcards she recalled writing a while back. She loved that heart. All this remembering made her tired again. She just wanted to sleep, but something was bugging her. Why couldn't she sleep yet?

"Sir, she's in here." Aurelie heard footsteps coming into her room. Didn't sound like the others. She wondered whose they might be.

"Oh Benji, I'm so glad you made it. It won't be long now. I think she's been fighting it so she could see you," Riley said.

Benji. Yes! That's it! That's that little boy in the photo with the messy hair and glasses that kept falling down. Phew. Now if I could just figure out why he's so important. I'm so tired. So very tired.

Aurelie felt the weight of her bed shift and warm, strong hands grabbed hold of her feeble, bony ones that were getting colder by the minute. "Momma Aur. It's me. Benji. Sorry I'm so late. I was the keynote speaker at the national cancer research conference in California. I just flew in. I'm so sorry I was almost late. But I'm here now."

"Benji, Bri and I have already said our goodbyes. We'll step out and give you some privacy. Let us know if there is any change. It could be any moment now." Riley took Brianna's arm, and they walked out of the room, together.

"Oh Momma Aur, I knew this day would come, but I ...shit. That sounds so common. Let me try this again." Benji took a deep breath and Aurelie followed. She felt this would be important.

"Momma Aur, you saved my life. You helped me find my purpose, and you taught me how to play. To be a kid. I don't think I would have ever survived into adulthood without you. Honestly. I am so grateful to you, for finding the human in me. You gave me the greatest gift I ever received. Your love. Your unconditional, supportive, free-spirited, love." Aurelie felt something warm and wet fall on her arm, but again, the fog was rolling in.

"So, thank you, Momma Aur. Please forgive me. I forgive you. Continue to love me as I love you. Goodbye." He bent down to kiss Aurelie on her forehead just as she had given to him a million times before. "Momma Aur, your purpose here is done. You're free to go," he said while he wept.

In that moment, Aurelie felt a warm and bright sensation hitting her face, slowly moving toward her feet and she swore she heard the light say to her, "Aurelie, come with me. It's time." Suddenly she felt lighter. She could open her eyes with ease, and she reached out her hand and let the light guide her from the bed and above the commotion. Aurelie couldn't understand why the people were coming into the room and crying over that old, wrinkled woman with the silver hair. She felt a calm come over her and when she looked down at her hands, they were tan and supple. The pain was gone. It didn't hurt to breathe. Her brain didn't feel all foggy. She was confused, but that was because she'd never had this kind of experience before.

It seemed like she and the light were floating up higher than a human would ever be able to on their own. But she wasn't afraid of the unknown. Now she was curious. When the light let go, she heard the lovely lilt of a woman's voice in front of her. "Welcome, Aurelie, we've been expecting you."

Aurelie touched down on the silkiest patch of green grass she'd ever had caress her bare feet. She looked down expecting to see pale, tissue paper thin skin with those atrocious varicose veins in her feet and legs. Instead that thin, pale skin was replaced with the bronzed smooth skin of her youth. Interestingly, Aurelie found she was wearing a short sleeve, crew neck white cotton dress, fitted with pockets. She twirled around and relished the feel of the flowy dress flouncing around her. Then she looked down and noticed they were at the edge of a crystal blue lake. Curiously, Aurelie looked into the water and saw her face and hair. It was her in her thirties. That spunky, curly black hair she loved. Her eyes were that bright and sassy, emerald green, and her lips were full and pink. Her favorite version of herself.

"I've been looking forward to meeting you for such a long time." Aurelie gazed up and into the eyes of a woman, about her age, but paler, lighter hair, straight and shoulder length. But she was wearing a similar dress to Aurelie's.

Just then, a little girl with long black ringlets and striking green eyes came up and tugged on the woman's dress. "Can she play with us yet? Is she ready?"

The woman chuckled and then hugged the little girl before she spoke. "She just got here. I promise, I'll give you a signal when she's ready to play with all of you, Angelina."

Aurelie was shocked to attention. She knew that name. But she didn't recognize the girl. "What's going on? Who are you, and where am I? Why am I here?"

"Of course, you have a lot of questions, Aurelie. I had plenty myself. I had a guide to help me when I arrived, and I very much appreciated it. So, I asked if I could be the one to guide you." They started walking toward a tree. A very large oak tree with vast branches filled with sage green leaves, so thick it blocked the sun from certain angles.

"My name is Corinne. Corinne Clark." Aurelie looked quizzically at the lovely lady and thought very hard. Then it clicked.

"Your Dillion's first wife! You died of cancer!"

"Yes. Yes, I did."

"So, I'm here because I died?"

"You could say that."

"I don't understand. Why did you want to be my guide? I married Dillion after you. I adopted your kids. Why would you want anything to do with me?"

They stopped walking when they got to the shade of the tree and Corinne put her hand on the trunk of the oak. "Does this tree remind you of anything?" she asked.

Aurelie walked around it, felt its rough bark and waxy leaves. "It does look familiar. I saw it in a photo once. Were you the woman pushing Benji on a tire swing? Was this your tree? With Benji?"

Corinne smiled. "Yes. Yes, that's right."

"So what does your tree have to do with me?"

"Well, before I died, Benji asked God to make a promise to take care of me up in heaven. The second part of the promise was to give him a sign that I was watching out for him. Do you remember that?"

"Hmm, was that the North Star?"

"Very good. So, the North Star is a very special star. It has magical powers. It is the star that led the wise men to Jesus. It is also the star that led you to him. And Brianna, Riley, and Dillion."

"I'm sorry, I'm still confused. You're saying that this tree and that star led me to the Clark family? Why?"

"Because when someone is loved so much, their love lives on through eternity and it is granted 'special powers.' Benji's wish and my promise combined with those special powers gave me the opportunity to find a unique woman who would help heal the family that I left broken. When I found you, just as lost and struggling as they were, I knew you were meant to be together. So that's what I did."

"Did what?"

"Brought you and Dillion together. I had the idea for Dillion to have the cancer event and invite your dad to speak. Well, first I had to test you to make sure you could take care of someone, something other than yourself. So, I guided you to–"

"Mumford!"

"You got it. He's such a great dog. He's perfect for the children."

"You mean he *was* great for the kids. Yes, he was."

"And he still is."

"Sorry, but I'm lost again. So, you guided me to Mumford and then what?"

"Well, anytime you needed a little help, I was there."

"How? When?"

She shrugged her shoulders and pulled a leaf off the tree. "It depended on what the situation called for. Sometimes I was a phone call from an old friend. Other times I was a breeze that welcomed you in the forest. Or a cold breeze to keep you from making a big mistake. And sometimes … "

Aurelie remembered something. "Sometimes you were the north star."

"Yes, ma'am. I think that was one of my most brilliant ideas." Corinne grinned.

"But why me? Why did you choose me? I was a mess. I didn't even know if I could or would ever get married, want kids."

Corinne sighed and looked across the grassy field at a small group of children playing in a field of wildflowers with a very large dog. "I wanted you to raise my babies for me. I left them too soon. They were shattered. Broken. You were, too. You all were grieving at the same time. Different reasons, but grieving the loss of a loved one, just the same. I knew you'd be perfect for them. So, I promised to take care of your babies here, in heaven, because you promised to take care of my babies on Earth." Then Corinne raised her hand and waved at the group playing. The girl, Angelina, saw the signal and ran up the hill towards the two women.

Aurelie's mind was going a mile a minute. Scenes from her life flashed before her. Memories that confirmed everything that Corinne just told her. It was true. All true. "Wait a second,"

"Yes?" Corinne still watched the group playing.

"If all you're saying is true then Angelina," a lump formed in Aurelie's throat.

"Yes, Aurelie. Angelina is your baby girl. And down the hill playing with Mumford are your other two babies, a girl and a–"

Aurelie finished it. "Boy." *Oh my God!* Aurelie said to herself. By then, Angelina had reached the two women. Looked up at Corinne, Aurelie, and Corinne again. "Is it time? Can she play?"

Corinne smiled at the little dark-haired girl and moved an unruly curl from her face. "Yes, Angelina, Aurelie can play with you now."

Angelina walked up to Aurelie and offered her hand, "Would you like to come play with us, Momma?"

Though there are no tears in heaven, Aurelie felt overrun with emotion. She reached out and accepted the small chubby hand. "Yes, Angelina. Yes, I would love to play with you."

Aurelie mouthed the words, "Thank you" to Corinne, leaving her underneath the oak tree before she followed her own baby girl, skipping down the hill to play with her children. For the first time. For always and forever.

Author's Note

Canoodling Always & Forever is the amalgamation of women who have asked me to write Aurelie's story, women who have shared their personal stories of loss, and women who are labor and delivery experts--among other experts who have helped me craft Aurelie's journey into motherhood. I always knew that Aurelie would suffer the loss of a child. However, it wasn't until my niece, a labor and delivery nurse, told me about an article she read in USA Today, that I knew how I'd present Aurelie's loss in this book. In summary, the article follows a couple who is excited to have a baby but finds out the pregnant woman's water broke at 17 weeks—too early for the baby to survive. She lives in Missouri and was negatively impacted by the abortion law that prevented her from receiving care to save her own life.

When I read the article, I was haunted, moved, and inspired by this quote, "If this was a year ago, they could have induced labor and I would have been able to hold her [the baby] and say goodbye," (Szuch, 2022). It was this quote from the baby's father that plagued me. Though it was a quote from a man, it was Aurelie who told me this was her heart song. Dillion also expressed his own wish--that I write about his grief as well. He emphatically did not want to lose another young wife and how he would do anything to save Aurelie's life. Period.

Acknowledgements

Canoodling Always and Forever wasn't even a thought in my head until the *Canoodling* focus group asked me, "What happens to Aurelie?" at the end of writing *Canoodling Out West*. Thus began this book's journey in 2019. Four years later, I wrote the last word in the third book of *The Canoodling Series*. However, I didn't get this far without a tremendous amount of help.

I am grateful to the women who made up the first *Canoodling* focus group for putting the idea in my head that I needed to find Aurelie's voice: Nicole Bessert, Kris Engaas, Kristin Freiberg, Julia Jaegersberg, Nicole Kerneen, Kathleen Marshall, Tammie Quarrie, Marcia Rupp, Joy Sinclair, Donna Tronca, Erin Verdoni, and Lu Wilson.

Canoodling Always and Forever had its own focus group because, after four years, people's lives moved on and others came into my orbit to help provide me with a new perspective and insight as to what story I wanted to tell. Here are the people whose diligence and honesty brought this book to the next level: Kris Engaas, Melinda Dejewski, Kathleen Marshall, Rod Vick, and Erin Verdoni. Thank you!

While this is a work of fiction, I did my due diligence to try to get the story right. There were many hours of research via firsthand testimonials and interviews with subject matter experts which framed Aurelie and Dillion's trajectory in a way I didn't know when I wrote the first words to their love story. It is their input that has given Aurelie and Dillion's story so much more depth than I could have ever created on my own. I owe a great deal of gratitude to:

Jonah Verdoni who educated me on bass fishing, as the last thing I caught with a fishhook was his hoodie. Needless to say, I am not allowed to fish any more.

Gabrielle Verdoni, BSN, labor and delivery RN and Jennifer Verdoni, BSN, former labor and delivery nurse who were incredibly important to flush out the medical terminology, diagnoses, clinical timelines and outcomes that provide credibility to the storyline. An additional note of appreciation to Gabrielle as she led me to the article that changed the entire trajectory of Aurelie's journey.

Jim Jelinek, retired Episcopal bishop, was a Godsend. Once I set out to tell what happened to Aurelie after Cat and Damon's wedding, very quickly I committed to having her love interest as an Episcopal priest. However, I didn't know very much about the Episcopal religion except for the one or two times a year I join my friend, Kathleen, for Sunday mass and *donuts for Jesus*, as my kids have dubbed the gathering after service. While I focused on attending Sunday mass at a variety of Episcopal churches in Wisconsin while conducting research for this book, it was Father Jim who was invaluable for helping me develop a plausible storyline that didn't break with Episcopal law.

Shawn Lund, former special education instructional assistant, provided me with insights and nuances into the autism spectrum which brought a depth to Benji's character I never knew he needed. Thank you!

To this group of women, I owe the soul of *Canoodling Always and Forever* to you. I am humbled and honored that you shared your stories of physical, emotional, and spiritual trauma as well as unfaltering hope with me. I can never repay you for what you've offered me, to guide me through your harrowing experiences. I am in awe of how you still came out on the other side of tremendous loss and grief with hope and a commitment to move forward. I am forever in your debt: Jennifer Rolfson, Lynn Schweikl, and Vicki Verdoni.

I am blessed with a family member who was willing to share his professional expertise in family law. I call him Uncle Bill, but you can call him Your Honor; William E. Hanrahan, Chief Judge

CANOODLING ALWAYS & FOREVER

5th Judicial District of Wisconsin, retired. Thanks, Uncle Bill! On the other side of family law, I wish to acknowledge Dan and Deb Danowski for sharing their personal story and timeline with me.

One of the reasons people tell me they like my books is that I pepper them with real places and experiences. Thank you to all the business owners who gave me permission to use their official names in this book. To be able to do so brings a sense of reality to this work of fiction.

My dear friend, Meg McCormick, will take my professional head shot for a homemade pizza. Thanks for making me look so good! Jody and Jim Schmitz, Jr., I appreciate your willingness to lend me your sweet Great Dane mix, Jocelyn, for the photo shoot. She's a perfect stand-in for Aurelie's rescue, Mumford. Also, I love that you included the photo of Jocelyn in the dinosaur snood in your Christmas photo montage!

Publishing and promoting *Canoodling Always and Forever* is a labor of love that was made that much easier because of work and encouragement provided by my publisher, Mike Nicloy of Nicol1 Publishing and Design, as well as Melissa Blair and Stephanie Blair of Cultivating Sales PRO, and my editor, Marla McKenna.

Finally, to my own personal dream maker, my husband, Rich Verdoni. I am eternally grateful to you for always finding a way to say "yes" to make my dreams a reality. I love you always and forever!

Works Cited

Doolin. (2024). *Stay and Discover More*. Retrieved from Doolin: https://doolin.ie/

East Troy Railroad Museum. (2024). *History*. Retrieved from East Troy Railroad Museum: https://www.easttroyrr.org/history.html

Failte Ireland. (2024). *Your guide to the perfect Dublin break*. Retrieved from Visit Dublin: https://www.visitdublin.com/

McEwen, J. (2016, April 19). *Why raising your vibration increases serendipity*. Retrieved from TEDxTalks: https://www.youtube.com/watch?v=SLSsqCI7NIE

Szuch, S. (2022, October 15). *She had 'a baby dying inside' her. Under Missouri's abortion ban, doctors could do nothing*. Retrieved from usatoday.com:

https://www.usatoday.com/story/news/nation/2022/10/15/missouri-abortion-ban-pregnancy-complications/10496559002/

The Aran Islands. (2024). *Go Back In Time*. Retrieved from The Aran Islands: https://www.aranislands.ie/the-aran-islands

Trinity College Dublin. (2024). *Welcome to Trinity*. Retrieved from Trinity College Dublin: https://www.tcd.ie/

Author's Bio

Shawn M. Verdoni is the author of *Canoodling Up North—Book One, Canoodling Out West—Book Two and Canoodling Always & Forever—Book Three.* She attended the University of Wisconsin-Whitewater for her degree in secondary education and the Milwaukee School of Engineering to complete her master's in business administration. Her best days are spent with her husband, children, and two dogs just hanging out. She loves living in Wisconsin, especially in fall when you can find her in a pumpkin patch or an apple orchard collecting tart baking apples for her famous crumble crust pie.

Printed in the USA
CPSIA information can be obtained
at www.ICGtesting.com
LVHW022302060624
782362LV00004B/11